Praise for Vero

"A poignant story . . . It explores family, friendship, revenge, obsession, and the power of love to heal deep wounds."
—*RT Book Reviews*

"Profoundly touching and emotionally searing."
—*Fresh Fiction*

"Wolff writes a story that will grab you from the first word and not let go."
—*Night Owl Reviews*

"Passionate and magical."
—*Publishers Weekly*

"Refreshing and intriguing."
—*The Romance Readers Connection*

"Powerful, riveting, and vibrant. A must-read page-turner destined to be a keeper."
—Sue-Ellen Welfonder, *USA Today* bestselling author

"A rich, beautifully written love story that will haunt your heart long after you turn the last page."
—Penelope Williamson

"[A] beautiful romance."
—*Romance Reviews Today*

Berkley Sensation titles by Veronica Wolff

MASTER OF THE HIGHLANDS
SWORD OF THE HIGHLANDS
WARRIOR OF THE HIGHLANDS
LORD OF THE HIGHLANDS
DEVIL'S HIGHLANDER
DEVIL'S OWN
SIERRA FALLS

Anthologies

LADIES PREFER ROGUES
(with Janet Chapman, Sandra Hill, and Trish Jensen)

Sierra Falls

VERONICA WOLFF

BERKLEY SENSATION, NEW YORK

THE BERKLEY PUBLISHING GROUP
Published by the Penguin Group
Penguin Group (USA) Inc.
375 Hudson Street, New York, New York 10014, USA

Penguin Group (Canada), 90 Eglinton Avenue East, Suite 700, Toronto, Ontario M4P 2Y3, Canada
(a division of Pearson Penguin Canada Inc.) • Penguin Books Ltd., 80 Strand, London WC2R 0RL,
England • Penguin Group Ireland, 25 St. Stephen's Green, Dublin 2, Ireland (a division of Penguin
Books Ltd.) • Penguin Group (Australia), 250 Camberwell Road, Camberwell, Victoria 3124, Australia
(a division of Pearson Australia Group Pty. Ltd.) • Penguin Books India Pvt. Ltd., 11 Community
Centre, Panchsheel Park, New Delhi—110 017, India • Penguin Group (NZ), 67 Apollo Drive,
Rosedale, Auckland 0632, New Zealand (a division of Pearson New Zealand Ltd.) • Penguin Books
(South Africa) (Pty.) Ltd., 24 Sturdee Avenue, Rosebank, Johannesburg 2196, South Africa

Penguin Books Ltd., Registered Offices: 80 Strand, London WC2R 0RL, England

This is a work of fiction. Names, characters, places, and incidents either are the product of the author's
imagination or are used fictitiously, and any resemblance to actual persons, living or dead, business
establishments, events, or locales is entirely coincidental. The publisher does not have any control over
and does not assume any responsibility for author or third-party websites or their content.

SIERRA FALLS

A Berkley Sensation Book / published by arrangement with the author

PUBLISHING HISTORY
Berkley Sensation mass-market edition / April 2012

Copyright © 2012 by Veronica Wolff.
Excerpt from *Timber Creek* by Veronica Wolff copyright © 2012 by Veronica Wolff.
Cover design by George Long. Cover art by Jim Griffin.
Interior text design by Laura K. Corless.

ISBN: 978-0-425-24795-2

BERKLEY SENSATION®
Berkley Sensation Books are published by The Berkley Publishing Group,
a division of Penguin Group (USA) Inc.,
375 Hudson Street, New York, New York 10014.
BERKLEY SENSATION® is a registered trademark of Penguin Group (USA) Inc.
The "B" design is a trademark of Penguin Group (USA) Inc.

PRINTED IN THE UNITED STATES OF AMERICA

10 9 8 7 6 5 4 3 2 1

ALWAYS LEARNING   **PEARSON**

To Robin Rue,
with sincere thanks for the invite
to the twenty-first century

Acknowledgments

As ever, I'm tremendously grateful to my editor, Cindy Hwang, for helping me discover Sierra Falls—with her encouragement and support, I always seem to find new stories to tell.

I'm also thankful to Robin Rue, for cheering me on and suggesting I try my hand at contemporary. Thanks to Beth Miller, too, for being such a careful reader and a treat to talk to, even when we're just discussing cover copy.

I also owe a huge thank you to my early readers and brainstormers: Jami Alden, Teresa Grant, Rachael Herron, Connie O'Donovan, and last but not least, my amazing critique partner, Kate Perry.

Finally, thanks to Adam, for always getting us safely over those high, snowy passes. If it weren't for him, I never would've discovered my love of the mountains.

One

"Come on, Dad. It's called a frittata." Sorrow scooped her egg, potato, and bacon creation onto a plate and held it out to her father. "It's the same food *you* just ordered, just a different shape. See?" She prodded it with a fork. "Bacon, eggs, and hash browns, only all mixed up."

Bear Bailey gave it a quick, skeptical examination. "*Mangled* up, more like. Nothing beats Sully's scrambles." He gave their fry cook a conspiratorial wink. "Ain't that right, Sully?"

"Yes, sir." Sully spared him a sharp nod before getting right back to work, his entire focus on a griddle jammed full of pancakes. The man found ways to express his independence, but going against his employer wasn't one of them. Sorrow supposed you could take the man out of the military, but you couldn't take the military out of the man.

"More for me then." She stepped around Sully, but at the last minute, snuck a bit of her frittata onto a plate for him, giving the man a pointed look.

What her father didn't know wouldn't hurt him. He'd never change the menu at his Thirsty Bear Tavern, but Sorrow's life would be dull if she didn't steal her moments of quiet rebellion.

Sully just shook his head. He'd witnessed some version of this same father-daughter argument for years.

Speaking of arguments . . . "Where's Mom?" Sorrow asked,

plopping onto a stool next to her dad. She'd overheard him railing on about something the night before, and it hadn't exactly sounded like a two-way conversation. The silence from her mother had been deafening—she might as well not even have been in the room. Not that her father was prone to yelling. Bear Bailey just liked to . . . hold court.

"She's at the front desk," he said, swabbing a piece of bacon in a puddle of syrup. We got two guests coming in this morning. Young couple from Sacramento. Snowshoe types, most like."

"They'll need a helluva lot more than snowshoes if this keeps up." Sully wiped his hands on his apron and leaned against the pass-through between kitchen and tavern.

Sorrow followed the direction of his gaze. What had started as a light dusting of snow that morning had thickened into dense flurries in the past half hour.

"It's really coming down now," her father said, swiveling on his stool to look out the window. "Looking like a slow one for business today."

"Maybe so." She felt light at the prospect. Maybe things would be calm enough for her to roast a nice cut of meat for dinner. Maybe even bake a pie for dessert. Her dad wouldn't be able to complain about *that*.

Helping run her family's lodge and tavern wasn't exactly Sorrow's dream come true, but her older sister and brother had fled the nest, and then her father had his stroke, and she'd been left holding the bag. Though her mother was a definite help, by no means was she strong enough to do all the work on her own. It was Sorrow's opinion that her mom too often let Dad call the shots anyhow.

With her siblings gone, family dinners gradually became a thing of the past, and increasingly it was Sully who served up their meals. For Sorrow, what'd started as an aversion to the man's "Turkey Loaf" blossomed into a passion for cooking.

It started slowly with tricks she picked up on TV cooking shows. Pasta dishes that relied on more than a jar of Ragú. Soups came next—she still marveled how you could add some meat, salt, and veggies to a pot of water and end up with the tastiest dinner ever.

Soon the kitchen became her refuge. She loved the creativity of it. Loved the different flavors. She was stuck in a small town, living with her parents, helping run their inn, but when she was in the kitchen, she could make enchiladas and take off for Mexico. Or whip up a simple bruschetta and whisk herself off to Italy. Though one of these days, she'd settle for whisking herself off to a fancy restaurant in the city, with white tablecloths and big goblets of wine.

She loved cooking so much, she could even imagine doing it professionally—and what a dream that would be. Not that she'd ever get the chance.

Alone in the kitchen, her problems dropped away. Cooking demanded focus—stirring before something burned, chopping the veggies just right—and it always managed to push all other concerns from her mind. And she had a lot of concerns.

Stupid stuff nagged her, and she hated all of it. Housekeeping issues, plumbing issues, money issues . . . *all* the issues that cropped up in the running of a creaky old lodge in the foothills of the Sierra Nevada mountains.

"You sure I can't make you a side of bacon?" Sully's voice startled her from her thoughts.

"Hmm?" she asked, catching him watching her.

"Bacon. I can make it crispy. You used to like that."

She gave him a warm smile. "Good memory."

Sully had arrived in Sierra Falls when she was a kid, rolling into town on a Harley. He was a quiet sort, a restless and rambling soul, but theirs was a very live-and-let-live sort of town, and he'd taken to the place.

He stayed on as cook for the tavern attached to her family's Big Bear Lodge. Folks shortened his name from Tom Sullivan, so as not to confuse him with Tom Harlan, who ran the hardware store across town. And like that, it was as though Sully had been in Sierra Falls forever.

He wasn't exactly prone to sharing—Sorrow knew he'd done time in Vietnam and that he'd been married a few times, but that was about the extent of it. Even so, he was a good man, and she'd come to think of him as an adoptive uncle figure.

She shook her head. Time to get going. It was already 8:30,

and her days didn't so much begin, as they tended to explode out of control. "I'm good, Sully. But thanks."

Sorrow scraped the last of her breakfast to the center of the plate so she could mash it into the tines of her fork and savor every last bite. Next time, she'd try adding tomatoes—maybe sun-dried, so the eggs wouldn't get too runny.

She pushed away from the counter and bussed her dishes, catching sight of the conditions outside. "I should get going."

They hadn't had much snow over the holidays, but now that it was January, winter seemed to have begun in earnest. It was accumulating fast out there. While a light dusting was great, too much snow on the road became a hassle, and she worried this was headed toward *hassle* territory.

Being in the foothills, they didn't get as much weather as Lake Tahoe to the northeast, but still, there was snow and ice aplenty, and it plagued her. Keeping the lodge standing was trouble enough—keeping the place warm and weatherproofed through the winter months consumed her. "Duty calls," she said with a sigh. "The floor's all yours, Dad."

Sully dinged the small bell on the window between tavern and kitchen. "Order up."

Bear looked around for the woman who worked as their bartender and waitress. "Where's Helen?"

"I'll bet she's stuck in this mess." Sorrow shook her head sympathetically. "She's got three kids at two different schools, and if it's a snow day . . ."

"Well, someone's gotta do her job." Her father began to stand.

She put a hand on his shoulder. "You sit, Dad. I got this one." Ever since the stroke, Bear hadn't moved around as easily, and Sorrow would just as soon give him the chance to finish his coffee in peace.

She grabbed the plates from the pass-through and served their handful of diners, all of them locals. Visitors to Sierra Falls were few. It was a small gold rush town, too remote to take advantage of the Tahoe resort area, and too far from Route 50 to catch any tourists coming from Sacramento or the San

Francisco Bay Area. It was too out there to be on the road to anywhere, really.

If her family hadn't owned the lodge and restaurant outright, they probably would've gone under years ago. They saw the occasional hikers, hunters, and fishermen, or folks who'd gotten stuck on the snowy mountain pass and been forced to double back and stay the night. But other than that, the Bailey family income relied mostly on serving predictable meat-and-potatoes dishes to the residents.

She served Sheriff Billy Preston last. He looked up from the morning paper as she approached. "Morning, Sorrow."

"Sheriff." She softened her greeting with a smile.

She liked the man—there was something quiet and maybe even a bit haunted in his eyes. She'd heard he was a widower, and she tried to meet those eyes whenever they spoke, tried to give him a genuine smile to compensate for whatever demons the man was harboring.

The sheriff hadn't lived there long, and time would tell if his troubled look ever went away. She hoped it would. She wished the man well. He'd gotten on her good side from the start by being one of the few whose first words to her hadn't been to remark about her name. *Sorrow* was a family name, but sometimes she felt saddled with it, as though in being called a thing, she might be fated to a life of it, like her hard-luck ancestors before her.

Her father always prattled on about those ancestors—grandmother, great-, and great-great-grandmothers Sorrow. They'd known hard lives that, according to Dad, she herself was destined to relive if she didn't marry right, or dress better, or hell, if she didn't clean out the garage and call the plumber.

"I've told you before, it's Billy." Though his words were gruff, his tone was polite, in that way that seemed unique to men in uniform. He took his plate from her hands, lightening her load. "Looks good." He added in a low voice, "But I'd have liked to try that frittata."

His conspiratorial tone surprised her. That he—or anyone—wanted to try her food was a kick. She smiled a real smile then.

She'd love to cook for people someday, and how kind of Billy to sense it.

She gave him a piercing gaze—was he truly sad or was it just a trick of those dark eyes? His smiles were genuine, and though they lit his face she wondered if they truly shone any light on his heart.

Those dark eyes narrowed, and she realized she'd been staring. She gave a little shake to her head. "If you want frittatas, you'll have to take it up with the man." She tilted her head toward her father. He was still seated at the bar, yammering at Sully about something, and he'd likely be in the same spot when she returned at noon for lunch. "Bear Bailey isn't a fan of change."

She didn't know Billy Preston well, and she wasn't interested in him in *that* way—she had a boyfriend after all—but she enjoyed how they always exchanged a few words. He'd been a lieutenant in the Oakland PD before being recruited as sheriff for Sierra Falls, and she loved his occasional mention of big-city life.

An idea hit her. "Hold on," she said, and darted back into the kitchen. She'd baked bread the night before, and the last thing she needed was that many carbs lying around.

She returned, handing him a small foil-wrapped bundle. "It's not a frittata, but my apple cinnamon bread is a close second."

"Sorry," he deadpanned, patting his belly. "We law enforcement officers only eat donuts."

"Well . . ." Biting back a grin, she pulled the bread out of his reach, doing her best to look offended. "See if I ever try to feed *you* again."

"On second thought, it smells too good." He laughed and snatched it from her hands. "Give me that."

She laughed with him, not caring that the others were looking. It was gratifying that she'd been the one to draw out the humor. For the first time that day, the muscles in her shoulders felt like they might relax.

A hideous sound caused her to seize right back up again.

Outside, there was the long whine of creaking timber, followed by a loud crash.

She and the sheriff locked eyes. For the flicker of a moment, a feeling of comfort cut to her heart, and Sorrow was grateful she wasn't in it alone.

Which was crazy, of course. She didn't even know the man.

But those thoughts came and went in the blink of an eye, and she was dashing out the door, Billy and the rest of their patrons hot on her heels.

Two

Billy Preston's first thought was that somebody had crashed a car into a tree. His second was of his wife.

Every other thought was.

Only this time, he felt almost guilty when the memories of her slammed back into his mind. He'd been sharing a few friendly jokes with a pretty woman—as though he'd forgotten his past and were a regular guy.

But he wasn't a regular guy. Three years ago, his wife had been struck and killed by a bus while biking to work. And he hadn't been there for her.

There was never any predicting what would return him to that day. No knowing when the odd questions would creep in to haunt him. Things like, what had *she* eaten for breakfast that day? Had *she* looked at the newspaper before she'd left that morning? And a desperate curiosity would seize him, plague him.

This time, it was the sound of crashing from outside that called her back.

Normally, he held a shield in place through the daylight hours. It let him deflect those bad thoughts, hoarding them for the wee hours. But he'd met Sorrow's eyes, and the raw connection there startled him. It shattered his guard, sending his mind spinning for an instant.

Spinning back to those days when he drove his wife to work every day. Every day except for *that* day. He'd been up late the night before with paperwork—police did reams more of it than they showed on TV—and Keri had insisted he snag the extra twenty minutes of sleep.

A beat cop delivered the news hours later, just as he was racing out to grab a bite for lunch. It'd taken that long to identify Keri, to track him down as her next of kin.

While he'd been showering, and swilling back the rest of his tepid coffee, contemplating whether or not he could get away with skipping his morning shave, his wife had been on the side of the road, dying. While he'd been bitching to the guys about paperwork, she was already gone.

He'd endured six months of personal leave, a few years of phoning it in, and countless hours at the gym lifting till the muscles in his arms trembled, before an old buddy hooked him up. The small town of Sierra Falls had lost the sheriff they'd known for decades, and did Billy want to step in to fill his shoes? Like that, he was tapped for the ballot, running uncontested, and before he knew it, he was packing up his belongings and heading to the mountains.

He'd been anxious to get away from the city, from the reminders that lurked everywhere, and now, living in the shadow of the Sierra Nevadas, a part of Billy was able to find some peace.

The other parts, he simply shut down.

Sharing that moment with Sorrow had unsettled him. He'd had the eerie feeling that, locking eyes as they had, she could see into his soul, reading his guilt, his pain.

Billy shoved such silly notions to the back of his mind. He bolted up from his booth. Ran out the door.

Sheriff once more.

He and Sorrow stood shoulder-to-shoulder, and it took only a second to realize what'd happened. A tree branch had crashed through the roof of the Big Bear Lodge.

Billy shook his head slowly. A goodly chunk of the roof had caved in, and it was now one devastated mass of snow, timber, and roofing. If he craned his neck just right, he could see through the hole clear to the attic window on the other side.

"Oh, shh"—Sorrow swallowed the tail end of the curse—"sugar."

"Go ahead and say it. Looks like you could use a good round of swearing." It seemed the woman managed most every aspect of her family's business. He guessed this would fall square on her shoulders, too.

Her arms were crossed tightly across her chest, like she might fly apart if she let go. "It's the *Sorrow* thing."

"The what?" If she was speaking about herself in the third person, maybe she was more upset than he'd realized.

"It's my luck. The *Sorrow* luck. All the women in my family who've been named *Sorrow* have had atrocious luck. With men. With money. With pretty much everything. Why they keep using that damned name is beyond me."

Edith Bailey burst from the lodge, a crocheted shawl clutched at her chest. "What on earth—?"

"The roof." Sorrow spared the briefest glance for her mother then looked back at the devastation. "How much is *this* going to cost?"

They all stepped closer. Billy rested a hand on the pine towering overhead. Peering up into the branches, he said, "Looks like you've got some dead branches."

"I knew we needed to trim the deadwood." Sorrow pinned her mom with a look. "I told him we needed to trim the deadwood."

Billy didn't need to ask to guess that by *him* she'd meant her father, but he knew to mind his own business. Instead, he backed up, shaking clumps of snow from a row of low branches. "This is some wet snow. And on top of last week's storm? Too heavy, even for this gorgeous old giant."

Sorrow's mother remained silent, chewing on her thumbnail.

He hardly knew the Bailey family, but at that moment, her tense presence seemed like the last thing Sorrow needed. Putting his hand at Edith's back, he gently guided her back toward the door. "You're going catch a chill, ma'am. I can help your daughter while you go find yourself a proper coat."

Edith stopped in her tracks. "Oh good Lord, the hope chests." In a panic, she called to Sorrow, "Your grandmother's trunks. The attic will get soaked. You've got to go take care of all the trunks."

"We'll take care of it." Billy continued to herd her back inside, then returned to Sorrow's side. "What trunks?"

"There's ten tons of junk in the attic. As if I don't have enough on my plate." She turned, trudging toward the lodge entrance.

The woman looked suddenly so drawn, so alone, Billy couldn't help himself from falling into step with her. "Can I help?"

As she opened her mouth to reply, the wind gusted, enveloping them in a cloud of white. He instinctively reached for her, taking her arm to stop her. It was silly—the cars in the lot were parked, there were no more snow-laden branches overhead, it was perfectly safe—but he couldn't stop himself.

They stood like that for a frozen moment. Sunlight caught the snow and it sparkled as it swirled around them. It kissed the fabric of his shirt, damp and clinging to his shoulders.

When the cloud settled, he found Sorrow's gaze on him. Watery light cut through the branches and reflected off the snow, and he saw that her eyes were more green than blue.

Guilt speared him, and he pulled his hand back abruptly. He felt like he was cheating on his wife. Logically, he knew that was ridiculous, but something in his chest told him otherwise.

There was a brief, awkward silence, and then they both spoke at once.

"What do—"

"How is—"

They each huffed out a humorless laugh. He tried to smile, but suspected he didn't quite manage it.

Crossing her arms over her chest, she gave a self-deprecating shrug. "Just my luck, huh?"

He cleared his throat, anxious to be back to business. "It might not be so bad."

They studied the damage. Snow was still falling, steady and quiet, drifting into the attic in a way that seemed almost diligent.

"Or not," he said, correcting himself.

"Yeah." Pain flickered across her face, before she schooled it to a careful, bland half smile. "It's kinda bad."

He put aside his own pain for a moment, confronted with hers. "Seriously, Sorrow. Are you okay?"

She sighed. "Complaining won't stop the snow."

She was no nonsense. He appreciated that. Just then, he didn't think he could deal with an overwrought female. "What can I do to help?"

"Unless you're a roofer, there's nothing you *can* do." She bit her lip, deep in thought. Something about it made her seem so alone. "Damien—he's my . . . friend—he's got contacts."

Damien. Billy recognized the name and guessed it was the good-looking guy he'd seen around with her. He'd spotted the two of them doing things like eating lunch, or driving in his car, headed out of town.

Clearly, more than friends.

Billy wanted to help. He almost offered to help her sort through the attic. But he reminded himself it wasn't his place. Sorrow already had a man to help her, while Billy had work to do.

They said their good-byes, and he headed back to the tavern. He needed to pay his bill and get back to it. And then he'd push this strange episode from his mind.

Three

Sorrow had sent the sheriff on his way. Something about the look on his face made her feel pitiable, and she hated that feeling. She might need help, but she wasn't helpless.

She especially didn't want *him* thinking of her in that light. Billy Preston was once a big shot police lieutenant in a major city, and she hated feeling like she might be a small-town yokel in comparison.

And anyway, she had a man in her life already, and he *loved* to help. Maybe it was because Damien was stuck in a suit, sitting behind a desk at his family's business, but he seemed to relish coming to her aid as much as any knight of old had loved crusading on a white horse.

Whatever the reason, he was always happy to roll up his sleeves and do things like chop wood, or fix a clogged drain, or perform any of a variety of manly man tasks she might need. Sometimes he was a little *too* happy about it, smothering her with his manly manness when she didn't necessarily need it.

Though there was one task she liked him to perform, and she blushed to think of it. A wistful sigh escaped her. She sure could use a heaping dose of *that* sort of help right about now. But she pushed the thought aside—this latest crisis was a doozy. She barely had time to shower these days, much less canoodle with Damien, no matter how yummy he looked in his suit.

She sat on an old stool. Staring blindly at the attic wreckage, she phoned him.

"Hey, Bailey," he said, answering his cell the way he always did when she called. He had a smile in his voice, and it was a relief to hear him, even though she never did love his penchant for calling her by her last name. But it was a habit he'd started in middle school, and those things died hard.

"Hey yourself." She heard background noise, like the sound of wind and gears shifting. She frowned. "Are you driving?"

He paused, hesitated. "Maybe."

"Oh, Damien, you know I hate when you talk and drive." Even as she said it, she hated even more the naggy sound of her own voice. But he could be so reckless sometimes, acting the bad boy, and she had enough troubles without him wrecking his car. "God forbid," she muttered, putting such thoughts to rest.

"Relax. I'm using that ear thing you got me."

She held her tongue for a moment, and decided she'd pretend to believe him. "Okay."

"What's up? We're still on for tonight, right?"

She heard the sounds of spitting gravel and the whine of a rapidly downshifting engine. He drove like an eight-year-old playing with Hot Wheels, but she'd vowed not to henpeck. Instead, she told him, "It's the roof."

"The what, babe?" He cut the engine, and she heard the dinging of the opened car door. "Tell me."

Hearing the focus in Damien's voice, she completely forgave and forgot his crazy driving. He'd work his magic and save the day. She knew a momentary pang—was she taking him for granted?—but she nudged away the feeling. Sorrow was strong and could handle what came her way, but finding a roofer willing to work in this weather was another thing entirely. And Damien, with one phone call, always managed to pull a rabbit out of his hat.

"The roof," she repeated, getting up and wandering to the center of the attic where she could stand fully upright. Snow was blowing in, and she shielded a hand over her eyes, squinting against it. "A branch from that old pine smashed through, into the attic."

"Yeah, it was dumping pretty hard this morning," Damien said, and she heard his car door slam. "I told your dad he needed to cut back that tree."

"I know, I know. But what Bear wants—"

"Bear gets," he finished, with an irreverent laugh.

Everyone in Sierra Falls loved her father, but they also knew how set in his ways the man had become. As far as Bear Bailey was concerned, there was only one way to run the Big Bear Lodge and Thirsty Bear Tavern, and it was *his* way.

"Don't you worry," Damien said. "We'll have you patched in time for happy hour. What's the damage?"

She spun in a circle, assessing. Thankfully the snow was slowing, but the sun was coming out and the temp was rising, and snowmelt had already begun to drip in a steady *plop-plop* on the attic floor.

Sometimes she didn't want her boyfriend to keep swooping in to save the day—but this was definitely not one of those times.

"It's pretty bad." Snow piled in little drifts around the room, while the lodge's ambient heat had puddles forming in random cracks and valleys along the warped timber-plank flooring. "I called Jack Jessup, but he said he's booked solid and can't come out till next week."

"I'll call him," he said, and she knew that was enough to settle it. Damien Simmons was the son of Dabney Simmons, CEO of Simmons Timber, a company that provided the bread, butter, and livelihood for much of their town. The Simmons clan owned much of the land in Sierra Falls—if someone in the family wanted a roof patched, it got patched.

"Thanks, Damien."

"My pleasure, Bailey. I'll be sure to get my reward later."

He laughed suggestively just as he clicked off, and the sound reverberated in her belly, her body's response instant. It wasn't love she felt for him—at least she didn't think it was—but that didn't matter. If she ever wondered why she was with the guy, all she had to do was see him in person, and . . . *yowza*.

Damien had a knack with women—he'd had it as a teenager,

and he had it in spades now. And though it felt wonderful to be the center of his attention, there was something about it she didn't trust. Maybe it was leftover from high school, when he hadn't spared her the time of day.

But he was hot, she was lonely, and besides, everyone in the town expected it. He'd been out of her league for years, but now that she was one of the few from their class who either hadn't left town or wasn't married, everyone expected her to fall head over heels for "the Simmons boy."

Everybody knew him, of course. He was the pride and joy of the Simmons family. Oddly, that was one of the things that appealed to her. Not that he had money, though she sure could've used a whole lot more of that in her world. But Damien understood family expectations and responsibilities, and she liked that. Sorrow had family obligations coming out of her ears.

She just wished he weren't so heavy-handed with her sometimes. He took care of business for his family, but she didn't necessarily like the feeling that she was an obligation for him to deal with, too.

She raked a hand through her hair. "Damien, Damien," she murmured, not quite sure what to do with him. But now it was time to get back to business.

Knowing Damien, the roofer would be there within the hour. In the meantime, she might as well do as her mom asked and rifle through the generations of old junk not valuable enough to have a place in the rest of the house.

"What a disaster." She kicked at one of the old trunks. It was the "hope chest" of one of the women on her dad's side. If it'd belonged to one of the Sorrows in his family tree, it was no wonder the thing was still filled with dusty and forgotten hopes.

She nudged it from the wall to see how even after death, these women had bad luck. The sides were already rippling and peeling, the wood turning cherry-red with damp. Getting ruined on her watch.

"My apologies, Grandma Sorrow. Or old Auntie Sorrow. Or whoever you were." Sinking to her knees, she jiggled the old hinge, trying to unfasten it despite years of rust.

"Too bad they didn't name *Laura* after you," she grumbled.

Why her parents hadn't saddled her big sister with the name Sorrow was beyond her. If they had, maybe *Laura* would be the one kneeling there in a freezing puddle. "If I'd had a different name, then maybe *I'd* be the one off gallivanting around California. I'd be the one with the fancy job and car."

But no, her siblings hadn't been able to run out of Sierra Falls fast enough, abandoning her with things like leaking roofs and rotting trunks. "Maybe I'll find some treasure and then *I* can have *my* turn."

She finally pried open the lid, and was hit by a wave of mildew and mothballs. "Oh, jeez." She rubbed at the twinge in her nose, looked up at the bright hole in the roof to catch a sneeze. She was going to be sneezing all day, she knew it.

"All right," she muttered, digging through the contents in search of whatever needed saving first. "Gotta start somewhere."

Family photos, important papers—she went through each trunk, systematically setting aside anything that couldn't be washed or replaced. Most of it was junk, though. Her father had inherited the lodge from his father, who got it from his father, and so on, and much of this stuff was the forgotten, meaningless bits of life that accumulated when you weren't paying attention. Old ledgers, musty afghans, mildewed picture frames, a warped guitar . . . she hoped to convince her parents to toss it all in the Dumpster, but knowing Bear and Edith, she feared it was a pipe dream.

"Seriously?" she exclaimed as she opened an old Kinney shoebox, revealing stacks of ancient receipts. She shoved the whole thing into a paper bag, planning to sneak it and the rest of the worthless papers to the recycling center in Silver City. "Do they seriously need this stuff?"

What she saw at the bottom gave her pause, though. The prettiest lace shawl, with ivory crewelwork, yellowed to a color that told her it'd been at the bottom of the trunk for a long time. She pulled it out, afraid the cheap wood might bleed color onto it.

Something tumbled from the shawl, and she scooped it up. A stack of letters. She held them up to catch the light. "Hello there."

They were as yellowed as the linen, but otherwise miraculously spared of damage, still bound by a strand of rickrack gone crispy with age. The handwriting was old-fashioned spidery loops, and she got a shiver, knowing in her bones that she held a piece of history. A very intimate piece of history.

Carefully, she slid off the ribbon and unfolded the first page. The writing was dense, but two lines at the end popped out:

Sincerely, and ever your Loving,
Sorrow

"Well, what do you know?" She'd known all her life that hers was a family name, but seeing it written by the owner's own hand felt thrillingly personal. "Which Sorrow were you?"

She plopped onto her bottom. An icy puddle seeped into the seat of her jeans, but she didn't care. She'd read the date at the top of the letter—1851. This could be from none other than her three-times great-grandmother, the first and saddest Sorrow of them all, Sorrow Crabtree.

Four

Marlene Jessup sat behind the wheel of her Ford pickup, shaking. She'd skidded off the road right into a snowbank.

The old truck acted light as a feather—or at least the back end of it did—and it had the nasty habit of fishtailing all over the road at the first hint of flurries. By the end of winter, there was always a bed full of snow to weigh her down, but these early season dustings were always tough.

She'd have loved a nice car, something fancy and European-sounding like *Volvo* or *Audi*, but when her husband left, he'd taken half of their already lean bank account and stuck her with the pickup.

He and his new squeeze lived in Pinole now, in some well-to-do development, probably driving some fancy *new* pickup. The hell of it was, his new wife wasn't even that much younger. It would've stung less if he'd left for some fresh-faced bimbo—she could've pointed the finger in blame. But Frank had left her for some late-fifties professional type—something to do with pharmaceutical sales—and soon they'd both retire, at which time they'd probably buy that boat Marlene and Frank had always talked about, and they'd travel the world.

Some other woman was getting her boat.

And Marlene was left with the old Ford, two elderly aunts,

and an ailing mother to care for, haunted by questions of where she went wrong.

Not going there, as her grandson would say. She put the truck into reverse, willing her hands to stop shaking. It wasn't even *that* cold, dammit. She hit the gas, and there was a horrible whirring sound, her tires spinning uselessly.

Damned pickup. It had one of those mini backseats that took forever to wrangle her aunts into. She'd wanted a sedan, but Frank had insisted. She slammed her hands on the wheel. She had no use for a damned pickup.

If she couldn't get unstuck, she'd be late to pick up the ladies. Her aunts and mother were a trio, the famous Kidd sisters, Emerald, Pearl, and Ruby, the youngest a spry eighty-two.

And if she was late to pick them up, they'd *all* be late for the historical society meeting, and then she'd never hear the end of *that*. The ladies lived for their meetings.

Marlene had enough trouble on that front, as it was. She'd stupidly taken on the role of chairwoman, and they were a day late and a dollar short planning and funding the annual Sierra Falls festival.

It was one of the many quirky events Northern California was known for. Gilroy had their Garlic Festival. Other towns had cherry blossoms, chili cook-offs, art walks, and quilt shows. For Sierra Falls, it was the Spring Fling held every May. It was just January yet, but their coffers were empty. They could host town hall bingo till they were blue in the face, and it wouldn't be enough to cover a pie-throw much less a whole festival.

No, she needed to get to that meeting. She petted the dashboard, coaxing, "Come on, girl. Just back us out of here, and I'll buy you a nice set of snow tires."

Marlene hit the gas only to hear that horrible, high-pitched whirring again. With a heavy sigh, she sank her forehead against the wheel.

She'd have to call one of her boys, but which one? Though Jack and Eddie lived the closest, she'd hate to bother them— they'd started Jessup Brothers Construction and had been running around like one-armed paperhangers ever since.

There was always Jack's wife, Tina, but she was never

around during the day. Or maybe her daughter-in-law only *seemed* to disappear whenever Marlene needed her. God only knew how the woman occupied her daylight hours—their son was a senior in high school and almost completely independent, so it wasn't that she was toodling around, driving carpools. Regardless, Marlene wasn't about to call *her*.

She couldn't call Mark either—he was a doctor in Silver City, and as she recalled, this was his on-call day.

That left Scott. He worked as a park ranger for the Sierra Nevada Conservancy—*his* truck would surely be able to get her unstuck. He was her second oldest, her easy, smiling boy.

She rifled in her purse for her phone. Where had the years gone? Her *boy* had turned thirty-four on his last birthday.

It was getting real cold, real fast in the cab of the truck, but she had to pull off her gloves to dial, and her fingers fumbled over the tiny cell phone buttons.

There was a rapping on the window, and Marlene jumped about a foot off the seat. "Oh!"

She wiped the condensation off with her sleeve, revealing the new sheriff. He was a big man, filling her view, and adrenaline exploded in her chest. She glanced at the rearview mirror and, sure enough, he'd pulled his sheriff's SUV right up behind her, the white four-wheel drive looming on the narrow shoulder.

Why did the sight of a police car make her panic? She told herself to calm down—she couldn't have been speeding, she hadn't even been *moving*. Marlene rolled down the window. "Did I . . . is there something wrong?"

"Everything all right, Mrs. Jessup?" Billy Preston's eyes were warm and concerned.

She put a hand to her chest, relieved. She wasn't in trouble—he was *worried* about her. This new sheriff was a nice young gentleman.

"Please," she said. "Call me Marlene. Jessup was my husband's name. There's another Mrs. Jessup now." That last bit had come out a bit snappier than she'd meant it to.

"All right, *Marlene*," he said slowly. His eyes went to her hands, and she realized they were shaking even more than before. "Are you okay?"

"I think I am . . . I don't know. Maybe not." She wriggled her fingers, then tried to put her gloves back on. Why was her body not cooperating? "It's hell growing old. Beats the alternative, I suppose." She gave a shake to her head. Maybe the cold was getting to her—she was rambling like a crazy woman.

The sheriff opened the door and escorted her out. "Let's get you in my truck. You warm up, I'll shovel you out, and we'll get you on your way."

She looked back over her shoulder at her pickup. The snowbank wasn't high, but she'd managed to get her front wheels firmly entrenched. "The darned thing was skidding all over the place," she explained.

Cars whooshed by as they walked along the shoulder, and she found her legs were trembling, too.

"Easy, Marlene." He chafed warmth into her arm.

She leaned into him, a reassuringly solid man at her side. "I think I'm just cold is all."

"I'll blast the heat. You'll feel better in no time." He settled her in the front seat, and as promised, he cranked the heat all the way up.

She put her hands over the vents, relieved to feel the hot air blowing up the sleeves of her coat. How had she gotten so jittery? She wasn't a jittery sort of woman. She breathed deeply, trying to calm down.

"Something sweet is what you need." Billy pulled a foil-wrapped sack from atop the dash. "Apple cinnamon bread. Still warm from the oven."

She looked up, eyes wide. "You cook?"

He laughed. "Not me, no. I got this from Sorrow Bailey, down at the lodge. She baked it." Seeing that she took a bite, he gave her a firm nod, and shut the car door.

Marlene chewed slowly. It *was* good bread, just a little bit of sweet, yet substantial, too. Now the question was: how did the sheriff end up with homemade bread from the Bailey girl's kitchen? Sorrow was with Damien, and a young girl would be a fool to step out on the rich and handsome Simmons boy. She'd pelt Sorrow's mama with questions next time she saw her, that was for sure.

A bite of food spiced with a bit of speculation perked Marlene up, both in body and spirit.

Billy grabbed a bag of gravel and a small shovel from the back of his SUV and set to work freeing her front wheels. It was a testament to the Sierra Falls community that the sheriff's snow shovel got more action than his sidearm ever did.

He bent down to spread the gravel evenly at the base of the tire. Marlene tilted her head . . . my, my, but the man had a fine set of shoulders. He was built like a bull. A strong, solid sort of man.

Fishing another slice of bread from Billy's stash, she nestled deeper in the front seat, nibbling at the snack like it was popcorn at the movies. The sheriff shoveled and spread gravel, got into her truck, and sure enough, he was able to back it out. Marlene was almost disappointed to see the thing freed from the embankment.

Billy opened her door. "Feeling better?" His cheeks were flushed and damp from the cold and flurries.

There was nothing like seeing a man after a job well done. If only she were thirty years younger.

Marlene gave him a broad smile as she let herself out of his truck. "Much."

He returned her smile, wary surprise in his expression.

She thought she must look like a loony bird and toned down her grin. "You've been too kind, Sheriff Preston, and I thank you for it."

"If I get to call you Marlene, then you've got to call me Billy." He gave her a wink, and her heart thumped in a way that had her wishing she had a daughter she could foist onto the man.

"Then thank you, *Billy*." Marlene handed him the aluminum foil. She'd folded it into a careful square. "Homemade bread is good for what ails you, I always say. Sorry I didn't leave you any."

"Don't you worry," he said as he walked her back to her truck. "I had my fill earlier. Once you start eating the stuff, it's hard to stop." He opened her door, and the old hinges creaked. "You sure you're all right to drive?"

She checked her watch. "I'm sure I won't be all right if I'm late to our monthly meeting."

He ushered her into her seat, a true gentleman. "Meeting?"

"The historical society."

"Of course," he said. "The Spring Fling women. The last festival happened just before I moved into town. Can't wait to go to my first—your BBQ cook-off is the stuff of legend."

"If there even is a festival," she grumbled. He raised his brows, waiting for more explanation, so she continued, "We're broke. I swear, sometimes it feels like the town's dying. We can hold bake sales and bingo nights till the cows come home, and it won't be enough to cover our expenses."

He leaned against the open door, looking thoughtful. "Well, if there's any way to save the tradition, my money's on you ladies to find it."

Marlene smiled as she drove off. Money or no money, the festival budget needed to include one of those strength testers—she bet their new sheriff would be one of the few who'd be able to pick up the sledgehammer and ring that bell.

Five

Sorrow sat on one of the attic trunks, ignoring the flurry of activity around her. She'd been sneaking peeks at the letters all morning, reading snatches of lines here and there. She couldn't wait to dig in that night. The one she was reading looked like a love letter, written to someone who'd left her ancestor behind.

She could certainly relate to that—her siblings and just about everyone she'd gone to school with had left town, abandoning her in Sierra Falls.

Scooting her feet out of the way of one of the roofers, she flipped through the stack. Were they all love letters? It was so frustrating—all she wanted to do was curl up with a cup of tea to read them, but she was stuck with a bunch of careless construction guys instead.

A horrible slam tore her from her reading. She flew up, scuttling across the attic, hunching so as not to hit her head on the low sloping ceiling. "No! I mean . . . please. Oh! Watch the dollhouse."

The guys had shown up like bats out of hell, Jack Jessup's crew more interested in getting the job done than in having a care with any of the Bailey family possessions. She stood protectively in front of the dollhouse from her childhood. "I'd just like to move some things aside, if you don't mind."

Apparently the men did mind, as they continued to barrel up and down the stairs, managing to tromp gritty, blackened snow throughout the place. They'd cut away the damaged portion of the roof, and big wet clumps of snow had fallen straight into an opened trunk. So much for her careful piles—between the swirling wind and all the activity, her neat stacks were in shambles.

Tucking the letters inside her jeans at the small of her back, she grabbed an armful of what looked to be vintage dresses and hustled them to her room and out of harm's way. There was still a trunk she hadn't gone through, and she was wrestling it to the far corner when Damien's head appeared at the top of the attic stairs.

"Bailey," he greeted her, but his eyes went straight to the roof and widened. "Holy crap, you weren't lying. The roof caved in."

"It didn't cave in," she snapped. "A dead branch crashed through. And your guys are doing a bang-up job at destroying the rest of it."

"Whoa, whoa, whoa." He practically leapt up the remaining stairs, his fit body effortlessly closing the distance between them to pull her in his arms. "Easy, babe. What do you need? You want me to help clear this stuff out of the way?"

Sorrow let herself sink into him, her body shuddering in a big sigh. She should hold her tongue—Damien was there to help. She nodded.

Keeping one firm arm around her, he shouted at the crew to haul every single trunk, suitcase, and box downstairs. He pulled her out of the way as they jumped into action. Naturally, the place cleared before her eyes.

She put a hand on his chest, pushing away to look up at him. "Thank you."

He pinched her chin. "Anything for a lovely lady in distress. And they're not *my* guys," he added with a laugh. "They're *Jack's* guys, and they're doing me a favor. They want to patch it up and get out of here as fast as you do."

He hugged her close, then pushed back again, snaking his hand up the back of her sweater. "Whatcha hiding?"

She playfully swatted his arm away, self-conscious about

Jack's crewmen looking on. "Come downstairs. I'll put on a pot of coffee and show you."

The Bailey family kitchen was sunny and warm, heated by an old woodburning stove that probably broke all manner of environmental laws. The yellow walls and gingham curtains had the feel of something that was in need of a modern renovation, but it was Sorrow's favorite room in the house, and if anyone wanted to touch it, they'd have to go through her first. Good thing her dad didn't like change.

Of course, it had undergone *some* changes since she was a kid. The tavern was separate from the main lodge, and to keep up with codes, they'd needed to revamp the restaurant kitchen in the nineties.

Sorrow had been much younger then, but even as a teenager she'd seen her opportunity, and had convinced her dad to upgrade a few of the family's appliances while they were working on the tavern. Their avocado-green Amana fridge became a nice GE one with ice and water in the door, and the ancient stove had become a decent model, with six burners and a griddle option.

It was her refuge.

She prepared Damien's coffee the way he liked it—black, with just a splash of half-and-half—and brought it to him at the table. Loud crashing and scraping sounds came from above, and she gave his shoulder a distracted squeeze. "Can I get you something to go with that? I made my apple cinnamon bread."

He took a sip and, putting his cup down, stood to embrace her. He nestled his face in her neck, his hand sweeping down to cup her backside. "I know what I need, and it's not food."

"Jeez, Damien." She pushed away with a laugh. "You're a machine."

He pulled her back. "You know it."

For some confusing, illogical reason, she pictured the sheriff again.

Unsettled, she stepped away. Needing something to do with her hands, she pulled the letters from where she'd tucked them. "I wanted to show you something."

"I'll show you something." He reached for her again.

She flinched away, annoyed. She was feeling a total

disconnect. They had a physical connection, and the sex was always good, but more and more it wasn't as satisfying. There was just something missing. It made her feel ungrateful, because he really was a great guy. He was always there for her, especially lately.

Mustering her patience, she tried to make herself heard. "Please listen, Damien. For once, I've got something to think about besides the lodge."

He traced a finger along her collarbone. "You know what I think about?"

"Be serious." She walked to the counter and began slicing her bread.

"I am serious," he said, and she felt him stand behind her. Looking over her shoulder, he spotted what she was doing. "Hey, I wasn't kidding. No bread. I've been feeling loose in the cage." He patted his already hard belly. "I'm cutting out bread and beer for the week."

She put her knife down. "*Loose in the cage?* The only thing loose on you are a few screws."

The guy was all discipline—except when it came to nookie. She turned and saw the hunger in his eyes, and scooted to avoid him. "Damien." She attempted a playful laugh, but there was an edge to it. "I really want you to see this. I'm excited about it. Besides, you cannot expect me to get"—she lowered her voice—"you know, *in the mood*, with all this going on." She pointed at the ceiling.

"What better time?" He fingered a slice of the bread, considering it, then shoved it away decisively. "All that hammering, babe. You could make all the noise you wanted, and nobody would even hear you."

"I'm showing you what I found." She sat at the table, effectively putting an end to his seduction, and settled the stack of letters before her.

Damien sighed and sat across from her. "Okay, Bailey—shoot. What'd you find?"

"Letters." She untied the quaint rickrack and sifted through to find the one she was looking for.

He squinted at them in disbelief. "I'm being denied a booty call for a bunch of old *letters*? Come on, Bail." He reached across to take her hand and swept his thumb in circles along her palm. "I've gotta get back soon. We're wasting time."

Normally, her blood would heat at that touch, but she had things on her mind. She tugged her hand free. "No, really. They're not just any old letters. They're from my great-great-great-grandmother, Sorrow Crabtree."

"Poor woman," he said, tapping his fingers on the table.

His tone drew her eyes up. "Huh?"

"Sorrow Crabtree . . . that's some name." There was a short *bzz-bzz* sound, and he pulled his cell phone from his pocket. He considered it for a second before putting it on the table.

"No, listen. There's a story behind it." She'd heard it since birth. She guessed it was the consolation prize—she got a weird name but a good story. "There's a reason behind the name. Her father had loved his wife so much, that when she died in child-birth, he named their child *Sorrow*."

"Huh. Is that what's in the letters?" Damien reached distract-edly for them, and something about the gesture had her feeling protective.

"Wait," she said, scooping up the stack before he did. She needed to make him understand the importance. She wanted *somebody* to get it—she'd tried to explain to her mom, but she hadn't wanted to listen either. "Let me read a bit. Get this: it's dated April *1851*. Can you imagine?"

"Cool," he said automatically, but it didn't sound like he meant it.

"But *wait*. That's not the crazy thing. Listen." Scanning down the page, she found the line she wanted and read, " *'You may be fancy, Mister Buck Larsen, but my mama told me to stay away from men like you.'*"

She looked up at him expectantly and caught him stealing a surreptitious glance at the screen of his cell, checking the time. Apparently Damien had a lot more time for sex than he did for old letters.

"*Buck Larsen*," she repeated, emphasizing every syllable. In the ranks of Old West legends, Buck Larsen was right up there with men like Kit Carson, or Davy Crockett, or Daniel Boone even. Pioneer, frontiersman, and later, author and statesman—he was a California legend. She jabbed the table with her finger. "He lived *here*. In Sierra Falls. During the gold rush. Before he became, you know, *Buck Larsen*."

A light finally clicked on in Damien's eyes. "Cool," he said, and this time it sounded like he meant it.

"I *know*," Sorrow said triumphantly. "But it gets better." She rifled through the pages. "Every single one of these is written to him, from Sorrow Crabtree. I guess she was too chicken to send them. Ah"—she placed one sheet at the top—"here's where it gets really good. *'If I'd told you the boy was yours, would you have come back to me?'*"

"Wow, they had a kid? That is pretty cool, Bailey."

"Not just any kid," said Sorrow. "Don't you get what this means? It means *I'm* related to Buck Larsen."

Her mother appeared at the door. "She tell you her news?"

"Hi, Edith." Damien stood to greet her, as well-mannered and articulate as his parents. Dabney and Phoebe Simmons were the Sierra Falls answer to royalty, and they'd raised their prince right. "Your daughter was just telling me. Very exciting."

"We didn't know before, who the father was." As Sorrow spoke, she watched Damien pocket his phone in a way that told her he was about to make his escape.

She felt an unexpected breath of relief, and the reaction surprised her. But she wanted to be alone to finish her work so she could curl up with her great-great-great-grandmother.

Her mom noted the same thing, and said, "One favor before you leave, hon?"

Damien tipped an imaginary hat. "Anything for you, ma'am."

"I'm late for my hair appointment, but the car won't start."

Sorrow shook her head, marveling. First the roof, now this. "When it rains, it pours."

"I've got cables in my car," Damien said at once. "I'll be right there."

As her mom went for her coat, Sorrow repeated a thank-you. Damien seemed in the business of saving her family's collective hides.

"No prob. I'm happy to jump-start the car, seeing as I'm not getting jumped in here." He winked and gave her a quick kiss. "Seriously, Bailey. It's all good. Congrats on those letters—pretty cool. Don't forget us little people when you're a famous California icon." He shouldered into his coat. "You need anything—and I do mean *anything*—just give a call."

And with that last flirty comment, her boyfriend breezed out the door.

Six

Unloading all this meat in the slushy parking lot was a pain in the neck. Or in the lower back, to be precise.

Sully hauled another side of beef from the trunk. He'd driven the Jeep to Reno for his monthly stocking up, and he supposed he should be thankful he could still do this at his age. There were plenty of men who couldn't. Look at Bear, shuffling around with his bum leg after that stroke.

Still, sometimes he wanted to get back on his bike and ride off. It felt like he'd wandered for years, searching for something, but he could spend his whole life waiting and that mysterious something would never appear.

Damien breezed out the door, with Edith on his heels. They spotted him at the same time, calling out their hellos.

Edith stopped short and faced Damien. "I didn't know Sully was back. I'm sure he can give me a jump. I don't want to trouble you."

Sully had plenty on his plate already but kept his mouth shut. He knew as well as Edith that her offer had been merely a formality. Lately, Damien seemed to take every opportunity he could to help anyone even remotely related to Sorrow. The kid was worse than a rent collector, coming around like he did. The thing of it was, Sully had begun to wonder just how much the girl even wanted his help.

Sure enough Damien told her, "Edith, you know helping you is never any trouble."

He certainly was a smooth operator. But Sully was happy enough to be left out of it all. He hid his amusement as he pulled a pallet of bread and buns from the back and carried it to the tavern.

Granted, Sully appreciated the fact that someone was looking out for Sorrow, giving her a hand. But there was something that wasn't perfect about the fling those two were having. And by the way some of the women acted around Damien, you'd have thought things would be *perfect*.

He supposed a girl wouldn't exactly be overwhelmed with dating options in a small town like Sierra Falls. Especially someone like Sorrow, who was too busy to get to nearby Silver City to experience any sort of nightlife.

His eyes cut back to Damien. He liked the kid well enough, but he was a smidge too suave. Maybe that was why, when Sully saw the two of them together, he just didn't get it.

Damien popped Edith's hood. "Did you leave the lights on? That'll burn out the battery in no time."

"I *never* do. It beeps if I try."

"Even the interior lights," he said. "That'll burn through the juice, too, if they're left on all night."

Sully heard Bear's heavy step and turned to find him staring at Damien and Edith.

Bear's cheek jumped, just a little tic. "That boy's got the town charmed."

"And your women seem to be at the top of the list," Sully said, but his comment made Bear scowl, so he added, "Hey, Sorrow could do worse. It's nice for a woman to have a man around. Buy her dinner, tell her she's pretty."

Bear's expression didn't change. "My fool daughter seems to want to cook her own dinner."

"You know what I mean. A girl likes to feel appreciated." Sully grew serious, thinking how *appreciation* should start at home. "She's a special girl. Good on Damien that he noticed."

"That damned sheriff seemed to be doing some noticing earlier. He's been coming around more than usual."

Sully pondered that. "Yeah, I suppose I have seen his eyes on her once or twice."

"Don't know if I should encourage it or punch the man," Bear said.

He laughed. "It's never wise to hit a lawman."

Edith's car engine roared to life, and Damien hit the gas a few times to rev it.

"Looks like Superman saved the day." Bear said it with a bitterness that sounded like *he* still wanted to be Edith's Superman. At least to Sully's ears.

"No surprise there," Sully said. Whatever he thought about Damien Simmons, the guy *was* capable.

Bear turned his attention to the Jeep, peering in the back. "Hey, Sergeant, these groceries ain't going to unload themselves."

"That's Major to you." Shouldering past Bear, he hauled a couple of beef tenderloins from the back. When Bear bent to help him, he saw the man's hands tremble and gave him a sharp look. "And I'm ordering you to get your hands off my ground round."

A cloud darkened Bear's features. "Seems to me, *I* paid for it, and I'm perfectly able to carry it, too."

Sully counted to ten in his head. Bear hadn't been the same since the stroke—no man would be after such a thing. But he fought his weaknesses, as well as everyone else who was there to witness them.

Edith scurried over. "Bear, I need you."

That got his attention—the woman knew her husband, that was for certain. Bear raised his brows in silent question.

She said, "Damien says we need to keep the car running for a half hour to recharge the battery."

He narrowed his eyes. "And?"

"And would you do it, honey? Sit in the car for me? I'm so chilly, and these gloves aren't doing anything." Edith flexed her fingers to prove her point. "I need to go in and find my good driving gloves. The lined ones make all the difference."

Sully saw what the woman was doing and wondered if Bear did, too.

The man scowled. "Can't we just let the damned car run?"

"I'm afraid of leaving it on with nobody in it. Come on, I turned on the radio, so you can listen to the game while you wait. I'll just be a second." She paused significantly. "Unless you're cold, too?"

That got him. "I don't get cold easy, you know that."

Bear shuffled to the car, and Edith caught Sully's eye and winked. She did a good job keeping her husband busy, making him feel needed in little ways.

He got back to unloading the Jeep. He'd wasted too much time jawing with Bear, and now telltale wet spots were starting to form on some of the cardboard boxes as food began to thaw.

Tucking a couple of tenderloins under his arm and a case of corn dogs in the other, Sully thought how he genuinely didn't mind the work. Physical labor was good for a man. It cleared the mind. And with three tours in Nam under his belt, there'd been a lot of memories to clear.

Besides, he liked helping the Bailey family. Truth was, he'd come to love them. He'd been kicking around there long enough—he'd have to be one hard-hearted son of a bitch not to love someone like Sorrow as his own kid.

There was Bear Junior, too, though he was away on his second tour in Afghanistan. Sully had felt as proud as Bear Senior on the day the boy announced he was going ROTC, and even more so when the kid made the cut and joined the Corps after graduation. Though, as an Army man, Sully could never resist getting in a ribbing around the annual Army-Navy game. *Hooah.*

They didn't see Laura enough either. The eldest Bailey girl sure did have piss and vinegar running through her veins. Even though her apartment in San Francisco was just four hours away, she didn't visit all that often. And when she did, she had a habit of waking up after a few days with eyes like a trapped animal, ready to cut and run back to life in the city.

But cutting and running was something Sully understood. *Just passing through* had been his motto when he arrived in Sierra Falls a few decades back. He'd been a lethal combination of aimless but exhausted, roaming the country on his bike, trying to make sense of what'd happened between the years 1968 and 1972. Or maybe just what'd happened to *him*. He'd gone straight from West Point to Vietnam, and when the time came for the "coming back" part of *hell and back*, it was a whole other world he found waiting for him.

A couple of wives. A couple of motorcycles. A couple dozen jobs and a couple thousand miles later, he'd rolled into Sierra Falls. Something about the place had made it hard to leave.

He slammed the Jeep doors shut. His eyes went to Bear, sitting in the car, peering at that radio like he might be able to alter the destiny of the San Francisco Forty-Niners. The Baileys had come to be like family to Sully, up to and including that grumpy old son of a bitch.

As Sully made his way back into the tavern, he breathed in deeply. The mountains had air so pure he felt cleaned down to his soul. He always thought he'd leave Sierra Falls, but he kept putting it off until one day he realized he had a job. A place to live. A *place*.

After the war, he'd cut himself off from the world. But here he was, caught up in life again, and it felt good. He didn't know when it'd happened, but he'd woken up one morning to realize he had friends. Family.

Sully hoped some good would come of those letters that had Sorrow so jazzed. The girl needed something to spur her out of the rut she was making for herself.

And then there was Bear Junior—he owed the kid an e-mail. BJ had heard about Damien and wanted to make sure he had good intentions. What would the boy think if he found out the sheriff had also been sniffing around his sister?

There was another person who'd been coming around the lodge a lot lately. *Marlene Jessup*.

Pausing at the door, Sully shook his head in appreciation. Sassy eyes, shapely legs, and a mouth that could bring a man to his knees. Now *there* was a person he'd like to get friendly with.

Seven

Billy closed his cell phone and sat in the SUV, parked along the thin, gravelly strip that was the tavern lot. He and Scott Jessup were supposed to meet for an after-work beer, but the ranger just canceled last minute.

Scott was an unexpected mix of thoughtful and boisterous, a good man with an easy laugh. They'd first met several months ago, both called in on the same missing person report. When it turned out to be nothing more than a stoned, wandering hiker, they'd gone for a beer.

He'd been one of the few with nerve enough to ask about Billy's late wife—for some reason, most other people avoided the topic altogether, as if it might've slipped his mind otherwise. But Scott received the story with a heartfelt word and an unwavering eye, and the sheriff had held him in high regard ever since.

Friday night beers had become their routine. Except tonight Scott couldn't make it. Something about a bear breaking into someone's garage, devouring everything in their chest freezer.

He peered over at the main lodge but couldn't see the roof from where he sat in the car. Had it been fixed? He kept putting it out of his mind, but something about the Bailey girl kept popping it back in his head again. For an instant, she had looked so desolate. Had her boyfriend helped her? Had she been able to seal off the attic? It'd been just yesterday when the branch fell through, but if nobody had helped her yet, the whole house would be freezing by now.

How was she? There was something about her that seemed forgotten, or overlooked. Like people noticed her, but didn't really *see*.

He slammed his hand on the steering wheel. What was his damned problem? "What the hell," he grumbled, cursing himself. Sitting there thinking about some girl.

He'd had his girl. He'd married her. And now she was gone.

Billy put his key back in the ignition. Buckled his seat belt. With Scott canceling, there was no need to go inside. He'd drive home, back to the place he'd rented, and get in a good workout. He had a bench and free weights in the garage, and a killer session was always good for keeping the ghosts at bay. Maybe he'd top it off with a beer in front of the tube. Nursing a cold one in front of late-night television until he was too tired to think was sometimes the only way he could get to sleep.

He hoped the Bailey family could sleep with the wind howling through a gaping hole in their roof.

"Dammit." He unbuckled again. Got out and slammed the door shut.

It was just a friendly visit, to satisfy his curiosity. To make sure everyone was safe and sound. It was something a sheriff would do, and he liked being sheriff. He liked feeling part of this community.

He knew in his gut he'd done the right thing leaving Oakland for Sierra Falls, shoveling cars out of snowbanks instead of working crime scenes. There was peace to be found in small-town life. It felt right to make a difference in little ways, helping good people, like Marlene or the Baileys.

He pocketed his keys. He'd just pop in, say hi, see how things were coming along. Maybe have a club soda.

With so much work to do, Sorrow probably wouldn't be around anyway. And if she was, he'd keep it formal with her, of course.

A pack of young twenty-somethings spilled from the tavern, and Billy got out of his vehicle to give them a hard stare. Most folks in search of burgers and beer gathered at the Thirsty Bear, but the younger crowd always migrated to Chances, a noisy bar across town. That was probably where they were headed now.

His eyes narrowed on the kid taking the driver's seat. Billy had zero tolerance for drinking and driving. The lone cell at the sheriff's office was empty. His deputy, Marshall McGinn, was still on duty and would be all too happy to process a DUI offender for the night. But then the kid bid him good evening, and Billy's shoulders relaxed—he was clearly sober.

Entering the tavern, he was greeted by a blast of warm air and classic rock coming from the jukebox. He looked around, registering the familiar faces—he believed recognizing people was part of his job. He noted Jack Jessup with some guys from his crew. Helen was behind the bar. Sully was off duty, sitting next to Bear, who looked like he hadn't moved since yesterday.

Sorrow didn't seem to be there, and the brief stab of disappointment caught Billy off-guard. Guilt came on its heels, and he tamped it down. Just a friendly visit—nothing to feel guilty about.

Helen stopped wiping down the counter to lean against it, cradling her breasts in the fold of her arms. "Evening, Sheriff. What's a man like you drink after a hard day?"

He darted his eyes away—to the bar behind her, to the kitchen pass-through, anywhere but at her. "Just a club soda please."

The woman was a flirt, and it made him uncomfortable. It wasn't just that she was too over-the-top for his tastes, but she was married, with a few young kids, too. He imagined she'd probably been something else when she was a teenager, but hers was the sort of cute that didn't age gracefully. Or at least, not in a way that appealed to Billy. By the slack jaws of several of the other men, he guessed his opinion was in the minority.

He turned his attention to Sorrow's father. "How's that roof coming along?"

Bear spun on his barstool and tipped his bottle of Bud toward Jack in a toast. "Fixed up, nice and tight. Marlene's boys know their business. Too bad the other two Jessup brothers didn't join Jack and Eddie. They'd be rich."

Billy couldn't picture Scott Jessup as anything other than a park ranger, outside all day, beholden to no man. And he didn't think the fourth brother, Mark, was hurting for money working as a doctor in Silver City. "Either way, you're lucky. Getting someone to patch a roof in this weather? I don't care how many Jessups there are to choose from, that's some feat."

Bear puffed his chest. "Damien—he's my Sorrow's boyfriend—he's got his fingers on the pulse here. You'll learn, if you haven't already."

Was Damien's power in the town what appealed to Sorrow? Billy found himself asking, "Where *is* Sorrow this evening?"

Just being friendly.

"Where she always is. The kitchen." Bear scowled, pausing for emphasis. "Where she doesn't belong."

The comment caught him off-guard. "Now there's a twist. You a forward-thinking man, Bear? Because isn't the old-school line that a woman's place is in the kitchen?" Billy chuckled at the thought of Bear Bailey as a women's libber, but by the look on the man's face, he didn't seem to think it was funny.

"The girl's got her mind on things." Bear took a long pull from his bottle of Bud. "She always cooks when that happens."

"As a man who's eaten one too many Marie Callender's meals this month, I've got to ask: how is that *not* a good thing?"

"If she made some real food, things might be different," Bear grumbled. "God only knows what it'll smell like when I get home. I have to sleep in that lodge, too, you know. Last time she had her mind on something, the place smelled like curry for a week. Disgusting." He polished off the rest of his beer, and with a nod to Helen had a fresh one almost instantly.

Billy considered him. The man's main source of pride appeared to be that Sorrow had landed Damien for a boyfriend. It made him feel defensive on her behalf. "You should be proud," he said, even though he knew better than to goad. "She is something in the kitchen."

Bear went on alert. "When'd she cook for you? Sully's in charge of cooking around here. Nobody makes a better fried chicken. All Sorrow wants to do with chicken is put weird sauces and mushrooms on it. They grow those things in shit, you know."

"Nah, it wasn't like that," Billy said. "She gave me a few slices of her apple cinnamon bread before I went on patrol."

"I thought cops only liked donuts."

The comment had been grumpy, but instead of annoying Billy, it gave him a laugh. "I like donuts, too, sir. I just like Sorrow's bread more. Have you tried it? You put it on the menu, I guarantee it'd make you a small fortune. Best bread I've had in some time."

Bear only grunted *hmph* in reply. He seemed to be formulating a fervent reply, but when he turned in his stool to deliver it, his foot caught and he stumbled sideways off his seat.

Billy reached out, catching his elbow to steady him. "Easy, sir."

The man flinched away, impatience wrenching his features. "I had a stroke. I'm not an invalid, boy."

He understood the flare of anger. He guessed Bear had once been as fierce as his name—such a man wouldn't appreciate growing feeble.

But the behavior also worried him. The man had tottered on his feet. Was Billy witnessing one too many Budweisers or something else? He was well-versed in first aid—all sheriffs were—and he was particularly on alert where a history of stroke was concerned.

He decided to keep the man talking to assess. "What's on her mind then?"

"Huh?" Bear settled back on his stool, leaning both elbows on the bar.

The man had a startled look on his face, and Billy knew a wave of sympathy. He kept his voice light and easy. "You said your daughter has things on her mind. What's got her so preoccupied she was forced to retreat into the kitchen?"

The man sniffed. "She found some letters and has it in her head we're all related to Buck Larsen."

The unexpected turn in the conversation took a moment to register. "Pardon?"

"Yeah. Who knows with that girl?" Bear's expression softened. He spun his bottle around and around on the counter, shaking his head. "She found some old letters in the attic, and now has a bee in her bonnet about the whole thing. Says my great-granddad was the natural child of Buck Larsen."

"*The* Buck Larsen?"

Bear shrugged, but the faint smile on his face said maybe, just maybe, there was indeed something about Sorrow that made him proud. "She's at the house, doing her stirring and chopping. Go see for yourself."

Eight

She dried her prized butcher knife till it gleamed. It was German, used by professional chefs, and had cost her a pretty penny. She hated when even the most minor of water spots marred the surface. Sorrow tilted it up to the light, wondering if it could use a sharpening. After all, a chef was only as good as his—or *her*—sharpest blade.

"Remind me not to cross you."

The voice in the doorway startled her. Her knife froze, midair.

Sheriff. The man filled the doorway, those broad shoulders making her pounding heart skip a beat.

She darted her eyes back to her task, giving it her whole focus. The sauce was simmering, and she'd taken a moment to clean up. A dirty kitchen was one of her pet peeves. "You know better than to surprise a woman wielding a big knife."

"It's safer than a woman . . ." His eyes flicked in the direction of the tavern as he made a funny, frightened sort of face. "Well, never mind that."

She smirked. "Been at the bar, have you?"

"How'd you guess?"

She shrugged, sliding her tools back into the knife block. She knew what he'd been about to say. Helen worked as their part-time waitress and part-time bartender, but she was a full-time flirt. Billy Preston was a fine man—the woman had probably been on him like white on rice. The thing with Helen was, most men seemed to run *to* her. All except for her husband. And that, Sorrow guessed, was the crux of the issue. But it wasn't her place to gossip.

Although she did file in the back of her mind the fact that Billy appeared the sort of man who ran *away* from such a woman.

He wandered closer and gave her knives an appreciative nod. "Nice."

She *loved* her knives and had to temper her smile as she thanked him.

He glanced around the kitchen, quietly taking it all in, and Sorrow wondered what he might be thinking. "Your mother let me in," he said after a moment. "I hope you don't mind me showing up so late in the day."

"On the contrary." The sound of a rapid boil startled her from her thoughts, and she jumped to turn down the burner. She stirred her sauce, relieved it hadn't burned. She used an arm to brush the hair from her brow. "Your timing is perfect. You're just in time to clean out that dish for me."

He gamely jumped into action, shrugging out of his coat and rolling up his sleeves. "What are we making?"

"Beef bourguignon."

He scraped bits of onion and bacon fat from the casserole into the sink. "Don't you mean *boeuf*?"

With a laugh, she tapped her spoon clean. "Impressive."

"Hey, I saw that Julia Child movie."

She wiped her hands on her apron then grabbed a sieve from a cabinet under the island. "So that means you won't complain if I ask you to hold this for me?" It was time to strain the sauce into the casserole dish, and balancing everything always gave her arms a workout.

"I'll do you one better." He took up both sieve and saucepan with an easy confidence that surprised her. "I've got this, you just scrape."

She couldn't help but think of Damien, who was so powerful and in control in other aspects of his life, but magically turned useless whenever he got near a kitchen.

Billy added, "I'll only complain if you don't let me eat it when it's done."

She raised a brow. Taken aback, but not in a bad way. "Sorry, Sheriff. If you saw that movie, you'll know this sucker doesn't go in the oven till tomorrow."

He inhaled deeply. Straining the sauce had spread the rich aroma into the air even more than before. "Well, I'll just have to take a rain check. I'd cross an ocean for a good beef bourguignon."

Sorrow paused at that. "Would you really?"

He gave a hearty nod. "I love Sierra Falls, but . . . good restaurants? That's the one thing I miss about living in the city. No offense to your tavern," he added quickly.

She laughed. "Believe me, no offense taken. I'd rather . . . I don't know . . . set my hair on fire than eat Sully's 'Prospector's Pie' one more time."

Billy's laugh was loud and deep. "What on earth is that?"

"Meat pie," she said, scrunching her face.

"Hey, sounds good to me. What kind of meat?"

"All kinds." She shuddered.

He laughed at that. "Just how many kinds can there be?"

"Oh, you'd be surprised." She brought the casserole dish to the refrigerator.

He jumped to open the door for her. "Is that why you learned to cook? An aversion to mystery meats?"

She bumped the fridge door shut with her hip. "Necessity is the mother of invention." But as she washed the dirty sieve, she found herself giving him a real answer. "If I can't whisk myself off to another country, well, cooking is a way to bring other countries to me. It lets me travel to other places in my head."

Wiping her hands, she turned around, and her smile faded. He stood so close, his body a commanding physical presence suddenly so near, in her private space, the kitchen.

The silence hung.

She racked her brain for words and automatically asked, "Can I get you something to eat?"

"I . . . I think . . ." His stomach took the opportunity to rumble, and they both laughed, the awkward moment passed.

"I'll take that as a yes," said Sorrow.

"If your apple bread and the smell of that sauce are any indication, I must confess, I'd love a taste of what you're serving." A look washed over his face, and it gave his words a double meaning. "I mean . . . if you're sure you don't mind. I don't want to be an inconvenience."

"Not at all. I have to eat, too." She ducked back into the fridge, rifling more than was strictly necessary. The cool air was a relief on her warm cheeks. What was wrong with her? "How do you feel about pasta?"

"I feel good about pasta."

She smiled. Finally a man who didn't shy away from carbs. "I can pull together a quickie Aglio e Olio."

"Sounds fancy."

She grabbed the olive oil and made sure there was enough garlic. "It's just Italian for 'garlic and oil.' Nothing to it."

Billy reached up to grab her colander and big spaghetti pot from their hooks. He held them up in silent question.

"Perfect," she said, a little surprised. "Thanks."

He began to fill the pot with water. "While the pasta's boiling, you can tell me about those letters."

She froze for the merest second. "You know about the letters?"

"Your dad told me."

And he was interested in hearing more about them? Disbelieving, she poured olive oil in a saucepan and added a decent glug of a Pinot Grigio she'd had in the fridge. Her arm hovered in the air a moment. *What the hell?* She showed him the bottle. "Do you want a glass of wine?"

"Why not." He seemed surprised he'd said it. And a little uncomfortable, too.

She gave him an extra glug for good measure. She knew she needed one herself. She was feeling a little uncomfortable, too, but in an excited-uncomfortable way. Because she kind of liked having the sheriff in her kitchen.

The sauce was reducing, the water put up to boil, and it was time to wait. As she joined him at the table, he put a careful fingertip atop the small stack of letters. "Are these the ones?"

"They are," she said. "Dated from the 1850s, from my three-times great-grandmother."

He shook his head at that, marveling. "When I see something that old, it's impossible not to imagine the person who owned it. Them picking up this paper—it probably cost a lot back then. And then taking their pen in hand."

He'd voiced thoughts she'd had a hundred times herself. Mostly she burned to know exactly who this woman was, this first Sorrow. She was a family mystery. A woman who'd given birth to at least one child out of wedlock, at a time when such things weren't to be considered. A story had been woven through the generations—but had Sorrow Crabtree really known as hard-luck a life as the tale went?

Photography wasn't common back then, and she couldn't even summon a mental picture of the woman. Sorrow had found a couple of old dresses in the attic and fantasized they'd belonged to her ancestor. A dress did much to describe the woman who wore it, and this woman had been curvy—not unlike herself—with a penchant for low necklines and tight bodices. They were the sorts of dresses a lady didn't wear on a stagecoach. Instead, they were for dancing, or for shots of whisky at a saloon. For bawdy jokes and hands of poker.

"I wonder what kind of pens they used then," Billy said, calling her from her thoughts. "Do you know?"

She smiled to herself. "I'd like to find all that stuff out, I think."

He skimmed a finger along the side of the stack, and she appreciated his care. "Are they really written to Buck Larsen?" he asked. "Did he write back?"

"That's the thing." She inhaled deeply, back in the moment, and reached for them, taking a few from the top. "My great-great-great-grandmother Sorrow never sent them. From what I can tell, Buck Larsen lived here, then took off for the capitol, and well, you probably know the story from there."

"Me and every fifth grader in California." His eyes caught hers, and there was a look of amazement there. "Now, what they *don't* teach is how he left his pregnant lover behind . . ."

Sorrow felt a flare in her belly as she locked eyes with this man, heard the word *lover* come from his lips. She cleared her throat. "Looks that way. I'm reading the rest of them, but it's slow going. The handwriting is pretty tricky to make out."

"May I?" He reached his hand out, and she handed him a random letter. Billy studied it for a moment. "Handwriting is a lost art."

She leaned in to look, and he edged toward her, moving the page to where she could see. The movement had been automatic, as had the way she'd scooted closer for a look. Only now their shoulders were touching, and Sorrow found she couldn't focus on the words.

But apparently Billy could. She was grateful when he laughed, pointing to a spot low on the page.

"She sure does give him what for," he said. "Listen to this: *'I'm nothin but a Grass Widow, left for dead. Folk been sayin how grand you are now, living in Sacremennto. I say your nothing but a coward, Buck, runnin like you did.'*" Billy leaned back. "Hoo-boy. She must've been something else, your great-great-great-grandmother. Them's fightin' words."

"Wow. 'Grass widow?' I'm not even sure what that means."

He carefully picked another few from the stack, rifling through. "This is remarkable. Have you read all of them?"

"Not yet." She realized the excitement buzzing through her was from having another person actually show some enthusiasm. "So, you're interested? I mean . . . you think they're interesting?"

"What, the letters?" Billy shot her a look. "Who wouldn't be?"

Damien. Her dad. Her mom. Pretty much everyone else. "I wonder if there's a way to use these to bring more business to the lodge, but I'm not sure how."

"You should take them to the historical society."

It'd come from out of the blue, and a quick laugh escaped her. "What do *you* know about the historical society?" Generally, the only person she heard discuss such things was her mother. The other members probably discussed their society ad nauseam during their weekly bridge night, but Sorrow always steered clear, terrified she might get pulled into a round.

He scooted his chair to face her, looking earnest. "Seriously, they'd probably be able to help leverage the Buck Larsen connection. And answer other questions for you, too, like about pens, and grass widows, and such. I was talking to Marlene just yesterday—"

Now she really did laugh. "*You* were talking to Marlene?"

"Yes, *I* was talking to Marlene." His eyes twinkled, and Sorrow wondered if she and the sheriff were flirting. "Apparently they're having financial trouble. This would be of great interest to them. I take it you're not a member?"

"Me? No way. That many older women in one room—it's like a cabal. Each woman's sole goal to introduce me to their grandson, or grandnephew, or paperboy or whatever."

"Paperboy?"

"They've known me forever," she said, waving that one off. She sipped her wine, thinking. "You know, though . . . you might actually be on to something. I'll have Mom bring it to the Kidd sisters." At his puzzled look, she clarified, "Marlene's maiden name was Kidd."

"Marlene has sisters?"

"No, no, no." She gave a grand shake to her head. "I forget how new you are around here. Marlene has *aunts*. Two of them. And her mother's still alive, too. They're all in their eighties."

Billy's brows furrowed. "I don't think I've met them."

"Oh, you'd know if you had. Emerald, Ruby, and Pearl. The grandes dames of Sierra Falls."

"Oh, my."

"Oh, yes." She shared a smile with him. Suddenly she realized how intimate it all felt. Suddenly she wondered what it'd be like if he lowered his lips to hers and kissed her.

He looked like maybe he was wondering that as well.

Her heart beat hard in her chest.

The angry sound of water boiling over and sizzling onto the burner broke the moment. Sorrow shot to her feet. She ran to the pot and tossed in some linguini.

"That's a lot," he said.

She smiled secretly over the stove. "You seem like a man with an appetite."

"How'd you guess?" He picked up his wine and joined her, looking over her shoulder into the pot. "Except that might even be too much for *me*. Though I've always believed nothing beats leftover pasta in the morning."

She nodded her agreement. Nodded, and found herself wondering what it might be like to serve this particular man breakfast.

Nine

Marlene surreptitiously smelled her wrist. She hoped she wasn't wearing too much perfume. She hadn't *thought* it'd been too much, but when she'd walked into the tavern, so full of the aroma of beer and fried things, she'd begun to worry that her Estée Lauder stood out.

She *hated* having to worry about such nonsense. One would think a sixty-three-year-old woman would have a little confidence by now. But the divorce had thrown her.

One would think a sixty-three-year-old woman didn't have to worry herself with nonsense like blind dates, but there she was.

Her eyes adjusted to the dark, and she sensed the slightest lull in conversation as folks turned to see who'd come in. Cheeks burning, she walked to the first empty table that was neither too conspicuously close to the door, nor tucked too secretively in the corner.

Normally she wouldn't have chosen the Thirsty Bear—it meant meeting her prospective beau in front of everyone and their brother, for goodness sake—but she'd hoped to grab a word with Edith. There were no secrets from anybody in Sierra Falls anyway. She could've driven all the way to Sacramento to meet the man, and still folks would've heard about it.

Pulling off her scarf, she smoothed her hair into shape. She dyed it and had regular blowouts, but no matter how much money she threw at it, gray hair had a life of its own. She hated that almost as much as the lines that seemed to etch themselves on her face overnight.

"Marlene!" Edith caught her eye and waved.

She waved back, giving her friend a smile that she had to force. Edith looked as effortlessly attractive as ever—*Edith* never had to work at it, and *Edith's* husband clearly wasn't going anywhere. Marlene only hoped the dim tavern lighting was working the same magic on her.

Edith gave one last word to Helen behind the bar before scampering over to join her. "I've ordered us a couple of glasses of wine," she said. "It's that sauvignon blanc for you, right?"

Marlene half stood to offer her cheek for a quick air-kiss. "That's perfect." And of course it was—her friend seemed to remember everything about everyone.

She'd been a conundrum to Marlene since they'd met as girls. Edith always silently watching the world, noting everything. And just when she thought the woman was as passive as a lamb, she'd roar like a lion. Not that she needed to do much roaring—Edith and Bear had been together forever, and he did his fair share of bellowing for the two of them.

Helen came over with two glasses of white wine, looking put out that she had to step from behind the bar. The two women shared a quiet chuckle as the bartender walked away.

"She's a piece of work," Marlene whispered. "Flirts with everything in pants. And then's a witch with a capital *B* to the rest of us."

Edith sighed, watching Helen get back to work behind the bar. "She is, isn't she?"

"So why not cut her loose?" Marlene didn't understand why she kept the woman around. There were any number of people in their town who'd do backflips to get some extra work.

"We all of us have our troubles," Edith said mysteriously.

"Ain't it the truth." Marlene raised her glass to toast *that* bit of obvious wisdom. She took a big sip, but the wine suddenly tasted too tart. Her friend's relentlessly forgiving and openhearted outlook made Marlene feel jealous and small. She tried to be kinder in her thoughts, adding, "To women with troubles."

Edith sipped, but shook her head. "How can you say you have troubles when you're looking so pretty?"

Marlene smiled, not expecting the compliment. "Oh, Edith," she replied with grudging honesty, "it's *you* who's looking pretty. As always."

Edith had blond good looks, and she'd given them to her daughters, too. Weren't fair-skinned women supposed to age more quickly? Marlene touched her own forehead—she wondered how that Botox stuff worked. She was certain there were any number of doctors in Reno or even in nearby Silver City who worked with it. Maybe it was time to give it a try.

"Enough about me. So"—Edith leaned close to whisper—"you're meeting a *man* here tonight? How exciting."

Hardly. She remembered her blind date and smiled stiffly, nodding. *Exciting* wasn't the word she'd use. What would be *exciting* was if she'd already met the man, and he'd been a classy, gentlemanly sort of fellow. Someone who'd had a good, respectable career. A widower judge, perhaps. Or maybe a retired doctor. Someone who was kind, with a full head of hair, a healthy nest egg, and a nice sedan. Something foreign maybe, with a leather interior that was a color named something like *ebony* or *champagne*. She could put this Internet dating nonsense behind her.

And the next time Frank visited Sierra Falls, he'd see her, and see how well she was doing, and how spoiled she was, and he'd be jealous and realize what a fool he'd been to leave her.

"But aren't you worried about this online stuff?" Edith asked, pulling her from the fantasy. "I've heard stories."

Marlene had heard them, too, and a big part of her was terrified about all the crazies out there. But instead she made herself sound bravely nonchalant. "Oh no, it's perfectly safe. All the singles are carefully screened." She hoped. "And what other choice do I have? I've lived here my whole life, and as far as I know, there aren't any retirees zipping around Sierra Falls in any sports cars, looking for wives."

Edith slumped at that, unable to muster a rebuttal. "Forget men, then. How are *you*?"

Marlene sipped her wine, considering. How *was* she?

She was a sixty-three-year-old woman on a blind date. She was struggling to keep hold of her dignity. The last time she'd dated, she hadn't needed to figure out how to balance her reading glasses on her face in order to put on eye makeup. The last time she'd dated, it'd been with boys she'd grown up with, nice boys her parents knew, not a bunch of strangers who might or might not be kooks.

She'd gone straight from raising four kids—four *boys*—to taking care of two elderly aunts and an ailing mother who was in the early stages of Alzheimer's. She shouldn't be sitting in a bar drinking Bear Bailey's crappy sauvignon blanc.

That's how she was.

What she said instead was, "I'm plugging along, Edith. You?"

Edith glanced around then leaned in close, looking conspiratorial. "I have *news*."

Marlene leaned close. The best cure for depression was *gossip*. Her friend looked happy—it was good news then.

Dark thoughts were replaced with a flurry of speculation. A smile crept across Marlene's face as she realized what it must be. "It's Sorrow, isn't it?" She slammed her hand on the table, a lightbulb going off. "She and the Simmons boy finally got engaged."

"Oh . . ." Edith looked momentarily puzzled. "Oh, no, not that. But it does have to do with Sorrow. She found letters."

Marlene deflated. *Letters* wasn't nearly as exciting as *engagement*. "Letters?" she asked, trying to sound intrigued.

When Edith got to the word *affair* Marlene perked back up. Turned out, Bear's great-great-grandmother had a child out of wedlock with *Buck Larsen*, of all people. She'd written, but never sent, a stack of letters that featured some pretty juicy details.

Edith's face was lit up in a way that Marlene hadn't seen in some time. "It's just what the town needs."

Marlene hated to play devil's advocate—why was *she* always the one to put a damper on things?—but she couldn't keep herself from asking, "How do you know they're real? I mean, those letters must be over a hundred years old."

"Over *one hundred fifty* years old." Edith beamed proudly, adding definitively, "The woman had no reason to lie."

Marlene still didn't buy it. It was a woman who'd connived her Frank out of a marriage that'd spanned almost four decades. Who knew what women had been capable of back then? "All the more reason she could've made *any* old thing up."

"Why would she go and do something like that? Especially since she never even sent them." Edith waved away the notion. "Don't you see? It means we can turn our Spring Fling into a *Buck Larsen Festival* instead. Get some publicity, some new tourists."

That gave Marlene pause. Edith did have a point. The town sure could use some livening up—and not just financially. This discovery could bring new people into Sierra Falls. And with the average age of their historical society hovering somewhere around seventy, their group could use some fresh blood, as it were. Maybe it'd even bring in a wave of older, single men. Visions of tweedy historical types flitted through her mind.

Finally convinced, Marlene smiled. "I can't wait to see their faces when I tell them."

Edith didn't have to ask to know the "them" in question were Marlene's mother, Emerald, and her two aunts, Ruby and Pearl. Three women whose preacher daddy had scared away enough boys that they'd aged into thick-as-thieves spinsters. Marlene's mother had been the wild one of the group, running off as a girl, but she'd returned home with a belly full of baby and a mouth full of secrets and had never left town again. They were the backbone of the historical society and a permanent fixture in Sierra Falls.

"I'll get them going on a special gold rush quilt," Marlene said.

"We could have a raffle!"

Marlene nodded, her mind spinning. If they played up the gold rush aspect, they could really milk it. "We could make a book of old California recipes."

Edith's eyes lit up. "We could put on a show, too. From the look of the dresses we found, Sorrow—that was her name—was a dance hall girl. We could have a performance, maybe an exhibit, too."

Edith bustled off, anxious to start her list of to-dos.

Which left Marlene alone again, waiting for Mister

Wonderful, who had yet to make his appearance. She checked her watch for the umpteenth time. She'd come a little early, but now he was starting to feel a little late. She nursed her wine as slowly as possible—she didn't want to sit there with nothing to sip on, nor did she want to order another drink. This one was hitting her too much already.

Edith's news had been exciting, and Marlene was feeling residual optimism. Maybe she'd have a great time on this date. Maybe he'd be The One.

She adjusted her shirt, waiting. Why hadn't she worn a sweater? It was chilly, and she'd sat too close to the door. Damned old age—most days, she was either too hot or too cold. Well, it was too late to move now, it'd just look funny.

Rubbing warmth into her arms, she decided she knew full well why she hadn't worn a sweater. She ran a mental catalog of what was in her drawers, and it was all ancient cardigans. Sure, they were well-loved, having been hand-knit by her mother once upon a time, but all of a sudden they seemed too frumpy for something like dating. Too fusty.

She *resented* that feeling. She loved those sweaters—why *weren't* they good enough? Did it mean *she* wasn't good enough? That got her thinking about Frank again. This was all his fault.

Her optimism was fading fast. Her nerves getting more jangled by the minute. Where *was* this man?

"A woman like you . . ." A male voice said from behind her.

Marlene turned to find Sully standing behind her. There was a devilish light in his eyes that brought a quick smile to her face. *That*, she knew, was her vanity, pure and simple. Sully was a quiet man, but he'd always had a word or two for her, and as the years passed, her ego appreciated the attention more and more. "A woman like me *what*, Tom Sullivan?"

He put a glass of something sparkling on the table in front of her. "A woman like you shouldn't be kept waiting."

"A woman like me should do lots of things. Take *this*, for example," she said, pushing away the glass. "I definitely shouldn't."

"I know you shouldn't." He edged it back toward her. "That's why it's just a club soda with a twist."

She inhaled, the knot in her chest easing a bit. A club soda with a twist sounded perfect right about then. "How'd you guess?"

"You were wearing a hole in the table, spinning your wineglass all around. Thought you could shift that nervous energy to a nice cocktail straw instead."

"I'm not nervous." Did she really appear nervous? And how'd *he* known?

"You're the boss." He gave her a mysterious smile. But he didn't leave, and he didn't sit down either.

Why didn't he just sit down? She narrowed her eyes on him. "If anything's making me nervous, it's you hovering over me."

"If I'm hovering," Sully said, "it's because you haven't invited me to join you."

Would Sully really join her if she asked, or was he just ribbing her? Did she *want* him to join her? Why was he being friendly? He couldn't be interested in her, could he?

She dismissed the possibility at once. A man like Tom Sullivan would attract someone saucier and wilder. An older, big-bosomed version of that attractive bartender they had. *She* wouldn't be his type.

Not that she knew who he ran around with—she'd never heard that sort of gossip about him. The only rumors about Tom Sullivan were about his past, how he'd come back from Vietnam a changed man and had spent years on the road like something out of *Easy Rider*. It was probably all romantic speculation.

"I'm meeting somebody," she said. With a subtle shift of her shirtsleeve, she checked the time again. She needed a rich man, not someone who flipped burgers for a living. A wealthy retiree who'd buy her a sedan. A silver fox. She was in search of a *classy* boyfriend. Not someone who rode around on a motorcycle, looking too young for his age.

Tom didn't get the hint. "Seems he's late."

Marlene bristled at that. Even though it was true, it was a presumptuous thing to say. She took in his tight, white cook's T-shirt, the Army infantry tattoo on his forearm. He sure did look strong. Not a silver fox at all, but vital and vigorous. And when had she started thinking of him as Tom? She took a sip of that bubbly water.

His tattoo put a thought into her head. She was anxious to change the subject anyway. "They say you went to war."

"So I did," he replied, his tone wary.

The pain that flickered across his face told her to tread carefully. "Would you talk to my grandson?" His face crumpled into something that looked highly skeptical, and she continued quickly, "He wants to enlist right out of high school."

His eyes narrowed, pinned on her. Goodness, but they were a dark and vivid blue, like indigo. It put her on the defensive.

"Don't you get that look with me, Tom Sullivan. Hear me out. I had a cousin from my grandmother's side who served—you should know that. You were here when we flew to Arlington to bury him, may he rest in peace, and if you don't remember, you just need to listen to Ruby and Pearl for half a minute to hear his memory invoked." She grew half concerned that the wine had made her too emotional, but pressed on, anxious to be understood. "There's nothing that'd make me prouder than to see Craig serve his country. But I get nervous that he doesn't see that side of it. The service side. I'd love to see the boy shape up and put on a uniform, but for the right reasons. He doesn't understand how seriously it should be approached. How hard he'll need to work. I worry he thinks it's just a chance for him to appear in one of his video games."

Sully was silent for long enough she began to worry. But finally he nodded. "I understand. Bring him by, Marlene. I'll be happy to talk to the boy."

She unclenched something she hadn't realized she'd clenched. "Thank you, Tom."

A gust of wind blew in as the door opened. Sully looked up and that stony look was back in his eyes.

"It's not right," he muttered. His dark blue eyes locked with hers. "This date of yours had better pay. I see him try any nonsense like splitting the check, I might need to come back over."

Marlene felt her cheeks blush. And *Good Lord*, when was the last time she'd blushed?

Ten

"Sorrow!" she heard her mom call from the hallway a moment before she appeared in the doorway of the laundry room.

Mom had that tone—the one that told Sorrow she was going to be assigned another duty she didn't want. Whatever it was, it had to be better than ironing linens. She hated ironing.

"Did you hear me, Sorrow?" Her mother had a white-knuckle grip on her purse, and that alone had her putting down the iron. Her mom never looked that tense. "I need you to call your friend again."

"Who? You mean Damien?"

Edith nodded. "The road is closed. I thought he could make some calls. Get it plowed."

"Wait, *our* road is closed?" The lodge was on Irish Camp Road, an old mining road off Route 88. It wasn't exactly a major thoroughfare, but it wasn't a small street either. "I'm sure it was plowed hours ago. Why would Caltrans close it?"

As far as Sorrow was concerned, Caltrans—aka the California Department of Transportation—were the unsung heroes of their area, plowing through the night, clearing rockslides, and managing avalanche control in the higher elevations. They might be experiencing the first real weather of the season, but it was nothing compared to what Caltrans could handle.

"It's not the snow," Edith said. "There's something blocking the road."

What was she supposed to do about something blocking the road? Why did everything fall on her shoulders? Why couldn't her *mother* call Caltrans? Better yet, why wasn't her *sister* around to enjoy this indentured servitude, having to deal with things like ironing the tavern's tablecloths? Or how about her brother, for that matter?

She felt a pang of guilt at that last thought. BJ was deployed in Afghanistan . . . ironing was a walk in the park compared to what he was going through.

She sighed. "Fine. I'll call Caltrans."

"Maybe you should call Damien."

Sorrow hesitated, reluctant to ask for his help on this one, especially since she'd been having inappropriate thoughts about another man. She felt guilty about Billy and heating things up in the kitchen—because the things she wanted to heat up had nothing to do with food. "Caltrans will take care of it."

"Please," Mom pleaded. "It's just that, I think Damien would be able to call someone in charge over there and get it cleared faster than you could."

She turned off the iron, defeated. It was unlike Mom to get this impassioned about something. "Okay, sure. I'll call Damien." She reached over to unplug it—the way her luck was going, the whole lodge might burn down otherwise. She edged past her mother in the doorway in search of the phone.

Edith followed right on her heels. "This is very important, Sorrow."

She had to chuckle at the uncharacteristic intensity. "I said I'm on it, Mom."

"I'm going to present your letters to the historical society. Marlene thinks that it might be just the thing to breathe some life into this town."

"Good," she said distractedly. Girding herself, she dialed and put a hand up to signal quiet.

Unfortunately, she didn't need to keep quiet for long. Damien was in a meeting and not to be disturbed. Sorrow had a good guess what the meeting was about, and if her hunch was right, he'd be unavailable for some time. Simmons Timber was ready to thin several overstocked acres, clearing debris in a fire-prevention effort, a huge concern in the Sierras. The problem was, his father was trying to use the program as an opportunity to clear more acreage than necessary.

The stance felt a bit uncharacteristic for the kindly Dabney Simmons, but she supposed you didn't get to be rich without being aware of the bottom line. And for a timber company in a paperless era, that bottom line was getting progressively smaller. As a result, father and son were butting heads more often than not, with Damien increasingly outspoken about the responsibility they owed to the environment, while Dabney was preoccupied only with keeping food on his employees' plates.

"He's unavailable, and . . . oh, crap." Sorrow shut her eyes as she hung up, turning her head heavenward to take a deep breath. A road closure had much bigger implications than her mom missing the historical society meeting. If their road was closed, nobody could drive to the lodge or tavern. It would mean a day's business lost. "Crap," she repeated vehemently. "We've got two groups of hunters coming in tonight, and I already bought a few sides of salmon to serve in the tavern."

"Well Sully can't cook it," Edith said. "He hasn't even made it in yet. That fool man insists on riding a motorcycle at his age."

"He drives the Jeep in this weather, Mom."

"Well, what are we going to do?" There was an edge to her mother's voice that she didn't often hear. "I don't want your father getting upset. And I especially don't want him going out in the car to check on it himself."

Sorrow grabbed her coat and scarf from a hook in the mudroom off the garage. "Don't borrow trouble. I'll check on it and see what's going on. Dad's still watching the headlines—he won't even know I'm gone." Her father's CNN addiction came in handy at times like these. The constant hum of the television was aggravating, but she knew he was safely ensconced in his den, apart from the lodge's public area.

She was slipping on her snow boots when she heard the main entry door open. It was a slow creak followed by a tentative knock—someone polite enough to realize that, even though it was a lodge, a family lived there, too.

"Anybody home?" a man called.

She recognized Billy's voice, and found herself putting a hand to her hair. She'd tugged it back that morning into a messy ponytail. So much for looking presentable.

Why should she care anyway? He was just a man like any other.

But he wasn't just a man. He was *Billy*.

She pulled out the elastic and gave her head a shake as she finger combed some life into her waves. And *then* she went out to greet him. "Hi, Billy."

Something in his face softened. "Hi, Sorrow." His eyes went to her snow boots. "You know your road"—he stopped, seeing the look on her face—"you *do* know."

"Yup. The road is closed."

He nodded, frowning. "There are signs posted, but somehow nobody notified Caltrans. I called it in, and it should be cleared by this evening."

"This *evening*?" So much for their guests.

"But I need to get to my meeting," Edith said.

That again. The historical society meeting was the last thing on Sorrow's mind. All *she* could think about was a hundred dollars in salmon that wouldn't freeze well.

Edith began to sound frantic. "I told Marlene I'd drive her and the Kidd sisters. All she has is that pickup. You know the women hate climbing into *that*."

"Mom, I'm sorry. You're going to have to miss the m—"

Billy cut her off. "I'll take you in the truck, ma'am."

Sorrow shot him a look, waiting for an explanation.

He jingled his keys. "How do you ladies think I got here?"

Sorrow shook her head. "You're nuts."

He shrugged. "I had to see if today was the day Sully finally put his Prospector's Pie on the menu."

That startled a laugh out of her. "Now I *really* know you're nuts."

"Hey, a little off-roading is good for the soul."

"You mean driving off the road?" Edith asked. "Is that allowed?"

"Are you suggesting I give myself a ticket?" The sheriff put an arm around her mother's shoulders, leading her to the door.

"Now button up that coat and let's go. I guess I'll just have to wait for that Prospector's Pie." He looked back at Sorrow and winked.

A zing of excitement stabbed her chest. "I can do you one better," she heard herself say. "You like salmon, Billy?"

Eleven

Marlene's date had gone south fast. She'd had plenty of time to contemplate that sad fact, seeing as he'd sat across from her, this total stranger, talking at her the whole time. There was not one single question he had to ask her. The blasted man just droned on and on about *fishing*. And he hadn't even called it *fishing*—he'd corrected her every time she dared say the word. *"Angling, Marlene. It's called angling."*

He started in on "bite indicators," and that was when she'd tuned out completely. She'd already had a man who'd chewed her ear off about fishing, and look how *that* had turned out. She certainly didn't need to go out and find herself a new one.

But the whole situation had made her think. All these men had their leisure activities—watching sports, going fishing, playing golf. So what were *her* passions? Some days it felt like she'd gone straight from raising four young boys to caring for three elderly women. Unless she counted dusting and laundry among her pastimes, she had a sad absence of interests in her life. Interests that were hers and hers alone.

Sometime during the *bite indicators* conversation, she made her decision. She'd forget men for the moment and pour her heart and soul into the historical society instead.

That was how she came to be early, prepared, and waiting

when folks started to arrive at the town hall for their weekly meeting. It'd been some feat getting her elderly aunts and mother ready sooner than usual.

Now that they had these letters, the meeting promised to be a rip-roaring one. She hadn't yet told the ladies the news about how Buck Larsen had spent time in Sierra Falls and was making a great show of a grand secret to be revealed. So with promises of high drama ahead, she'd managed to wrangle Ruby, Pearl, and Ma into their coats.

The drama began even before they got to the meeting. Marlene heard an unfamiliar car outside and opened the door to find Billy Preston parking in their drive.

"Oh, good heavens." Her aunt Ruby's eyes widened, seeing the big sheriff's SUV. "The law is here."

Pearl sidled into the doorway. Her gloved hand had a death grip on Marlene's arm. "What do you think happened?"

Ma piped up, "Did he find out about that lipstick I took?"

"Oh, hush Emerald. That was back in 1946."

Marlene spotted Edith in the front seat and patted Pearl's hand. "I think what happened is Edith had car trouble again."

Billy hopped out of the car. "You're all looking lovely today." He bounded up the porch stairs, taking an aunt on each arm. "Your chariot awaits."

Marlene locked up the house and, taking her mother's arm, followed him to the car. "Sheriff, you probably have a dozen other important things to do."

"Maybe so, but this was at the top of my list." With a smile, he helped her climb into the additional row of backseats. "You going to be okay back there?"

"Yes." She settled herself, but her mind was churning. Now here was a considerate man. She'd sensed it the day he'd helped free her car from the snowbank. *This* was a man who wouldn't chew off a woman's ear about bait lines. She wasn't used to getting help, though, and twice in a row from the same man no less. She felt bad putting him out. "You don't need to drive us old biddies to our meeting."

"I don't see any biddies here." He gave Pearl a wink.

The moment she was buckled in, Ruby leaned forward to

study the complicated control panel that was nestled between the front seats. The police radio crackled to life, and distant, unintelligible chatter filled the SUV.

The ladies gasped. Marlene had a chuckle to herself. They'd be talking about this for weeks.

They talked about it now, seated in the Sierra Falls Town Hall, waiting for the meeting to come to order. She and Edith sat at the front, and she could sense that her friend was dying to gossip about the sheriff, but Marlene silenced her with a look. They were the heads of the historical society, and it was up to them to project an official air.

As chairwoman and de facto treasurer, Marlene was the one who got to use the gavel, and she banged it. "Time to get this meeting to order. First item of business is our budget."

They addressed their dwindling bank account, and as was often the case with money talk, the discussion dissolved into grumbling and fretting.

Edith shushed them, and Marlene's head swiveled to give her friend a startled look. "Marlene and I think we have a solution," Edith said. "We found letters."

Marlene gave a quick pat to her friend's hand. It wasn't like Edith to put herself out there like that. It looked good on the woman.

"Letters?" a woman in the back asked. "How are a bunch of letters going to help us?"

"They're *historical* letters," Edith said.

Other voices chimed in. "What kind of historical?"

"Maybe they're just old."

June Harlan spoke louder than the rest. "How do you know they're real? It's impossible to date things with the naked eye."

Pearl turned in her seat. "You listen up, June, and let her tell it. If Marlene says she has letters, there are letters."

"Well, where'd she find them?"

Marlene banged the gavel again. "The Bailey family found them."

Edith gave a proud smile. "And we think our next festival should be a Buck Larsen festival."

June was looking frustrated. She turned to Pearl, asking in a loud whisper, "Did she say Buck Larsen?"

Ruby spoke up, sounding confused. "Buck Larsen's dead. He can't come to the festival."

"No," Pearl said. "He *wrote* the letters. Isn't that what you're saying, Marlene?"

"No." Marlene regretted not telling this news to her aunts and mother in advance. She'd thought it'd be a fun surprise, but the real surprise was how the meeting was crumbling into chaos. "The letters were written by *Sorrow Crabtree.*"

Emerald turned to Ruby. "Isn't that Edith's child?"

Ruby nodded and piped up, "What's that about Sorrow?"

"Sorrow wrote letters." Pearl was hard of hearing, and her whisper had echoed down the aisles.

"Not *our* Sorrow," Edith said, exasperated. "Our Sorrow *found* the letters, from her great-great-great-grandmother."

As understanding dawned, female voices swept across the hall like a sigh. "Ahh."

Marlene put down her gavel. "Turns out, Buck Larsen was one of the pioneers of *our* town. If we theme our next festival around Buck Larsen and the gold rush, we might draw more tourists."

Edith leaned in to add, "More tourists means more money for Sierra Falls."

Ruby got it and nodded enthusiastically. "So you're saying Buck Larsen is *Bear's* kin."

Emerald looked aghast. "Bear skin?"

Pearl patted her sister's hand. "Bear Bailey. They're talking about his ancestors."

Marlene couldn't take the circus anymore. What this crowd needed was a spectacle. She cleared her throat and spoke in her best assembly voice. "Sorrow Crabtree was one of the early residents of Sierra Falls. It looks like she had . . . an *affair.* With Buck Larsen. She had his baby." She paused dramatically to let that sink in, and sure enough, another wave of female *oohs* and *ohhs* swept the room.

The meeting fell apart from there, the excitement too great to get any more business done. Marlene spotted Billy Preston waiting at the back of the hall and quickly wrapped it up.

Standing to put on her coat, she turned to Edith. "You never did tell me what the sheriff was doing at your house to be offering you a ride." The buzz in the hall drowned out her voice, and she leaned close to speak into her friend's ear. "Seems Billy Preston has an awful lot of business to tend at that tavern of yours."

Edith puffed up. "He just happened to be there."

"Mm-hm." Marlene buttoned up. "Lucky you. Or should I say, your lucky daughter."

Edith was winding her scarf around her neck, but her hands froze in midair. "Sorrow, you mean?"

"Yes," Marlene said impatiently. *"Sorrow."* First she caught the sheriff toting around her apple bread and now this. "Seems to me like I've seen the two of them together a lot lately."

"Oh no, not him," Edith said. "He's a widower."

"Well, that's a silly thing to say. It's his wife who died, not him." They both studied the man. He stood like a cop, straight and tall. His sheriff's jacket made his broad shoulders look even broader. "Seems to me, he's still a young man. Not hard on the eyes neither."

Edith made a little *hmm* sound. "No, he's *not* hard on the eyes, is he?"

Marlene squinted her eyes to focus better. "He reminds me of . . . I don't know . . . a cowboy from a TV movie."

Edith finished tying her scarf around her neck. "Not as handsome as Damien, though."

"Maybe not," said Marlene. "Though he makes Damien look like a kid in comparison."

"Damien isn't a boy. He's Sorrow's age, and I say twenty-three is old enough to start thinking about settling down." Edith's eyes drifted back to the sheriff. "Are you saying *he's* looking to remarry?"

"I didn't say marriage." Marlene abruptly began to gather her papers into her handbag.

All this talk of spouses made her think. If she'd been a widow, would *she* have remarried? Would the pain have been this deep? Sometimes, when she was feeling small-hearted, she wished she *were* a widow. That her husband had died instead of divorcing her. In her low moments, she told herself that burying him would've been easier to bear than the shame of his leaving.

Pearl approached the table. The woman wore a contented smile—the meeting had been as dramatic as promised. "Are we leaving now?"

The other two Kidd sisters were close behind, still bundling up. Marlene's elderly mother was having trouble with her coat sleeves, but before she could help, Billy appeared at the woman's back.

"Let me get this for you," he said, guiding Emerald's arms into the sleeves. "You got all turned inside out."

"What a gentleman," Ruby exclaimed.

Edith met Marlene's eyes, a significant question there. *Was* there something between Billy and Sorrow?

Marlene studied him. Whether or not he was a widower, whether it was Sorrow or somebody else, someday, some lucky woman would find herself turned inside out by this sheriff.

Twelve

Billy felt kind of awkward. He'd gone home to change—nobody wanted their guest to show up for dinner wearing a sidearm—but he worried he looked as though he were trying too hard. He refused to think on the fact that simply thinking on such things *was* the very definition of trying too hard.

Was he trying?

Of course he wasn't. The last time he'd tried with a woman had been with Keri. For years, they'd been colleagues, then friends, and it was a slow courtship that'd turned them into lovers. He'd bought flowers. Symphony tickets. Dinners at the latest *in* restaurants. Things he didn't necessarily enjoy but had thought his wife would. Sitting through a three-hour avant-garde opera? Now *that* had been trying.

No, this was a friendly visit, all part of small-town living. Sorrow's mother led him into the lodge's private living quarters. He'd never eaten in the lodge before—tourists and lodgers ate at the tavern—and he was looking forward to seeing how the family interacted.

"You're looking handsome this evening," Edith told him as they joined Sorrow's father in the den. The man sat in his recliner, watching a college basketball game on mute.

Billy had settled on wearing jeans with a sweater, but seeing Bear's scowl, he'd begun to regret the absence of that sidearm.

"Bear"—Edith nudged her husband—"say hello to Billy. If it weren't for him, I'd have missed my meeting."

The older man nodded a greeting then turned back to the game.

"Evening, sir." Billy's eyes went to the action on TV as he settled onto the giant sectional couch. Its old brown leather was as comfortable as it looked. "Kentucky came out strong this year."

Bear's eyes narrowed. "You a Kentucky fan?"

That seemed like a minefield if ever there was one. For all he knew, Kentucky fans weren't allowed in the Big Bear Lodge.

"I went to Colorado State," Billy said, sidestepping the question. A topic change seemed in order, so he added, "It's where I discovered my love of the mountains."

"Why go all the way there?" Bear was skeptical, obviously not the sort of man who thrived on travel.

"Football scholarship."

Bear pulled his eyes from the screen to study him. "Really now?"

Billy sat up straighter, feeling a little uncomfortably checked out. "Running back," he clarified.

"Ahh." A smile spread across Bear's face. He nodded thoughtfully. "Yeah, I see it. You got that stocky sort of look of a man who played ball. I played ball, too, once upon a time. It was different then. We didn't much bother with nonsense like pads."

"You play in college?"

Bear was quiet for a second. Finally, he said, "Nah, didn't go. Didn't need it. I played high school ball, then played around here. Town stuff."

They watched the game for a few minutes, then the older man surprised him, saying out of the blue, "I appreciate you driving Edith. I'm sure you got better sheriff duties to tend to."

"Not a problem," Billy said, and he meant it. It'd been a break from his routine and a pleasure to boot. In fact, small favors like that were how he kept it together these days. By being relentlessly friendly and occupying himself with the needs of others, he could keep the ghosts—one particular black-haired ghost—at bay.

When he'd doubled back to drive the women home, they'd invited him in and plied him with a lot of coffee and Danishes, but surprisingly few questions. He could tell they wanted to ask more and couldn't blame their curiosity—a young widower like himself? He imagined the average Sierra Falls female retiree would view him as a project. Oddly, rather than mind it, Billy found it touching.

"I don't know what it is with women and meetings," Bear said. "You meet the Kidd sisters yet? All I know is, you driving my wife saved me from having to deal with those old birds. They're going to use our letters, though. It'll turn this town around, you'll see."

"Thanks to Sorrow," Billy said. At Bear's questioning look, he added, "I mean, thanks to your daughter for finding them in the first place and seeing their worth. Not everyone would appreciate such a slice of history. Most folks would've dumped the lot of them straight into the trash."

Bear shrugged. "I guess."

"Can I get you a beer?" a voice asked from behind him.

Billy turned to find Sorrow standing in the doorway. Her blond hair hung loose and wavy at her shoulders, and the light coming from the fireplace made her eyes sparkle.

The world stilled around him. Sorrow had the sort of looks that demanded his attention. She had some meat on her bones, and her snug sweater clung to that spot between the dip of her waist and the curve of her hip. His mind went to an image of his hand tucked just there.

He swallowed hard. "Yes, ma'am, I think I could use a beer."

He hadn't been with a woman in a long time. He'd indulged in one or two mindless hookups—outside town limits, of course. He was a man after all, and thirty-five was far from dead.

But this was Sorrow. There was no *mindless hookup* with Sorrow. And anything more would feel like . . . cheating.

He needed to stop looking at her curves so he dragged his eyes back to her hair. It was different. He realized she mostly wore it tied back. Not that he didn't like it that way. She was a natural beauty, with a peaches and cream, fresh-faced complexion that looked as good with makeup as without. Though tonight, in the warm firelight, her hair loose and her sweater tight, Sorrow was quite stunning indeed.

She gave him a perplexed smile. "Is there a problem, Sheriff?"

Billy realized he'd been staring. "You look . . ." *Edible*. His eyes went to the oven mitt in her hand. "Like you could use some help."

Was that disappointment that flashed on her face?

He stood abruptly. *Get a grip*. "Tell you what. Let's get that beer, and I'll give you a hand in the kitchen."

Bear shot him a look that Billy caught from the corner of his eyes. It'd probably never occur to her father to lend a hand with the dinner prep.

They went into the kitchen, and she handed him a bottle of Bud from the fridge. "Sounds like a good trade."

"Give me a job," he told her, cracking it open. Because if he stood there staring at her, he might be tempted to find out just how soft the sweater—and what lay under it—really felt.

She looked around, deciding. "We'll ease you in slow, how about? Want to set the table?"

"Table setting? Child's play." He pulled out the cutlery and plates. "What does a man have to do to get respect around here? You'd have thought I proved my worth helping strain that sauce of yours. And I didn't even get to taste it."

"You'll have to settle for my salmon. It's better for you anyway."

He breathed in deeply. "Wow, that's like no salmon I ever smelled."

"It's with bamboo shoots and green curry."

"I love green curry," he said, genuinely impressed. He went into the attached dining room to set the table, and she joined him, taking the napkins from his hand to spread them around the table. He caught her eye from across the table. "One question, though. Is Bear going to go for that?"

She laughed. "He'll go for it, or go hungry."

"A rebel, huh?"

"I'm making up for my teen years."

They ended up side by side at the head of the table. He said, "Well, I'm just happy I'm the one who gets to benefit."

She opened her mouth, looking like she wanted to say something, but didn't quite know how to phrase it. He waited patiently, curious to see what this woman might say.

"Did your wife like to cook?" Her question surprised him, and she quickly added, "I hope you don't mind me asking."

"I don't mind at all." Oddly, it was always a relief when people asked him about Keri. So many folks tiptoed around the issue, but what they didn't know was that Billy longed to talk about her. He missed her terribly, and it was the sort of grief that made him feel set apart from everyone else. But talking about her always brought him one step closer, back among the living.

He leaned against the dining table. "My wife—Keri was her name—she wasn't much for cooking. She was a lawyer. That's how we met, in court. Anyway, between her long hours in the DA's office and me being on the force, we spent more time at our local sushi bar than we did at the corner market. Then, when she did cook, it was always some fancy salad. They were good . . . she'd use crazy ingredients, like goat cheese, or blood oranges, but truth be told, they always left me hungry."

He laughed at the memory, and it was good to be able to remember it, and talk about it, and actually have a smile about it.

Sorrow held his gaze with a warm, open look. She didn't say anything, didn't scramble to come up with any of the standard-issue condolences, and he was glad of it.

Talking about his wife like that, it was impossible not to note the differences between the two women. They were physical opposites—Keri's chin-length black hair and bangs were such a contrast to Sorrow's feminine dishevelment. This woman seemed like she'd be most at home in a long, flowing skirt and flip-flops, while his wife had been all about power suits and heels.

He'd adored his wife, and man, she'd been something to see. Especially in the courtroom. A snapshot memory came to him—polished nails, quick retorts, strong stride, and confident delivery. It stabbed him. What a loss, what a waste.

He realized he'd been staring at Sorrow. She had such kindness in her eyes. Soft where Keri had been hard. The sort of woman who might twine her fingers through his hair, pull him to her, and make him forget his troubles.

A barking dog broke the moment. It was a relief. He'd put women out of his mind. Best to keep them out.

"I didn't know you had a dog," he said.

She tensed, looking in the direction of the den. "No. We don't."

It was an odd reaction. "Not a fan?"

"What?" Sorrow caught his eye again. "Of course not. I love dogs. I just . . . I think I know who that is."

The animal burst into the kitchen. He was friendly and high-energy, with a lean, medium-sized body and short, white fur covered with cartoon-cute brown spots. He looked like he might've come from central casting for a Hollywood dog movie.

Billy squatted to call him over. "Hey, little guy. Who do you belong to?" He glanced up, and Sorrow was stiff as a board.

The owner strolled in, and the dog forgot about Billy, galloping back to his master's side.

It was Damien Simmons. *The boyfriend.*

Thirteen

❧

"Hey, Bailey. You look great." Damien stepped in close.

Sorrow fought the urge to flinch away, self-conscious of Billy standing right there next to her. She and Damien had a thing. He was her *boyfriend*. So why was this situation stressing her out? She tipped her head so Damien could brush a kiss on her cheek—she wasn't about to give him a full-on mouth kiss with the sheriff standing *right there*.

Billy stepped forward, reaching out to shake hands. "It's Damien Simmons, right?"

The two men gripped hands, and if the white knuckles were any indication, it looked like a squeezing contest was going on.

"Hey, Sheriff. Good to see you." Damien's smile was wide and easy, Sierra Falls poster boy. "Thanks for taking care of our Edith today. The woman does love her meetings."

Our Edith. Sorrow felt her back go rigid. What was up with *that*? Helping out around the lodge was one thing, but laying claim to her mother was entirely another. She bit her tongue. *Boundaries, Damien.*

"My pleasure," Billy said. "That's a cute dog. What kind is he?"

"Just a bird dog. Aren't ya, Coop?" Damien scratched between the dog's ears, then smoothed his hand back to give a firm, affectionate pat to Cooper's side. "He was a rescue mutt . . . a pointer, most likely. He loves to hunt, don't you, boy?"

The dog wagged furiously. That creature sure did love Damien . . . he could get in line with the rest of the town.

Damien's clothes finally registered. He was wearing his top-of-the-line gray and white camouflage jacket. "You went hunting?"

"You were out hunting in *this* weather?" Billy asked at the same time.

"I did and I was." Damien directed his smile at her. "Quail season doesn't end till February."

"Oh." So that was the important meeting that couldn't be interrupted? "You held all your calls so you could hunt?"

The sheriff laughed. Good that someone found it amusing. "Isn't it kind of wet for that?"

She must've been scowling because Damien chucked her chin, telling her, "Don't look so bummed. I brought you a few quail in the cooler—you can cook us up one of your gourmet feasts."

Damien wandered back into the den, and they followed. His sudden presence had her feeling a little smothered. She told herself she was *glad* he'd had a good day. But it would've been nice if he'd at least fielded her call, instead of ignoring her and then showing up unannounced for dinner.

Billy went to the window and pulled back the curtain. It was full dark, and the snow glowed like a white blanket in the moonlight. "I still can't get over that you were hunting in this weather."

"Not a hunter, Sheriff?" Damien settled on the couch. She sat stiffly on the end, and he scooted closer.

Billy seemed to be taking in every detail of their interaction, and it made her intensely uncomfortable. "Sure, I've hunted," he said. "I still have some venison in my freezer from the fall. And I love the snow . . . skiing, snowshoeing, it's all good. But choosing to *sit* in it? All day? Not my thing."

"Me neither," her mother chimed in.

Sorrow had to agree. If anyone was asking. Which they weren't.

"Don't knock it till you've tried it," said Damien. "We hike around, it's good exercise. I'll take you sometime."

This whole exchange had her feeling peevish. "You never offered to take *me*."

Damien faced her full-on, asking earnestly, "Would you like to go hunting with me tomorrow?"

"No," she admitted.

"A-ha! There you go." He addressed the whole room, saying, "I tell you, it's more *fun* in the snow. More of a challenge."

Billy asked, "What do you hunt with?"

"Twenty-eight-gauge."

"That's big for quail," her dad grunted from his recliner.

Damien turned to face him, not missing a beat. "Mister Bailey, when it comes to shooting, Rhett Akins gets it right." He warbled out the lyrics, " *'A gun's like a woman . . . it's all how you hold her.'* "

Her father's laugh was explosive. He nodded sagely, his eyes brimming with warmth.

Maybe *Bear* should be the one dating Damien. She stood. "Boy talk. I'm outta here."

But Damien snagged his hand in her jeans pocket, catching her before she could escape. The gesture embarrassed her.

He tugged her back to the couch. "What's eating at you, babe?"

She shifted out from his grip. That was the thing—she wasn't exactly sure *what* was eating at her. "I thought you were supposed to have a big meeting with your dad today."

With a gusty exhale, Damien flopped back on the couch. "Oh, that. Yeah, we tabled it for another day. It was the old man who convinced me to go hunting instead. What was I supposed to do? He's the boss."

Of course Dabney could convince his son to get out of the office—the world could be ending, and Damien would still jump at the chance to spend a day outdoors. The Simmons men had been butting heads over environmental issues, and Damien had been gaining support in the company. But the Simmons employees adored his dad, and Dabney probably wanted to buy time to remind them of that fact.

"He's just trying to distract you," she said.

Looking at Billy, Damien explained, "My dad and I have a long-running argument when it comes to how much we should cut down and where." He paused, mimicking his dad's booming voice, " *'People need paper, son.'* But there's a way to do it mindful of the native habitat, you know? That's just good PR. And hell, it's good for the wildlife, too."

The men got to talking about the logging business, and she took that as her excuse to finally make her escape.

Her mom followed her into the kitchen, her voice a frantic whisper. "Sorrow Ann Bailey."

Sorrow stopped. "Uh-oh. The middle name—I must be in trouble now. What is it, Mom?"

"You be a good hostess and ask that boyfriend of yours to eat with us."

"He knows he can eat with us."

"I didn't hear you *invite* him. A man needs to hear you say it."

She rolled her eyes. "What is this, 1950?"

"Hey, Bailey." Damien appeared in the doorway. "Got enough food for one more?"

Her mother gave her a pointed look before scurrying from the room. Something about this whole situation put Sorrow out of joint. She turned on Damien. "Do you *have* to call me Bailey?"

"I've been calling you Bailey since junior high." He reached for her hair, twirling a wave around his finger. "Sorrow's just such a . . . I don't know . . . a mopey name."

Mopey. "Yeah, and it's all mine."

He pulled her close, nestling her body against his. "C'mon, mopey. Give me a proper hello."

It was nice having a man who cared. Nice not to be alone. Wonderful how he'd gotten her out of so many jams. Was she taking him for granted? She should want him around when she didn't need his help.

She tried to put herself into the moment. That hard body of his felt good. She glanced up. Damien sure *looked* good, too. So why did she feel so put-upon? Shouldn't she feel all melty at his touch? It was nice, but shouldn't it be electrifying, too?

She gauged the talk in the other room. Billy's deep voice, her mother chatting away, and Dad's occasional *humph.* They were deep in conversation. It didn't seem like anyone would come in and catch them kissing.

As she stood on her toes, she wondered why she was feeling so self-conscious. She told herself it was just polite. It was a considerate thing, not kissing one's boyfriend in front of one's dinner guest.

Damien's hands were warm and sure, sweeping down her back to cup her bottom. "Shorty," he teased. "I need to pull you up to reach me."

He pulled her higher onto her toes, and she wrapped her arms around his neck for a slow kiss. She tried to forget herself, but remained overly aware of the hum of conversation in the other room. She wanted to push the voices out of her mind, but they weren't to be ignored.

Damien must've sensed it, because he broke the kiss to nip along her jaw, nuzzling in behind her ear. "C'mon, gorgeous" was a hot whisper in her ear.

A shiver rippled across her skin. The man definitely had some good moves.

"Sorrow," her mother called, "do I smell something burning?"

That was the problem—*nothing* was burning at the moment. Putting her hands on Damien's arms, she pulled away, and they both sighed.

"Mom won't want to keep hungry men waiting," she told him.

He touched his forehead to hers. "Are you saying you're blowing me off *again*?"

"Me cooking dinner is hardly blowing you off." Though she did find she was anxious to get back to her cooking, for more than one reason.

He gave her shoulders a squeeze. "It's okay. I'm a patient man."

Her mom bustled into the kitchen to toss a couple of empty bottles into the recycling bin. "I set another place, Damien. You'll be sitting right across from the sheriff."

A knot twisted in Sorrow's belly.

Not what she'd pictured for the evening. Though why that was so troublesome to her, she had no idea.

Fourteen

Billy studied the man across from him. If he had to be honest with himself, he might say he was a little jealous of Damien Simmons. Not the guy's looks, which were good, and not even his bank account, which seemed sizeable. It was the guy's ease, that nonchalant way he carried himself through the world.

Billy had lost his ease when he'd lost his wife.

But Damien was young, eager to take life by the horns. He was the sort of guy who flirted with every waitress and cracked jokes with strangers. As though he were a friend to all.

Which made Billy wonder how much *anybody* really knew the guy.

"So, this is actual bamboo?" Damien studied the food speared on the end of his fork. "Does that make me a panda?" He gave the table a cheeky smile before shoving a hearty bite in his mouth.

Bear chewed and swallowed, frowning all the while. "Why you didn't just toss the fish on the grill is beyond me. Some butter, a little salt, there's a good meal right there. Takes a lot less time, too."

"You seem to be enjoying it well enough," Sorrow said, not looking up from her plate.

Billy had to agree. The man complained a lot, but he sure

did seem to be clearing his plate. He watched her father bristle, and jumped in to defray the tension. "Well, I'm impressed."

"Me, too," Damien chimed in, not to be outdone. "Totally."

The compliment seemed rote, so Billy added, "I used to eat a lot of Thai, and this is as good as any I got in the Bay Area."

"Thank you, Sheriff." Sorrow put her fork down, seeming genuinely touched.

He leaned back in his chair, overcome by a feeling of contentment. It must've been a combination of good food, a cold beer, and general conviviality. And, he realized, it was because of Sorrow, too.

That she'd asked about Keri had somehow drawn an invisible thread, connecting the two of them. His grief set him apart from other people, but Sorrow's openness had offered him a bridge back. He waited for the guilt to hit, but oddly, it didn't come.

The thought was interrupted when the dog exploded into frantic barking.

"I'll go check it out." Damien scooted away from the table, nodding an apology. "Hey, quiet, Coop," he said, his voice carrying to them as he walked into the foyer. When he returned, he had a pretty blonde by his side. "Look who I found."

Edith jumped up from the table with a squeal, and a smile finally cracked Bear's surly expression. Sorrow, though, her shoulders tensed. It was almost imperceptible, but Billy had been trained to spot such subtle cues.

Edith hugged the woman over and over, exclaiming, "What are you doing here? Why didn't you call to say you were coming? You didn't drive all the way from San Francisco in this weather? Billy! You have to meet our Laura."

He pushed away from the table to stand.

"My older sister," Sorrow said, and he noticed she didn't jump out of her seat as quickly as her mother had.

"Laura, meet our new sheriff."

She slipped a tiny hand into his, smiling wide. "Ooh, you're much cuter than the last sheriff."

The comment took him aback. The sisters weren't just different, they were *very* different, and women like this put him on his guard. He wanted to come off as friendly, but not too much like he was taking her bait, and he fumbled for an appropriate reply. "I'm glad to oblige. Though I hear your last sheriff was a good man."

Laura shrugged and wandered to the table. She poked at the curried salmon, swishing it around with the serving spoon. "Is that hard-ass deputy still there?"

Billy chuckled at that. "Who, McGinn? He's a lamb, once you get to know him."

"No thanks," Laura said. She dropped the spoon into the serving dish, and it landed in the sauce with a *plop*.

Billy's smile turned speculative. If first impressions meant anything, this girl was a handful. It made him appreciate Sorrow all the more. He stole a look at her as she watched Laura with guarded eyes.

"Sit down, sit down." Edith shooed her eldest daughter to an empty seat, helping her out of her coat. It was a short, puffy thing that looked like it belonged in a magazine spread.

"You can eat bamboo with us," Damien said as he emerged from the kitchen carrying a fresh plate, napkin, and cutlery.

Billy had to give the guy props for being Boyfriend of the Year material.

They all returned to their seats, and Damien reached over to spoon some food onto Laura's plate, but she put a hand up to stop him. "I ate already."

"You're missing out," Billy said, using the opportunity to study her. Light from the wrought-iron chandelier caught her profile, and he saw the family resemblance. But although she had the same blond hair and delicate features as Sorrow, the similarities ended there.

Unlike her sister, Laura didn't have a hair out of place. Everything from her designer snow boots, to her skinny jeans, to the fake fur of her jacket collar spoke to urban-professional-goes-snow-bunny. She had a gym body, too, all taut lines to match her taut demeanor.

Not like Sorrow, who had the body of a real woman. He much preferred a girl with something to hold on to.

Damn, what was his problem? He took a big swig of his beer. He barely knew these people, and he was a guest in their home, for God's sake.

"So I guess this means the road is open again," said Bear.

"Thanks to the sheriff and his efforts," Sorrow said.

Laura's face lit, and she looked from her sister to him, and Billy sensed the female cogs turning. Had she read his thoughts? The possibility there might be a connection between him and Sorrow that was *that* obvious made him a little queasy.

They might've had a friendly spark, but no way could it ever be more than that. She had a boyfriend—who was sitting *right there*—and even if she didn't, he'd sworn off relationships. He'd learned the hard way how all the clichés were right. Love hurt, and he'd never put himself through it again.

Laura met his eyes. "You're making friends already, Sheriff. I'm impressed."

"A man tries." He made his voice as bland as he could.

"Tries *and* succeeds, apparently." She reached over and tweaked her father's ear. "It takes a lot to get a compliment out of grumpy old Bear Bailey."

Her dad did his darnedest to bite back a smile. Billy made a mental note: apparently a statement of fact followed by a noncommittal grunt could be counted as a compliment where Bear was concerned.

Laura continued her assessment, and Billy polished his beer off too quickly, nervous under the scrutiny. "I see you're not just strapping," she said, "you're also a can-do man." She looked to Sorrow with teasing eyes. "I'll bet Helen at the bar is all over him."

Sorrow looked as uncomfortable as Billy felt. She steered the conversation to another topic, her voice absent of emotion. "What brings you back to Sierra Falls?"

Laura's reaction was subtle, but it was immediate. A cloud crossed her features, dimming the light in her eyes. "I thought I'd take a vacation."

Sorrow sipped her beer slowly, and Billy felt tension crackle between them. "What about your job?" she asked.

Laura shrugged. "It's like a . . . sabbatical."

"Sounds like a nun thing," said Bear. He was following the conversation, even though he mostly remained focused on his plate of food.

Sorrow ignored her father. "Isn't that just for . . . I don't know . . . professors?"

"It was . . . it *is* a very high-stress job. You have no idea how cutthroat it is in Silicon Valley these days. Especially in Marketing."

Edith turned to Billy and beamed. "Laura is vice president of her department."

Laura looked down as she twirled her napkin. She'd gone from bubbly to cagey, and Billy half wondered if maybe she hadn't lost her job and was just too scared to tell her folks.

"How good you can take a vacation then." Sorrow kept talking, but seemed either unwilling or unable to meet her sister's eyes. "I don't suppose you'll be able to help around the lodge this time. I know you were too busy on your last visit. Reno, Tahoe . . . I understand there's a lot to do when you're on vacation."

Edith chimed in, "Now, that won't be necessary. We've got everything under control, don't we, Sorrow?"

Billy hadn't been coming to the lodge for long, but if this was under control, he'd hate to see when things got out of hand.

"On the contrary, Mom." Laura smiled wide. "I'd love to pitch in."

Sorrow stood abruptly to clear the dishes. "I made a pie."

Now Billy had to stare flat out. Laura had offered help, and wasn't that what Sorrow needed? And yet she seemed upset. He stood to help, too curious to do otherwise.

Damien made a move to get up, but Billy stopped him. "I got this one."

The other man raised his beer in a toast to thank him. "Works for me. I hate the kitchen."

Billy was right behind Sorrow with his hands full of dishes. "What was that about?" he asked the moment they reached the kitchen.

"Nothing." Her voice was tight. She turned her back to him, stacking dishes in the sink.

"It didn't seem like nothing in there."

She stiffened. Paused. "Every once in a while, my sister breezes in."

He wondered what she wasn't saying. He wasn't one for female drama, but something about this situation piqued his interest. "Seems like you could use the help," he ventured.

She dropped the dish she'd been washing and turned to face

him. "Trust me, the next time there's a problem around here, Laura will claim some personal drama and make a break for it, heading back to San Francisco faster than you can say *Miss Fancy-pants Vice President*."

Billy chuckled. "That so? Well, maybe that's a good thing."

Bear's belly laugh reached them from the other room, and Sorrow looked stricken by the sound of it. "Stick around long enough, Sheriff, and you'll see. There's a favorite daughter, and it ain't me." She'd tossed the comment off, but he heard the pain beneath her breezy delivery.

This Laura might sail in all charm and sass, but it was Sorrow who struck him as the backbone of the family. He met her eyes. "I don't have siblings, but I've done enough living to know that *favorite* and *most valued* are often two very different things.

"And besides," he added, "maybe she'll distract Bear long enough for you to start serving that frittata of yours in the tavern."

"Yeah, maybe so." She softened her features, giving him a grateful smile. Up close like this, the girl was so pretty she seemed to glow from within.

Such an errant thought, it struck him dumb for a moment. He wasn't looking for a woman. He had one, and he'd buried her. This one already had a man anyhow. He told himself it was purely neutral observation that had him thinking how much prettier Sorrow was than her sister, even though it was Laura who probably caught more men's eyes.

"C'mon," she said as she pulled a pie from the fridge. "You ever have Butter Pie?"

His eyes grew wide as a kid's. "You're kidding. There's such a thing as Butter Pie?"

"My specialty. Made just this morning."

"Is it really what it sounds like it is?" He stepped closer to take an appreciative sniff. "My life has been incomplete."

"It's exactly what it sounds like. Butter, sugar, vanilla, eggs. Some whipped cream on top. Some people add cranberries but—"

"Cranberries?" he interrupted. "Why mess with beige perfection?"

She giggled, and it was a good sound. "Should we go for broke?"

He gave her a hearty nod. "Hell, yeah."

"Grab some ice cream. A little more beige never hurt anyone." She pointed to one of the drawers. "Scooper's in there."

He snagged the ice cream, scoop, and a stack of plates, and followed her back into the dining room, practically salivating from the wonderful smell.

Laura peered at the pie dish, frowning. "Is that what I think it is?"

"Yup," Sorrow said, and the change in her attitude was visible.

Laura folded her napkin and put it onto her plate. "You know I can't eat that."

Sorrow's arms and shoulders were stiff as she put the dish onto a trivet. "If you'd told me you were coming, I'd have baked my famous Splenda and Air Pie instead."

Billy choked back a laugh, cheering inside. If the other woman was going to be so uptight, he was glad they'd added a big tub of ice cream to the spread. All the better to torture her with. As he sat back down, he told her, "I say you're crazy."

"Crazy, huh?" Laura got a glint in her eye that made him wish he'd kept his mouth shut. "Why am I crazy?"

"To pass up this food. Your sister's cooking is some of the best I've ever had."

Laura gave him a coy smile. "So you're saying, I *don't* need to watch my figure?"

What the hell *was* he saying? This woman was a wily one—was she baiting him? Flirting with him? All he knew was, he'd better watch out for these land mines. "I'm saying . . . I'm gonna shut up and eat some Butter Pie." And he took a giant bite to prove his point.

They all laughed. Except for Sorrow.

He looked over at her. If anyone was becoming a friend in this town, it was her, and he automatically sought her gaze to share the moment. But her eyes were flat, pinned on her sister.

He knew women. He'd been married. He'd had many women friends through the years, a number of female coworkers. He appreciated the fairer sex, listened to them, enjoyed their perspective, their company. And so he recognized her expression.

It was jealousy.

Fifteen

Laura pointed angrily at the TV. "What the hell is she making?" She was sprawled in one corner of their giant sectional couch and turned to glare at Sorrow seated stiffly in the other.

Sorrow grabbed the remote and made a show of upping the volume. "I don't know, Laura. I can't hear over your talking."

Laura leaned over and snatched it from her. "It's 4:00, there must be a talk show on. She's just *cooking*—how is that interesting?"

"Please. I just want one little break." Sorrow snatched back the remote. "I was working all morning. I'll be working in the tavern all night. What have *you* been doing all day? I have this one tiny window when I can relax, and *this* is what I want to watch. If you're so bored, why don't you go *do* something?"

"I don't know what to do," Laura moaned.

"You sound like you're twelve. You should finish unpacking. You brought enough stuff to clothe an army."

Laura slumped into the couch, ignoring the suggestion. "Do we *have* to watch the Food Network?"

"The host is discussing techniques for velveting tofu."

"Exciting," her sister said sarcastically. Then she made a grumpy *hmph* sound. "Do you *really* need to know this? You should just be a chef."

It was an offhand comment, but it made Sorrow feel like

her head might explode. Old resentments burbled to the surface. "Gee, Laura, I'd *love* to be a chef. But I'm stuck *here*."

"It was just a suggestion. No need to bite my head off." Laura shrugged. "Maybe if you spruced this place up a little, it'd be more interesting for you."

"Maybe if *you* hadn't fled Sierra Falls, this place wouldn't need sprucing." Sorrow angrily upped the volume. "*Sprucing.* Of course the place needs sprucing. *Duh.*"

"Easy, cowgirl. I'm just saying, if you livened it up around here, maybe you'd get more visitors. Keep you busy. I don't know how you survive out here in the woods."

Sorrow muted the TV to glare at her sister. "*Busy.* You don't know the meaning of busy. You cut and ran after graduation, leaving me holding the bag."

When Laura left, their brother BJ was already off at college on a ROTC scholarship, committed to serve upon finishing. By the time it was Sorrow's turn to make her life choices, her father had had his stroke, and somebody needed to stay behind and help run the place. Their mother definitely couldn't handle it; too many of their simple day-to-day chores—shoveling snow, unloading groceries, hauling guests' suitcases up and down stairs—were just too physical for her. And so Sorrow had given up on *her* dreams to stay behind.

"I'm not having this conversation again," Laura said.

"So now you can tell me what I can and can't talk about?" Sorrow had been holding her feelings in for some time. All she'd wanted to do was sit and watch her stupid program in peace. Her feet were killing her, and something about Laura's pouting pushed her to the breaking point. "You can tell your fancy coworkers what to do, but you're not vice president of me, so don't come here and think you can boss me around. You have *so* not earned the right to breeze in and tell me how I should be doing things."

"Jeez," Laura said under her breath. She looked away, back at the screen. "*Relax.* I'm not bossing. I was just making some friendly suggestions."

Sorrow ignored her and barreled on. "You left for bigger horizons, leaving me here, doing work I don't really want to do."

Laura rolled her eyes. "Look, don't do *me* any favors. Nobody said you had to stay home and live with Mom and Dad. If you don't like it, make a change."

"Seriously?" Sorrow turned off the TV—she was unable to follow it anyway—and scooted sideways to face her sister. "So, what, I was supposed to leave after Dad's stroke?" It'd happened when she was a junior in high school. He'd been laid-up for months. Gradually, she'd taken on responsibilities, until one day she was the one who was basically running the place.

"I don't know," Laura said. "You seem pretty happy to me. You're like queen of the castle here."

"Hardly," Sorrow snapped. "It's *hardly* unicorns and rainbows around here. But I do the best I can with what I've got. Unlike *some* people who visit their family so they have a whole new audience to complain to."

"Well you should feel free to complain to me, any old time," Laura said blandly. "You hold things in forever, and then explode when it's too late to do anything about it. How are people supposed to know how you feel if you don't let anybody in? Even Damien—it seems like you're keeping *him* at arm's length. And I don't know what's up with that sheriff. I saw you giving him googly eyes. The man's too old for you. You should just stick with Damien. You want help around the lodge, you need to go for the hot, rich one."

Sorrow thought her vision might go red. "Wait right there. Let me clarify something. So, your version of *letting you in* actually means letting you tell me what to do? Like I need *your* advice."

Laura gave her an evil look. "If the shoe fits . . ."

"Hey, thanks for being there for me," Sorrow said, sarcasm thick in her voice. "This has been awesome."

"Fine, forget the Damien-Billy thing. If you're so in over your head, I see some things you could be doing better. My life hasn't exactly been a fairy tale either, but I've got experience. You could actually try listening to me for once."

Sorrow glared. "Oh, so I should let *you* take over? Just the easy things, though, like having *Big Ideas*. Stuff like shoveling snow, I can still hang around to do that. You know, actually, Dad would love that. He and Mom seem to love you unconditionally.

Laura, Laura, Laura, she can do no wrong. Vice President Laura is *soooo* experienced."

Laura sat bolt upright. "What? *You're* the one Dad has running the show."

"I'm hardly running the show. He has his nose in everything. Second-guesses *everything.* Unlike you, who can do no wrong."

The phone rang, and Sorrow answered with a clipped "Hello?" It was Helen from the tavern calling. Their water heater had sprung a leak. "Of course it did," Sorrow said, hearing the news.

"Well?" Laura asked when Sorrow hung up.

"The water heater is leaking. It's a commercial model. That means a very *big* leak." Sorrow cradled her head in her hands, trying to think.

"What can I do?" Laura asked.

"There's nothing *you* can do."

"You should let me help. You're just being stubborn." Laura got up from the couch. "When you're done butting heads, let me know. I'm here."

Sorrow gave her a tired look. "Look, I appreciate the offer, all right? But when it comes down to it, you can't *really* help unless you live here."

"Fine. Whatever. Damien knows the place. You should call him."

Sorrow stared at the phone in her lap, wishing everyone would stop pushing her toward Damien. "It seems like all I do lately is lean on him for help."

Laura shrugged it off. "Eh, guys love swooping in on their white horses to give a lady a hand."

She might not trust her sister with the lodge, but Laura sure knew men better than Sorrow did. Damien did seem to like helping. Besides, whatever their relationship was, he had a genuine affection for her family. Still, she hedged. "It's taking advantage of him, calling so much."

"Damien Simmons is *not* the kind of man who lets himself be taken advantage of." Laura waggled her eyebrows. "Hey, I imagine if any advantage is taken, it'll be when he cashes in on your gratitude later tonight."

Sorrow blushed. *"Laura."*

"Seriously," Laura said. "Call him."

Maybe she was just being stubborn. Finally, she picked up the phone, hating the feel of Laura's eyes on her as she dialed.

They had a quick conversation, and he rose to the occasion like he always did. Her boyfriend loved saving the day. He was *great* at saving the day. He did it all day long in his high-powered job at Simmons Timber. A broken water heater was just one more thing for Damien to triumph over.

She hung up and told her sister, "He said we should get a tankless heater to replace it. His plumber is coming out today. The guy owes Damien some favor, so he's going to comp the labor."

Laura gave her a wicked smile. "Like I said. Hot *and* rich."

But Sorrow could only scowl at that, unable to shake the feeling that she and her problems were just more items on Damien's list to conquer.

Sixteen

Sully wiped his forehead on his sleeve, and the stink of fry grease filled his head. He could probably boil that shirt in bleach, and still the stench would cling to it. He was sick of spending every day smelling like burgers.

He peeked through the window into the dining area. Folks had begun drifting in for lunch, and it'd be mostly burgers and fries for the next two hours.

But he had a job, and he did it. A man didn't serve in the Army without learning a sense of duty and responsibility.

A wave of laughter swept in, and he scanned the room. He spotted Edith and her two daughters seated at a table. They hadn't been the source of the merriment, that was for sure. They were showing Laura those old letters, but instead of it being a happy occasion, the tension was as heavy as the stink of fry grease.

Edith was acting clueless as ever, pretending it was all good. But he knew better—she really knew every single thing that went on in the lodge, and acting oblivious was her way of making everyone work out their own problems. Genius, if you asked him.

They'd pulled over a few extra chairs. Would Marlene be joining them? He tuned his ear to their conversation.

"Listen to this part." Laura waved one of the letters, and she was practically vibrating with excitement. " '*Sierra Falls is like a bit of gold sparkling in a dry creek bed.*'" She slammed her hand down on the table. "See? We're the ones who've struck gold. We make a Web site and pull some of these Buck Larsen quotes to—"

"That's not a Buck Larsen quote," Sorrow said, and Sully heard the steel in her voice. "That's a Sorrow Crabtree quote. If you just read further"—Sorrow snatched the letter from her sister—"she writes, '*I don't understand how you don't see the beauty. How you could ever leave such a place. How you could leave me.*' If anything, it sounds like he couldn't get out of here fast enough." She gave Laura a pointed look. "Sounds like some people I know."

Laura waved it off. "It doesn't matter. People will get the gist."

"It *doesn't matter*? How can you say that? We can't rewrite history. It's enough that Buck Larsen lived in Sierra Falls for a time and that he left an illegitimate child behind. We don't need to make it some misty-eyed interpretation. In fact, I think the *real* truth is just as interesting as your version."

Laura snatched the letter back again. "It's *not* as interesting."

"Be careful with those," the younger sister snapped.

"This is called *marketing*, Sorrow. People love a love story."

"I know what marketing is, *Laura*. I'm not an idiot."

Popping grease brought Sully's attention back to where it should be, and he ducked back into the kitchen. It was just as he suspected—tensions were running high.

Growing up, the two Bailey girls had been near enough in age to be a nuisance to each other, yet far enough apart that their worlds didn't intersect. By the time Laura got to high school, she naturally hadn't wanted anything to do with her kid sister, and then she'd gone straight to college, and on to a high-powered job in San Francisco. She didn't get home much, and the girls had never really gotten to know each other.

And now that they were adults, their surface differences kept them apart. But *he* knew, they weren't so different in their hearts. If only they'd give themselves a chance to see it.

He quickly flipped his burgers and wandered back to the

window just in time to see Laura snatching the letters back. He couldn't help but smirk. Both girls had grown into strong, independent women, but this was turning into a childish squabble.

"Mom, tell her." Laura turned in her chair to challenge Edith. "I majored in marketing. I have a *degree* in it."

Edith gave her youngest a rueful look. "Honey, Laura *is* vice president of her company's marketing department."

Sorrow seemed ready to explode. "Well, I have a degree in *running this lodge*, which is just as real as *her* experience."

It was silly, pure and simple. The lodge was falling down around their ears, and they had a real find in these historical letters. Why they wouldn't just talk it out was beyond him. They were all nuts . . . just one big fruitcake sitting there, sipping their Diet Cokes.

The door opened, and Sully held his breath. It was Marlene's entourage, Emerald, Pearl, and Ruby Kidd. The three grandes dames of Sierra Falls were a slow-moving barge of white hair, colorful clip-on earrings, and the scent of powder. And where Marlene's aunts and mother went, she was never far behind.

He gave a quick check to the grill, and darted out from the kitchen to help usher them in. Flurries blew in on a gust of cold air, and he angled his body in the doorway to block it. It put him face-to-face with Marlene.

Hell, but she was a fine figure of a woman. Winter had finally settled in for good, but she didn't frump up like some of the others did. Her down coat was white and sleek, and her sunglasses reminded him of something Jackie O would've worn. The lady was all class.

"Thank you, Tom," she told him, and the sound of his Christian name on her tongue was good on his ears.

She pulled off her sunglasses, and the smile she gave him knocked his socks off. She hadn't done any nonsense to her face like he'd seen with other women their age. The years were plain on her face, and she was the more beautiful for it.

"Looking lovely, Marlene. As ever." Sully frowned. She deserved more than whoever that milksop was she'd met for drinks. Now *he* would know how to treat her right. Why shouldn't *he* meet a woman like Marlene for drinks? Why not

Marlene herself? Yet he couldn't seem to get away from flipping Bear's damned burgers.

"If you're sweet talking me, why is it you look like you just sucked a lemon?"

He had nothing to say to that—although he was sure that, come midnight, a half dozen good responses would come to him. Cursing his lack of words, he could only grin at her, feeling like a fool.

She carefully folded her sunglasses and put them in her bag. Giving him a polite smile in return, she glided across the room to join the Bailey women.

Sully headed back to the kitchen, but when Edith popped out of her chair to get the women their teas and sodas, he saw his second chance. "You sit," he told her. "I'll get your drinks."

Laura twisted around to look at the bar. "Where's Helen?"

Bear grumbled, "Yeah, where is that woman? Bar won't tend itself."

"Don't know," Sully said, "and I don't care to know." There was a saying for women like Helen: *a mess in a dress.* He'd spent years trying to find some inner peace, and getting embroiled in the dramas of his coworkers wasn't high on his list.

The man seated next to Bear at the bar grumbled, "Give the woman a break. I hear her husband's a real son of a bitch."

Deputy Marshall McGinn had been seated at the end of the bar, and he stood to put on his jacket. "It's morning yet, Bear. Pour your own damned coffee. Or *Sully* can pour it for you."

Sully shot him a snarling look. "Aren't you on duty?"

"Watch out," Sorrow said. "Or Marshall might give you a ticket next time he sees you."

"Just look at him funny and he'll give you a ticket," another said. "Ain't that right, Deputy?"

Marshall only shook his head at that, and a round of laughter followed him out of the tavern. McGinn was a by-the-book sort of deputy. Former military, with an honorable discharge after getting wounded in Iraq, he took his job in law enforcement more seriously than some folks in Sierra Falls deemed necessary.

Sully went behind the bar to pour the women their drinks.

There was no need to ask what they were having—the older ones always had iced tea, and the younger ones their diet colas. The women's chatter resumed, and he gave it half an ear.

His mind was on one thing: Marlene Jessup's perfume. It beat the smell of fry grease any day of the week.

Seventeen

Marlene watched Tom as he walked to the bar. The way he'd looked at her . . . it'd been a *look*. And she hadn't had one of *those* looks in years.

She'd sworn off men. She was going to live as an independent woman who followed her own passions. So if all that was true, then why was she sneaking a peek at him in return?

Ruby leaned in. "If you ask me, it's not right, not showing up for work. That Helen's a fast woman. Lord knows where she's off to." The woman's conspiratorial whisper hadn't been a whisper at all.

"You hush." Marlene nudged her aunt's arm. "That's not our business."

Pearl ignored her, adding, "Doesn't pay to be a fast woman."

"Our *Emerald* was a fast woman," Ruby said.

At mention of her mother's name, Marlene felt her cheeks go hot. She looked at her mother as she said, "Good on Mama for getting out of Sierra Falls and living a little."

Marlene's grandfather, Frederick Bose Kidd, had been a pinched old tough-as-nails preacher, and he'd raised the Kidd sisters with a heavy hand and a hefty dose of brimstone. It was no wonder they were all spinsters.

Her aunt pressed on and said with a definitive nod, "Fast living is what gave our Emerald the Alzheimer's."

"*Whoa*," Laura muttered under her breath.

Sorrow gave a beleaguered sigh. "Not this again."

But Laura only laughed. "So . . . having sex before marriage gives you *Alzheimer's* in your later years?"

Marlene wanted to say something to hush such inappropriate talk, but froze when she saw that Laura's comment had brought an unlikely, matching smile to Sorrow's face. Such sisterly goodwill was just too valuable to censor.

"I love their scientific theories," Laura said.

"Some things never change," Sorrow agreed.

"Emerald's the one who frittered away her youth," Pearl said. She and Ruby looked like a matched pair of bookends, shaking their heads in judgment.

Laura looked from Emerald to the other women, amazement on her face. Ma was wearing her usual pleasantly blank expression. "She's sitting *right here*."

Little did Laura know that she and Sorrow sounded just as callous when *they* fought. Apparently every generation of sisters had its fair share of trouble.

"She doesn't listen anymore," Ruby said. "Fast living took its toll."

Marlene couldn't keep it in any longer. "Good heavens," she erupted, "don't say such things. That's your sister you're talking about. And my *mother*."

"What's that, dear?" Mama asked, a smile in her voice. The old woman had spent a lifetime bearing her sisters' judgment with a mischievous good humor that never seemed to flag. Even now, even with the senility that encroached more each day, she still wore that smile.

Marlene fought the urge to hop up and hug her. Instead, she reached over and put a napkin under Mama's glass of iced tea where it'd sweat a puddle onto the table. One day soon she'd need to put her in a home. It was the hardest decision she'd ever faced. Some days Ma was the same woman as always, kind and playful. But other days, it was like a part of her was missing. The mind was a funny thing, solid but with blank spots, like Swiss cheese.

Edith finally joined in, speaking with an uncharacteristic edge. "Pearl, Ruby, you're sounding like your father."

Ruby sat erect in her chair, looking prim as ever. "*Emerald* was the one who ran off. Not us." Her aunt was as stubborn as the day was long, and Marlene wished for once she were disrespectful enough to tell her so.

"Met some man. In *Los An-ge-les*." Pearl said, elongating the words. "Got herself in trouble."

Laura touched her shoulder to Sorrow's, whispering, "Seriously? Emerald went to LA?"

Sorrow nodded. "Word is, she used to party with Olivia de Havilland."

Marlene had to unlock her jaw to speak. "You ladies are just jealous."

She put up with a lot, but this was getting to be too much. She'd used what meager nest egg she had to wall off the porch so the women could have a TV room. She'd put off vacations, and trips, and lunches with friends, always taking a backseat to what her aunts and mother might need. And it had gotten to be *too much*.

Tom hustled from behind the bar with the tray. "How 'bout some iced tea for you ladies?" He caught and held her eye. There was an earnest look on his face. He seemed anxious to change the topic. For her sake.

She pulled her shoulders back, suddenly self-aware. Earlier, he'd told her she looked lovely. She felt his continued scrutiny and wished she'd gone to the restroom to touch up her makeup before sitting down.

The thought had her gaze breaking from his. What was she doing, *flirting*? The man's nickname was *Sully*, for goodness sake.

"Sully!" Bear's bellowing voice rose stopped the chatter. "What the hell are you doing? I don't pay you to pour drinks. Is that something burning? Get on those burgers, man. Beef ain't cheap."

"On it." Sully was back in the kitchen in a flash, but not before Marlene heard him whisper, "I never burned a damned burger in my life."

He returned a few minutes later with a handful of red plastic baskets, carrying orders of burgers and fries, a couple of chicken clubs, and one grilled cheese.

Marlene couldn't resist one more exchange. When she caught his eye, she said, "Look at you, Tom. Serving the women. What will Bear say?"

"I don't give a good God damn what the man says." His delivery was deadpan, but the wicked look he gave her made her giggle.

She covered her mouth. When had she last *giggled*? Trying for a little poise, she said, "Cooking, tending bar, and now this? Seems to me you need a day off."

Her mother looked up at Sully as he served her a club sandwich. The powder on her face had separated, settling into her deep wrinkles, but Mama's smile was just as bright. "Aren't you a gentleman?"

He tipped his chin. "A table of gentle ladies requires no less."

"Tom Sullivan," Marlene exclaimed. "You surprise me."

Apparently, she *was* flirting with the man. She was out of practice, but it felt good.

He put her grilled cheese before her. "More tea for you, Marlene?"

"Any more and I'll float away." She made her smile broad and confident, eager to show Sully and the world that her ex-husband was a fool.

Sully put Laura's lunch in front of her. "Eat up," he told her, giving the girl's shoulder a squeeze. "I'm watching you, kid. You need to live on more than just Diet Coke and carrot sticks. You're wasting away to nothing."

The man was considerate. He *noticed* things.

He gave Marlene one last look, and she gave him her most pleasant smile. Maybe she could have a man in her life *and* her interests, too.

When he went back into the kitchen, Marlene got down to business. "Sorrow, did you bring the letters?"

"I did," she said proudly, and began to hand a small stack to each woman.

"Those letters belong to the family," Bear said from his perch at the bar.

Sorrow deflated like a balloon.

Sully poked his head from out of the pass-through. "Bear Bailey. Give the girl a break."

Marlene couldn't agree more. Even when Sorrow was just a kid, she'd had those wise eyes that betrayed her as the type who felt responsibilities down to her core. Marlene had known then that someday the girl would suffer for it, taking on chores she didn't have time for, running errands for folks who, given an inch, would take a mile. Sorrow's was a dependable nature, and such a thing sometimes led a woman to betray her own heart.

Laura rolled her eyes. "Why does *Sorrow* need a break? Just because she has the same name doesn't mean those letters belong only to her." She turned her attention back to the table. "It's time to plan, and you ladies need to forget about your past festivals. The Buck Larsen Fair is going to be *big*."

"Yes," Sorrow said with exaggerated patience, "a Buck Larsen festival is exactly what we've been talking about. *Before you came*."

"I think we should get the lodge involved," Laura said. "Run a special weekend rate. Include discount festival tickets or something."

Sorrow glared at her. "You let *me* worry about the lodge."

"I thought you hated the lodge."

"You are totally twisting my words."

The girls were starting to snipe again, and it just made Marlene tired. She'd endured enough sniping for the day. She caught a glimpse of Sully through the pass-through. What would he do if she just up and joined him? She could lean against the counter and sip her tea.

She tore her eyes away. The last thing she needed was a *fry cook* for a love interest. Best to stick to her previous plan: pouring heart and soul into the historical society. Which meant planning the best festival the area had ever seen.

"Maybe we should advertise this year," Marlene interjected. "What do you girls think?" She purposely included both Bailey sisters.

"I have all kinds of ideas about how we could handle it," Laura said. "I'll do a press release, of course. Maybe align ourselves with some celebrity figure."

The ladies cooed at that. Laura was a handful—not like Edith at all—and when she was in charge, she was something else again. She'd always been ambitious that way, must've gotten it from Bear. Even back in her high school days, Laura was the kid who'd sneak out after curfew and still make honor roll. It was clear why she was so successful as a career woman.

"How do you know all this?" Pearl asked, her voice awed.

Laura brightened. "I have tons of marketing experience."

"So we've heard," Sorrow muttered. "Five thousand times."

"That's wonderful," said Ruby.

"Edith, you must be so proud," Pearl added.

Edith smiled and reached across the table to pat her daughter's hand.

The gesture gave Marlene the tiniest of pangs. She loved her boys, but had always wondered what it would've been like to have a daughter. Her sourpuss daughter-in-law definitely didn't count.

"I'd be thrilled to take over publicity," Laura said, positively beaming. "We could do some online promotions."

"That sounds fabulous," Marlene told her.

"With what money?" Sorrow's voice was flat, and it gave Marlene pause. The girl looked like steam was about to pour from her ears.

Laura waved off the question. "We won't need much. We'll use Twitter. Make a Facebook fan page. Guerilla marketing stuff."

"Gorillas?" Mama took that moment to tune in, sounding alarmed.

Pearl snuck a skeptical look at Ruby. "I don't think we have a permit for those."

"I don't think the fairgrounds will allow wild animals," Ruby agreed.

Marlene choked back a laugh and almost spat out her tea. "She meant *guerilla*, like in warfare."

Pearl gave her head a prim shake. "I think Buck Larsen is enough of a theme."

"Yes, dear." Ruby gave Laura a soothing look. "We don't need to include things about wars, too."

Marlene rolled her eyes. This wasn't exactly going as planned.

Sorrow scooted her stool back with a loud scrape. "You

know, you ladies have at it. My fearless sister seems to have this under control." She sidled up to the bar, calling into the kitchen, "Sully, I'd love you forever if you made me one of your cookie sundaes."

He peeked out from the pass-through, a smile warming his face. "You got it, kid."

Marlene thought back. The last time *she* had a sundae she'd been a kid herself. It made her think, Sully was so great with the Bailey kids, it was too bad he didn't have children of his own.

Her heart stuttered. *Maybe he did.* The man might have two dozen kids out there somewhere—how was she to know?

She suddenly lost all interest in the conversation happening at the table and strained to catch every word of Sully and Sorrow's exchange. She studied his profile as he scooped the ice cream—the man had a strong, clean-shaven jaw.

He peeked out again. "You still like whipped cream?"

Sorrow made a face. "Duh. It's not really a sundae if there's no whipped cream. And please, will you do that thing with the chocolate sauce?"

Marlene held her breath, waiting to hear his response. But none came. All the man did was smile a knowing smile. Take off that apron, put him in a collared shirt, and he'd be downright dashing.

The women's conversation became a meaningless drone around her. That was it. She had to find an excuse to join them.

He was sliding Sorrow's treat toward her when Marlene came up to the bar.

"You make desserts, too?" She'd made her voice breezy and self-possessed, but it cracked to see that Sully's *special chocolate thing* was to squirt a big, cursive *S* with chocolate sauce along the top. She sucked in a breath, murmuring, "Adorable."

Sorrow grinned. "*S* for Sorrow." She plucked the cherry from the top of his creation and popped it into her mouth. "Sully's cookie sundaes are *to die for.*"

Marlene studied it. "Cookie sundae?"

"Yup, there are cookies all along the bottom. He bakes them himself." Sorrow shoveled in a huge bite and sighed with pleasure. She covered a hand in front of her mouth to say, "I make a mean Crème Brûlée, and it still couldn't compete with Sully's chocolate chip peanut butter cookie sundae."

"Hell, woman. I'll make you one." Sully leaned against the bar. He had biceps like no sixty-something man should have.

"I couldn't," she said, considering both the ice cream *and* the strong arms.

He narrowed his eyes on her. "You can't eat ice cream?"

"Well, I *can*. I just shouldn't."

He refused that answer. "If it's your figure you're worried about, you can throw those concerns right out the door." There was something assessing in his eyes. The way he'd spoken with such intensity about her *figure* heated her blood. "I say you need some ice cream."

Sully grabbed a spoon, and Marlene's mouth went dry. This man was a far cry from her husband, who'd never given two hoots what she needed or wanted.

"Try this," he said, as he assembled a spoonful of ice cream, cookie, and whipped cream in careful proportions. "The secret is mixing the dough in with the ice cream."

"Be sure to break off enough cookie from along the bottom," Sorrow told him.

She reached for the spoon, dumbfounded. Her *husband* had never tried to feed her ice cream. Her husband had thought she needed to watch her waistline.

But Sully didn't hand her the spoon. Instead, he reached it toward her mouth. "Have a taste." His voice was like gravel.

Her heart kicked to life in her chest. The last time a man fed her something, she must've been in her twenties. She hesitated, then opened her mouth. Risking eye contact, she saw Sully's eyes were riveted on her.

And then she tasted the ice cream. Shutting her eyes in bliss, she sighed a purring, contented sound. When she opened her eyes, she couldn't stop the grin from spreading across her face. "You've got a way with food, Tom."

There was a moment's lull in the tavern as the women read the letters and Bear stopped talking to sip his beer. Sully's voice filled the silence. "I want a day off." There was something intense in his voice, something driven.

Bear put down his glass and gave him a blank look. "What's that?"

Marlene watched avidly.

"I said I need a day off, Bear."

What *did* Sully do on his time off? Did he date women he met on the Internet? Take them out for drinks? Would he ever ask *her* out for drinks?

"I'm taking a night off." And then Tom Sullivan met her eyes, and it was as though he'd read her mind. "A man needs to live his life."

Eighteen

"Oh, God . . . what now?" Sorrow was trying on one of the old dresses she'd found in the attic when a loud thud reverberated through the house. As she raced for the stairs, the heavy fabric swirled between her legs—how had pioneer women managed?—but she galloped down, doing her best not to trip, half expecting to find the walls caved in.

She darted from room to room, stopping short at the door to the den. *Her sister.* Of course.

"What the . . . ?" Her eyes goggled, catching sight of a giant black workout contraption. A couple of men in blue-shirted uniforms were rearranging the furniture to make room. "What *on earth* is that?"

Laura smirked and pointed at her dress. "The question is, what on earth is *that*?"

She shrugged, embarrassed, tugging the low neckline up and the tight bodice out. "I asked you first."

"It's an elliptical trainer." Laura gave her an aggravatingly innocent smile. "You're looking pretty saucy, baby sister. Is that one of Sorrow Crabtree's dresses?" Then her eyes lit. "Hey, I know. We should have people *dress up*. You know, for the festival."

As if Laura cared about the festival, really. Getting dolled up in costume would probably be just another way for her trim sister to get attention. "*You* just want to dress up for the festival." She turned her glare at Laura's contraption. "What's that doing here?" Just the sight of it made her chest tighten. Moving the furniture had revealed more than she cared to see—the brown carpet was five shades darker where the couch had been, and the baseboards were caked with dust. Just more things for her to deal with.

"Cardio," Laura answered brightly.

"Put it in *your* room."

"It won't fit in my room."

"Of course it won't, because it's *ginormous*. Careful!" Sorrow dashed between her dad's recliner and the wall. The moving men were hauling the huge leather chair out of the way and getting too close to the television in the process. If they damaged either, *she'd* be the one to pay the price. She swung on her sister. "Laura, this *cannot* go in here."

"I thought Dad could work out in front of CNN. It'll be good for him."

Sorrow crossed her arms at her chest. Anything to keep it from exploding. "You mean, you thought *you* could work out." She walked a circle around it. "You know Dad's never going to use a treadmill."

"It's not a *treadmill*. It's an elliptical trainer. They're better for your knees." Her sister continued to use that overly chirpy tone, and it was infuriating.

"Try *walking*. It works for the rest of us."

Laura shook her head. "It's not the same as cardio. You could use it, too—you need to get your heart rate up."

"Are you kidding? Chasing down problems is all the *cardio* I need."

Laura's expression said she disagreed. "If you say so."

Did her sister just give her figure a once-over? Sorrow sucked in her belly, feeling outraged. The snug saloon-girl dress wasn't helping matters. "What are you doing here *really*?"

"I told you. I'm rearranging the den. Since when did that become a federal offense?"

"No, Laura. I mean, why are you *here*? Home. Don't your minions need you back in San Francisco? If this is just a visit, then why are you installing an elliptical machine?"

Doubt flashed in her sister's eyes, and Sorrow wanted to exclaim *a-ha*. Her sister avoided the subject, as expected. "Speaking of rearranging furniture, I can't believe you all still have that stuffed bear."

Sorrow rolled her eyes. The black bear had adorned the foyer since they were kids. And yeah, it was disgusting. But she chose her battles, and her dad's prized bear wasn't one of them. "It's a hunting lodge," she said flatly.

"It's disgusting is what it is."

"Of course it's disgusting. But you're nuts if you think Dad will let us deep-six his bear. His name *is* Bear, after all." Sorrow crossed her arms. Her sister was a master at changing the subject, but she wouldn't be deterred. "Would you please stay on topic?"

"You tell me," Laura said. "What's the topic?"

"Maybe if you'd eat once in a while you wouldn't have such trouble paying attention."

"Maybe if *you*—"

"The *topic*," Sorrow interrupted, not wanting to know what her thinner, fitter sister was going to say, "was, *why are you here?*"

"To visit," Laura said, but she'd replied too quickly. "What's wrong with a simple visit?"

Her big sister had fled Sierra Falls the moment she graduated from high school. There was never a "simple visit" where she was concerned. "You *never* just visit. So tell me: why's the big-deal VP taking a so-called sabbatical? What do you want?"

Laura's eyes narrowed to slits. "I don't want anything from you. Jeez, Sorrow. Why do you always feel so put-upon? No wonder Damien hasn't sealed the deal with you yet."

Sorrow practically shrieked. "*What?* What the hell does *that* mean?"

"You know exactly what that means. It's time for Damien to put a ring on it, but why would he when you're such a nag?" Laura's face became the picture of calm.

Sorrow recognized her sister's expression. She'd known it from their youth—it was the look of battle. Well, she could play this game as calmly as Laura. Mastering her emotions, she kept her arms crossed tight, curling her fingers into her biceps. "Who says I want Damien to put a ring on it anyway?"

Saying the words, Sorrow realized the thought of a ring and *Damien* made her feel more alarm than anticipation.

Laura tipped the movers and shooed them out the door. "Don't tell me you're into that *sheriff.*"

"I'm not *into* anybody." Sorrow began to put the den back to rights, shaking out a throw blanket with a sharp snap, folding and smoothing it probably more than was necessary. But her stomach gave a little flip-flop at the thought—*was* she into the sheriff?

"Oh, God." Laura gaped. "You *are* into him. He's kind of old for you, isn't he?"

How was it her pesky sister was always able to read her mind? Sorrow straightened, facing Laura head-on. "Billy is *not* old. He's in his thirties. Since when is that old?"

A slow smile spread across Laura's face. "You want some sisterly advice?"

Sorrow's response was instant. "No."

She continued anyway. "Go for someone your own age."

"I told you, I'm not *going* for anybody."

"I've told you before, Damien is cute *and* rich," Laura insisted. "Keep your head in the game, kid. Eyes on the target."

"I'm not a *kid.*" Sorrow was feeling trapped in this conversation—she didn't feel like discussing *either* man. How did Laura always manage to get the upper hand? "And what's with all the bad sports metaphors? Some people aren't in it to win something. We're not all as ruthless as you are."

Laura studied her for a second with an annoying smirk on her face. "If nothing's going on, why so defensive?"

There was a knock at the back door, and the sisters exchanged a withering look.

"Saved by the bell." Sorrow dashed from the room to get the door, wondering who it could be. Folks usually used the front door and walked right in.

Unfortunately, she heard her sister's footsteps close behind. She looked over her shoulder, telling Laura in a quick, hushed voice, "Nothing is going on with Billy. Damien and I are just dating. I'm not marrying anyone that I know of, not now, not in the near future. Thanks for your interest." That should shut big sister down. She opened the door, and it was *him*.

Billy.

Stopping behind her, Laura chuckled. "Speak of the devil."

Evil. Laura was evil. Devil spawn. Sent to torment her.

Billy's eyes zoomed to Sorrow's breasts, which were currently popping up out of the low neckline like two plump orbs desperate for air. She did her best to gather her wits, despite feeling very conscious of the cold air on her décolleté. "Hi, Bill—"

But Laura's chirpy voice cut hers off. "Sheriff! What can we do you for? You here to see Sorrow?"

Billy looked suddenly wary. He wasn't dumb; he was an intuitive guy. He probably sensed how he'd walked smack-dab into the onset of World War III. "I'm always happy to see Sorrow," he said slowly, clearly thinking through his words carefully, "but I'm here because your father sent me."

Laura leaned against the wall, giving him a playfully saucy look. "Aren't you happy to see me, too?"

Sorrow would've kicked her sister had she thought she could do it unnoticed. Instead she glared.

Laura was so easy with Billy, and it irked her. *But why?* Was she jealous of how good her sister was with men? Or was she jealous that Laura might be good with *Billy*?

She realized how she'd begun to crave the man's attention herself. Shouldering in front of Laura, she asked, "What's up?"

"I just got off duty and was grabbing a coffee when all hell broke loose." He kept his eyes on her as he added, "I'm afraid they need you at the tavern."

Of course they do. "Give me a sec to change."

She forgot her girl trouble and had her jeans back on in no time. What could be going wrong now? Explosion, maybe? Plague of locusts? "What is it this time?" she asked as she grabbed her fleece and shouldered past Laura out the door.

"The freezer died."

"Oh. Okay." She wasn't expecting that one. Not so bad. Her mind flipped through the contact list in her head, deciding who to call to get it fixed. Meantime, they'd need to move the food.

"Can't Sully just transfer the food to the chest freezer? We've got one in the garage."

"No," Billy said, "that freezer's down, too."

"*Both* of our freezers?"

He nodded.

Her sister piped up, "Weird." Clearly not in touch with the gravity of the situation.

Sorrow shot her a look, feeling surprised and a little annoyed to find that she'd followed them. "Thanks, Sherlock."

She felt her sister's eagle eyes boring into her and the sheriff, scrutinizing every move. Why *was* she tagging along? The girl was a varsity flirt, and that she was even around for this interaction made Sorrow intensely uncomfortable.

"There's more," Billy said. "The food's all spoiled. The units must've been down for a while before anybody noticed."

That stopped her in her tracks. "Crap." Hundreds of dollars in frozen patties, chicken tenders, corn dogs . . . all the junk her dad insisted Sully cook up; not much of it was fresh.

She felt a rock settle in the pit of her stomach. "All that food . . . that'll cost us a fortune." And then something else hit her. There weren't many lodgers these days, which meant the family relied on the tavern for income. They couldn't afford to turn people away. "What are we going to *feed* people?"

"Can you call your distributor?" Billy asked. "Have an emergency delivery made?"

"We don't really have one."

Billy pinned his eyes on her. "What do you mean you don't have a distributor?"

"Well, stuff like bread gets delivered. But Dad says he doesn't trust the distributors. He likes me and Sully to pick out the meat ourselves."

"Wow," said Laura. "That sucks."

"Yeah, thanks." Sorrow rubbed her temples and took a deep breath. *Just go away*, she wanted to tell her sister. *Or help out.*

Having Laura there to witness this latest crisis, feeling her scrutinize every aspect of this interaction with Billy . . . it all made her so uncomfortable. And in a way that went beyond the usual sisterly annoyance.

Could that mean she *did* have a thing for the sheriff?

He spoke in a low voice, aimed for her ears only. "Don't worry. We'll handle this one problem at a time. I have some business in Silver City tomorrow—why don't you come with? We'll hit one of those big box stores in the morning, you can stock up, maybe even buy a small freezer unit to tide you over till you figure this out. I'll be driving the SUV—it's more than big enough to fit whatever you need."

Relief washed through her. "Okay."

She took another deep breath. A plan—she liked plans. They made her feel in control. She attempted a smile, having found humor the best way to deal with this ridiculous string of bad luck. "The Sheriffmobile, huh? Does that mean we can speed?"

"I won't tell if you won't."

She looked up at him to express her thanks, but what awaited her stole her breath. Billy was staring down at her, such a solid male presence, his rich brown eyes trained only on her.

Oh, crap.

She *did* have a thing for him.

Nineteen

Had he seriously just told the woman he'd *speed* to the store for her? And in an official vehicle, no less. What the hell had gotten into him?

Billy jogged to catch up to Sorrow, striding purposefully to the tavern. His eyes grazed down her back—God help him, *that* was what'd gotten into him. Her fleece jacket and jeans hugged every curve, and he fantasized about giving that rump a good squeeze.

He rubbed a hand over his eyes. What was his problem?

He'd had a few flings since Keri died. Emotionless hookups. And they'd been enough to satisfy the part of him that, though grieving, was still a man. But never had he been so *curious* about a woman. Through the day, he found himself wondering how Sorrow was, if she was hanging in there, what she might be cooking up next.

The only trouble was, the pangs of guilt and regret were always quick to follow. Why should *he* get to enjoy and feel and live his life while Keri hadn't been given half a chance at hers?

The sound of yelling drifted out to them. Sully and Bear, shouting at each other. Sorrow's face fell, and their eyes met. "Sully never fights," she said, sounding a little lost.

He got the sense the man was like an uncle to her. So now she had drama to add to the current crisis.

Laura caught up to them—he hadn't realized she was following. "Wow, check it out," she said. "Sully actually has a voice."

He shot her a look. Big sister didn't seem to *get it*, obviously too concerned with her own issues, whatever those might be.

Laura caught his expression. "Seriously. If you Googled 'strong, silent type,' you'd find a picture of Sully."

They made their way back into the kitchen just as Sully was saying to Bear, "The girl didn't touch your freezer."

Bear scowled. "Freez-*ers*." He spotted his daughters. "Sorrow. What the hell have you done? Why are the freezers busted?"

Billy clenched and unclenched his hand. He didn't consider himself a violent guy, but just then he wished he weren't an officer of the law. Just then, he longed to get in one good punch. Instead, he stepped forward. "Calm down, Mister Bailey. I'm sure your daughter knows nothing about it." It was beyond him why that boyfriend of hers hadn't nipped Bear's attitude in the bud. Maybe Damien lent a hand around the place, but it sure didn't seem like he stood up for her enough.

Sully growled, "Neither of us knows about it."

"Well, it can't be coincidence." Bear kicked the huge industrial freezer. "Both of them are dead, and the food's all spoiled. Somebody must've done something to overheat 'em."

Laura opened the door and shut it again quickly, scrunching her nose against the smell. "Did you take a look, like, under the hood or whatever?"

It was the first semireasonable thing the woman had said all day.

"Good idea." Billy nodded at Sully. "You get that side," he told him, and they pulled it from the wall. Dust was a thick, gray blanket along the baseboard, carpeting the floor in thick rolls like tumbleweeds. A dark puddle glistened along the floor.

"Is that melted ice?" asked Laura.

Billy touched a finger to it. "Freon."

"I can't look." Sorrow hoisted herself up to sit on the counter with a sigh. "I wish BJ were here."

Now there was an unfortunate name. He peeked from behind a panel of stainless steel to give her a questioning look.

"My brother," she said.

"Bear Junior," Laura clarified. "He's got the magic touch when it comes to machines."

"He's in Afghanistan," Sorrow added, "flying copters."

Sully grunted. "And if he ever gets tired of that, the kid could just as easily fix them."

"My boy knows his way around a motor," Bear said proudly.

Billy had another question for Sorrow and looked at her just as she unzipped her fleece. His mind blanked.

Damn. When had thermal underwear shirts become so sexy?

He darted his eyes from her lush body to focus on the freezer instead. He struggled to remember his question. "You got a screwdriver? I'm not as gifted as your brother, but I can take a look."

Everyone stared silently, except for Sorrow, who hopped down and grabbed one from a junk drawer. Was she the only one who knew what was what in this place?

Their eyes held for a second as she handed him the tool, and he felt a clench in his gut he hadn't known in years. He turned his entire attention to unscrewing the back panel.

He didn't have to be an electrician to see the problem at once. Condenser tubes ran in an S-pattern along the back, and Freon dripped from them, a slow, glistening ooze.

Bear saw it too and exclaimed, "What the hell?"

Sorrow stepped in. "What is it?" She smelled like shampoo, or lotion maybe—some female smell.

"The condenser," said Sully.

"Yup." Billy had to force himself to focus. He studied it closely, wishing the light were better. "It must be cracked or . . ." His voice trailed off as he concentrated, running his finger along the tubes. Then he felt it—a sharp edge. Too sharp to be just a crack.

"Regular wear and tear?" asked Laura.

Sorrow challenged, "That wouldn't explain *both* freezers dying at once."

"Not wear and tear." Billy stood and wiped the grime from his hands. "I think it was sliced."

"Someone *cut* it?" the girls asked in unison.

With a nod, he faced Bear and said, "Looks like you have a vandal on your hands."

Bear laughed outright. "Vandal? There are no vandals in Sierra Falls. Everyone knows everyone. This is just how it goes around this place." He looked at his daughter. "Isn't that right, Sorrow? All hell breaking loose on a regular basis."

Billy didn't buy it for a minute. Those wires had been cut, and it called into question every other thing that'd been going wrong lately. He'd stake his badge that the Baileys were up against something more menacing than just the usual chaos of a family business.

Bear may not have wanted to hear it, but Sorrow did. She seemed to get it, and was looking at him with widened eyes. "Who would destroy our freezers?"

"Nobody destroyed our damned freezers," her dad said. "You're not in the big city anymore, Sheriff. There's no crime out here. It may bore you, but all the suspicions in the world aren't going to make any criminals appear."

"Not to interrupt," Sully said, "but what are we going to feed people?"

Sorrow pulled her shoulders back. "Billy said he'd drive me to Silver City for supplies." There was something in her voice—Resolve? Camaraderie?—that made him happy he'd offered.

"We can stock up," he added. "Get a small replacement freezer till you can get a bigger one delivered."

"That doesn't feed people *right now*." Bear checked his watch. "Hell's bells, girl. It's 4:30. People are going to start showing up for Sully's early bird any minute."

There was a moment of tense silence, then Sorrow said, "*I* could cook."

Bear shook his head. "Ain't you been paying attention? All our food is spoiled."

"Just the frozen stuff. I can make pasta."

He loved how she stood up to her dad. The way she snapped right back at him had a way of defusing the man's temper, till he seemed like nothing more than a harmless grump. "She makes a good pasta," Billy said with a grin.

Sorrow's sister pinned him with a wicked look. "When have

you had her pasta?" Something in her voice made him self-conscious.

He was grateful when Sorrow broke in, "I've got all I need in the pantry. Some garlic, olive oil, a couple of cans of olives, some capers . . . I can make a puttanesca."

Bear hooted. "What the hell's that?"

"Give the girl a shot," Sully said, his voice almost comically somber.

"You, too?" Bear looked from his cook to his daughter and stiffened. It was like witnessing a lightbulb flicker to life above the older man's head. "You're serious."

Sorrow crossed her arms at her chest, and Billy fought the urge to gently pull them apart and give her shoulders a quick rub. *And then stroke down her back to the curve of her waist . . .*

Hell. He really needed to stop thinking like that.

"I've been meaning to tell you," she said. "I want to start cooking one night a week."

"You'll do no such thing," Bear said instantly.

Sully shrugged. "I told you the other day. I could use a night off."

Bear looked aghast. "What the hell? It's a conspiracy, that's what this is."

"The girl can cook, and you should give her a shot," Sully said, which for him seemed tantamount to a speech.

"If it weren't for Sorrow's cooking," Laura added, "I'd have been five hundred pounds overweight when I graduated high school."

Sorrow caught her sister's eye and gave a self-effacing shrug. Billy could see she was pleased and touched. Just how long had the woman been toiling in the kitchen without thanks?

Sully bristled. "Wait a minute. My food's not *that* bad."

Laura gave a gusty sigh. "We love your cooking, Sully. You know what I mean. Sometimes a teenage girl wants soup and a salad instead of cheesy chili fries."

"I can cook." Sorrow stood tall, and Billy felt a spurt of pride. "People *like* my cooking, Dad."

Bear scowled. "So everyone tells me."

"Who else has told you?" she asked, sounding genuinely curious. The girl was too modest for her own good.

"Him, for one." Bear pointed his way.

Billy gaped. "What?" The attention flustered him, and he was at an utter loss for words. "I . . ."

Sorrow got the cutest perplexed smile on her face. "*You* told my dad I could cook?"

The way she'd asked tugged at something in his chest. He tried to formulate something cool and collected to say, but Sorrow's father didn't give him a chance.

Bear turned on her. "Girl, I don't know what you fed our sheriff, but he's been crowing about . . . I don't know . . . *bread* or something. All that time in the city, maybe he forgot how to eat meat."

Billy laughed. "I love meat. For the record."

Sully added, "Sorrow does do a fine brisket, sir. Her secret is to add Coca-Cola, if you can believe that."

"Fine, fine." Her father waved impatiently. "Sorrow can cook. One night a week. Tuesdays, how about. We'll call it Ladies' Night."

"Ladies' Night?" She rolled her eyes. "Should I feel insulted?"

Billy couldn't help it—he couldn't keep his hands to himself anymore. "Hey." He squeezed her shoulders, telling her in a quiet voice, "This is a good thing. He's saying you can cook."

"You start tonight." Bear walked to the window and shoved aside the lace curtain. "And you better get a move on. Jack Jessup's truck just pulled into the lot."

Twenty

Marlene stole a peek into the kitchen and knew a surprising wash of relief to see Sully. She didn't know why she was being so silly. After all, the man was *always* there. It was only that she wanted him to talk to her grandson, Craig, of course.

For a brief second, she wondered what it was Sully did when he left the tavern, driving away on that noisy motorcycle of his. Where did he go? Was there a woman waiting for him at home?

How was it she could know positively nothing about a man she'd seen and said hello to for over two decades now?

There was some to-do in the kitchen, and she dallied, remaining standing to spy as she touched up her hair. She pulled off her scarf and cupped a hand along the bottom of her do, making sure her bob was still curling under.

It looked like the Baileys were having some sort of appliance trouble. Bear had his usual crotchety face on, though for once his girls weren't at each other's throats.

The door that led between kitchen and dining room swung open, and she hopped aside, letting out a little "Oh!"

Laura stopped short before running into her. The girl put a startled hand at her chest and did a quick side step. "Sorry, Marlene. Gotta run get some ingredients from the house kitchen."

The door flapped shut, and as the girl ran off, Marlene stole a glimpse through it. Sorrow and their new sheriff were exchanging words. *Quiet* words.

She bit back a smile, pleased that she'd insisted her family dine at the tavern tonight. If there was something afoot, she'd not miss a second of it.

She went to the table to join her son Jack and his family. Her daughter-in-law, Tina, was wearing that sourpuss face she always had on—*she'd* wanted to go somewhere else for dinner, naturally. If Marlene said tomato, Tina would say *tomahto*. They never seemed to see eye to eye on anything. Especially money. Tina had a taste for the fancy restaurants in Silver City, and though Marlene's boys Jack and Eddie made a good living running Jessup Brothers Construction, Tina clearly had yet to understand that money didn't grow on trees.

Jack stood to scoot her chair in, and she gave her son a warm smile. "Thank you, dear." Her ex-husband might be a son of a bitch, but they sure had raised themselves some lovely gentlemen.

"I'll go grab us some menus," he said.

"No need for that," Bear said as he burst into the dining room.

Sully was on his heels. "Freezer's down."

Marlene made herself not look at the cook, focusing instead on unfurling and smoothing her napkin in her lap. She'd raised four gentlemen, and *she*, too, would be genteel.

Jack stopped, midstride, a handful of menus in his hand. "Want me to take a look?"

"No need," Bear said. "They're *both* down."

Marlene finally looked at Sully, and his eyes were already on her, riveted, like he might be able to see straight through her. She cleared her throat. "So, you're not cooking then?"

"Sorrow's trying her hand at it tonight," Sully said, and his expression softened.

It gave Marlene pause. What else made his expression warm like that? Was there a woman in his life who got to see that face? She felt a twinge, like loss, and brushed it off as foolish.

"*Sorrow's* cooking?" asked Jack.

Tina added under her breath, "And pigs must be flying."

Marlene shot her daughter-in-law a look. The girl could be short on manners.

Bear shrugged. "She's cooking up some putanleska pasta. You don't have to eat it."

"Oh," Marlene exclaimed, delighted. "A *puttanesca*. That sounds wonderful. Of course we'll eat it, Bear. Good heavens."

She felt Sully walk over and wished she had a drink to sip on. There wasn't much more she could do to arrange the napkin in her lap.

Why was she feeling this way? Lord, but the divorce had thrown her. What had happened to her confidence?

"Evening," Sully told the table. "How are you folks doing? It's Craig, right? I didn't recognize you at first. Kid's growing like a weed."

Forgetting herself for the moment, Marlene looked up at him. When it came to her grandson, she was 100 percent focused. "Yes, this is my grandson, Craig. And I think you already know my son Jack, his wife, Tina."

Jack scrunched his face at her. "Come on, Mom. Of course I know Sully. Join us," he said, gesturing to the chair next to him.

"It'd be an honor."

Marlene watched, mesmerized, at this different side of him. She'd seen the man for much of her life, but somehow she'd never really *noticed* him. Something was different tonight. First off, he wasn't wearing that apron. Instead, he wore a pair of khakis and a snug navy blue polo. Goodness, his eyes were dark blue . . . deep, almost purple, like lapis.

He turned his attention to Craig. "I hear you want to join the service, son."

Her grandson beamed. "Yes, sir."

"Good for you."

There was a notable silence. Tina's eyes turned to frost, glaring from Marlene, to Sully, to Craig. She told her son, "I thought this discussion was over. My son is doing no such thing."

It seemed suddenly that Sully was a million miles away, separated from them by a gulf of cold wariness.

Was it a mistake to have asked him to talk to Craig? Had

she crossed a line? But she knew . . . the boy would be eighteen soon, and then he could make his own decisions. He was almost a man now, and pretending otherwise was the worst they could do.

Someone needed to say something, and it fell to her. "I thought Tom . . . you know, Sully . . . could tell Craig about the service."

She was probably making an enemy of Tina, but this wasn't about her daughter-in-law. Craig was stubborn, and she wanted to make sure he was informed and thoughtful about the very life-changing choices he was facing.

"We don't want him to go," Tina said, shutting her down.

Jack's hand snaked across the table, finding his wife's. He nodded his agreement. "The boy's too young, Mom."

She could tell her son was trying, and she appreciated it. But she had the wisdom of her years to tell her, the boy would do what the boy would do. And all they could do was love him and guide him as best they could.

She doubled her resolve and turned to Sully. "How old were you? When you enlisted, I mean."

"I didn't enlist. I was a West Point man."

"You were?" Marlene felt her eyes widen. It sounded so . . . masculine. Like something from a movie.

Sully looked amused. "Yes, ma'am."

Marlene put a hand on his arm to interrupt. The gesture surprised both of them. "Good God, do *not* call me ma'am. You make me feel positively elderly." She felt his arm tense. Hard ropes beneath wiry muscle. Tom Sullivan stayed in shape.

She pulled her hand back and touched it to her temple. Why did Bear insist on keeping the tavern so warm?

"Fine. *Marlene.*" He gave her one of his rare smiles, and it was like the sun broke out and warmed something in her chest.

What was wrong with her? She hadn't had a hot flash in years.

Sully turned his attention back to Craig. "Have you thought about college? It's a good way to go."

The boy slumped back in his chair and scowled at his folks. "Not if there's no money, I can't."

"First thing you'll learn in the service is not to talk to your parents that way." Sully's tone was one Marlene didn't often hear. It was more than simply strict, it was commanding, and yet he hadn't needed to raise his voice to get there. It was an *officer's* voice.

Craig's eyes widened.

"You'll sit up like a gentleman, too," Sully added quietly. "Elbows off the table."

Damned if the boy didn't sit bolt upright and put his hands in his lap.

Jack and Tina gaped, and Marlene bit her cheek not to smile.

"If money's tight, you could do ROTC like Bear Junior did." Sully pronounced it *rot-see*.

Tina looked like she'd swallowed a lemon. "Only kids with decent grades get scholarships."

Jack shot his wife a quelling look before calmly adding, "You can join the construction business with me and your uncle. Nothing to be ashamed of in that."

"It's not like I don't want to go to college," Craig grumbled. His eyes were flat, staring at the table. "I just want to enlist first."

Tina sat so rigidly, she looked ready to snap in half. "I don't want my boy to get killed."

"He doesn't have to see combat," Sully said, with understanding in his voice. "There are lots of jobs where—"

"I *want* to see combat." Craig glared defiantly at the table.

Tina's face turned beet red, and Marlene knew a pang of sympathy for the woman. This was clearly a conversation that happened on a regular basis. Her daughter-in-law turned on her, speaking with raw pain in her eyes. "*You* raised boys. Can't you understand what I'm going through?"

"Craig might be your son," she said quietly, "but he's *my* grandson. Don't you think for a minute I don't understand." She reached across the table to take Tina's hand. "I might seem like a dried-up old prune to you, but with age comes wisdom. I know what it is to be protective. But a mother has to let go sometime. The boy's got to do what he needs to do to become a man. And all *we* can do is make certain he understands the choices he makes. I don't know Craig's heart. Only *he* does. What I do know is that replaying this same argument won't do the boy one bit of good. And it won't change his mind either. In fact, it could very well backfire and push him in a direction he's not ready for."

She squeezed her daughter-in-law's hand, and Tina squeezed back like she was gripping a life raft. Marlene's throat clenched, and she swallowed back the ache. Tina would discover that, too—how a mother's job was learning to swallow back the ache.

"Why don't you let us talk for a while?" Sully said gently. "You and Jack go grab a glass of wine."

Marlene nodded to the bar, trying to muster some chirp in her voice. "I see Edith running around back there. You two need to ask her about those letters. You still haven't heard the full story. It's a juicy one. Don't worry, you can trust Tom . . . *Sully*, I mean, to talk to the boy."

Tina bit her lip, her chin quivering. Marlene braced for a challenge, and was surprised when the woman nodded and let Jack escort her to the bar, his arm wrapped protectively around her shoulders.

Marlene had faith in her son. There was something in Tina that spoke to him. Someday maybe the woman would let *her* in on it, too.

As his parents settled on stools at the bar, Craig turned a wary eye to Sully.

"You can still go to college," the older man told him. "You enlist now, you get free schooling once you're out. Which branch are you considering?"

Her grandson was struggling not to fiddle with his napkin. "Huh?"

Sully stayed patient. "What branch of the military are you thinking about?"

"I don't know. Maybe I can be a Marine like BJ."

Sully nodded slowly, and Marlene could see the cogs turning. The boy hadn't given this enough thought. She guessed Sully's mind and decided some humor might ease the growing tension. "Well, Tom, it seems you've had trouble convincing any of these boys to go Army."

The sternness of his expression cracked a bit, and he spared her a half smile. "I suppose I have." But then he turned back to Craig, and his intensity returned full-force. "This is a big commitment, son. You're not enlisting just because . . . you don't want to do construction, or you think big guns are cool, or it'll be like a video game, or any nonsense like that, are you?"

"No sir." Craig laughed. "Though I do hear they give a sweet enlistment bonus." He'd lingered on the word *suh-weet*.

Sully stiffened. "That's *not* what I wanted to hear."

The boy tensed, on his guard, and his sullen expression made him seem younger than his seventeen years. "They think it's a joke. Like *I'm* a joke. The whole family does. They'll take it serious enough if I bring home a fat check."

"The family thinks no such thing," Marlene said automatically, then checked herself. Craig was still a boy, and boys said thoughtless things.

But Sully kept on topic, pressing him, "People *take you seriously* when you make decisions like an informed adult. Money doesn't make you a man. Serving your country is not a path you choose for the paycheck."

At words like *adult* and *man*, Craig snapped to attention, captivated. Marlene decided to listen in silence, letting Sully handle it. He had a way with the boy. Though that made sense, if it was true that he used to command them.

"You don't join just because you think you're some tough guy who's good at shoot-em-up video games. Now, I don't care if you go Army, Navy, whatever. Wherever you enlist, they'll chew you up and spit you out. They'll break you and build you back up again. So you best be serious, son. Now tell me. I'm listening. Why do you want to join?"

Craig paused and when he spoke again, the boy's voice was gone, replaced by the voice of a man. Her grandson was transforming before her eyes, this child crossing the gulf into adulthood. "Because," he said carefully, "I want to be a part of something bigger than myself. Because I believe in this country. Men before me fought and died so I could play those shoot-em-up games, and now it's *my* turn to serve."

Sully got that answer and more, and every one of them sounded more articulate than anything *she'd* ever heard come out of the child's mouth. She sat and listened, imagining how

Sully might have looked in a uniform. In fatigues. In his dress blues. Picturing him at West Point, in Vietnam. He'd probably walked through ranks of uniformed boys no older than Craig, shouting orders. Getting answers.

Marlene sat and watched Tom Sullivan, watched him in a new light.

Twenty-one

"No, I said *I'm* cooking." Sorrow nestled the phone at her ear as she tried to talk to Damien, chop olives, and sauté garlic all at the same time. "The freezers went down and the food spoiled, so I'm making pasta for everyone."

"We've got reservations," he said, and she strained to understand across his warbled cell phone connection. "I'm taking you to Silver City."

"We need to cancel. That's what I'm trying to tell you." In a way, she was relieved. Not because she was looking forward to cooking, but because she needed to have a conversation with Damien that she was dreading. A breakup conversation.

The kitchen door swung open, and it was Laura and Billy with an armful of canned olives, a big jar of capers, and a few bottles of red wine.

Sorrow whispered an enthusiastic "Thank you!" She nodded to the counter. "Put it there. Could you open the olives?"

"What's that, babe?" Damien asked.

The phone slipped, and she inched it back up, crooking her neck to hold it in place. A stitch zinged up her shoulder. "Sorry, but I really need to make this quick. I was saying, dinner and a movie isn't going to happen with me cooking for a restaurant full of people."

"Can't you just get it started, and Laura can dish it out?"

"No, I can't." She frowned. This was the chance she'd been waiting years for, and he wanted her to let Laura take over? "It's not that simple, Damien." There was a lot these days that wasn't that simple.

She worried she'd been thinking about that sheriff one too many times a day. It was just that, when she was with Billy, she felt like she could let it all hang loose. That she could be herself, and best of all, he understood.

She held her breath, making an exaggerated grimace she knew nobody could see. She should really break it off with Damien, and tonight. "Why don't you come here instead? You can have some of my puttanesca." Her cheek pressed redial, and there was a rapid beeping as the phone redialed Damien's number.

"What?"

"Sorry, sorry. This is driving me nuts."

Billy came up behind her and silently showed her the olives. He was trying to help. He knew how this was her big moment. He got it. He got *her*.

He'd opened several cans and silently gestured, asking if she wanted him to drain them. He'd turned up the cuffs of his red flannel shirt, exposing solid forearms. His muscle flexed beneath skin as he moved. He was a *man*.

She *had* to stop thinking about him. Had to stop her mind from wondering what else about her he'd understand. How those muscles would feel beneath her hands. How he might touch her. Hold her.

She came to, and glanced up to find Billy watching her. He lifted one of the cans, repeating his silent question. She gave him a grateful nod, feeling the heat flood her cheeks. Putting a hand over the mouthpiece, she mouthed, "Save some of the juice."

"I'm losing you, Sorrow. What was that?"

That was it. This whole situation was just too unfair to Damien. She'd break it off with him tonight. "Come over, you can try my puttanesca. It's a tangy pasta." She'd talk to him over dinner.

"You know I don't eat pasta."

"Of course you don't." She couldn't deal with this right now.

She had a job to do. She began to chop in earnest—her knife slamming against the cutting board like it might save her life. "I really should go. *Ow*"—she'd sliced her thumb and sucked it into her mouth—"Damn." Sloppy chopping wouldn't do her a bit of good—she needed to calm down. *She* was the one who'd wanted to do this.

Damien sounded genuinely concerned. "You all right, babe?"

"Yeah, I just cut myself."

The sheriff put down the can opener and took her shoulders in his hands. Her breath caught. His touch managed to be both gentle and sure. He led her to the sink, holding the phone so she could wash her cut.

"Is it bad?" asked Damien. "Can't your sister help?"

"It's no biggie." She rummaged in the junk drawer for the little zippered kit she kept there. Billy took it from her, and she gave him a weak smile as he applied a glop of antiseptic cream and a couple of Band-Aids. His hands *were* gentle, and deft, too.

She cleared her throat, back at the cutting board. "So, you coming over for dinner then?"

"You know, it sounds like it's crazy for you over there. And honestly, it's crazy for me here. I'm buried. Can we take a rain check? I think I'll just work late. Let you have your moment in the sun. Save me some leftovers, though, okay?"

She hung up with Damien, feeling a weird mix of disappointed, unsurprised, and relieved. Now that she had it in her head that they needed to talk, she needed to just do it and get it over with. Otherwise, it felt like an ax poised to fall.

That was the last real conversation she had all night, as she was quickly swept up in kitchen insanity. Somehow word had spread through Sierra Falls that Sorrow was cooking, and more folks than usual came by for dinner.

She'd salvaged beets, goat cheese, and some candied walnuts from her own pantry to pull together a beet salad. Some random veggies, a couple of cans of white beans, and chicken stock had made up a nice soup. And for a finishing touch, Billy had cored over a dozen apples, and she'd made baked apple for dessert. That she'd had to serve all of it in tiny portions had impressed the customers all the more; they thought it was some sort of fancy citified preparation.

Her mom carried in the last of the plates. "Have *you* had a chance to eat anything?"

Sorrow ignored the question, her eyes only on the teetering stack of white dishes. "I don't have to do the dishes, too, do I?"

Billy walked through the swinging door, taking the stack from her mother's hands and putting them in the giant stainless steel sink. "Don't think you can sneak away from me, Edith. I got these."

"Hey, Sheriff." Sorrow said his title playfully, and rather than something formal it'd felt intimate. She didn't care—she was in a giddy mood, going on adrenaline, and was genuinely pleased that someone who wasn't family was there to witness her triumph. "I didn't know you were still around. It must be midnight."

Her mom checked her watch. There were digital clocks all over the place, but her mom had been relying on the same Timex for twenty years—tan face, frayed brown band. "It's 10:30, and Sheriff Preston has been helping us shoulder the load. You'd think the town had run out of food."

Sorrow watched as he poured a big glass of wine. "Were you here all night?" Though thinking about it, she could picture Billy at various points in the evening, getting glimpses of him opening bottles of wine, clearing dishes. Yup, he'd been there all night.

He handed her the glass. "And miss your grand debut?"

The man really was thoughtful, and she gave him a grateful smile. She sipped and exhaled a blissful sigh. "Thank you. I'm ready to drop on my feet."

Her mom scraped the last of the pasta from the big pot. "There's a bit left, honey. You better eat up before the Jessup boys come in for fourths." She handed her the plate. "Now I best get back out there. I think your dad is trying to muster up a poker game, and I'm sure it breaks all kinds of gambling laws." She gave Billy a panicked look, realizing she was speaking in front of the *sheriff.*

Billy winked. "Did you say something, Mrs. Bailey? I'm afraid I didn't hear you."

As her mom bustled from the room, Sorrow hopped onto the counter and dove into her pasta. "I didn't realize how starved I was."

Billy peeked under lids, scrounging for leftovers. He salvaged a cup of soup and half a baked apple. "I'm afraid there's not much left."

He dished it out for her, then started on the dirty plates, making quick work loading them into the industrial dishwasher.

"No, it's perfect." All that'd been left in the pot was a small serving of pasta and the dregs of the sauce. It'd cooked down to thick, tangy glops of capers and olives. She held up her fork. "This bit is my favorite."

A memory sideswiped her, and she swallowed back the sudden ache in her throat.

It didn't escape Billy. "You all right?" he asked, concerned.

"Yeah, just thinking about my brother. BJ loves my puttanesca." She laughed. "Though he always drives me batty. Even though I buy these awesome Italian reds, he insists on washing down whatever I cook with a Budweiser."

Billy shook his head. "An abomination."

"Totally."

"Everyone knows *Miller* goes best with Italian."

She hopped down and nudged him with her shoulder as she slid her plate into the dishwasher rack. "Heathens. All of you."

Her voice had come out sounding distracted, and Billy caught it at once.

He wiped his hands on a rag, and pinched her chin in his fingers, tipping it up to face him. "Uh-oh. I see cogs turning."

That touch sent an electric charge from his fingertips straight to her belly. The intense night left her feeling drained and emotional, and a powerful urge swept her—the desire to lean into Billy and let him take care of her like she'd been taking care of everyone else.

But there was Damien to consider. Until she broke up with her boyfriend, she couldn't allow herself to sink into this other man, as much as she wanted to. She stepped back. "I'm just tired."

He put soap in the tray and turned on the dishwasher. He

faced her, looking deadly serious. "This is more than just you being tired."

"Jeez, Sheriff. Remind me not to get pulled over by you."

"Hey, don't make me break out the tough-guy act." His voice had taken on a pretend stern tone, and yet something dark glinted in his eyes. Something that made her think of things like getting pulled over, frisked, and patted down by the likes of Billy Preston.

She felt her cheeks blush. What was *wrong* with her? She couldn't help but compare him to Damien. She'd been very attracted to her boyfriend—physically, they clicked. They'd had some great times. But he didn't make her feel this way. This sensation of her skin tightening around her body, her breath catching with the need to step closer. To ask more. To tell him everything. To feel his skin against hers. To *know* Billy, and be known by him.

She had to break up with Damien, like, yesterday.

"You're not going to distract me," he said, "so you might as well spill it."

"What?" Her eyes widened. Had he somehow read her thoughts?

"Your eyes give everything away," he said gently.

Something about his tone, about being alone in the kitchen with him after a long day on her feet, intensified the growing intimacy between them. She wanted to know Billy, and he wanted to listen.

She'd been feeling so isolated—surrounded by loved ones and yet still alone. Nobody seemed to notice how she was frantically paddling to stay afloat. How close she felt to breaking sometimes. How often she dreamed of different places and different things.

But in walked Billy, and somehow he'd seen. He'd listened and heard. It was a simple connection, but it did so much to make her feel better. Getting to know him, she'd begun to sense how happiness was there for her to find, she just craved a partner to share it with. Not a man to hold her up like Damien tried so desperately to do, but someone to stand with her, by her side.

"Tell me," he whispered.

She heard the care in his voice and knew she couldn't stop

herself from sharing with this man if she tried. She missed her brother—was racked with worry for him. Sometimes she hated her sister, and got so angry with Dad, so frustrated with Mom. But here was Billy, waiting, wanting to know what she was thinking. Wanting to know *her*.

She let out a long sigh, letting it all go. "I told you about my brother. The thing is, he always knows how to handle Dad." She had to stifle a stab of guilt. "He's a good man. Dad, I mean. His stroke . . . it was hard for him. But still, he drives me nuts. He's so old school. Take the whole 'Ladies' Night' thing. I mean, should I be offended? That I can only cook if it's *Ladies' Night*?"

She risked a glance into his eyes, half expecting him to brush it off. Damien would have brushed it off. But instead, Billy's brow was furrowed in thought.

"Don't let the man offend you," he said. "He's from a different generation. It's a chance for you to cook, and you should take it. Let me guess, it's been Bear's way or the highway all these years. Am I right?"

"I suppose you don't need to be a rocket scientist to figure that one out."

"And *his* dad ran the lodge and tavern before him?"

Sorrow sighed. "I see where you're going with this."

"Do you?" he asked gently. "Think about it from your father's perspective. I'll bet the things he's able to do—hell, the things your mom *lets* him do—have changed since his stroke. Changed *a lot*. He was once the master of his universe, and now I bet your mom doesn't even let him out of her sight without a cell phone in his pocket."

It was true, and it gutted her. "Yeah, that's pretty much the whole of it." She'd only been thinking about her own perspective. She stared at the floor, ashamed of her selfishness. *Dad's stroke*. It'd changed him, but the changes had come about so slowly, it was something she hadn't considered, not like that. "He worked timber when he was younger—he was once a pretty physical guy."

"I know his type. Change is hard for a guy like him. But aging is something that happens to every man—if they're lucky." Billy tucked a strand of hair behind her ear, and the sweep of his finger sent her blood pounding. "Besides, he's in for a big awakening. Wait till Bear realizes that Ladies' Night draws every male in Sierra Falls just for a taste of your cooking. He'll see. As it is, I think he's floored by how much business you did tonight. More people jammed into that tavern for dinner than I ever saw on Sully's watch."

Billy's hand still hovered by her cheek, and she fought the urge to turn into his palm, leaning into his warmth. How had he done it? With just a few words, he'd made her feel more sensitive to her dad *and* better about herself, all at the same time.

What else could a man like that do, what else could he make her feel?

His hand was right there—just one slight shift of her head, one step closer to his body, and she'd take this conversation to a whole different place. What would he do if she did?

The door swung open. It was her sister. Laura froze at the sight of her and Billy, standing so close to each other in front of the sink. The blood pounded in Sorrow's cheeks.

Laura waggled her brows in a way that she found intensely annoying. "Kudos, kiddo. Your pasta was a hit. Even *I* loved it."

Sorrow turned her back and pretended to finish up some chore by the sink, rinsing out a sponge that didn't need rinsing. Waiting for breathing to be not so difficult. "I thought you didn't do carbs."

Laura reverted to her high school big-sister voice. "Shut. Up." She put a stack of dishes in the sink, nudging Sorrow as she passed. "I *don't* eat a lot of pasta. But I *did* have some of yours. Duh."

Sorrow gave her a grudging smile. "I'm honored."

"No, seriously," Laura said in a more adult tone. "It was fantastic. Better than anything I ever got in North Beach," she added, referring to San Francisco's Italian district, but then she put the tease back in her voice. "Isn't that right, Sheriff?"

Billy smiled, not taking the bait. "I've been to North Beach a time or two myself. Your sister's right."

"Wow, okay." Sorrow put the sponge down and turned to face Laura. Now she really was blown away. "Thank you. Both of you."

Laura winked. "And someone else is here to taste it."

She recognized that wicked look. She should've *known* that Laura's sweetness came with a price. "Who?" Sorrow asked blandly.

"Damien's here," Laura said in a voice dangerously close to a singsong. "He's getting a game of pool going with that Neanderthal, Eddie. I told him you'd be right out."

Sorrow felt her shoulders tighten. She wasn't sure what bothered her most about the exchange with her sister, though she could work up a list.

Billy reached out toward her, and her heart soared, but then he squeezed her arm in a way that meant good-bye, and her stomach fell. He said, "I'll leave you to it, then."

A part of her wished he'd show some typical male reaction—jealousy, competitiveness, *something*. But instead Billy just looked vaguely amused. It made her feel like a kid. But she was twenty-three—young, sure, but definitely well past teenager. Hell, she'd been *running* the lodge nearly single-handedly.

And yet, hearing Damien's voice booming from the other room, she felt embarrassed. It was a strange feeling. There was definitely no need to be self-conscious—Damien was hot. He'd been an all-around sports star. He was from the wealthiest family in the area. So why this strange, jangly feeling in her chest?

She tried not to look as crestfallen as she felt. Damien was here, but she wanted to play a round of pool with *Billy*. Wanted *Billy* to be the one to walk her back to the house after they closed up.

Billy's hand on her arm had felt so broad and firm. *That* was the hand she wanted to take.

She gave a shake to her head. This was not good. It was time to talk to Damien.

But what if the connection she felt with Billy was a figment of her imagination? He was a widower, after all. What if he mourned his wife too much ever to move on?

Or what if he *were* interested in a relationship—what would *that* imply? Would it mean he hadn't mourned *enough*? She was treading water she had no idea how to navigate.

Billy's voice brought her back to herself. "I'll see you tomorrow?"

"Tomorrow?" She let herself study him, and his gaze didn't waver from hers. Faint lines at his eyes, mouth, and brow spoke to spending much time outdoors. She imagined him squinting against the sun as he got out of his cruiser for a routine traffic stop. Those eyes would be hard on someone who'd broken the law. But they were warm on her now.

He was so different from Damien, his features not technically as handsome, those eyes not as young. But Billy was so in control of his world—he was steadiness, strength, and wisdom, and to her those things were more vital, more necessary, more *attractive* than anything she shared with Damien.

"You remember." Amusement tinged his voice. He tilted his head, studying her. "Silver City?"

Their shopping trip to Silver City—she'd forgotten. Excitement snapped through her veins. "Right. Of course. Totally. *Tomorrow.*"

From across the kitchen, her sister snorted an unladylike laugh.

Sorrow blushed. She'd answered a bit too giddily, and Laura had noticed. She made a mental note to ask next time they were alone just when it was her big sister planned on returning to the city.

Billy didn't seem to notice. "Good news," he added. "I've got a buddy in the restaurant business there. He talked to his supplier. Usually they're closed weekends, but we can get you into the warehouse tomorrow morning. He said he'd give you a new industrial freezer at cost."

Hearing that news, Sorrow forgot all about her sister. Appliances cost a fortune, and she was still in denial about just how much a new freezer was going to run them. "At *cost*? Really?"

"One that won't break down." He winked and, for an instant, that rugged tough guy was just plain cute.

Cute, steady, strong, wise, and now *thoughtful*. She resisted the urge to fling herself into him.

"Rack 'em up," she heard Damien shout. His voice

reverberated clear into the kitchen, followed by the laughter of other men. Damien had always been able to make the other men laugh.

But in that moment, Sorrow knew. She didn't want Damien. She wanted Billy.

Twenty-two

When Billy showed up early the next morning, Sorrow was waiting for him in the tavern. He spotted her at once. That tousled, wavy blond hair hanging down her back. A flannel shirt tied around her waist. From behind she seemed relaxed, perched on a barstool, chatting with her father. By the smell of things, Sully was there, too, frying up some hash browns.

Bear spotted Billy and nodded a greeting. "Sheriff."

"Bear," he replied.

Sorrow turned and gave him a bright smile. "Hey, Billy."

His pulse jumped.

She might've looked casual, but Sorrow was no tomboy. In fact, she was all woman. Her smile was open and easy, that of a confident, capable woman. Of somebody who knew what she was about. It was the smile of a woman who'd be as confident in the bedroom as she was lounging on that stool.

He needed to stop *going there* in his head.

Last night he hadn't been able to stop himself. He'd gone there in his head all night, until his stomach was in knots, through the night, until finally he hadn't been able to stop himself. He'd touched her. He couldn't help not touching her—he'd had to know what that hair felt like, how those waves might give beneath his fingers.

And once he'd touched her he'd had to touch her again. Her

chin. Her arm. He'd had to turn and face the sink, running cold water over his skin to stop the ache.

It'd taken all he had to look casual. To pretend to be easy when all he'd felt was a fist closing around his heart. Pained, wanting her, then guilty because of it. Guilty because of Keri. Because of Damien, Sorrow's *boyfriend*, who'd been just in the next room.

He inhaled deeply to gather himself, trying to look more nonchalant than he felt. "Morning, folks. Sorrow, you ready?"

The way she lounged on that barstool—leg swinging, leaning against the counter in a way that pulled her shirt tight. Self-consciousness overwhelmed him. Like a damned teenager with a crush, he became overly aware of his approach, of his step. Of where he should look and how broadly he should return her smile. It was a feeling he hadn't felt . . . well, since he was a teenager.

It'd been different with his wife. He'd known Keri for years before they hooked up. She worked in the DA's office, and with his role in the department, they'd moved in the same circles. They'd had a long time in which to get to know each other over coffee, over posttrial beers. By the time he and Keri realized there was a spark between them, he was as comfortable with her as he'd been with his closest friends.

Sorrow, though, she was different. This was different.

He pushed aside the thought. Women like her weren't for him. Crushes and hope had died with Keri.

Billy leaned on the bar next to her, ignoring the smell of her shampoo. The scent of Sorrow in the morning.

"Good news," she told him. She was happily working through a stack of pancakes.

Her eyes were bright and her mood contagious. It was like sunshine burning through the cloud over his heart, burning away the shadows. He couldn't help but forget his dark thoughts and give himself to the moment.

"Sock it to me," he said, stealing a triangle of her toast. He had to admit—he loved a woman who loved to eat.

"Our cupboards are full. Or rather they will be. No need for us to go shopping after all."

Disappointment needled him, and he tamped it down. He told himself he was just concerned for her safety. He was suspicious of all the unusual accidents lately. If he wanted to hang around Sorrow, it was simply that he wanted to keep an eye on things. "That is good news," he said.

And he tried to believe it. Not having to shop for food meant he'd reclaim several hours from his morning—he should be happy. It was his day off, and there were any number of things he needed to tend to in his personal life.

He just needed to think of them.

She nodded and swallowed. "It means I don't need to bother you *too* much this morning."

"It wasn't going to be a bother." If the way this disappointment kept surging to the surface was any indication, a shopping trip with Sorrow would've been a pleasure. But he was being a fool. He grabbed another slice of toast, and it was too dry in his mouth. "What happened?"

"Damien heard about our troubles when he was here last night." Her eyes flicked to his, as she quickly added, "He left pretty much right after he found out."

Was she trying to tell him something with that look? Had there been a message in her eyes?

He looked away. Pretty, young women didn't telegraph hidden messages to men like him. More fool he.

"Damien has some friends," Sorrow continued, and he could've sworn he heard something like guilt in her tone.

Bear interrupted with a smirk, "*Some* friends?"

"Yeah, okay," she said flatly, "Damien has *a lot* of friends. He knows a few restaurant owners—"

"Some as far away as Reno," Bear boasted.

Billy forced his pleasant expression not to fade. He'd offered his help, but *restaurant owners*? How could he compete with *that*? All he had to offer was a buddy who worked as a line cook in Silver City.

Her smile was gone now, her mouth a tight line. "Yes, Dad. Some as far away as Reno. So anyway, apparently any minute now, men will start showing up with food. Enough to tide us over, but not so much that it won't keep in the regular fridges."

Billy said, "Well, that's wonderful." So how come he didn't feel wonderful? He was disappointed, and the reaction surprised him.

"It is, isn't it?" Sorrow crumpled her napkin and dropped it onto her plate. Did she look disappointed, too? "Though I can't imagine what Damien offered to convince them to sell us food from their own kitchens."

"What'd he *offer*?" Bear put down his coffee hard enough that some sloshed over the edge of the cup. "The guy *offered* not to kick their asses if they helped you."

Sorrow stood and patted her dad's shoulder. "Easy there, cowboy." She met Billy's eye. "I may not need to buy food, but if that other offer still stands . . . ?"

"The freezer?" Something in Billy's chest unclenched. "You bet."

She grabbed her purse from atop the bar. "It's as good a day as any to spend a ridiculous amount of money on appliances."

Bear handed his daughter her coat. "You help her, Preston. Have her pick out a good one."

Billy helped her shrug into her layers. "I'm sure your daughter is perfectly capable of picking out her own appliances, but I'll be happy to offer my help if she asks for it."

Was it his imagination, or was that a mischievous glance she just shot him? He resisted the urge to put his arm around her shoulders as they walked out to his SUV.

It was a long drive to Silver City. Forty-five minutes in which Billy would *not* notice the curve of Sorrow's thigh on the seat next to him. To not savor the smell of her, something like vanilla and shampoo. To not allow his gaze to be pulled over and over again to the slash of sunlight that cut across her face, sparking her blond hair to a thousand shades of gold.

His mind went to Keri again, and he knew his usual grief, but this time it was cut with something else. He felt the sadness, but oddly, it didn't sear through him like it usually did.

Was this him moving on? Because for the first time, he was glimpsing what it might be like to turn the page on that chapter of his life and step into another.

Was that what Keri would want him to do?

He stole a look at Sorrow. His heart was heavy, but something in his mind felt lighter than before. More open. He imagined it was hope. It was a heady feeling.

Sorrow was like those rays of early morning light that cut

through the windshield, and he was a creature emerging from darkness, blinking at this new reality, feeling a tentative fascination.

She was so different from his late wife. Keri would never ride in the car with her shoes propped on the dash. She'd never sit with her face turned toward the sun. His wife had shied from the sun, slathered herself in sunscreen, worn designer hats.

But there was Sorrow, with a faint dusting of freckles across the bridge of her nose, wearing jeans, a T, and a flannel shirt layered overtop. Fitted and purple, it was definitely a women's shirt, but it made him think how good she'd look wearing *his* flannel shirt. Romping around his apartment in his ancient red plaid. Wearing nothing else but her panties.

Damn.

He needed to stop thinking. He wasn't ready for this.

Talking. *Talking* would stop this thinking. "We should be in Silver City by ten. Stroke of luck Damien knows so many people. Good thing I'm not competing with him," he said, attempting a joke. "Money, charm, *and* powerful friends . . . a guy could get easily outmatched."

Sorrow gave him a blank look.

The line had been funny enough in his head. Hell, he needed to stop talking *and* thinking. He turned on the radio, and an old rock song filled the truck.

"Yeah," she muttered, "Damien's something else." She leaned forward, peering at the complicated police console. Her hair slipped from behind her ear, sending a waft of flowery shampoo scent his way.

He stared hard at the road. Maybe talking *had* been better.

He'd told himself he wasn't interested. That he couldn't *allow* himself to be interested. He'd sworn off relationships— he'd barely survived getting gutted by the last one. He wouldn't survive another loss like that. *Couldn't.*

But could he survive his current life? Going on like he'd been, closed to all but the most superficial of interactions.

He'd come to Sierra Falls, hoping to find peace in a small town. To find solace dealing with small things. But in the past weeks, he'd discovered the most peace while spending time with *her.*

He stole another glance. She was so different, so refreshing.

And so beautiful. Long hair tucked haphazardly behind her ear. Fresh, rosy cheeks. A love of life, a passion for food, and a smile ever on her face, even as she dealt with the most challenging of issues—finances, the lodge and tavern, her father.

She was just right.

But would a woman like that want a man like him? He felt like an old shell sometimes, but there Sorrow sat, a woman of appetites, fresh and ripe and . . .

It sheared like a bolt straight through him. He *wanted* her.

Was this him deciding to live again? Because where his mind went, his body eagerly followed. If he were honest with himself, he'd wanted to get to know her all along, had enjoyed learning about her. But what consumed him now was something else entirely.

It was desire.

He adjusted himself in his seat, racking his brain for idle chat.

This was no good. The woman had a *boyfriend*, for God's sake. He might want Sorrow, but that wasn't his decision to make.

The current station went to a commercial, and she reached over the console for the radio. "May I?" she asked.

He nodded, desperately trying to come up with some topic of conversation. "You like music?" Lame conversation, apparently.

"I like a little of everything." She zipped through, searching for a good song. The scent of her hair wasn't so much flowers as it was flowery vanilla.

He cracked the window.

Cooking. That seemed safe enough territory. "Why do you cook?" It was the best he could come up with, though he could guess the answer. He'd tasted what Sully called pot roast.

But he was surprised when her answer was slow in coming.

"The kitchen is my solace," she said finally. "It's a place for me to go. You know, in my head. I mean, there's not much else to do around the lodge." She gave a rueful laugh. "Though you'd never be able to tell with how crazy things have been lately.

But usually it's just me sitting long hours behind the desk, or cleaning the rooms—"

He shot her a look. "*You* clean the rooms? When do you sleep?"

She sighed, sounding older than her years. "It's not like we have tons of people in and out of there. It's not that much. Anyway, planning menus, all the kitchen prep . . . it helps me imagine traveling to a place. When I cook, tasting Indian curries, or stir-frying Chinese, it's a way to visit there. In a way." She got quiet.

"You've never left Sierra Falls?" He cursed the disbelief in his voice—he would hate to think he sounded patronizing.

"Well, sure I've left," she said quickly. "Class trips to Sacramento, San Francisco. That sort of thing. But real traveling . . . I guess that's not in the cards for me."

He wanted to tell her she could determine her own *cards*. That she needed someone to help prod her father. Why Damien didn't apply some friendly pressure on her behalf was a mystery. Hell, *he'd* been pressuring Bear on her behalf since the day their road caved in. Billy wanted to say that and lots of other things, but instead he just kept driving.

She shifted in her seat, and he felt her eyes glued to his profile. "How about you?"

The bald way she'd asked it took him aback. "How *about* me?"

He gave a little laugh, but when he turned to catch her eye, he wished he hadn't. She was watching him avidly, her expression serious, like she might be able to uncover something he hadn't realized he'd been hiding.

He wanted her to turn and look out the window instead.

He wanted to reach across the seat and sweep the hair from her face. Then he'd take her hand and tuck it in his, to hold it nestled in his lap.

"You were a high-ranking police officer," she said. "In *Oakland*. It must've been so exciting."

He put his entire focus on the road. That'd been another time. Another life. His voice was tight when he replied, "*Exciting* is one word for it."

"It must pale in comparison to what we've got going on in Sierra Falls."

He shot her another look. He was so in control in all aspects of his work. His whole *job* was getting people to confess to things they wanted kept secret. And yet Sorrow always caught *him* off guard, always got *him* talking—how did she manage it? "Hey, we were talking about *you*. How'd the tables get turned?"

She gave him a wicked smile that would've worked on any perp, in any interrogation room. "I'm not done with my questions yet, Sheriff. So you decided to leave gangs for grandmas?"

"Thank God."

"You don't miss it?"

He wasn't even sure what that meant, *miss it*. It was so much more complicated than that. Of course he missed it. Just as he never wanted to go back. He avoided the question. "I'm happy putting myself out to pasture."

She laughed. "You're hardly ancient."

He sighed. Some days he felt it. Billy sat there, waiting for the familiar weariness to swamp him again. Only this time it didn't. Catching a glimpse of her sneakers on his dash, smelling her sunshine scent, he had to admit, this was not one of those days.

Twenty-three

Sully kept one eye on the kitchen as the men carted away the old freezer and rolled in the new. The appliance guys worked fast, hooking up the water line and electricity, and rolling that big beast into place.

He occupied himself with busy work, because he didn't really need to be there. Not with Billy Preston there supervising things. Sully leaned on the pass-through for a glimpse.

Billy and Sorrow were in the kitchen, but it was Billy who'd asked the men to sweep away their trash before pushing the freezer into place. Billy who'd told them not to ding the door. Finally, it seemed there was someone else around the place looking out for Sorrow.

Sully eyed the sheriff—he sure was hanging around a whole helluva lot lately. He had to admit he liked the guy. As former military himself, Sully understood a man who'd chosen a uniform as his vocation. Respected him.

It put him in mind of Damien, who had yet to command Sully's respect. *His* uniform was a pair of khakis and a button-up shirt, and Sully had always thought Sorrow could do better.

The door swung, catching Sully's eye. The installation guys were headed out. "You're all set," one of them told him. "Give a call if there's any trouble."

Sully nodded his thanks. Curious about the new freezer—and, he hated to admit, excited, too—he went into the kitchen to check it out.

But Sorrow and Billy were already checking it out, and they were standing close. *Real* close. Though they didn't look like they might kiss, they were speaking quietly, like two people who'd definitely thought about it.

Sully cleared his throat. "Excuse me."

They hadn't even been touching, but Sorrow and Billy sprang apart like they were two magnets with opposite poles.

Unsure what to do, he snatched a rag from the counter, turned on his heel, and headed right back out. It'd been an adolescent maneuver, but he'd needed to do something. Those two were close and looked like they were thinking about getting closer. Better for Sully to feel like a moron than catch Sorrow and Billy in a lip-lock.

Especially when one of them had a boyfriend. He was surprised they hadn't broken up yet, though lately Damien had been making himself scarce, almost like the guy knew something was up. The sheriff, meanwhile, seemed to be there every time Sully turned around, and from what he just saw in the kitchen, it looked like where there was smoke there was fire.

Well, hot damn. He let the notion sit for a bit. The sheriff was older than Sorrow—he better not be taking any advantage. Sully considered the possibility, then dismissed it just as fast. Billy Preston struck him as a good man. A widower—not the type to be dallying with girls' affections. Quite the contrary—Billy would be *serious*, with serious intentions.

And what exactly were those intentions? Sorrow deserved to have someone in her life who wanted to ask just that. He didn't trust Bear with the task—the man wouldn't know subtle if his life depended on it. No, it'd be up to *him* to ask what Billy had in mind where Sorrow was concerned.

It wasn't long before he got the chance. Sully heard the phone ring, and Sorrow strode out of the tavern not a minute later. Billy stood at the door, shouldering into his coat.

"Hey, Sheriff," Sully called. "You got a second?"

With a curt nod, Billy hung his coat back on the hook. "Sure thing." His look was quizzical as he joined him in a booth.

"Sorrow head out?" he asked, unsure where he was going with all this or how to begin.

"Some emergency at the lodge." Billy noticed his concern and added, "Nothing major. I get the impression that a light's out and Bear can't find the bulbs."

Sully let out a belly laugh, relieved it wasn't something more. "Good thing he's got Sorrow around. If it weren't for her, the man would probably just sit in the dark and bitch about it."

Billy chuckled, adding, "Probably gripe about how it was her fault."

"Something like that." The irreverent talk had broken the ice, and there was a moment's comfortable silence.

Sully took a deep breath. It was now or never. "I've known Sorrow since she was knee-high to a grasshopper. She was a good kid, and she's grown into a good woman." He looked Billy in the eye—it'd be cowardly to do anything but. "You're a lawman, and I respect you, but I've got to ask . . ." He faltered. He didn't have kids, and definitely no experience with daughters. He could command a battalion of soldiers hailing from every background, every race, every walk of life. But this? He was no good at this overprotective thing.

"What my intentions are?"

Sully let out that breath. "Yeah. That's the one. I'd like to know what your intentions are."

It was Billy's turn to falter. "She has a boyfriend," he answered finally, and though his words said one thing, his eyes told quite another story.

"Doesn't mean you don't like her."

Billy nodded, hesitated. "Sorrow is special."

"You have feelings for her."

Billy nodded. Looked down at his hands on the table. There was something else.

"But there's something else, isn't there?" Sully prompted.

When Billy looked back up, his gaze was distant. "It's more than just the boyfriend." He gave a humorless laugh. "I'm a broken man, Sully."

"Don't seem broken to me."

"All right, not broken, but . . . my wife, Keri. I can't seem to forget her."

Sully had some experience on that front. Not with women, no. But he was haunted by faces—dozens of them—young men who'd died while he lived. "I don't know that we ever forget the past. Just so long as we keep moving forward."

They sat with that thought a moment. Billy looked like he needed to say more, so Sully just waited for his words to come.

Eventually they did. "Keri cast a long shadow," Billy began. "She was powerful. A lawyer in the DA's office. And man, could that woman make the most hardened felons quake." He smiled at the memory. "She was something else. Never would I have cheated on her." He laughed then. "Hell, I was afraid to disagree with her."

The smile bled from his face, and he leaned his elbows on the table, struggling to put words to his feelings. "It isn't just moving on that's hard. The feeling that I'm somehow breaking my vows if I look at another woman. It's that I was a different person when I married her. That man is long gone. And that feels like a betrayal, too."

"Men change." As Sully said it, he wondered if it was time to make some changes *himself*. But he pushed the notion away to focus on the man across from him. "You've got to keep going. Experiencing new things. That's how you honor her memory— by living your life. Otherwise you might as well have died with her. Something like that—losing your wife so young—it'll make you different. You'll live different, and you'll love different, too."

"I *am* different," Billy said. "There's a quiet inside me that I didn't have when I was with Keri. Like peace. My whole life, I didn't realize it'd been lacking. Until I came here and met Sorrow."

Sully knew a little something about that. "I think some folks call that wisdom."

"Maybe so." Billy shrugged. "All I know is that, for the first time in a long time, I feel like there might be things out there I could look forward to. And it's because of her. Sorrow. When I'm with her, I just feel . . . happy." He'd spoken the word as though he'd never said it before. But then a dark glint flashed in his eyes. "And I feel a whole hell of a lot more than that, too, obviously."

Sully recognized that glint. He growled, "I'll have to caution you there, son."

Billy laughed. "Understood." He leaned back in his seat, looking lighter. More at ease. "You ever lost anyone, Tom?"

Sully blew out a sigh. Why hadn't he poured them something to drink first?

"I've known loss," he said carefully. "Not a wife, though. Not that. But they were losses just the same. I felt a lot of guilt when I stepped off that plane back in '72. Coming home when so many didn't. But those boys, my friends, they'd have wanted me to live. They'd have kicked my ass if they thought I'd given up on my own life. Strong woman like your Keri? I imagine she'd do the same."

"Kick my ass from the great beyond?"

"You bet," Sully said, but then it was his turn to go quiet. He sure was free with the advice—advice he should consider taking himself. Because what he was doing—flipping Bear's burgers day in and day out—that wasn't exactly taking life by the horns. It was time he made a change. Time he did a little living himself, maybe ask Marlene out on a proper date.

"It's time to let go and give in to your feelings," Sully said, but then he paused as it hit him. Those words applied to himself as much as to Billy. He nodded, clear now on his own feelings. Billy was lucky—the guy was a kid in comparison, with another lifetime ahead of him. "You'll never lose the grief," Sully added, "but you're young yet. You can move through it. It's no dishonor to your Keri if you move on with your life."

Billy's eyes met and held his. Something moved between the two men, connected them. It was respect.

The sheriff was good people. Solid. Sully could see him and Sorrow making something work. Which meant she needed to do something, and fast, before she had a situation on her hands. "Now she just needs to deal with that boyfriend of hers." He wished there were a way to broach it with her, have a talk like he was having with Billy, but if he brought up her love life, she'd probably look at him like he'd grown horns.

An evil smile curled onto the sheriff's face. "I could always arrest him for something. That'd take him out of the picture."

He barked out a laugh. "No need to resort to that. I've had

my eye on that girl. I've seen how she is with you. If I know Sorrow, that boy will be getting his walking papers any day now."

When Sorrow returned, she plopped next to the sheriff in the booth. "Let there be light," she pronounced.

Talk about lightbulbs—Billy's eyes were a thousand watts when he looked at her. "All good?" he asked.

"All good." She leaned against him with a sigh. "But boy, am I beat."

Sully watched the exchange in silence. He was sure they were blissfully unaware how obvious the fireworks were that crackled between them. He'd said Sorrow could handle Damien, and he hoped he was right. She was, in her way, a bit of an innocent with men, unaware of her effect on them.

Damien, though, he was a pro. Not manipulative, but a smooth talker, that was for sure. Sully had tried to like him, *wanted* to trust and respect him, but as far as he could tell, the guy earned his money mostly by wearing those fancy clothes and talking on his cell. Born into the richest family in Sierra Falls, he'd had a lucky birth, though with the way women treated him, you'd have thought he was in line to be king of England.

The front door opened, bringing in a gust of crisp winter air. *Speak of the devil.*

Sorrow sat bolt upright. "Damien, hi," she said, her voice overly bright.

Damien stiffened. "Hey, Bailey. Sheriff." He gave a curt nod toward the back of the room. "Sully, congrats. I hear you got a new freezer."

A crazy grin was pasted on Sorrow's face. "What a surprise to see you. I thought you had to work."

He took in the whole scene. "I like to keep you on your toes," he said carefully. "I wanted to check out the new setup." He shot a pointed look at Billy. "See if you need anything."

Looked like things might come to a head sooner rather than later. Sully suppressed a smile—this was more fun than he'd had in some time. These kids, figuring out their lives. Youth really was wasted on the young.

She stood, looking brittle enough to snap in two. Damien wrapped an arm around her and leaned down, taking a kiss that struck Sully as longer and firmer than necessary.

Sorrow pulled away. "Well, come see."

Damien strode straight back into the kitchen, leading the way. And of course he did—Damien was the sort of guy who never second-guessed himself.

Sully couldn't help but follow, and he felt Billy at his back. The word *guarded* came to mind.

Damien gave the freezer a once-over. It was a professional model, with great stainless steel panels. "She's a beauty."

"A friend of mine is in the restaurant business," Billy said evenly.

Sully frowned. "Nobody better tamper with this one." He met the sheriff's eye, and they exchanged a meaningful look.

"I'm going to talk to Bear about installing a security system," Billy said.

"Good luck with that." Damien opened the door to take a look. "This whole thing must've cost him a fortune already."

Sorrow was nodding away like a bobblehead doll. "Billy's friend got it for me at cost."

"I'll bet he did," Damien muttered.

Sorrow and Billy were so focused on staring inside that freezer that Sully was the only one to notice the smirk on Damien's face. He wasn't sure if the kid was getting ready to laugh or punch the sheriff.

"Well, Sheriff, nice work." Damien shut the door. "It sure is a big one. Sort of reminds me of those Transformer movies. Like it might spring to life."

"Yeah, right?" Sorrow tried to sound playful, but there was tension in her voice.

Damien put his hands in his pockets. "So I guess you don't need me."

"No—" Sorrow stopped herself with a dispirited laugh. "I mean, of course we *need* you, but this is all taken care of."

Sully noted it was "*we* need you" instead of "*I* need you."

He backed away slowly. Seemed like a good time to run out and do an errand. Maybe make a quick stop by the house. Marlene's grandkid wanted to see his Vietnam medals.

Folks said all was fair in love and war, but at the moment, war sure seemed the easier of the two.

Twenty-four

∾

Billy's friend had moved heaven and earth to deliver the freezer so soon, and Sorrow contemplated the big, whirring beast as she cleaned the kitchen, scouring away grease and the dust that'd exploded from beneath the old one when the appliance guys had done their thing.

Cleaning was usually such a good, mindless activity, and yet she couldn't stop fretting about what the heck she was supposed to do with her love life. The timing kept being off, and there hadn't been a good moment to have her talk with Damien. He'd probably be fine with a breakup—he was the sort of guy who had two dozen women waiting in the wings. Maybe he was even thinking of breaking up with *her*.

She had to admit, though, he'd looked ready to throttle Billy this morning. She was sure his jealousy had nothing to do with *her*—Damien just didn't like to lose. However she looked at it, there was no question—she needed to end their fling the next time she saw him, no matter what.

Because she couldn't get Billy out of her mind. She was surrounded by people she loved, people she knew who loved her, and yet it was only when she was with Billy that she felt like she wasn't in it alone.

She'd thought she was into Damien, until Billy had come into her life. The two men posed such a stark contrast. Damien seemed like such a . . . *guy* sometimes, a dude who told jokes over the pool table, made public moves on his girl, and drove his car too fast. But the sheriff was all man—thoughtful, kind, strong, experienced—and all man was exactly what Sorrow needed. What she *wanted*.

Laura had ribbed her about Damien putting a ring on it, but as she got to know Billy, Sorrow realized how Damien wasn't the sort of man she'd want for a husband at all. She was young even to be thinking the word *marriage*—some might say too young—but she'd borne such responsibility for so long, sometimes she felt far more ancient than her twenty-three years.

It was old enough to know Damien wasn't the one. The man she'd spend her life with would be someone who stood tall, stood for what was right. Stood up for her. A man like Billy Preston.

Her fling with Damien had been fun, but now she saw how that was all it'd been—good, physical fun. Granted, Damien was a great person—he'd done so much for her and her family, and she didn't doubt he cared for her. But her stolen conversations in the kitchen with Billy, the quiet way she felt him ready to catch her if she fell, how he always wanted to know about her day before anything else . . . she saw how love could grow there. And love was what she wanted.

The problem was *him*. He'd said he wasn't competing with Damien. *"Good thing I'm not competing with him"* to be exact. If Billy wasn't even trying, that meant he wasn't interested, right?

It's not that she expected Billy to make a move. He was a gentleman after all. A good guy. And a good guy never moved in on another man's woman.

Which meant it was up to her to make a move. Only she didn't have any inkling what his feelings toward her might be. She knew he liked her, and she definitely knew *she* was feeling something. But was she in it alone?

Maybe he still felt too much grief over the loss of his wife. A part of him would surely grieve her for the rest of his life. Would he ever see his way through it? And, if he did, would there be a place left in his heart with room enough for someone to find a home there? Could that someone be *her*?

Billy was older, though. Might he want someone more experienced?

Dealing with her dad's stroke at such a young age had certainly made her feel older than her years. She'd had plenty of emotional experience. And she had the real-life experience of running the lodge almost single-handedly. Yet she didn't feel *worldly*. While Billy, with his life in the city, and his fancy restaurants, and his lawyer wife . . . he'd lived a lifetime before he'd even arrived in Sierra Falls. And it'd been a lifetime that seemed pretty worldly to her.

Either way, it was definitely past time to break it off with Damien, and only then could she figure out this thing with Billy. If he wasn't interested, that was something she needed to find out pretty quick, because she was spending way too much time daydreaming about the man.

She managed to get Damien alone when he swung by for lunch. By the look in his eyes, she could see he knew what was coming. It made her nervous. Damien was smooth, he was quick on his feet. He'd try to trip her up. She needed to focus. End it quickly, kindly, with no debate. Like pulling off a Band-Aid.

"It's that sheriff," Damien told her. "You're breaking up with me because you've got a thing for Billy Preston."

"No, that's not—"

"Sorrow Bailey, I've known you my whole life. You can't bullshit a bullshitter. I see what's going on. I get it."

"I . . . you do?" Relief plumed through her. Damien understood. Maybe he'd make it easy on her.

"Of course. And I don't buy it."

Her relief was short-lived. He wasn't going to make this easy at all. She'd just have to toughen up. "Well, you *have* to buy it."

Surprise flashed in his eyes. Good. He was hearing her. Only he decided to take a different tack. He stepped closer, tugged at the front of her shirt. "Look, babe. You've been so swamped around here. And I've been swamped at work. What we need is to get out of town, reconnect. We'll take a mini-vacation. Drive someplace warm, like Sonoma or Napa. We could go wine tasting. French Laundry is out that way, too—I could get us a reservation. It's one of the best restaurants in the world."

She knew an instant of temptation, but then pictured Billy

in her mind's eye. She might not know how the sheriff felt, but she had to be free to find out. She took a step back. "I can't. I'm sorry."

"Why can't you? I'll whisk you away." He stepped forward, leaning down to whisper in her ear. "There's a spa in Sonoma. You can get a facial. Maybe a hot stone massage."

Wow, he was good. It'd be so easy to say yes. Hot stone massages and floating in hot mineral pools. She could go. He'd love to take her.

But she knew she couldn't. She shook her head. "It wouldn't be right."

"What do you mean, not right?" He shook his head, baffled, like she was speaking gibberish.

That nonchalant attitude of his girded her. Damien had always gotten what he wanted. But not this time. She stood tall. "I'd feel like I was taking advantage of you."

"It's not taking advantage when it's something I *want* to do. For you. For us."

"I can't, Damien. I'm just not feeling it."

He opened his mouth to speak, and for once nothing came out. She felt a pang of guilt. Damien was a good guy—she cared for him. She really did. And she hated hurting him. Because, she was surprised to discover, he looked genuinely hurt.

"What about me?" he asked, his tone subdued for once. "What if *I'm* feeling it?"

"No," she said, and the word brought with it a stab of sadness. It was more than the discomfort of delivering bad news—this breaking up thing was hard. She genuinely cared for him, would genuinely miss him. "This is it, Damien. You're great— *so* great. You've done so much for us. But . . ."

"Let me guess," he interrupted. "The old 'it's not you it's me' line?"

Her shoulders fell, and he laughed, a rueful, regretful sound. "It's okay, Bail. I've given that talk a time or two myself." He chucked her chin. "It's not done yet, you know. It ain't over till the fat lady sings."

As breakups went, it felt oddly incomplete. He'd see, though. In time, he'd come to understand that she'd meant every word.

She moped around the house after that, and Laura found her later, sitting on their brother's bed. It was a good place to think. Representing hope and melancholy both, there was no better spot for wallowing than BJ's room.

He'd gone to Quantico for Officer Candidate School right after college, and though he'd been away for years, everything was just as he'd left it. A Metallica poster. San Francisco Giants baseball memorabilia. A snapshot of him with his high school girlfriend.

She peered at that photo for a while. Strange that he'd kept it, they'd been broken up for so long.

"Hey," Laura said, and Sorrow startled.

She put the picture frame back on BJ's bedside table. "Hi."

"What are you doing in here?" Laura wandered in, glancing idly at the books on his desk. But then she froze, paled. "There wasn't any news, was there?"

"No," Sorrow said quickly, having instantly understood the question. A loved one fighting a war on the other side of the planet tended to make normal things like doorbells, ringing phones, and somber visits to the bedroom cause for alarm. "No word from BJ."

"Jeez. You scared me." Laura plopped next to her on the brown corduroy bedspread. "So then what's got you so droopy? You look like you just lost your puppy."

"Damien and I broke up."

Laura smirked. "You mean, *you* broke up with *Damien*."

Sorrow cast her eyes down and picked at the comforter. "How'd you guess?"

"Who *hasn't* guessed? You and that sheriff are practically joined at the hip."

She snapped her head up at that. "We are not."

"What's up with that, anyway? Some sort of older man complex?"

"He's, like, ten or eleven years older than me," Sorrow said. "That's hardly *old*."

"Whatever." Laura flopped onto her side, leaning on her elbow. "So, you and Damien. Spill it. How'd it all go down?"

"He didn't believe me."

Her sister laughed. "Of course he didn't. I think the last

person to break up with *Damien* was Paula Richardson in the third grade."

Sorrow gave her a rueful smile. "Yeah, I think you're probably right."

"So, what'd he say?"

"He said he wanted to take me away somewhere."

"Like on a vacation?"

Sorrow nodded. How she'd dreamed of a vacation. But she'd never take advantage of his money that way. "Yeah."

"So what'd you say?"

"That I just wasn't feeling it."

Laura waved her hands, beckoning for more. "And then?"

"And then he said he *was* into it, and what could he do, and it went on pretty much like that . . ."

"So what are you going to do? Are you and Billy a thing now?"

Sorrow gave her a sharp look. "Billy doesn't *have* 'things.' He doesn't seem like the type. I don't know if he's even interested."

"Duh. Of course he's interested." Laura sat up, looking riled. "If I hadn't lived with you for so many years, I'd have thought you were born yesterday."

"Why do you say that?"

"Why do you think he comes around here? For what, Sully's cooking? To chat with Dad?"

A tiny match lit in Sorrow's chest, a small flicker of hope. "I guess not."

"She guesses not." Laura shoved her shoulder. "Well? Do you *want* him to be interested?"

Sorrow felt the blood heat her cheeks.

Laura barked out a laugh. "Sorrr-ow likes the sherrr-ifff."

"Shut up," Sorrow said, shoving her sister back. "What about you, Miss Know-It-All?"

"What *about* me?"

"You're quick with the love life advice," Sorrow said. "Anyone you've got *your* eye on?"

Laura looked taken aback. "In this town? No way."

"Why do you say that? There are lots of great men in *this town*."

"Yeah, it is like walking into the land of low-hanging fruit . . ." Laura laughed. "But none of them are for me."

"Why not?"

Laura shrugged. "I don't know. The guys around here are all so . . . *townie*."

The attitude was classic Laura, and as usual, it drove Sorrow nuts. She crossed her arms at her chest. "Just because a guy lives in the mountains, doesn't mean he's backwoods."

Laura bristled. "I didn't say that."

"You implied it. *You* were born here, Laura. What, you spend a few years in San Francisco, and all of a sudden you're better than the rest of us?"

"Not at all," Laura said, and seemed actually to mean it.

Maybe her sister was being sincere. Maybe *she* was the one with the chip on her shoulder, reading too much into Laura's off-the-cuff comments.

"Whatever." Sorrow waved it off. "It's just men. I didn't mean to jump down your throat."

Laura puffed up playfully. "An apology. Well, then." Her eyes narrowed to an evil glint. *"It's just men*, my ass. Little sis, I think you need my help."

"Help," Sorrow said flatly, but then she felt suddenly shy. She hated to admit it, but what Laura knew about men could probably fill an encyclopedia. "Okay, say I am interested in him. What do I do next?"

Laura laughed. "Some things you need to figure out on your own."

"Be serious. What should I do?" Her sister never had guy trouble—she was confident in a way that attracted men. Sorrow had always been confident, too, but until Damien, that'd meant she'd always ended up as the buddy. Everyone's favorite girl. "I need your help." She was stumped enough that it didn't even sting to say it. "You're good with guys."

"You're good with guys, too."

"Yeah, maybe at playing the part of the girl next door."

"Jeez," Laura said with a scowl, "how'd you ever land Damien?"

Sorrow shrugged. "You know Damien. Damien landed *me*. I think he must've been bored."

Her sister's eyes hardened. "Don't say that. You have *got* to stop thinking crap like that."

Laura's vehemence took her aback, touched her. Her sister was right; Sorrow *was* prone to being too self-effacing.

She considered confiding more, but decided not to go there. The trust just wasn't there yet. She waved it off. "Okay, okay. I didn't ask for a therapy session."

"Well then, here's a question," Laura said. "Is *Damien* going to need a therapy session when you're done with him?"

He wouldn't, she knew that. Their relationship had been complicated in its way, offering something they each needed. For Damien, it was that she *got* him. Being with Sorrow let him imagine himself something he longed to be. He wore a suit, sat behind a desk, was a power player, but that success came with a price—it kept him under his father's powerful thumb. Whereas she'd understood that a part of Damien longed to roll up his sleeves and be a man's man, doing things like jumping dead batteries and thawing frozen pipes.

But she wasn't about to explain all that, so Sorrow just shrugged. "It wasn't exactly true love with us, you know?" Feeling vulnerable, she flopped onto her back, staring at the ceiling instead of meeting her sister's probing stare. "Please. I just need some advice. I'm not good at this flirting thing." She put a hand out to stop Laura's denials, meeting her eye. "Listen. You don't understand. It comes naturally to you. Me, I'm the girl guys confide in. I've always been Sorrow Bailey, The Buddy."

"You're being serious, aren't you?" Laura's expression softened as she seemed to see Sorrow for the first time. "Well . . . first off, you've got to let him know you're interested. Give him a sign."

"What kind of sign?"

"Guys don't need much. Billy looks at you all the time. Next time you're alone, just . . . don't look away. Trust me. The man will take it from there."

"Okay. I can do that. Wait." Sorrow's heart skittered in her chest at the thought. "Where should I be when this happens? Tell me how I should begin, *exactly*."

"How, *exactly*?" Laura scanned her critically. "Change that shirt, for starters. And wear something other than hiking boots."

Sorrow stuck her legs in front of her, rolling her ankles. "These aren't hiking boots. They're all-weather sneakers."

"Yeah, whatever. Lose them. And wear a shirt that fits."

Sorrow tugged at her hem. "This fits."

"Okay, check that. I meant, wear something *fitted*." Laura popped from the bed and grabbed her sister's arm. "Come with me. We're raiding my closet."

"Really?" Sorrow stumbled down the hallway behind her. "You'll help me?"

Laura flung open her closet door. "If you mean, will I dress you up then shove you out the door, then yes, gladly. I'll help you."

Sorrow briefly registered the surprising amount of clothing Laura had brought for what was supposedly a "short visit." But then her sister's words sank in. "Wait, you're going to shove me out the door? Where am I supposed to go?"

"To his house, dummy." Laura flipped through her closet, grabbing random items and tossing them on the bed.

She felt a fluttering in her belly, excited to be getting actual help, but a little nervous, too. "What should I talk about when I get there?"

Laura stopped what she was doing to give her a long, hard look. "You really don't know, do you?"

She gave her sister a rueful shrug. "I can talk, I've just never gotten how to, you know, flirt."

Laura turned and, putting hands on hips, studied her. "You know how to flirt. You just don't know that you know. You know?"

"Um, not really."

"Just talk about something you feel strongly about. Like food. Only spice it up."

"Spice up the food?" Sorrow asked.

"No, dummy. Spice up your banter. Make it *sex-ay*." Laura raised a naughty brow, making Sorrow laugh. "And make some sexy food while you're at it."

"Sexy *food*? You mean, like how they say stuff like oysters and foie gras are aphrodisiacs?"

Laura grimaced. "It needs to be easy and edible. Like, something drizzly and chocolaty and whipped creamy."

"Got it," Sorrow said. Food was her domain, and talk of it gave her confidence. "And then what?"

Laura rolled her eyes. "Seriously? If you haven't figured *that* part out yet, you're in more trouble than I thought."

"You know what I mean." She joined Laura at the closet and picked out a purple dress, holding it in front of her before a mirror.

Her sister snatched it away and flung it on the floor. "Makes you look like an eggplant."

Sorrow plopped on the edge of the bed. "So, what will my excuse be, for showing up?"

"I don't know. Make it up. You bought too many groceries or something." Laura picked out one black high-heeled boot and tossed through her closet to find its mate. "Isn't the fastest way to a man's heart through his stomach? You're the chef, so . . . go *chef.*"

She nodded. She could do that. "I can do that."

"You can do that." Laura's eyes lit, and she plucked a gauzy black top from her closet. "A-ha."

Sorrow frowned. "You want me to wear *that*? It's see-through."

Laura foisted it at her. "Wear it. And don't leave until he kisses you."

Twenty-five

Billy knew he should do *something*, but there was nothing he felt like doing. It was too early in the evening to pop in a movie. He'd already gotten in a workout, just the free weights he kept in his garage, but his heart hadn't been in it. Considering he wore only an ancient pair of jeans, it seemed he couldn't even finish getting dressed.

He hadn't been able to get events at the lodge out of his mind. The Bailey family had scoffed at his suspicions. Fallen trees, the errant road closure, car and appliance troubles galore—they blamed it all on coincidence. Just a slew of innocent incidents that came with mountain living. But the cut freezer lines had cast all those emergencies in a new light. He had a hunch something was going on. Somebody was playing a dangerous game.

And, one of these days, one of those innocent incidents could turn lethal.

He couldn't bear the thought that Sorrow might get caught in the cross fire. He'd done some poking around, but it'd been no good. Bear had been right on one count: Sierra Falls *was* a friendly town, where everybody knew their neighbors. So who on earth would want to mess with the lodge?

He balled up his T-shirt and tossed it onto one of the kitchen chairs. As much as it killed him, he had to let it go for the night.

All he wanted to do was storm the lodge and protect her, but it wasn't his place.

He *had* to get his mind on other things before he drove himself nuts. He opened the fridge to stare inside. Food. He needed food.

There was nothing to eat. And he didn't feel like cooking anyway. He slammed the door shut.

He'd already had pizza once that week, which just about covered the delivery options in Sierra Falls. He thought about the tavern, but there was no way he could go there.

Even though that was all he wanted to do.

The early birds would be showing up for dinner right about now. Sully had probably made some sort of meaty special—meat loaf, Prospector's Pie, or maybe his Southwest burgers. He hadn't made those in a while.

Billy could get a hot meal, keep his eye on things. Sorrow would be in and out, probably working on her own creation in the family kitchen.

Sorrow. If he went for dinner, he probably wouldn't even see her. He could just swing by, grab a quick bite, make sure nothing was amiss. It wasn't like he'd be paying her a visit. If he saw her, he saw her, and if he didn't, well, it'd be no big deal. He grabbed his T-shirt, decided.

And then he stopped. He wadded the shirt back up and tossed it back onto the chair. He couldn't go back to the tavern *again*. People would start to talk, if they hadn't already. He'd lost count of the number of times he'd "dropped by" the Bailey place that week.

Something had happened on that car ride. A shift. It went deeper than him wanting to keep her safe. It was that he wanted *her*.

More, that it was okay to want her. That maybe he even *needed* her.

Except there was that damned boyfriend. He'd never compete with someone like Damien Simmons. Rich, young, powerful, good-looking . . . the list went on and on.

But then again, Sully *had* said Sorrow would be giving the guy his walking papers any day now. Could that possibly be true? And, if it were, would she possibly be interested in *him*?

He could always look elsewhere. If he'd made his decision to start dating again, he could try going to that bar across town—what was that ridiculous name, Chances?—and stop spending so much time at the tavern.

But who was he fooling? Sorrow was the only woman he had his eye on. Sorrow, who'd managed to burrow her way beneath his shell.

The doorbell pulled him from his thoughts. He glanced at the clock. Five was late for someone to be showing up at his doorstep. He raked his hand through his hair a couple of times. People come by a man's house after hours, they had to take what they got.

He opened the door, and his jaw dropped. It was *her*. "Sorrow. Hi."

"Hey, Sheriff."

He drank in the sight of her. Her cheeks were flushed from the cold and her sandy blond hair danced in the breeze. She was wearing a fuzzy bluish green hat that was an exact match to the color of her eyes.

She got prettier every time he saw her. Was there something different about her today, or was it just *him*, seeing her differently?

"Laura kicked me out of the kitchen, but I bought too many groceries," she said, sounding nervous, "and they'll spoil if I don't do something with them, so I was hoping maybe, I mean, I thought that maybe you might be hungry. If you're free. And hungry. I could cook for us."

He'd been feeling listless, but now he felt rooted to the spot, his entire focus consumed by her. Seeing her there before him, it struck him just how powerful a presence she'd been in his thoughts. And now she was *here*. On his doorstep. It was strange—like he'd summoned her somehow.

Her gaze flicked down, taking in his clothes—or lack thereof.

Damn. He wasn't even dressed.

"I hope I'm not bothering you," she said hesitantly.

"God, *yes*. I mean . . . no, of course you're not bothering me. And yes, I'm hungry." *Hungrier than you realize.* He laughed and stepped back. "I'm sorry, let's try that again. Hi, Sorrow, please come on in." He noticed her canvas bag overflowing with groceries and took it for her. "Let me get this."

What was she doing there? She was like an angel who'd appeared at his door, and now she was walking through his house as though it were something she did all the time.

As they headed to the kitchen, he caught her surreptitiously scanning the place. He darted a look around. A blanket was wadded on the corner of the couch. Some mail was tossed randomly on the coffee table. There was a stack of kindling and newspaper where he'd been readying a fire. A bit messy, but not dirty.

"It's kind of rumpled," he told her, "but it's home. And the kitchen's clean." He put the groceries down and quickly snatched up and pulled on his shirt.

"Not rumpled at all." She followed him into the kitchen and put her purse on the counter. "I was just thinking how homey it is. Comfy. Plus there are no heads anywhere," she added with a laugh, referring to her dad's penchant for wall-mounted antlers.

"Yeah, I'm not big on dead and dusty animals." He looked at her. She was so damned beautiful, and she was standing there in *his* kitchen. "So, are you really making me dinner?"

She froze. "If you want. Is that weird?"

"Are you kidding? Not at all. Just before you got here, I was wondering what I was going to feed myself."

"Hungry?"

"Starving," he said.

She looked pleased at that. "Good."

He began to empty the groceries from her bag. He needed to do something with his hands, something other than trace those errant wisps of hair from her face, or smooth his hands down her back.

As he unpacked, he grew more and more impressed. Melons, prosciutto, lamb, tomatoes, strawberries, *champagne*. "What did you bring us?"

"We've got melon and prosciutto skewers to start. Then I thought a rack of lamb with *herbes de Provence*, and some berries for dessert." Doubt flickered in her eyes. "Is that okay?"

He laughed. "Are you kidding? More than *okay*." He

tempered himself—he needed to stop sounding so enthusiastic. This was another man's woman. And it was *Sorrow*, no less. She was guileless, not at all a flirt. If she was there because she said she'd bought too many groceries, then that was why she was there.

She still wore her jacket, and he went up behind her. "Hey, take off your coat and stay a while."

He slid it from her shoulders and had to choke back a curse. Her shirt was sheer and black, and it gave him a glimpse of her black bra underneath. It was the sexiest goddamned thing he'd ever seen.

He coughed, feeling mighty glad he was standing behind her so she couldn't see his face, or any other parts of him for that matter. "You're looking *fine* this evening."

As she turned to face him, her hand fluttered at her hem, like she was fighting the urge to adjust her shirt. "Am I too dressed up?"

His eyes went to that part of her shirt that wasn't smooth, right where the lacy cups of her bra covered her breasts. His jeans grew tight, like he was a damned teenager again. Thank God he'd at least changed out of his sweats, or his condition would be ridiculously obvious. "Hell no." He laughed at how vehemently that'd come out. "I mean, not too dressed up at all. You're *gorgeous*."

But then an icy rock formed in the pit of his stomach, giving him pause. Was she *staying*, or did that fancy shirt mean this was a cook and run sort of thing? "Are you . . . have you got a date with Damien later?"

For an instant, she looked panicked. "No," she said quickly, then added in a more somber tone, "I mean, no. We broke up."

"Oh." His pulse thrummed hard in his neck, his throat suddenly dry. "I'm sorry. You doing okay?"

"Yes, I am, actually." She stood at the counter, arranging groceries that didn't need arranging. "I'm the one who broke it off."

The full impact of the situation hit him. Sorrow was single.

"So . . ." He hesitated on the question he knew he needed to ask. "Does that mean you didn't love him?"

She got a funny, faraway look. "I don't think I did." Those

blue-green eyes cleared, coming into focus to meet his. "I mean, I know I didn't. I guess I wanted it to be love. I've never been in love." She opened her mouth like she wanted to say more, and he held his breath.

He'd love to see this woman in love. Heat flared in his chest, long-stoked embers raging into flame. Billy would love to see this woman in love with *him*.

"I see," he said.

She'd put on that killer shirt. Filled a bag with food. And come to *him*. It wasn't love maybe, not yet. But maybe it could be.

There was something between them. He realized there had been, from the first cup of coffee she'd ever poured for him at the tavern. He'd felt the instant connection of two like minds, followed by a spark of attraction. But he'd been too muddled, or too guilty, or simply too long numbed to know what it was he'd been feeling.

He knew it now, though. He'd been nearly dead inside for years, but now he felt awake and alive. And like a bear emerging from hibernation, he was hungry and ready. His wanting was fierce, a thing that clenched his chest and tightened his groin.

His gaze went back to that shirt—the neck was a low *V*, with a row of delicate buttons down the front. A man would need to undo each one slowly, carefully.

Or simply tear the thing off her.

She looked around. "So . . . we should get started."

Oh yes, they *should*. He stepped closer, forcing himself to breathe slowly. They'd be lucky if they made it to the first course.

"Do you have an apron I could wear?" She glanced down at her shirt. She wore a small locket nestled between her breasts.

Someday he'd be the man to sweep the hair from her neck to clasp her necklace as she got ready. He'd stand behind her and rest his hands on her bare shoulders. He'd turn her to face him. He wouldn't give her a chance to finish getting dressed.

Billy licked his lips. He could taste her already. He could imagine what it would be like between them, and he was a goner.

"This is Laura's shirt, and I don't want to mess it up."

"Of course," he said, though his mind was still in his fantasy. And in his fantasy, he'd be careful with that shirt. No ripping this one. He'd take each tiny, shiny button one at a time.

She looked at him expectantly. "So . . . apron?"

"Apron," he repeated. He had an old one wadded in the pantry, but he'd be damned if he let her cover up that shirt. "I'm afraid there's no apron."

"I hope you're not too, too starving," she said as she readied the lamb. "I'd like to marinate this for an hour or so before I cook it."

He'd rather she marinate it for a good ten hours—there were other things he was much hungrier for than dinner—but instead he said, "That suits me just fine."

Once she finished her prep work, he let her take the lead and followed her into the living room. She stopped and spun, and he nearly walked into her. It put them standing close enough that he could feel the heat of her body pressing along the length of his.

"I didn't even call before I came," she said. "I'm totally interrupting your evening."

The normally self-possessed Sorrow sounded nervous, and it ignited an urge deep inside, to protect her, to put her at her ease, to let her know she'd be his.

He told her. "You're making my evening, not interrupting it."

"Did you already have plans?"

He couldn't fight it any longer—he put his hands on her shoulders. "I did. Grand plans. I was going to spend the next several hours poking at that fire. Care to join me?"

A broad smile spread across her face. Her eyes were so bright when she smiled. It was all he could do to not cup her face and kiss her. But he'd take this slow. She'd showed up with food, not propositions. Not yet.

He turned his attention to the fire, stoking it to life. He sensed her wandering toward the couch to study his stuff. Her presence was heavy in the room, and he felt her every pause, her every move at his back.

He mentally cataloged his décor. What would she make of it all? And his photos of Keri—what would she think about those? It wasn't as though the walls were blanketed with them, but they were here and there. Tacked over his desk, a black and white photobooth strip, shots of them making silly faces. There was a framed photo in the hallway, too, Keri's formal headshot from the DA's office. He felt Sorrow stop to study it.

"Your wife was beautiful," she said. "Very elegant."

"She was." He stood, wiping newsprint and ash from his hands. For the first time, thoughts of Keri weren't cold and sharp with grief, but had mellowed into something warmer and wiser, a melancholy. He'd loved his wife, more than anything. Her memory would forever be a gift in his heart, him all the richer for having had her for even a short time. He thought of Keri, of her foibles—the ones he'd loved, and the ones that'd annoyed him, too—and he smiled to recall the lot of them. "She was a city girl, born and raised."

"City girls must be pretty appealing."

He heard the subtext there—he'd need to tread carefully. "My wife *was* something else. But women from the city are just like women anywhere else . . . some are appealing, some not."

He walked across the room to stand at Sorrow's back. He studied Keri's photo, seeing it anew. Her severe black bob. Those dark eyes that once crackled with energy. She'd narrow those eyes during cross-examinations to go in for the kill, and witnesses never knew what hit them.

She'd been hard where Sorrow was soft, a razor-edged wit to Sorrow's bemused insightfulness.

"Do you miss the city?" Sorrow asked.

He didn't even have to think about that one. "Honestly, no, I don't miss it one little bit."

Sorrow was silent, so silent he wondered if she held her breath. He sensed she wanted to hear more, *needed* more.

It was time to dredge his memories, to let this woman in. He took a deep breath. "In some ways, it's the city that took her from me. She was in a . . . an accident." He cleared his throat, gathering his emotions. He owed it to Keri to tell her story. "I had no idea it'd happened. It took them a while to ID her. To track me down. And the thing of it was, I'd heard them talking about it over the scanner. Bus versus bike. One fatality."

"I'm so sorry," was all Sorrow said. There was nothing else *to* say, and she knew it.

His focus shifted, from the image of his wife to Sorrow's reflection in the glass. Her expression was drawn, pained. Sorrow was feeling his grief, opening her heart to him. She might've been different from Keri, but she was no less extraordinary.

Billy wanted to open his heart in return, but he also wanted to put her at ease, so he shifted back to the original question. "I always liked the country more than she did. We used to argue about it, over where to spend our vacations." He shook his head, remembering. "Keri's idea of camping was staying at anything more downscale than the Marriott."

"She'd have *loved* the lodge," Sorrow said in a flat, deadpan tone.

"Sorrow," Billy whispered, chiding her. He put his hands on her shoulders and gently turned her to face him. "*I* love the lodge."

Standing this close he saw the flecks of gold in her eyes. Her lashes were thick and brown. He imagined them fluttering closed during a kiss. His gaze shifted to her mouth. Her lips were parted, surprised at his touch.

The sight brought with it a revelation. He was alive again, and it was time to seize back his life. And that meant he *would* kiss Sorrow. *Tonight.*

Which meant he needed to steer her from these somber topics. "Come sit by the fire," he said, his voice hoarse.

She nodded, but the look she gave him was sad. Instead of sitting down, she wandered in front of the fireplace. Amber firelight cast dancing shadows on her face.

He read the question in her eyes. She'd want to know if he was ready to move on.

She put words to her thoughts, and he had to credit her courage as she asked, "Do you think you'll ever marry again?"

She wanted to know if he was still in mourning. Was a person ever done mourning? The answer was complicated, but it was one his heart finally understood.

"I will marry again," he said firmly. He'd thought those words before, but now, for the first time, he truly felt them. "It's been over three years since her accident. She'd want me to move on." For the first time, he *felt* the truth of those words.

Sully had been right. Keri—tough, smart-as-a-whip Keri—would have kicked his ass from beyond if she'd caught him wasting one more night wallowing. "She'd want me to find love again."

"But do you . . . can you . . ." Sorrow was struggling for words.

"Let's find out." Billy cupped the back of her head and leaned down. And then he kissed her.

Twenty-six

Billy's strong arms were around her, and she felt herself pulled onto her toes, her heart soaring even higher than her body.

After spending so much time looking at him, it felt so good finally to *feel* him. She wrapped her arms around him, greedily touching the stubble of his jaw, stroking his hair, squeezing the thick muscles of arms and shoulders, savoring each texture, memorizing the size of him.

She felt his hardness straining against her already, pressing hot and insistent along her body, and a whimper escaped her throat. Her desire was immediate and consuming, an ache in her belly. She was mad with it.

For months, she'd been kissing Damien, and it was a shock to be kissing someone else. Even though they'd broken up, the newness, the revelation of this other man made her feel dirty and hot.

Because whatever she'd fantasized about Billy, it hadn't been *this*. He was so gentle and kind in life, she'd expected a gentle, kind kiss. But *this* . . . this kiss was anything but hesitant. He was demanding. Confident.

And so big.

She felt his size as a visceral thing, his heat and strength imprinting along her body. She'd known Billy was a large man—he was broad and solid in his sheriff's uniform—but when he'd opened the door *shirtless*, she'd had to force herself not to stare. The man was ripped, and her hands roved him, eagerly feeling what she'd seen with her eyes. He was so firm and sure, and she felt so small in his arms. She felt safe.

She felt *taken*.

They kissed with desperation, and still it wasn't enough. She wanted Billy to take her, to take it all.

She'd had questions for him, but she no longer remembered them. All she knew was the throbbing between her thighs, the tightness in her breasts. All she wanted was to leap into his arms, wrap her legs around him, and quell this urgency.

A timer sounded in the kitchen.

No no no.

Sorrow wanted to ignore it, wanted it to go away. She couldn't stop kissing him, not now. She did ignore it, and instead scraped her fingers along his scalp, twining his hair into her fists. Her heart pounded till she felt she might not catch her breath. She wanted him completely, wanted completion. She wanted Billy to kiss her forever.

But the timer continued to ring.

Finally, slowly, he parted from her and touched his forehead to hers. *"Damn."*

She shut her eyes, pained. Inhaling deeply, she pulled away. When their eyes met, they shared a slow smile—it began as something wicked and naughty, like a shared secret, but as the timer continued to blare in the background, the moment grew more conspiratorial, until they were laughing. Stepping back, she slapped a hand to her forehead. "Sorry."

"Don't worry. The potatoes might be done, but we're not." He wrapped an arm tight around her shoulders, walking her slowly into the kitchen. "You and I are far from done."

He didn't ease away from her, wouldn't let her go, and the feel of him, the sensation of being so *coveted* transformed something deep inside her. Sorrow wanted another kiss, and more than another kiss. She'd show him what she was *really* made of.

When she'd arrived and seen photos of his wife, it'd scared her. Losing a spouse so young—a person might never recover from a thing like that. Her first thought was, how could she ever compare to such a pretty, sophisticated, powerful woman?

But that kiss. He'd kissed her, and instead of doubt, all she'd tasted was *hunger.*

All through her dinner preparations, Sorrow's skin buzzed, sensing his eyes on her, feeling his occasional touches grazing along her shoulders, down her back, leaving trails of fire along her body. Her whole being was attuned to him. Every look between them, every move, charged.

If she were being honest, it was something that'd started weeks ago, that night she'd cooked for him for the first time. Their bond had been instant, and the sparks, too. Meeting in the kitchen like this had felt like a secret courtship. Getting to know Billy over homemade food and loaded glances, till one morning she'd woken up to realize she was falling in love with him.

They had the intimacy, the connection. And now it was time to bring it to a different level. A level where she'd get to see that bare chest again.

Slowly, she sliced the shallots. Using her shoulder, she pushed the hair from her eyes. "Too bad we have to eat," she said shyly.

He stepped close to sweep his hand along her neck, smoothing the hair from her face. "A man needs his strength."

He repositioned himself behind her, until his body touched hers. The contact was light along her back, but she experienced it like a sizzling in her blood. His closeness weakened her knees, and she leaned on the counter for support.

His arm grazed hers as he reached over her to grab a couple of tomatoes. "Can I chop these for you?"

At that moment, she could think of a hundred things she wanted him to do. Chopping was at the bottom of that list. But instead she said, "Yes, please."

Billy made quick work of the tomatoes, and seeing there was no obvious job for him to do, he leaned against the counter, bringing all his attention to bear on her. "I still can't believe you're here. What did I do to deserve this?"

"I like cooking for you." She was rubbing her herb mixture into the lamb, but spared a glance up and caught his eyes raking over her shirt. His gaze was heavy, and a bolt of desire speared her through.

"I was about to say I couldn't think of anything better than your cooking. But," he said, in a voice thick with innuendo, "I think I could."

His banter was sexy, and it made *her* feel sexy. "Food first," she chided.

"You're lucky I'm so famished," he told her in a rasp, "or I wouldn't let you finish."

She put the lamb in the broiler and washed her hands. "Just a few more minutes now."

He walked up behind her and ran his hands down her arms, threading her damp fingers with his. "I'm going to take more than a few minutes."

Her breath caught.

The aroma of roasting lamb filled the room, and he breathed it in, exhaling with a satisfied moan that reverberated through her body. "How did they spare you at the tavern? Your father's a fool not to let you cook every night."

She loved his focus on her, loved the feeling of being seen and understood. And she loved that—with the possible exception of her sister—nobody had any idea where she was. "They don't even know where I am," she said. In some ways, *she* had no idea where she was—she felt like she was spinning out of control, falling fast.

"Their loss, my gain," he said. "Your dad is lucky you don't leave the tavern and get a professional chef's job."

She shrugged. "Nah."

"Nah," he mimicked affectionately and turned her to face him. "What do you mean, *nah*?"

She thought of the lodge, the tavern, her parents . . . all the responsibilities that tethered her in place. "My time has passed."

He traced her brow to sweep her hair behind one ear, his gesture softening the expression of wry humor on his face. "What on earth do you mean, *your time has passed*?"

"You know." She crumpled her face into a half smile. "It's too late for me to do anything new like that."

His face became dead serious. "You're young, and you can do whatever you set your mind to."

"I'm stuck." She paused, expecting him to speak, but he waited as though he were hanging on her every word, and so she continued, "Think about it. How am I supposed to follow any dreams from here? Laura and BJ were the ones who got free of this place. They left me to run it all by myself." Though *abandoned* would've been a better word for it.

The timer sounded, and putting on the oven mitt, he pulled the pan out himself. "You're cooking one night a week at the tavern—that's a start. We'll convince your dad to up it to two, then three."

She molded aluminum foil into a tent over the lamb. "That's all well and good, but then who'll do *my* job?"

"Around the lodge? Get Laura to help."

"Yeah, right." She smirked. Even if she could get over her resentments, she still hadn't gotten past the fact that her sister's attempts at "help" felt like an intrusion. Around the lodge, planning the festival—it was like Laura had something to prove. That she had more experience, that she knew better. That she was smarter, older, superior.

"I'm being serious," he said. "You need to ask people for help. You need to *make* people help." He popped a prosciutto-wrapped melon ball into his mouth, sighing with pleasure. "Hell, *I'll* help, if it gives you time to come up with more food like this."

She had to laugh at that. "It's sweet how you encourage me. My cooking is a dream, but it's a *pipe* dream, Billy. I'll never get help from Laura. Not any help I want, at any rate. I don't even get why she's here or for how long."

His gaze bored into her. "Something's been nagging me."

"Uh-oh." She looked away. How had her intended seduction turned into *this*?

He took her chin and tilted her face up to his. "I need you around me more, Sorrow."

"I . . . you do?" She'd been ready to go on the defensive, and his bold statement had thrown her. Stolen her breath.

"I do. Why do you think I've been hanging around that lodge? It was for glimpses of you."

Her heart soared till she thought her smile might split her face in two. "Really?"

"Really. But you're so busy, and there was Damon."

She giggled. *"Damien."*

"Whatever his name is." He shrugged playfully, barely concealing his smile. "All I'm saying is, I want to take you on a real date. You deserve the best. But you're always running circles around that damned lodge. I hate the thought of you dealing with *everything*. Repairs, budget, food, staff, *and* the cleaning? It's too much. We're hiring you a cleaning service."

"A cleaning service?" It was the last thing she'd expected to hear. She shook her head doubtfully. "In Sierra Falls?"

"I'll find one for you. You won't even have to think about it."

The prospect tickled her. But she was a realist. "Not possible," she said. "My dad would have a conniption."

"Your dad can deal with it." The steel in Billy's tone gave her pause. "I'm serious," he added. "If Bear gives you any trouble, tell him I'll cite him for child endangerment. Forget that, *I'll* tell him myself."

"I get it, I get it." She laughed. "I get your point."

"It's time to demand more help from your family. What do you have to lose?"

"You're right." She'd been accepting Damien's sporadic favors for months, so why was she afraid to ask for help from the people she cared for most? She was thoughtful as she assembled their dinner on plates. "All right then. What the hell?"

Her next thought, one that remained unspoken, was why hadn't *Damien* ever helped her get to that conclusion? How was it this new sheriff had come into her life, managing to turn it—and her—upside down in such a short time?

She raised a brow, feeling saucy. "If you help me, I'll of course need to figure out a way to express my gratitude." For the first time, she felt in control, felt how powerful she was in her femininity. She decided she'd make Billy wait, until he was crazy with wanting. She wouldn't spend the night. Not tonight. But she knew it'd be soon. Her skin pulled tight at the thought, the blood pounding hot, just beneath the surface. "I'll try to make your efforts worth your while."

She looked up, expecting to see humor on his face, but Billy's eyes were dark, pinned on her. She sucked in a breath, his intensity staggering. He was kind and thoughtful. But he was also a man's man, desiring and demanding, and that was what she read in his gaze now.

Her pulse kicked as some essential part of her wakened to life. Billy Preston was a lawman, but he kissed like an outlaw. She was desperate to discover just how he went about *other* things, too.

Twenty-seven

Marlene assembled her guests in the sitting room. Facing west, it was the brightest and warmest spot in the house and had a comfortable seating area with antique occasional tables that made serving tea and finger sandwiches convenient.

It was also her mother's favorite spot. And though the women had gathered to discuss historical society business, it was what to do about Ma that weighed most heavily on Marlene's mind.

Emerald was having an off day, staring silently, and it worried Marlene. Usually, her mother looked more *present*, like she was in there somewhere, wearing an expression that was bland but pleasant. But not today. Today Ma just sat, blankly.

Marlene had made her mother's favorite French toast, played her old music, and shepherded her into the TV room to watch one of her programs, but none of it had worked. Nothing engaged her.

Sorrow came to stand beside her, and Marlene remembered herself. She had guests who needed her attention. "Make yourselves at home," she said.

"Thanks for having us." Sorrow took off her hat and fluffed her hair, and it crackled with static.

"I thought a change of scenery would do us all good," Marlene said. Truth was, they had business to tend to, and she'd wanted to meet on neutral ground. Though with the tension that flared between the two Bailey girls, sometimes it seemed that not even Switzerland would be neutral enough.

Her eyes returned to her mother, sitting like a statue in the corner. Bailey family tension aside, she was happy not having to shoehorn three elderly ladies into that blasted pickup.

Sorrow caught her line of sight—the change in Ma's condition would soon be obvious to everyone, if it wasn't already. She gave Marlene's shoulder a comforting squeeze. "I swear, this is the *prettiest* room. So cozy, especially with all that snow outside."

She was a sweet girl, that Sorrow. Marlene gave her a heartfelt smile. Having a house full of women might be just the thing to take her mind off her troubles.

"Snow?" Laura flopped down on one of the wing chairs, stretching her feet in front of her. "Gray slush, you mean. I am *so* over this weather."

"The spring festival will be here before we know it," Edith said.

Sorrow cringed and went to the buffet. "Don't remind me. There's too much to do. I need food first."

Marlene had assembled their favorites—sandwiches made with olives and cream cheese, pimento spread on triangles of thin white bread, mint Milano cookies, and those crispy chocolate tubes Aunt Pearl loved.

"Oh, yum," Sorrow said, grabbing a plate. "I'm thinking we need to meet here more often."

"That town hall is too chilly." Pearl buttoned up her cardigan, as if the mere recollection made her cold, even though the gas fireplace had the sitting room downright balmy. "And Bear's restaurant can be so gusty."

Bear was a tightwad when it came to his heating bill. But then she smiled to herself, thinking how she never felt cold when that Sully was around.

"It's a treat to get away from the tavern for the afternoon," Edith agreed, ignoring the jab against her family business.

"*Totally* good to get away." Laura caught her sister's eye. "Did you see Dad this morning?"

Sorrow laughed. "The man was on a rampage."

That tidbit engaged Ruby's attention at once. "Why was your father on a rampage?"

A broad smile lit Edith's face. "We got a letter from my boy today."

"That's wonderful news, but . . ." Marlene frowned at the nonsensical connection. "I don't understand. Why is Bear in a sour mood if you heard from BJ?"

"Hearing from him always does it," Sorrow said.

"Thank God he hasn't figured out how to Skype BJ over in Afghanistan," Laura joked. "That'd really put Dad over the edge."

The sisters shared an amused, understanding look. It was good to see them getting along. Hearing from Bear Junior sure had put the Bailey women in a good mood. But Bear's inexplicable mood swings remained a mystery. "I still don't see why it should make him so crotchety," she said.

Laura raised a brow. "You mean more crotchety than usual?"

"BJ is spending more time near the front lines," Sorrow explained. "His unit's in Kabul now. I think it worries Dad."

Laura grew serious. "He's doing stuff like air reconnaissance and troop transport in that giant helicopter of his."

The barrage of military words put Marlene in mind of Tom Sullivan. He'd shown Craig some of his Vietnam memorabilia. Not that Sully had told *her* about it—the man wasn't exactly a big talker, and she'd had to hear the report from her grandson. According to Craig, Sully had a *stack* of medals.

She had no idea he'd been such a hero.

Apparently, there were other things in his collection, too. A few photos, something called a boonie hat—whatever *that* was—and his dress uniform. Her mind drifted. The man kept himself in great shape—she bet he could still fit himself into that uniform.

Marlene gave a shake to her head, clearing *those* thoughts. They were talking about BJ's letter, not aging retired officers.

She began to pour the women tea from her great-granny's old silver service. "Well, I'd just think Bear would be thrilled to hear from the boy."

"He was," Edith assured her brightly. "*Absolutely* thrilled."

She gave her friend a probing look, though what she wanted to do was demand what gave Bear the right to be such a sour-puss. And Edith enabled it, too—she acted like Bear's chief apologist. They had a curious relationship, those two. Marlene had known the Bailey family for decades, and she suspected more happened behind closed doors than people knew. Bear acted, well, like a *bear*, but she guessed it was really Edith who called the shots in her quiet way.

Edith must've sensed Marlene's opinion, because she added, "He *lives* to get those letters."

"It's true." Sorrow sat in the window seat, balancing her plate on her knees. "He's practically memorized this one."

"Well, I just think it's the strangest thing," Ruby said, trundling over to the buffet.

Pearl was right behind her. "If he misses the boy so much, he certainly has a strange way of showing it."

Judgment was thick in the women's voices, but nobody took issue. Disapproval was a downright hobby for the Kidd sisters, and everyone was used to it.

Marlene eyed her aunts as they assembled their food, wondering how different their lives might've been if *they'd* married, had children, and gotten a taste of how difficult the whole business was. She wagered they wouldn't have so much spare time in which to pass judgment.

Edith sighed. "Bear Senior is just . . . frustrated. He wishes he could do more—we all do. He hates that we're not in more contact with our boy."

"Nah," Sorrow said with a shake of her head. "Dad just wishes he could put on a uniform and go fight with him."

Edith gave a doting smile. "My husband is a man of action."

"Action?" Laura blew on her tea, stirring in three packets of Sweet'N Low. "A man of temper is more like it."

"Well, he should just say a little prayer when he feels his temper coming on," Ruby said definitively, though she was mostly focused on assembling her selection of goodies.

Laura eyed the older woman's plate. "How on earth do you stay so thin?" She caught Sorrow's eye and muttered, "Maybe *I* should start praying more."

"It's genes, dear." Pearl settled herself in the armchair and upped her voice a notch to address her ailing sister. "Isn't that right, Emerald? We Kidd girls have good genes."

Marlene went to the table to make a plate of food for her mother. She saw that Laura still had only a cup of tea. "Aren't you going to eat?"

Laura pulled an apple from her bag. "I'm eating. I'm good."

"An apple's not eating," Sorrow said. "Though it *does* look good." She picked at her cucumber sandwich. "I cannot wait till winter's over—produce has really been sucking lately."

"Berries will be in season soon," Ruby said cheerfully.

Marlene pulled a table over to her mother's chair and put a plate of sandwiches and cookies before her. Patting her shoulder, she prompted in a clear voice, "Time to eat, Ma. I've got your favorites."

Emerald looked at the plate, and Marlene peered hard, anxious to see something flicker in the woman's eyes. But still, there was just that horrible, devastating blankness.

Laura glanced at the clock on her cell phone, looking impatient. "We should get this show on the road." She pulled a manila folder from her bag. "So, for the festival, I went ahead and created a marketing plan. Nothing major, just some milestones that we'll need to meet in the next few weeks, a tentative schedule of events, and a list of tasks and who they should be delegated to."

Everyone looked at her, shell-shocked expressions all around.

Laura shrugged. "I couldn't sleep last night."

Sorrow held up a finger as she finished chewing, and the room seemed to hold its breath. "We need to learn more about her relationship with Buck Larsen before we finish planning. Like, did he ever return to Sierra Falls? That sort of thing."

Laura crunched her apple. "I still think we need a list of tasks and owners. There's so much more to do than just arranging the annual bake sale. Like, we should compile a program. We could pull together some good Sorrow Crabtree quotes, add some old-timey photos. It's easy to get a book like that printed up these days, and then we could sell it at the festival."

Sorrow gaped at her sister, and Marlene braced. Laura was

taking charge, and it was only a matter of time before the tension ignited between the two. But Sorrow surprised the room when she said, "Laura, that is an *awesome* idea."

"It is," Marlene agreed quickly. Anxious to keep the meeting so pleasantly civil, she steered them in a safe direction—one that didn't involve words like *publicity* or *strategies*. "But Edith tells me you haven't finished reading the letters yet."

"That's the thing." Sorrow flipped through them thoughtfully. "I've tried. But there are a bunch of passages I can't make sense of."

"That old-timey handwriting is a . . ."—Laura cut herself off, seeing Sorrow's glance that silently warned *language*— "it's a real pain in the tuckus."

"That's where you ladies come in," Edith said, addressing the older women.

Ruby pulled a lap blanket from the arm of her chair and draped it over her legs. "We're not *that* old-timey, dear."

Pearl poo-pooed her. "You know what they mean." She turned to Sorrow. "Why don't you read them, dear, then we can help make out the handwriting when you get stuck."

They spent the next hour enthralled, as Sorrow read her thrice-great-grandmother's letters. It was impossible for Marlene to hear the woman's words and not feel their universal truth. Sorrow Crabtree had been a woman who dreamed of greater things, stuck in a situation with no escape.

Sorrow stopped cold, calling Marlene back into the moment.

"What is it, dear?" Edith asked.

"Just a minute." Sorrow flipped the pages back and forth. "These are out of order."

Laura frowned. "What do you mean?"

Sorrow shuffled through some more, then just dropped on her knees to the floor, spreading out all the pages. "Okay, remember this gem? *'My Mama told me to live life for me. To follow my heart and love my kin and my God. And I'm going to do that, Buck. Just me and our boy. With or without you.'* That was dated 1851." She set it aside.

"Now check this out. We read this one first—remember? Where she went on and on about the dance hall and making a life for herself? At the end, she wrote, *'I've got a babe in my belly.'* We'd thought it was from that same time period. But it's not." Sorrow flipped through, matching page numbers and connecting sentences. "*This* one is dated *1853.*"

The women gasped.

"She had *another* baby," Edith said, marveling.

Pearl clucked. "That woman's luck was poor from the day she was born."

Marlene frowned at her. "Some see a baby as a blessing, Aunt Pearl."

Laura plopped onto the floor next to Sorrow, holding out her hand. "Let me see that." For once, Sorrow didn't hesitate and just handed over the pages without question, and Laura read for a moment. "Wow. You're right. Check this out, *'He moves in my belly. A boy, like your beautiful son. I'll raise them both to be good men.'*"

Edith tilted her head, peering at the pages scattered across the floor. "Was Buck the father?"

"No," Sorrow said, "Buck Larsen never returned. There must've been another man."

"She was a fast woman," Ruby said, shaking her head.

Pearl grunted her disapproval. "*Two* fathers, no husband."

"A life of toil and fatherless babies," Ruby said. "That's what being a fast woman brings you."

"That's enough," Marlene said. She was tired of this conversation. Tired of what they implied about her very own mother.

But Pearl wasn't done. She pursed her lips. "I wonder if it runs in the blood?"

Laura rolled her eyes. "That's us. We Baileys of the spoiled blood."

Sorrow shot Pearl an impatient look. "Who says she was fast? If she had another baby, maybe it means it got better for her. Maybe it wasn't a fatherless baby, but a secret love affair."

"Shush," Laura said, trying to concentrate. She grumbled, "How did you read this, Sorrow?"

"What does she say?" asked Edith impatiently.

"Give me a second," Laura said. "*Handsome . . . first sight . . .* blah blah. Okay, here it is. *This* must be the baby's father: *'My Silas is an angel. As dependable as God's love, he comes to town once a month, with letters in his bag and love in his heart.'"*

"Oh my God!" Sorrow shrieked. "She was in love with the mailman!"

"Those guys were actually pretty macho," Laura said. "Snowshoeing all over the wilderness. Think about it."

Edith's eyes went wide. "*First sight . . . angel . . .* When we read it before, I didn't really get it. I'd thought it had something to do with the baby."

"We all did," Sorrow said.

Marlene leaned forward in her seat. "And you're sure the date is correct? 1853?"

"Read more, read more." Sorrow waved her sister on.

Laura found her place on the page. "Okay, here we go. *'All's I need is a simple man. I thought I needed a man like you. But your promises are just as empty as that fancy suit you wear.'"*

Laura read on, but Marlene stopped paying attention. Those words had stuck in her craw.

She thought about her own situation—had *she* been wasting time on the wrong things? Had *she* been chasing men in suits with their meaningless boats and convertibles, when what she really needed was a man whose humble exterior held a heart filled with love?

If she were being honest, she'd always suspected there was more. She'd had a husband who was successful. She'd had a nice house. Shopping jaunts to Reno and a new designer coat every September. She'd devoted her life to standing by her man. But what had it gotten her?

She had her children, of course. And she'd do it all over again to have those four wonderful boys she'd raised into good and caring men. The love she held for them was fierce.

But what of her feelings for her ex-husband? After he took off, she'd begun to doubt herself. She often felt angry at being left holding the bag. But had she ever genuinely *missed* him?

Marlene looked at the three Kidd women and noted with a pang how her mother hadn't eaten, hadn't even moved. She just sat, not even looking out the window, with that same blankness in her eyes. Life marched on. One day these women would have passed and then Marlene would . . . *what?*

Everyone spoke at once, startling Marlene, and she tuned back in.

"You *have* to finish," Sorrow was demanding.

" *'The only things . . . the things . . .'*" Laura shook her head. "It's no good. I can't do it. This crazy handwriting is killing me."

Pearl held out a quaking hand. "Let me see it, dear." She slowly donned her glasses, kept on a beaded chain around her neck, and concentrated on the letter. After a silent moment, her face lit with understanding. "Ah! It says, *'The only things you regret in this life are the risks you don't take.'*"

Marlene felt herself pale. It was as though Sorrow Crabtree had reached across the generations to deliver this message just to her.

Her life was all about roads not taken. She'd spent her life caring for other people, first her husband, then her sons, and now her aunts and mother. Hers had always been the responsible choices—the sorts of choices where she'd *had* no choice. Her life had held no room for risk.

Sorrow's hand was warm on her suddenly chilled shoulder. "You okay, Marlene?"

"I'm fine." Pasting a smile on her face, she said, "Let's keep reading. We've been looking forward to it." She cut her eyes back to her mother. Maybe Ma was in there somewhere to enjoy it, too.

Her mother's life had been *all* risk. Leaving home, meeting a man, and returning heavy with child. Why had Marlene never asked her more about it? Asked her mother the hard questions. Ma sat there, across the room, empty as the prettiest of seashells, the one woman Marlene wished more than anything could give her wisdom.

Folks thought just because a family member was still alive meant there was no cause for grief. But Marlene knew different—Marlene grieved her living mother every day.

Twenty-eight

~

Sorrow's cell buzzed, and she had to juggle a lid, a ladle, layers of apron, and the rag she had tucked at her waist to reach it. It was worth it, seeing who the caller was.

"Billy, hey." She didn't even try to mask the relief in her voice. "You coming by soon? It's *Ladies' Night*," she added in a teasing voice. Tuesday was her night to cook at the tavern, and her dad had dubbed the evening with the silliest name imaginable. But she was heeding Billy's advice and taking her opportunities where she could get them.

"That's why I'm calling."

His somber voice alerted her at once. "What is it?"

"I've got to work a double shift," he said. "Marshall was hit with the flu—the guy looks like hell."

"How much crime can there be in Sierra Falls? Can't you just let people speed for one night?"

His laugh was gentle. "You know I can't. But I'll be thinking of you. Wish I were there to help."

"I wish you were, too—I'm using a Dutch oven that, I swear, weighs about a thousand pounds."

"What did you end up making? The chicken or the pork loin?"

"Chicken. Coq au Vin to be exact." Her sauce needed thickening, and she was stirring madly. "If I can get my roux to cooperate. It's broken twice already."

"Damned roux," he said in a perfect deadpan.

She laughed. She *missed* him. They'd had a few kisses, and already she couldn't wait for more. "I miss you." The words had slipped out, and she instantly knew a twinge of regret. They'd kissed, but she didn't know how he *really* felt. She suspected he was dealing with a lot of emotional baggage, and she needed to play it cool.

But he surprised her by saying, "I miss you, too." There was real affection in his voice, and it made everything okay. "Save me some," he added. "I'll stop by later. I promise."

She'd just finished searing the meat and had put it into the oven to braise when she sensed a hubbub in the tavern. Sorrow pulled off the red bandanna she wore in lieu of a hairnet, wiped her brow, and pushed through the swinging door.

"I swear, Helen," she said as she pushed through the swinging door. "I don't know how Sully does it. I am *roasting* in there. Could you please get me"—she spotted Damien and his parents settling into a window booth—"some ice water," she finished lamely.

Dabney and Phoebe Simmons—what were *they* doing there? If Damien was the prince of Sierra Falls, it was because his parents were its nobility. They were moneyed and sophisticated, and she wished she could hate them for it, but they also happened to be two of the kindest, most gracious people she'd ever met.

Dabney had been especially sweet every time he'd seen her, always joking how Sorrow needed to make his boy an honest man. It was like he was actually lobbying Damien to propose to her. She never could figure it, except to guess that Damien had been a hell-raiser as a kid and that maybe he'd mellowed a bit under her influence.

They'd have found out about the breakup by now. Had Damien sent them to convince her to get back together with him? She dreaded the conversation. Dreaded feeling like she'd hurt not just Damien but his parents, too.

As Helen handed her a big tumbler of water, she sang under her breath, "Oh yes, it's ladies' night, and you're feeling right."

She made a little snorting laughing sound that Sorrow didn't feel was entirely kind.

She glared at the bartender over the lip of the glass as she chugged and then put it down hard. "If you're quoting the song, I think it's *'and the feeling's right.'* And thanks for that. The only thing I needed more than seeing Damien's family was a Kool & The Gang song stuck in my head."

Phoebe and Dabney were kibitzing over the menu. Her mind scrambled for excuses, but it was no good. The chicken was in the oven—there would be no better time for her to go say hi.

"Need something stronger?" Helen whispered.

She had a joke on her lips when she met the bartender's eyes but kept her mouth shut when she saw that Helen was serious. Drinking might've been how the other woman dealt with her problems, but that wasn't how Sorrow rolled.

Still, the woman was just trying to be kind, and there was genuine gratitude in Sorrow's voice when she said, "No thanks, Helen. No drinks. I've got too long a night ahead of me."

She was girding herself to approach and say her hellos when Damien beat her to it.

"Heya, Bailey." He sauntered over to the bar, giving her a confident smile. Apparently, not even a breakup could get Damien down. Assuming he'd finally accepted that they'd broken up, which she didn't entirely believe. He wasn't the sort of guy to give up easily—showing up with a smiling face and his parents in tow had to be part of a master plan.

He was looking mighty fine, as always, and Sorrow gave herself a moment to study her own reaction to him. She was pleased to realize she didn't feel a darned thing—not a moment's regret, nor one iota of desire.

"You're looking good," he told her, echoing her own thoughts. "Cooking agrees with you."

She took the compliment for what it was and gave him a grateful smile. "Nothing like a hot, stuffy kitchen to put color in the cheeks." She and Damien weren't exactly going to be best chums, but he was a good guy, and maybe someday they'd get back to where they'd begun, as casual friends.

He gestured to the door. "Hey, your bear box is open." Everyone in the Sierras kept their trash in a bear box, lest they summon a several-hundred-pound scavenging visitor. "I tried to shut it, but it looks like the latch is broken. If you have some tools, I could take a look."

"Nah, I got it," she said, knowing she absolutely *could not* ask him to help her. She didn't want him to think they were slipping back into their old ways. And besides, she was perfectly capable of tending to her own bear box.

She went outside, and sure enough the door was swinging on its hinges. Not many bears this time of year, but the last thing she wanted was to awaken some hungry brute out of hibernation. Leaning her shoulder into it, she tried to close the latch, but Damien was right—it swung back open, broken.

She didn't have any tools, wasn't wearing gloves, and had two Dutch ovens' worth of Coq au Vin going. Now was not the time to deal with this, and she made a mental note to take care of the problem tomorrow.

She went back inside, and annoyance needled her. *Everyone* was in the kitchen, dragged back by her father who insisted on showing off their new freezer to the Simmons family.

Frustration joined annoyance—she had a ton yet to do. There was no time to give people the grand tour. She caught her mom's eye and gave her a pleading look, but Edith just shrugged as if to say *what can you do?*

It was true—there was no stopping Dad once he got going. He was droning on, clearly trying to make himself sound important by spouting an array of ridiculous product descriptions—gaskets and cam-lifts, solid door reach-in, electro-polished shelves—but there wasn't one iota of judgment on Dabney's or Phoebe's face.

She walked up behind Damien's mom and gave her shoulder a grateful squeeze. "It's a freezer all right," Sorrow whispered, rolling her eyes. "Not like it's going to feed any starving orphans or anything."

Her dad stopped midsentence, the light in his eyes dimmed. Mom shot her a disappointed look, and she instantly felt ashamed. *Bad daughter.*

"Very impressive," Dabney said, saving the day. Rich, land-owning, and in possession of a timber business that employed a goodly number of Sierra Falls townspeople, he was the town's resident benefactor. Dabney was something of a silver fox, too, in his convertible Jaguar and Italian driving loafers. "Damien tells me you got yourself quite a deal."

"I hear you have the sheriff to thank for it." Phoebe caught her eye and gave her a sad smile. Her next words were whispered for her ears alone. "He'd best be as good as he sounds, Sorrow. You were supposed to marry my Damien, you know."

But her husband had overheard. Dabney came over and wrapped an arm around Sorrow. "If that man doesn't treat you right, I'll have to go over there with a shotgun and see that he does."

She laughed, relieved that it was out in the open. "It's not like that. I mean . . . we had one date, that wasn't even really a date, and . . ."

A trickle of black smoke was the only warning they got. The oven door jumped as a fireball exploded to life, a boom followed by a raging, roaring blaze.

The kitchen exploded with screams. She felt a body pummel into hers. It was Damien, shielding her body with his.

"Get out of the kitchen," he yelled. Turning to his father, he shouted, "Get them out of the kitchen."

Edith pulled the faucet hose from the sink, and Damien pushed away from Sorrow to grab the woman's hand. "No! No water!"

"What the hell, boy?" Bear muscled across the room, grabbing for the faucet.

"It's grease." Flames licked up the back wall, the fire no longer contained in the oven. Damien squinted at the blaze, covering his nose and mouth with his hand, and barked out orders. "Call 911. Sorrow, fire extinguisher."

Everyone fled the kitchen, and Sorrow was across the room and back in an instant with the extinguisher. Damien snatched it from her and sprayed. Black smoke filled the kitchen as the fire alarm keened shrilly.

Coughs racked her, and Damien shot her an angry look. "Get out of here."

She shook her head. Struggling for breath, she grabbed their restaurant-sized bag of baking soda, but by that time the fire was out. She dumped it on the stovetop anyway, her body shaking with adrenaline.

Damien scooped her in his arms and half walked, half carried her to the dining area. They saw everyone standing in a cluster outside, shivering and talking a blue streak. He stopped her. "I need a minute."

"You and me both." Through the window, her dad's expression was as black as the smoke had been. "Guess who's going to get the blame for this."

Damien tipped her chin to face him. "I'll talk to him." He smudged soot from her cheek. "See, I'm good to have around, right?"

She went on alert—she'd need to tread carefully here. "I never said you weren't."

Damien's voice was husky as he slowly leaned down, bringing his face to hers. "So can I get you to come to your senses?"

Apparently he *hadn't* gotten the original message after all. Sorrow put a gentle hand on his chest and stepped back. "Damien, I'm sorry. It's still over."

"C'mon, Bailey. You *know* we're good together." He chucked her chin, as though she were being willingly unruly. "You need me, huh? Just a little?" His voice was teasing and light, and he wore his trademark grin, but now she saw how it masked something—Damien Simmons wasn't as confident as he made himself appear.

"I need you," she said. "As my friend."

His eyes shuttered. "You've already hooked up with Billy, haven't you?"

"Hooked up?" She prayed her voice hadn't squeaked.

As though in answer, Billy stormed through the door. The lights on his SUV were a red and blue strobe flashing on the tavern walls. His gaze went from Sorrow, to Damien, to Damien's hands on her shoulders.

At that moment, the sheriff looked eager to address Damien's question with his fists.

Twenty-nine

When the call went out over the radio—fire at the Thirsty Bear Tavern—fear exploded in Billy's chest. A horrific picture came to him—a bloodied body lying in the dirt, lovely limbs broken and twisted. His heart pounded, so hard he felt it slamming in his throat, choking him. Because, instead of seeing Keri's face like all those other times, this time he saw Sorrow's.

He'd suspected the depth of his feelings for her, but such a blast of panic and longing galvanized those feelings, illuminating the truth as bright as a lighting flash. He loved her.

He sped dangerously fast, beating the volunteer fire department to the punch. He had to get to her. They'd called only for the fire truck, not the ambulance, but he had to see for himself that she was safe.

It was clear now. Someone was terrorizing the Bailey family. She was in danger—they all were. If a fire didn't make Bear see the truth, he didn't know what would.

But when he charged in and found Sorrow's ex holding her, fear turned to fury.

He wanted to tear the guy's hands off her. Wanted to scoop her up and carry her from harm, away from this other man. He *had* to take her and have her to himself, someplace safe where he'd peel off every layer of her clothing to make sure every inch of her was unharmed.

Urgency boiled his blood, so powerful the desire to show Sorrow how much he wanted her, *needed* her. She'd snuck up on him, breathed life back into him, until the urge to tell her he loved her blinded him to all else.

It took everything he had to measure his step. He was in uniform, after all.

He flexed his hands—he would *not* physically remove this other man—but to his tremendous relief, Sorrow pushed from Damien and flew into his arms.

He wrapped himself around her, running his hands over her hair, along her back, up her sides. Let people think what they would. He had to check for himself that she was whole. His heart was thundering so hard, he felt certain she must've felt it reverberate through her own chest. "Are you okay?"

At her weak nod, he pulled her closer. He met Damien's eye. It was an adolescent thing to do, this urge to claim his woman, but he couldn't help himself. He met Damien's scowl with satisfaction, pulled her closer, nestled her head beneath his hand. *Mine*.

"What happened?" Billy demanded.

The door blew open, and Bear repeated the question, though more colorfully. "What in the goddamn hell happened in there?"

"Grease fire," Damien said. His expression was remote now. He was the sort of guy who'd need to save face at all costs.

Bear glared at his daughter. "I knew your cooking was a bad idea."

She tried to push from Billy, and though he loosened his arms, he refused to lose contact altogether. He would *not* let her face this alone.

"It wasn't my fault," she said. He heard the faintest tremble in her voice, and it nearly broke his heart. "Grease fires happen all the time."

"Not in my restaurant."

Billy cut the man off. It had been just one coincidence too many around the Bailey place. "I can't believe this was an accident."

The SFFD fire chief, Mike Haskell, burst in.

Damien spoke up. "It's okay, Mike. Sorrow and I put it out."

Billy was anxious to hear *that* story. He gave Damien a grudging nod of thanks.

Mike sniffed the air. "Trying to burn down the place, Bear?"

The fire chief's good humor did nothing to dispel Bear's glowering. "No, but my daughter is."

"It wasn't my fault." Sorrow turned to Billy, a pleading look in her eyes. "This wasn't my fault."

He ran the facts through his head. He knew Sorrow, and he knew Sully, too. They weren't careless. He'd seen one dangerous incident too many around the Big Bear Lodge and Thirsty Bear Tavern.

"Sorrow's right," Billy said emphatically. "This wasn't her fault." From the corner of his eye, he saw Scott Jessup pull into the lot in the old Parks Department Bronco. His friend was a volunteer firefighter in addition to his job as a ranger, and he'd be glad to have him there. Sorrow needed all the friendly faces she could get. "Something else has got to be going on here."

"Not with your theories again, Sheriff." Bear turned to scowl at his daughter. "I told you I didn't want you to cook. First you break the freezers and now this."

"I did *not* break the freezers."

Scott walked in the door and, sensing the tension, got a look on his face that was one part wary and one part bemused. "I hear you've got barbequed kitchen on the menu."

Bear looked like his head might explode, and Mike took the hint. He met Scott's eye. "Greetings, Ranger. About time you showed up. How about we have a look-see in the kitchen? Seems like these nice folks have some things to work out." He patted Bear's shoulder as he headed to the kitchen. "We'll leave you be."

Laura burst in. "I hear Sorrow burned down the kitchen!"

Billy shot her a warning look.

To his surprise, it seemed to have some effect, because she went to Sorrow and, looking cowed, squeezed her sister's shoulder. "Seriously, are you okay?"

She nodded, but her dad cut her off before she could speak. "Yeah," he said, "but my kitchen's not."

"I didn't do anything to your kitchen," Sorrow said, and

Billy was hugely impressed at how well she was doing under the pressure.

"Sully's been cooking in there for over twenty years and he's never had a fire."

Mike leaned on the pass-through and called out, "It was a grease fire, sure enough. Must've had some drippings on the bottom of the oven."

Bear's eyes narrowed, but Sorrow cut him off before he could speak. "No way. There is *no* way this is my fault. I keep a spotless kitchen."

Damien's parents came back in. "Sweetheart," Phoebe told her, "I am so sorry. Your big night was ruined."

Dabney turned to Sorrow, too, giving her a bolstering look. "She'll get another chance, won't you, kid?"

"She spilled grease in the oven," Bear said.

Sorrow's voice was dangerously calm. "Spilled *grease*? There's no grease in my Coq au Vin."

Billy put a protective arm around her. "Nobody keeps a healthier or cleaner kitchen than your daughter."

"Well something was in that *cocoa van* of hers." Bear shook his head as he told her, "I told you not to cook. That kitchen's too big for you."

The patronizing comment sent her over the edge. She crossed her arms tightly at her chest, edging one step closer to her father. "Too big? Too *big*?"

Dabney helped his wife shoulder into her jacket. "Listen here, Bear. If the girl said there was no grease, there was no grease."

"It's a shame." Phoebe gave her a hug good-bye. She held her chin and looked into her eyes as she gently said, "One of these days, this town will serve something more palatable than Tom's chicken poppers, and my money's on you."

Dabney went to the door. Looking back at Damien, he said, "Come on, son. I'm afraid you're our ride."

Billy had to give the guy some credit—at least he looked hesitant to go. Damien turned to Sorrow. "You sure you're okay?"

She nodded. The Simmons family left, with the rest of the crowd close behind.

"Grease fire," Chief Haskell said as he made his own exit.

"There's nothing much to do but clean it up. Believe it or not, the oven survived."

"Thanks, Mike," Sorrow said. "That's good news."

"Anything for a pretty lady." Mike gave her a wink.

Billy clapped him on the shoulder, giving him the hint. "All right, work's done here. Don't you have a wife to get home to?"

Mike laughed. "Understood. Hey, Sorrow, we'll see you at the festival. I hear it's shaping up to be a doozy, what with all the Buck Larsen stuff."

"Let's hope," she said, giving him a tired smile.

The sight stabbed him. Billy wouldn't stand idly by—he needed her father to listen to reason. "I wish I could convince you," he told the man. "First the freezers, now this. I don't think these *accidents* are accidents at all."

"That's enough for one night. I told you before, city boy. All we have in Sierra Falls is neighbors. No vandals, or gangs, or anything like that." Bear nodded toward the door. "Time for you two to get out of here. I'm closing shop. Gonna come some windows to air it out. Between the stink and the cold, we're pulling a goose egg on business tonight."

Sorrow stiffened. "It wasn't my fault."

"It was somebody's fault," Bear said.

Billy was quick to intervene. He was just as done with Bear as Bear was with his night. "We'll lock up here, Mister Bailey. You go join the missus."

Laura took her father's arm. "Come on, Dad. Let's go watch some CNN." She winked at her sister.

Her father sucked at his teeth a second, then with a stoic nod, let Laura lead him back to the lodge.

Sorrow gave Billy a sad half smile. "I think Dad could use some alone time to sit in his recliner and lick his wounds."

"Do you need to go back to the lodge, too?"

"Are you kidding? I'm not going back there until I know my father is sound asleep in bed."

He wrapped her in his arms. "I know it's not your fault. Not even a little bit."

She relaxed into him, sighing deeply. "Thank you. Though I can't imagine how something like that happened." She pushed back enough to meet his eye. "There's no *grease* dripping from a Dutch oven, and Sully keeps a spotless kitchen. So, what happened? Usually, the most exciting thing that happens in *this* town is when old man Ziegler has one nip too many and drives his snowplow off the road."

"Actually, that sounds dangerous."

"Yeah," she admitted, "it kind of was. But that was back in Christmas '95, and he hasn't done it again. I think the whole episode was why Marshall finally became a deputy when he got back from Iraq."

Billy chuckled. "That explains a lot." They grew silent, thinking. There'd been severed freezer lines, a roof cave-in, one downed tree, and now this. Fire was nothing to mess around with, and it shot his concerns to a whole different level. But how to address it with Sorrow without scaring the wits out of her? "Your dad thinks it's all just a run of bad luck . . ."

"A *lot* of bad luck."

"All at once," he said.

"To a *crazy* degree."

Their gazes locked, each reading the uneasiness in the other's eyes. She slowly shook her head. "These aren't accidents, are they?"

"There's no way they are," he said. "I just can't figure out who'd want to harm you."

"Harm *me*?" She gave a weak laugh. "Have you noticed how all this stuff started to happen when *Laura* showed up? Maybe I can blame *her*."

He couldn't help but laugh at her suggestion. "You're remarkably droll about this whole thing."

She sighed. "If that means I've got a sense of humor about it, then yeah, it's either laugh or cry." She dropped her forehead against his chest.

"You're a remarkable woman, Sorrow Bailey."

"So, what do we do now?"

"Without a suspect or clues, there's nothing we *can* do. The best plan of action is to keep you close." He slid his hands down her back. "You know, there *is* something we can do to deal with the stress."

Her head sprang up, and she mimicked a grave nod. "*And* the uncertainty. There's a lot of uncertainty."

Wrapping an arm around her, Billy steered Sorrow to the door, plucking her coat from the rack on the way out to his car. "Let's go."

"Whoa, cowboy." She halted to lock up. "I thought you were on duty."

"This *is* my duty." But then he paused—it'd been an intense night for her. He needed to be certain she wanted this as much as he did. "Unless you want to stay home, hang in for the night . . ."

"Believe me, Billy. You're all I want."

Hearing her resolve, he urged her back into a walk. "Then we're a pair, Sorrow. Because I happen to want you back. A lot."

She chuckled. "But what about all those speeders and lawbreakers?"

He ushered her into his SUV and walked around to the driver's side. "Calls get routed to Silver City dispatch starting at ten P.M. Until then, Marshall has one ear tuned to the radio and will call if anything comes up."

"I thought the deputy was sick."

"I offered him a raise."

She turned to give him a perplexed look. "So *this* is how a sheriff figures out who's up to no good?"

"No, Sorrow." He reached over and squeezed her thigh. "This is how a *sheriff* gets up to no good."

* * *

Once she'd made it clear it was what she wanted, Billy had put her in that car like he wouldn't take *no* for an answer. Which was fine by Sorrow. She had zero intention of telling Billy *no* to anything.

Not much time had passed since their first kiss, but Sorrow realized now just how long it'd been since she'd known deep down that she wanted to be with Billy. This was it. Tonight would be the night. *Their* night.

She'd wanted him for a while now, and after tonight's scare, she *needed* him. Needed to feel his strong body surround hers, to be safe in his arms. She needed to experience that feeling she knew when she was with Billy—the sense that she was no longer in it alone.

He drove them to his house. Her bag, their coats, his keys . . .

everything dropped to the floor the moment the door slammed behind them.

Billy was such a man's man, so *in charge*, and she'd barely gasped in a breath when he brought his mouth to hers. Her body exploded to life, every nerve, every inch of her wanting more from this kiss, deeper and harder.

Her hands roved eagerly along his body, fingers catching over foreign bits of his uniform. His belt, his cuffs. The newness of him turned her on in a way that startled her, excited her.

He unbuckled his belt, keeping his mouth on hers. Finally he pulled from her, and she heard the clatter of his gear where he put it on the entryway table. He was back at once and twined his fingers in her hair, tilting her face to lay kisses along her cheek and down her throat.

Oh God, he was good. But his hands, she wanted more of those hands. She'd never been good at the sexy banter, but she spoke now in a voice she didn't recognize, words coming from some unknown wicked part of herself. "You gonna frisk me, officer?"

His husky, sexy laugh sent a shiver rippling across her skin. "I'm going to do more than that." He took her shoulders in his hands and stepped forward until his body was hard along the length of hers. His leg pressed against her leg, guiding her backward.

"What are you going to do?" Her voice was weak—she couldn't catch her breath for the fire burning inside her.

He unbuttoned her top button, guiding her back another step. His head rose from where he'd been kissing her neck, her ear. His eyes were dark with intent. "I'm getting you naked." He nuzzled her neck again, popping another button. "You can stop me."

They went back another step. He popped another button.

"I can," she said breathily. She tangled her fingers in his hair, guiding his mouth lower. "But I won't."

"That's a good thing." He undid a third button, and cool air kissed through the lace of her bra. She sucked in a breath at the sensation, every inch of her skin pulled tight with desire. "I've been thinking about this moment for some time." He swept a thumb over the peak of her breast.

She hissed in a breath. "Me, too." She took another step back as he undid her last button, and her shoulders touched something hard—the doorjamb stopping her. She savored the feel of cool wood against her burning flesh.

His broad hand cupped her breast, kneading her and teasing her with his palm and thumb. He reached around her. Opened the knob. "Care to see my bedroom?"

Sorrow *did*. Though there was something she needed to see much more than that—his chest, bared again. She tugged his uniform shirt, untucking it from his pants. "Take this off."

"You got it." Billy swept her onto the bed, and she gave a little bounce as she landed.

She never knew she had a cop fantasy until experiencing the sight of a broad-shouldered sheriff stripping just for her. Legs parted slightly in a commanding stance, he stood over the bed, his eyes hooded and dark with hunger, swiftly unbuttoning. His gaze was unwavering. His desire, unwavering.

She'd enjoyed sex before, but never had she felt wanting like this. It seared her, set her body on fire. "I want you, Billy." She slid her jeans down to midhip, very aware of the sliver of black lace she revealed. "Now."

He practically ripped the rest of his clothes off and was on top of her, kissing her, touching her. She writhed with need, and he snatched her one hand, and then the other, twining his fingers with hers, sweeping her arms up over her head to give him unfettered access. "Is this what you've been hiding under those sweaters?" His mouth teased through the damp lace of her bra, sucking and nibbling her. "You're so hot. And now you're mine."

She arched her back, reaching her breast to his mouth, needing it closer, harder, more. "Get these clothes off me."

"Yes, ma'am." He slid his hand behind her back, flicked open the clasp of her bra, and tossed the black scrap of lace onto the floor. Her jeans and panties followed, his movements exhilaratingly confident and sure.

She wrapped her arms around his neck, pulling herself up, and him down, longing to feel his naked body press against hers.

When their skin touched, he hissed in a breath. He shifted,

holding the brunt of his weight off of her. "You're so perfect," he whispered.

She raked her fingers through his hair, kissing along his collarbone, up the strong column of his neck, to his jaw. Stubble scraped her tongue, and the erotic sensation amped her lust to a fever pitch. "Me? God, Billy, *you*." Desire made her weak, and she slid her hands from his hair to steady herself, grasping his upper arms, and moaned when her fingers met smooth, hard muscle. "You're rock hard." She gave a breathy laugh, realizing her double entendre, because another very hard part of him was an undeniable pressure against her leg. She wriggled beneath him, inching her hips closer to his, beckoning. She teased, a purr in her voice, "Rock hard."

"Condom," he growled, rolling from her. He was back on the bed in an instant, intense, focused, breathless. "I'll take more time . . ."

"No," she interrupted, guiding him to the perfect spot. "Now."

"Now." He plunged into her. "And again," he snarled with a thrust of his hips. "And later. And more. And forever."

And for the first time in her life, Sorrow felt completed. Complete.

Thirty

Marlene stole another glimpse of Tom Sullivan out of the corner of her eye. The theater was dark, but the movie's glow flickered over his features. In the starkly dappled shadows and light, he looked carved from granite.

He caught her looking, and she cut her eyes back to the screen, feeling herself blush a hundred shades of red. When was the last time she'd acted like such a schoolgirl? Probably the last time she'd been taken on an actual date, and she sure didn't remember when that'd been.

She'd felt like a girl again, when Sully picked her up to drive them to Silver City. He'd taken her to a nice Italian restaurant— not a chain—and had bought tickets to a movie *she'd* picked out.

The last time her ex-husband had taken her to dinner and a movie, they'd probably been in high school. It seemed like they'd gone straight from the Homecoming Dance to having babies to diaper and bills to pay. She'd lost both herself and him somewhere along the way.

She tried to pay attention to the film, but something began to buzz, and it took her a moment to figure out that it was coming from her purse. *The mobile phone.* She hardly used it, and on those rare occasions it rang, it always took her a moment to place the sound.

She slowly unzipped her bag, cringing at the loud sound, and slipped it out. It buzzed like an angry beetle in her hand. If someone were actually calling her, it was either a wrong number or an emergency. She prayed it was the former.

She glanced at Sully, uncertain. They'd announced that cell phones weren't allowed during the film.

Guessing her conundrum, he leaned close to whisper. "It's okay."

She barely registered his words, so focused was she on the feel of his breath on her cheek and the faint scent of his aftershave.

She forced herself to nod and peeked at the screen. The number was familiar, and it took her a moment to place it. *Ruby.* Her heart kicked up a notch. Oh dear Lord, what happened? There'd been much ado in her household over Marlene and Sully's date, and her aunt wouldn't be getting in touch if she didn't have a reason.

Sully guessed her distress, and with a steady hand, he guided her up from her seat and out of the theater. It was supposed to have been a simple, friendly date. Nothing big, just a Tuesday night—he'd had to talk her into it, for pity's sake.

And yet here he was, his warm arm around her shoulders the only thing keeping her propped up.

"Go ahead," he prompted gently, when they got into the lobby.

She blinked against the bright overhead lights, fumbling to press the button to answer. She was too late, and her hands trembled as she redialed. A person didn't act as caretaker to three elderly women without holding a part of her mind in constant reserve, always somehow expecting the worst.

"Ruby," she gasped, hearing her aunt's voice. "What is it?"

Marlene felt the blood drain from her head. She ended the call, met Sully's eyes. "It's Ma. She fell. They think it's her hip. An ambulance—" She choked on the last words.

Sully somehow had her in her coat and headed out the door before she knew which end was up. "They'll be taking her to Silver City Memorial," he said.

She nodded, grateful not to have to speak. Tom Sullivan just *knew.* Just as he somehow knew how to navigate the streets of Silver City, pulling into the hospital lot. She was on autopilot, grateful he was there to find the right attendant and ask the right questions, navigating them to the correct curtained room in the ER. Her mother had just arrived.

And then the waiting began. Time compressed until she felt as though she'd either just gotten to the ER or had been sitting there her whole life.

Ruby and Pearl showed up not long after the ambulance, having driven themselves there in Marlene's pickup. She would've found it shocking, had she not already been so swamped with emotion. She observed her aunts as though from a distance—them interrogating the nurses, bustling around, finding coffee—and she was struck by their calm. Their independence.

Suddenly it was nearly sixty years ago, and she was the kid and they were the adults. Snippets of memory returned in a flash, those times when her mother hadn't been home, and it'd been Pearl and Ruby feeding her dinner, making her wash her hands and finish her schoolwork.

Like sun shifting through a prism, a new light shone on her aunts, revealing a different truth, showing their quibbles and tics anew. She'd forgotten such large chunks of her childhood— the tiny details, the meaningless daily trivia. As the years passed, much of it had drifted from her mind like bits of ash on the wind. Those long-forgotten snippets came to her now, and she wondered, how had life passed so quickly? How had those memories slipped away? Weren't those day-to-day details what life was about?

Sully had been gone, and he reappeared now, sitting beside her to take her hand. He gave it a squeeze.

She looked at their twined fingers. His hands were so new to her, such an unexpected source of comfort. She'd seen in his eyes that he had word from the doctor, and she wanted to put off hearing it for another few moments. "My husband never held my hand like this," she said, stopping him before he could deliver any more bad news.

"Your husband was a fool," he said without hesitation.

She squeezed this strange man's hand as she remembered

Frank. How would *he* be acting right now? Her ex had never held her hand, never courted her, never taken her to fancy restaurants, and he definitely would never have tolerated a chick flick just because it was what Marlene had wanted to see.

She met his eyes. "I'm glad you're here, Tom." And she meant it. She was so grateful. She was an independent woman, a grown woman. She'd raised a houseful of boys. She was always the responsible one, including being responsible for her mother in a way Mama had never been truly responsible for her. She was a strong, self-reliant woman, and yet she found comfort in having a man beside her now. She drew a stabilizing breath. "What did the doctor say?"

"Your mother broke her hip. She's not responding, but that's the Alzheimer's. Technically, besides the hip, she's in good physical shape."

She swallowed again and again, trying to dissolve the ache in her throat. "Ma was always fit as a fiddle. Mountain living."

"Something like that." His left hand joined his right, until her cold fingers were cocooned in Tom's steady warmth. "They've hooked up an IV tube, Marlene, for feeding. But you're going to have some decisions to make."

She nodded, blinking back the tears. "Can I see her?"

"Of course." He pulled her to standing. "They're moving her now."

Walking into the hospital room, all Marlene could think was that she needed to get her mother out of there. Mama might be staring blankly, no longer in her body, but the woman she'd grown up with wouldn't want to be in a glaringly white and antiseptic hospital room—she'd want to be at home, where she could eat her favorite Pepperidge Farm cookies and watch her favorite afternoon programs. The younger Mama would've wanted to be in a car with the top down, laughing and angling for a picnic, even in the worst of weather.

"Hi, Ma," she said, and had to clear her throat not to cry.

Sully pulled a chair from the corner and brought it to the bedside. "You sit with your mother, Marlene. I'll go get you some coffee, find your aunts."

He was almost out the door when Mama's eyes cleared suddenly, pinned on Sully. "Wait," she said sharply.

"Ma?" The sound of her mother's voice should've been reassuring, but instead it alarmed her. She patted her mother's arm, and it felt like thin crepe draped over bone. When had Ma gotten so thin? Should she have put her in a home? Thinking on it now, she realized her mother hadn't been eating much, not really. Marlene knew a spurt of guilt and pushed it away. She beckoned Tom closer, saying in as bright and even a tone as she could muster, "You remember Tom Sullivan? Sully? Tom helped me. He drove me to see you."

But Marlene hadn't needed to bring him to her mother's attention—Emerald's eyes were glued to the man. Mama's voice was strong and steady when she said, "I don't regret you for a minute."

Sully shot Marlene a wary glance, but came to sit at Ma's bedside. "I beg your pardon?" He took her mother's hand without thinking, and Marlene thought him a good man for it.

When Emerald spoke again, an eerie clarity infused her eyes and voice, focusing on Tom like he was the only person in the room. Her hand trembled and knuckles turned pale with the grip she had on his hand. "I don't regret our running off. What I regret is that we didn't keep running."

"She thinks you're someone else," Marlene whispered.

"Gus?" The old woman became agitated, her tone turned frantic.

Marlene held her breath. *Gus.* She'd never before heard her mother say the name. The man who must've been her father.

Tom remained calm, though, his demeanor so warm and open. "Yes, Emerald? What is it?"

His equanimity calmed her mother, calmed *her,* and a question slammed to the forefront of Marlene's mind: *how on earth is this man single?*

Mama's chin quivered with emotion, but her voice rang clearly through the hospital room. "If I had it to do again, I'd stay. I loved you, Gus. And I love you still. And that's all there is. Daddy said I was reckless and I believed him, but my mistake wasn't that I ran off with you. It was heeding anything but my own heart."

She watched as Ma fell asleep wearing the most peaceful expression Marlene had ever seen. Sully silently disengaged his fingers and tucked her mother's hand beneath the covers. As he took Marlene's hand, she let her gaze meet his. The man behind those dark blue eyes was steadfast and strong.

It was time to learn from her mother. Time to let *her* heart run free. And as she held Sully's gaze, she knew. Her heart would be safe with him.

Thirty-one

Sorrow's eyes shot open, her heart pounding, unsure why she was awake and where. She knew a moment of sweet relief, feeling Billy at her back. *Billy.* Wondrous, amazing, hot as hell Billy. Then a ringing. *The phone.* The phone had woken her. Her heart kicked into double time.

Middle of the night phone calls were never good.

Billy sat up, as alert as if a switch had flicked in his mind. He answered the phone, and his voice might've been all business, but he put a warm, strong hand on her suddenly chilled shoulder.

Her first thought was of BJ—phone calls at odd hours were terrifying when you had a loved one at war. She told herself they never called—they came, first thing in the morning. Gray light filtered through the blinds—what time was it? Would her parents have gotten word and called her here? She glanced at the clock. 7:17 A.M. Early, but was it too early for some Marine Corps chaplain to drive out to Sierra Falls and knock on her folks' door?

"What's up?" he said, then mouthed to her, *Marshall.*

She bolted upright, cradling the sheet across her chest, unable to relax. Why was the deputy calling? Had there been another accident at the lodge? Billy worried the culprit was after *her*, but if they thought she was at home in her bed . . .

Billy and Marshall went back and forth, but then Billy looked at her. Hesitating, he said, "Yeah, she's here."

She leaned against the headboard, feeling numb. "What is it?" she whispered.

Billy didn't drop her gaze, but he didn't tell her what was going on either. "I'm sorry to hear that. We'll be there in no time."

She pounced on him the moment he was off the phone. "What is it? What happened? It's not BJ, is it?"

"BJ?" He had a perplexed look on his face. "Oh! God, no, Sorrow. BJ and your folks are all fine. It's Emerald. I'm sorry, she passed last night."

"Oh . . ." She slouched, letting the news sink in. "Poor Marlene." Emerald Kidd had been ailing for some time, but that didn't make it any easier on the family left behind. She frowned, thinking. "But why was he asking about me?"

"Your folks were looking for you. The lodge was up at dawn. Your mom apparently has a bee in her bonnet to hold a reception this afternoon. Emerald was well-loved."

"We all loved Emerald." Sorrow sighed, nodded. It was what you did in a small town—when crisis hit, you banded together and you ate. "Grief," she said sadly. "It's feed or be fed." She shifted to face him full-on. "But how did they know to call *here*?"

"When they realized you weren't in your bed, Bear called dispatch."

She slapped a hand to her forehead.

He laughed. "Our secret's out."

"I'm sorry," she said. His job as sheriff kept him in the public eye—would he shy away from the extra attention? The speculation? She was ready to jump in with both feet, but what about him? Was he even fully done with his grieving?

"Sorry?" He gently drew her hands from her face and pulled her close. "What kind of nonsense are you talking? *I'm* not sorry. You were here last night with me. I'm walking on air, Sorrow. I'm *thrilled* for people to know."

Walking on air. No man had ever said such a thing about her. "You are?"

"Absolutely," he said. "Not only that, do you honestly think anyone will be surprised?"

She gave him a shy smile. "No, I guess not." The question of Damien and *his* response was one she'd consider another time. With a sigh, she pulled off the sheet. "I guess we've been summoned."

"Oh no you don't." He tugged the sheet back up and burrowed deeper, snaking his hands around to grab her and roll her atop him. "They definitely won't miss you for another hour or so." As he glided his hands up and down her thighs, he told her slowly, "You need to shower, and do your hair, and eat breakfast, and lots of other things that will take you lots of time." His hands came to rest cupped on her bottom, nestling her into place.

Her hair fell in a curtain around his face. His body was already straining to meet hers, and she wriggled suggestively. "You sure we have time?"

"Life's short, Sorrow." Billy's face grew serious, the dark glint of desire in his eyes. "We'll make time."

* * *

Laura looked from her to Billy. "Well, lookee what the cat dragged in."

"Morning to you, too," Billy said, unruffled.

Sorrow felt herself blush, but refused to take her sister's bait. Today wasn't about them. "What happened?" she asked, redirecting the conversation.

Laura's teasing smile faded at once. "Emerald fell yesterday. She was on the porch, trying to go down the front stairs, wearing just her slippers and robe. Ruby and Pearl were in the kitchen when it happened."

"The poor women. I bet they feel horrible." It wasn't the first time something like that had happened, but there'd been no way to keep an eye on Emerald twenty-four hours a day. Not even a nursing home could claim that. "Where was Marlene when it happened?"

Laura raised her brows. "On a date. With *Sully*."

Despite the sad news, Sorrow couldn't help the smile that popped onto her face. "Really?"

"Yes, really." Laura sighed. "But talk about feeling bad. Marlene hates that she wasn't there. Thank God she was able to catch up with Emerald at the hospital. She passed in the night, very peacefully, I gather."

"What do you need us to do?" Billy asked.

Laura gave him an assessing look. "So you're sticking around, are you?"

"Marshall's on duty today, so you best get used to my ugly mug." He slid Sorrow's coat from her shoulders. "You go help your mom. I'll see if I can occupy Bear, keep him out of your hair."

When he left the room, Laura grinned shamelessly. "You *go*, girl."

What she had with Billy felt too special to gossip over, so she cut off her sister, saying, "Let's get to work."

Laura's shoulders slumped. "Fine," she muttered. "But you have no idea."

"What do you mean?"

"Just follow me."

They headed into the dining room, and her eyes widened at the devastation. It looked like someone had come and emptied their breakfront. Every piece of blue Wedgwood they owned was stacked on the buffet, the good silverware looked like it'd exploded over the dining table, a few cut-glass vases were waiting to be dusted, and blackened silver polish rags littered the place. "What's the story?"

"The story?" Her sister sighed. "The story is, Mom's losing it."

As if to illustrate the point, their mom bustled in, holding a tablecloth in each hand. "Which one?" she demanded, looking a little wild-eyed. "The gingham or Meemaw's table runner?"

"Meemaw's," the girls said in unison.

Edith looked doubtful.

"Meemaw was friendly with the Kidd sisters. It's a nice touch." Sorrow took it from her, and with Laura's help, moved the silver aside to spread it on the table. Before her mom could bustle back out of the room, Sorrow snatched her hands, forcing Mom to meet her eyes. "What's the plan?"

"It's a luncheon," Edith said.

"Okay," Sorrow said gently. She glanced over her mother's

shoulder, spying what was already a huge spread of food scat-tered across the counter. "But if people are coming over soon, we need to get this place cleaned up and put the food on the table."

"I loved Emerald," her mom said. "I want it to be perfect."

"I loved her, too. We all did. And it will be perfect—just perfect enough." She let go of Mom's hands and began to put the silverware back in its felted tray. "People won't notice if you're using the good silver or not."

"Amen," Laura murmured.

Sorrow shot her sister a look before turning her attention back to her mother. The woman looked like she'd aged twenty years in the night. "Have you eaten? You sit down." Sorrow steered her into the kitchen, hating the feeble, fragile feel of Mom's slack shoulders in her hands. "Take a minute to have a cup of coffee and make a list of what you need us to do. Lists are good." She sat her at the table and put a pad of paper and a pen before her. "Just tell us what you need, and we'll help."

Sorrow went back into the dining room. With a heavy sigh, she met and held her sister's gaze.

Billy reappeared. "Your dad is set up in his recliner. Lucky thing it's March Madness. Not only is he occupied, I'm afraid you'll need to unplug the TV to get him up from that chair."

He stood at Sorrow's side, resting his hand on her lower back. She looked up at him to give him a quiet smile—he man-aged to be loving and steadfast without being overtly affection-ate. At the moment, it was just right. She read total understanding in his eyes—Billy was more well-versed in grief than any of them.

They heard the scrape of the kitchen chair, followed by the clicking of the gas burner.

"Mom is wigging out," Laura said, and the uncharacteristic anxiety in her voice made Sorrow feel like the older sister instead of the youngest one.

"It helps her feel in control," Billy said. "Pouring herself into busy work is probably what's helping her keep it together."

Sorrow's eyes shot to his. The man was even wiser than she'd realized. Emerald's death might not have been a shock, but it *was* a blow. Even though she'd just passed the night before, everyone in the town—especially Mom—would want to pull together, keep busy, and most of all, *help*. "You're right," she said. "Mom loved Emerald. She grew up around the Kidd sisters. Putting together a big spread is the most therapeutic thing she could do, for all of us."

"She's been different since Dad's stroke," Laura said, her voice subdued. "I think she's clinging to life more than ever."

The insight was remarkable, and coming from Laura, it was a shock, too. Dad's stroke had been a reminder of how it could all change on a dime, and neither of her parents had been the same since.

"Yeah," Sorrow conceded. "I think that's exactly right." But then she sighed, checking the clock on the wall. "But all this talk isn't putting lunch on the table."

Laura led them into the kitchen. "I made a few plates of food this morning. Now that we don't need to polish the silver, we can start putting it all out."

Sorrow had braced herself to be the one to handle everything—especially the food—but when she saw the spread Laura had pulled together, she was shocked. "Wow," she said grudgingly. "Thanks. This looks great. How did you manage?"

Edith came over to stand between her daughters. "She did a nice job, didn't she, Sorrow?"

She looked at her sister, seeing her in a new light. She'd spent so many years feeling like she lived in Laura's shadow, resenting every minute she'd had to pick up the messes Laura left behind, that she'd lost sight of who her sister was, really—a bright, beautiful, capable woman. "Yeah, big sis. Nice work."

Laura shrugged, looking shyly pleased. "Luckily, I went shopping yesterday, and there was enough stuff like veggies, dips, and deli meats to assemble some buffet plates. Plus, I found some random frozen stuff in the freezer this morning—mini-quiches and pot stickers—I thought we could make those, too."

"That's a great idea." Sorrow gave her a sad smile. "Nothing like putting on a Costco wake."

Thirty-two

It'd been a week since her mother's funeral, and Marlene kept thinking about the picture that'd graced the easel at the front of the chapel—a black and white studio portrait of Ma, taken when she was much younger. Her dress was white with polka dots, and her lipstick was a dark and perfectly applied bow. It captured the younger mother she'd known, the vital one, who drank sparkling rosé and knew how to tell a cheeky joke. The woman who'd run away for love and returned home for the same reason.

"Marlene," a man's voice said. It was the sheriff, standing over her table, warm concern written on his face. "How are you doing?"

She considered the question, knowing he was the sort of man who'd see through a rote reply. "I'm . . . I think I'm doing okay." And actually, she was. She'd come to meet with the festival planning committee over an early dinner, and it was good to be out, to be in the tavern among her friends, even if it did mean the possibility of Bailey family sparring. It'd been a tear-soaked week, but she was grateful to feel all cried out for the moment. "Would you like to join us?" She'd been the first one to sit down, and gestured to the empty spot next to her.

"On duty, I'm afraid."

She noticed how his eyes found and tracked Sorrow through

the room. So that was why he'd stopped by the tavern, despite being in uniform. She smiled—it was just the sort of intrigue Mama would've enjoyed. Life went on, and it was good.

"You let us know if there's anything we can do," Billy added. "Sometimes it hits the hardest when all the vases are packed away and the well-wishers have gone."

He'd know better than anyone. She gave him a grateful smile. "I've got my family around me." *And Tom now, too.* She glimpsed Tom through the pass-through window. He was wearing his white T-shirt, and in the heat of the kitchen, it clung to his broad back.

"My mistake wasn't that I ran off with you. It was heeding anything but my own heart." Mama had wished to be her own woman. Marlene was sixty-three, and it was high time she learned what it meant to be *her* own woman. *Heed your own heart.*

There was a crash outside and the terrible shriek of metal scraping metal. Her hand flew to her chest. "What was that?" There was another crash followed by shouts, and she flinched.

Tom flew from the kitchen, right to her side. "Sounds like a couple of fender benders." He put a hand on her shoulder, acting nonchalant, but his eyes were bright as a hawk's when they locked with the sheriff's. "You sit tight, Marlene. We're on this. Don't you give it a second thought."

He was back in a flash, flanked by the sheriff, Sorrow, Eddie Jessup, and Helen, the tavern bartender. Dabney Simmons trailed behind them, an arm around his visibly shaken wife.

Laura had sat down to wait with Marlene. "What happened?"

"Black ice," Sully said. "A sheet of it on the driveway, smooth as glass."

"That's weird." Laura's gaze flicked to Eddie, giving him a quick once-over. "Nobody was hurt, were they?"

"No, nobody's hurt," Sorrow said, joining them at the table. "Thank God."

"Just some denting of fenders and pride," the sheriff added. "Eddie's new pickup is a little worse for wear."

"I salted out there yesterday, and it's been dry." Sorrow worried the edge of her apron. "I don't know how this could've happened."

Marlene caught the look that flashed between Sorrow and
Billy and was taken aback by the poor girl's intensity. "Don't
worry, dear," she assured her. "These things happen."

Sully looked doubtful. "It *is* strange."

"It's more than strange," Sorrow said. "It's a nightmare.
Mister Simmons's Mercedes has a huge dent in it. Poor Helen,
it was her old Dodge that glided right into it, like a big sled."

"Poor Helen is right." Marlene eyed the woman behind the
bar. She was tying on her apron with shaking hands. It'd take
months of tips to cover the bodywork on that fancy Mercedes.
"I hope she has insurance."

"We wouldn't think of making Helen pay for this," Phoebe
Simmons said from over Marlene's shoulder. The woman had
a white-knuckle grip on her Chanel quilted leather handbag.

There'd been a day when Phoebe's affluence would've made
Marlene writhe with envy. But not now. Not ever again. She'd
thought she wanted a BMW sedan and a retirement house on
the lake, but Ma's passing made her realize those weren't the
things she'd be mourning on her deathbed.

"Come join us," she told Phoebe. "Have something for your
nerves."

"I *am* a tad rattled." Despite those nerves, Phoebe was all
grace as she glided into a chair. There was no way to disguise
her caliber of wealth—she could be the most down-to-earth
woman in Sierra Falls and still she'd ooze class. "A sip of sparkling water should set me to rights."

"On it." Tom nodded and went to the bar. When he returned,
it was with *two* glasses—he'd brought a sparkling water for
Marlene, too. She gave him a shy smile.

Phoebe sipped, looking calmed. "Laura, it's such a treat
seeing you back in Sierra Falls. Edith tells me you might stay
for a while this time."

"I think I just might."

Poor Sorrow was stiff as a board, and Marlene willed the
girl to look her way so she could share a smile of encouragement. She'd heard about the girl's breakup with Damien and
didn't know if her agitation was due to the accident, to Laura,
or to the appearance of her ex-boyfriend's mother.

Phoebe was doing her best to ease the tensions, though, and

she met Sorrow's eye with a smile. "You deserve the help." The sentiment notched the woman higher in Marlene's estimation.

Laura straightened, brightened. "I'd love to transform this place from a dusty old hunting lodge into a cute destination resort."

"Oh, that would be charming. I've always thought the lodge had such potential." Phoebe's gaze swept the room, coming to rest on a pair of antlers over the dining table.

Laura laughed, catching her line of sight. "The first order of business would be to lose the animal heads."

Sorrow sat silently, practically quivering, and Marlene tried to ease the tension. "Some of us like a little local flavor."

"I'd keep some flavor, for sure. I'm talking to an old friend about designing a Web site, and it'd totally telegraph that gold rush town feeling."

Sorrow's mouth tightened. "Have you talked to Dad about this? Because you sure haven't talked to me."

"Not yet, not yet." Laura shooed her hand. "I'm pulling together the marketing plan now. It'll be comprehensive—addressing new interior design, an Internet presence—and it'll all tie into what I've got in mind for the festival. I thought we could even have a gold rush menu, with Sully's Prospector's Pie of course, and maybe even feature a special gold rush dinner that *Sorrow* could make. How about it, sis? You up for it? You could debut it at the festival."

Sorrow didn't get a chance to answer before Dabney came to gather his wife. Once the Simmonses left, she rounded on Laura. "If you haven't noticed, this *dusty old tavern* is open for business, so now is *not* the time to be gabbing about your grand takeover plans."

"Please don't—" *fret*, Marlene was about to say.

"It's never the right time for you," Laura snapped. "And I'm not trying to *take over*."

Marlene took a big sip of her water.

Sorrow crossed her arms at her chest. "Well it sure looks that way. You go around second-guessing everything I do. Don't you have enough to do in your fancy job? Do you need mine, too? Don't forget, *you* were the one who couldn't run for the door fast enough."

"How could I forget when you remind me every time I'm home? What is your problem, anyway? I'm just trying to help."

"You scheming about how to redecorate is *so* not helpful."

Laura pouted. "I thought you'd like my gold rush dinner idea."

"Sure, of course. It's cute. And it's not the point."

"Then what is the point? You've barely got a handle on things around here." She swept her arm, gesturing to the room. "Why are you so resistant to accepting my help? Like with the festival." Laura pinned her eyes on Marlene. "Tell her, Marlene. I feel like I've contributed a lot to the planning."

Marlene swallowed. "Oh dear, I . . ."

Edith appeared in a trice, aware of her girls' tension like a sixth sense. She gave them a scolding look. "Our dinners are up, and I'm sure Marlene is hungry. I know I am." She took her elder daughter's arm, tugging her up from her seat. "Laura, honey, would you help me bring out our plates? Helen is still too shaken up."

Sorrow and Marlene were left alone. The younger woman dropped her head in her hands. "I'm sorry. It was unacceptable to do that in front of you. I just . . . I haven't gotten much sleep, I think, and it's been a pretty emotional week. I'm so sorry."

"Oh, hush." She took Sorrow's hand. "Whatever are you apologizing for?"

"For me and my stupid sister." She sat up, but her shoulders remained slumped. "Nothing is going right today."

"Do you think this is the first sisterly fight I've seen? Don't forget who I live with." She had to smile. "Don't give it a second thought. You're young. You both are. You'll figure it all out." She watched Laura standing at the pass-through, balancing plates on her arms. "Consider forgiving your sister. The old cliché is true: life it just too darned short not to. Open your mind to your sister's ideas. I happen to think a little change around here would be a grand idea. And if Laura decides to stay in Sierra Falls for a while, then good on her for following her heart."

And, Marlene thought, it was high time she did the same.

Thirty-three

❧

Several days had passed since Billy and Sorrow had received their wake-up call that'd outed their relationship to the town. Now he was back in the Bailey house, sitting stiffly, wondering if it would be expected or frowned upon to grab a beer from the fridge. He'd already erred once, choosing what was apparently Edith's preferred spot on the couch. Not that Sorrow's mom was going to be watching any basketball with him and Bear.

When her dad brought up the Colorado/Brigham Young game, Billy had jumped at the chance to join him. He had a thing or two to say to the man, but so far, the bulk of the conversation had gone something like Bear grunting, "Colorado, huh?" and Billy replying, "Yes, sir. Econ major."

But he couldn't complain. In fact, he was shocked Sorrow's dad had even remembered his alma mater, and it made him think that there was more going on in Bear's head than the old grump let on. It was progress.

Sorrow popped her head in, looking mischievous. "You boys need anything in here?"

Billy let his eyes devour her for a moment. "Oh, I think I've got all I need," he said, but the look that passed between them said something more like, *when can we be alone again?*

She shot a glance at Bear to make sure his attention was on the TV, then gave Billy a saucy look meant for his eyes only.

He waited a full minute before he sprang up off the couch. "If you'll excuse me, I think I should see if your daughter needs any help."

And it wasn't totally a lie—he'd hoped his presence around the house might help Sorrow a bit, both with the general workload and with the sisterly and fatherly tensions that permeated the air, thick enough to cut with a knife.

He came up behind her where she was wiping down the counter, "I'm here to help."

"Are you kidding? Watching a game with my dad is above and beyond."

"Just getting to know the man better." He swept aside her hair, revealing a stretch of pale neck. Seeing tension in her shoulders, he snatched the sponge from her hand and tossed it aside, easing her arms to her sides to massage away her stress. "You know I'm in this for the long haul."

"I like the sound of that." She leaned back against him, releasing a huge sigh like the weight of the world slipping from her shoulders. She was so soft and inviting pressed against him, his body tightened, reaching for her. "Well hello, Sheriff," she said with a giggle. She nestled back against him. "I like the feel of it, too."

All rational thought fled his brain. He swooped her up, spun her around, and seated her on the counter. Slowly, he glided his hands up her thighs, separating them, pushing between her legs to stand closer. "You're lucky your dad is in the next room." He nuzzled his way up that luscious neck, whispering against her mouth. "Because I'm of a mind to have you right here, right now, on this counter."

She laughed wickedly, and he loved the sound of it, the sound of *her*, free and easy. "I thought you were here to help," she said.

"I'm not helping?" His hand found her breast, and she sucked in a breath.

"You're evil."

"Nah." He leaned close to nibble on her ear. "I'm a force for good. What do you say we head upstairs, and I can show you just how good?"

She grabbed two fistfuls of his hair and pulled his mouth to hers, kissing him deeply.

If he'd thought he was turned on before, the feel of her taking what she wanted from him sent him over the edge. "You're killing me," he said, when she parted.

"Now you know how it feels." She slid from the counter, a slow glide down the front of his body. "And now, I need to get this place in order. We have two parties of two coming in this afternoon. A Big Bear Lodge record."

The lights flickered, and it took Billy a moment to realize it was the faltering electricity and not some side effect of his desire, like his vision wavering from total frustration. But then there was sudden silence as the power shut down for good.

Sorrow's hands convulsed, gripping his shirt tight. He could see her eyes pop wide open in the darkness. "What was that?"

He smoothed his hands along her shoulders, easing her. "It's okay. I'm sure it's just a simple power outage." Actually, he wasn't so sure, and he wasn't about to take any chances.

She gave a nervous laugh, holding a hand at her chest, looking rattled. "Sorry. Just a little jumpy these days."

"We all are." He was attuned to her, but he sent a part of his senses outward, listening. "Where's the fuse box?"

"Garage."

That meant she'd be safe *inside*. "You wait here," he told her.

Bear shouted from the other room, "What the hell was that?"

"*That man*," Sorrow whispered, exasperated. She laughed again, sounding a little more like herself. "Well isn't this great? We've got guests on their way, and now no electricity."

He planted a kiss on her forehead and stepped from her. He had a hard time believing this really was a simple outage—where the Bailey lodge was concerned, nothing struck him as simple as it appeared. "I'll go see if you blew a fuse."

She grabbed the front of his shirt, stopping him. "Hey, rain check on the whole *force for good* thing."

"You got it, darlin'." He swooped in, stealing one last hard, quick kiss. "I *will* cash that rain check."

"Best get going then." She gave him a playful shove, then snagged him a flashlight from a kitchen drawer. "Just in case."

The living room was dim, and Bear was hauling himself to the edge of his lounger, trying to get up. "Wait," he grunted. "I got this."

Billy went to him, leaning down to give him a hand. "Let's go take a look."

The older man flinched back, angry. "I'm not an invalid. It's my house, and I'll take care of it."

"Of course. So how about I come with, in case you need me to hold the flashlight?" Someone could be waiting out there, and he wasn't about to risk Bear getting jumped in the dark.

The man shot him a suspicious glare, and as Billy watched him struggle from the chair, a puzzle piece clicked into place. Sorrow's father had been raised to be a man's man, spending his youth hunting for fun and logging for pay. That his body no longer cooperated had to be a blow to his ego and his manhood.

He might've been moving more slowly, but the man wasn't dead yet. It seemed somebody needed to apprise him of that fact.

Billy stood in front of the chair, blocking Bear's path. "Permission to speak frankly, sir?"

"Stop *sirring* me." Sorrow's dad teetered for a moment, getting his balance.

Billy bit back a smile. "Permission to speak frankly, you old hard-ass?"

Bear laughed at that. "I been waiting for you to speak frankly. Because I can't figure you out."

That wasn't the response he'd expected. "There's nothing to figure," he said, surprised. "What you see is what you get. I like your daughter, and I'm not going away anytime soon. At least, not if I have anything to say about it."

"I don't know how I feel about her breaking it off with that Simmons boy," Bear said, and he suspected the old man was testing him. "The kid practically prints money at that job of his."

The man wanted to be contrary. Fine. It was his right. But it didn't mean Billy would take the bait. "Damien has money, that's easy to see. Doesn't mean he's the right guy for Sorrow."

"Sometimes I wonder if the girl would know the right thing if it came up and bit her on the rump." Her father shrugged, wearing an expression of mild distaste. "So, this is you speaking frankly?"

"No. *This* is me speaking frankly: you need to stop being such a nasty old coot. Hollering at the women in your life doesn't make you a better man, it just gives us all a headache. I know your body isn't what it was, and I'm sorry for that. But, Bear, last I checked, getting old sure as hell beats the alternative."

Bear scowled hard at the word *old*, but Billy pressed on. "You want to be powerful again? You put that daughter of yours up on your shoulders. You support her, make sure she's set up to fly higher than you ever did. Now *there's* a weight that only a real man can handle."

Bear's features went utterly still, but whether it was anger or attentiveness had yet to be seen. "What are you saying?"

"I'm saying, you need to let your girl spread her wings."

The man frowned. "Last time she spread her wings, she almost set the tavern on fire."

Billy's response was instant. "I don't believe that was her fault."

"You *would* say that. New sheriff and all. We *pay* you to be suspicious."

"Look, Bear. Think what you like. But if you were to share more of the decision making, things would get better around here. If Sorrow wants to have more say in the tavern, give her a shot—what the hell, right? I'd bet good money Sully would *welcome* the help. Maybe it'd even prevent incidents like that fire."

"Girl's got no time for all that," Bear said.

"That brings up my next point."

"How many points you got, Sheriff?"

Billy ignored the gibe and pressed on, "Sorrow could use some help around the place. An assistant maybe." Bear's eyes goggled at that, but Billy refused to give him a chance to interrupt. "She runs around like a one-armed paperhanger. The girl is in her twenties, and as far as I can see, her closest friends are a bunch of retirees."

"Laura's back in town," Bear protested. "She's been helping." His tone was firm, but it sounded to Billy like the man was beginning to lose steam.

"You need to hire someone," Billy insisted. "In addition to

dealing with things like repairs, and budget, and reservations, you've got Sorrow on *room-cleaning* duty. For God's sake, Bear. If you hired someone, if you had more help around the place, you could handle more business. You'd eventually bring in more tourists. Think on it."

"You done?" The man's expression no longer made him look like he'd swallowed a box of nails.

Billy breathed a sigh of relief to see it. "All done," he told him with a decisive nod. He suspected he'd gotten through, just a bit.

Bear was the one person around here who could use some standing up to, and yet not many people did. His kids knew how to rebel against him, maybe. But rebelling against the man and *challenging* him were two different things.

"Then if you're finished flapping your jaw, let's go see what happened to my power." The man was proud; he wouldn't admit anything, but hopefully an attitude adjustment was in their future.

Billy clapped him on the back. "Lead the way."

They huddled in the dimness of the garage, with Bear flicking the fuses on and off. Billy tipped the flashlight, illuminating a tangle of frayed wires under the circuit breaker panel. "It's all chewed up."

Bear grunted. "Raccoon maybe."

"Maybe." Billy peered closer, certain that what he was looking at wasn't the work of any animal. Raccoons just weren't interested in fuse boxes. "Either way, you'll need to call an electrician."

Bear creaked to standing. "That'll cost a pretty penny." His lip twitched as he considered this news. He didn't look pleased. "Nothing for it, though. I'll get Eddie on the phone."

Just a couple of hours later, and it was all patched up. Eddie Jessup had come straight over—one half of Jessup Brothers Construction, his schedule had been miraculously open.

"You're all set," Eddie said, joining everyone in the living room.

"It's done?" Doubt was written across Bear's face. "All fixed?"

"Bear Bailey. When I say 'all set,' I mean *all set*."

Bear *harrumphed*, admitting under his breath, "I guess we didn't need Damien after all."

Billy looked over the man's shoulder to catch Sorrow's eye. They shared a smile. "I guess we didn't," he said expansively.

Suppressing a giggle, Sorrow stood and handed Eddie a foil-wrapped bunch of fresh-baked cookies. "I made these before the power went out. Spice molasses."

Eddie took them eagerly. "I'd have done the work for free if I'd known I was going to get some of your cookies. I swear they get better every time."

"It's to thank you for getting here so fast. We have some guests arriving tonight, and the last thing we need is a power outage."

"No trouble fitting you in," Eddie said. "I had a hole in my schedule."

Billy grinned. "I'll bet." It wasn't hard to guess why his schedule had a hole in it. "I saw those skis tossed in the back of your pickup."

Eddie laughed, and it was an easy, rolling sound. The guy lived and breathed outdoor sports, and had the snow-tan and premature smile and squint lines to prove it. He was the type to veer off the side of the road whenever he spotted a hill that looked dangerous enough to be interesting, hikeable enough to climb, and snowy enough to ski back down.

"You caught me," Eddie said. "What can I say? It snowed last night. Not much, but just enough for some fresh tracks out east of the falls."

Bear was staring at the cookies in Eddie's hands, apparently stuck on the concept that he might've somehow wrangled the electrical work for free. "That mean you're not going to charge extra for coming early?"

"Bear. I'm offended. But"—Eddie put down his toolbox and pulled on his jacket—"I *will* accept partial payment at the tavern in the form of something tall and cold." His smile froze as Laura walked into the room. His eyes tracked her, and Billy heard him mumble, "*Speaking* of tall and cold . . ."

The guy was looking slack-jawed, and no surprise there. Clad in only a pair of short shorts and a see-through mesh top over her jog bra, Laura was dressed—barely—for a workout.

"You can shut your mouth now," she said, not meeting Eddie's eyes.

That brought the guy out of it. A huge smile split his face. "Well, well, well. The Big Bad Bailey Sister is *still* here. Whatcha running from on that treadmill, little girl?"

Laura tossed a towel over the monitor and climbed onto the machine. Billy could've sworn she was blushing. "It's an elliptical trainer," she said primly.

Sorrow made a snorting noise that sounded suspiciously like a swallowed laugh.

Billy read her mind and began backing out of the room. "Well then. You all look like you've got it under control here."

"Yeah," Sorrow was quick to add. "I told Billy I'd help him with . . . a thing." Catching his eye, she jerked her head toward the door. The moment they were safe in his SUV, she said, "That was . . ."

". . . something else," Billy finished for her. When their laughing died down, he said, "At least I seem to have risen in your dad's estimation. I've gone from *accused* to merely a *person of interest*."

"I'm afraid Dad's a 'guilty until proven innocent' kinda guy."

Billy was thoughtful for a minute, then asked, "Was he that curmudgeonly before his stroke?"

"He was always a tough guy. But no, he's gotten worse. Isn't that what they say happens with age? Can't teach an old dog new tricks, and all that?"

"Maybe so." Though Billy wasn't entirely convinced. In fact, he thought he had the man pretty well figured. "Might be that he's just frustrated he can't get around like he did before."

She nodded, letting the idea sink in. "Yeah, I've been thinking about what you said before. It's got to sting, letting go of so many responsibilities." But then she laughed. "Either way, I thought his head was going to explode when he lost power to the TV."

"Hey," he said, "speaking of electricity, there sure were sparks flying between Laura and Eddie."

"Laura? No way. You thought my *dad* was proud? My sister will gain twenty pounds, sprout wings, and fly before she hooks up with a Sierra Falls man."

"I sure am glad you didn't get that whole dieting gene. A man likes something to hold on to." He reached across the car to squeeze her thigh. "And hey"—his fingers slid up to give that luscious rump a playful tweak—"what's wrong with Sierra Falls men?"

She squirmed away with a squeak. "You know there is *nothing* wrong with Sierra Falls men. We attract only the finest." It was her turn to reach across, resting her hand on his thigh, growing thoughtful. "Laura hightailed it out of here after high school and wants nothing to do with the place. I'm sure she pictures herself in some urban loft somewhere, shacked up with a dot-com bazillionaire."

Billy cut his eyes from the road long enough to give her a perplexed look. "Then why is she still hanging around?"

"Now *that's* the question." Sorrow leaned back, kicking her feet up on the dash. "Maybe she's hoping her dream bazillionaire will drop from the sky and check into the lodge."

"Maybe there's something else going on with her. Have you thought about just asking her?"

"I tried," she said, dismissing it.

"I don't mean in the middle of an argument. I mean, you could have a sisterly heart-to-heart."

"Uhh, no thanks," Sorrow said. "I've grown fond of my head and would prefer to keep it attached to my body."

Billy let out a laugh. "It's obvious she's wound pretty tight, but . . . I don't know . . . She *was* a pretty big help at Emerald's memorial. Maybe you underestimate her."

"I guess she has done a lot for the festival," Sorrow admitted. "She asked if I'd cook a special gold rush dinner."

"That's great."

"Yeah, I guess it kind of is." She shrugged. "She's constantly online, doing whatever she does. Some historical journal is even coming out next week to do a write-up on Buck Larsen and his days in Sierra Falls."

"That's cool," Billy said enthusiastically. "That's something. It'll bring in more tourists. It does seem like you have more guests than usual."

"I guess," she said grudgingly.

"So what's the problem, then? The festival is coming

together. You're drawing more visitors. Your sister wants you to cook for everyone. She must be good for something."

"All this buzz is great, sure. But I'm totally overwhelmed. The place is falling apart at the seams. Every time I fix one thing, something else breaks. Apparently, somebody may or may not be out to get me. Getting more visitors is all well and good, but it means more mouths to feed, more rooms to keep perfect, more things to stay on top of."

"You're overwhelmed, and it seems like Laura wants to help. It's not like you love every aspect of running the business. Why don't you let her have a crack at it?"

"Have a crack at it . . ." Sorrow's feet slid from the dash, hitting the floor with a thump. "Guess who's going to clean up the mess when her whole *crack at it* thing fails? Who's going to pick up the pieces when Laura decides she's done and takes off again?"

Alarms sounded in Billy's head. There was some tricky history between the sisters—Sorrow had been more hurt than he'd realized, harboring it more deeply than he'd guessed.

He made a snap decision to broach a topic that maybe wasn't ready for broaching. "Well," he said gently, "if she decides to take off again, I think we might have some other help for you."

"What do you mean?" Sorrow gave a rueful laugh. "First the Laura hard sell. You're not going to foist Ruby and Pearl on me, are you?"

"Better than that. Bear's hiring you an assistant. At least I think he will." He waited, excited and anxious to see her response.

But she looked at him as though he'd just spoken in Greek. "*Assistant? What kind of assistant?*"

"The helpful kind," he said. "The kind who'll make the beds, and answer the phones, and do the grocery runs."

"An assistant," she said in a dreamy voice. "How fancy. I'll believe it when I see it."

"Well, you'll need one. Because I'm taking you to Silver City."

"Cool." She paused. "Why?"

"Remember my chef buddy?"

It took her a second to follow him. "You mean the freezer guy?"

"That's the one. He's arranged for you to shadow him for a night at his restaurant."

"Get out! I'll get to work under him like a sous-chef?"

"Something like that, yeah." He stole a glance at her. The way her sweater clung to her curves gave him a good idea of what—and whom—he'd like to get under.

"Wow," she marveled. "Working with a real chef. How can I ever thank you?"

He practically skidded into his driveway. "I've got some ideas."

Thirty-four

"Can't sleep?" Billy asked, his voice low in the dark. He pulled her closer to cradle her body more snugly to his, and she felt him begin to rouse at her back. "I could try to take your mind off things."

She chuckled and rolled around to face him. "If you take my mind off of it any more tonight, I'm afraid I might have trouble walking tomorrow."

"Then stay in bed all day. *My* bed. I can protect and serve, and all that." He tugged her closer to prove his point, but reading the anxiety on her face, his tone turned somber. "You know you're safe here."

"I know it. But . . ." Sorrow tried to relax—Billy was being so charming and sexy—but her mind was going a million miles an hour. Someone had been *inside* her house, probably even while she'd been at home. The idea chilled her. It was too much like something out of a horror movie. "It's just . . . someone broke into our garage. While we were *home*. It feels so creepy. So personal."

"This has been personal all along. But I *will* protect you. We *will* find the bastard."

A sharp blade of moonlight shone through the slats in his blinds, illuminating him. She drew strength from those strong features—even in the shadows, she could see his resolve. She had every faith in him.

She couldn't help but think about her father and mother still at home. It seemed like one day her father had been the strong daddy swinging her up on his shoulders, and then the next she was fretting over his ability to walk up and down the stairs unassisted. And now he was acting so stubborn, refusing to accept these were more than simple accidents. What would happen if someone broke in again? What if next time whoever was after them did something worse than just snip some wires? "I'm worried about them."

"Your folks?" Of course he'd known exactly whom she meant, and at her nod, he told her firmly, "They'll be fine. Eddie said he'd crash in one of your spare rooms. Those Jessup boys are tough—he can handle whatever comes up." But then he laughed low. "The question is, will Eddie survive your sister? There are sparks between those two."

She felt a smile flicker on her face. "Laura totally denies it."

"What's the line . . . the lady protests too much?"

"Something like that, yeah."

They both grew quiet, and when he spoke again, his tone was grave. "I hate to say it, but without you there, I don't think anything else will happen tonight."

She shivered, chilled to her bones. "Who's doing this?"

"Whoever it is, I'll find him and throw his ass in jail so fast his head will spin. If I don't wring his neck first."

Sorrow had to laugh at Billy's vehemence. "Thanks. You know, I believe you will."

They lay in the dark a while longer as he idly stroked his hand up and down her back. She sighed—she felt safe with Billy. Safe in his house. In his arms.

But she still couldn't sleep.

"That's it." He slipped out of bed and pulled on his boxers. As he handed her his robe, he said, "You're coming with me." He grabbed an old pair of wool socks for her, too. "This time of night, you'll want these."

She swam in the green and navy plaid flannel robe, but there was nothing more intimate than the feeling of wearing her man's clothes. They walked downstairs hand in hand, and when she spoke again, she couldn't help the excited curiosity in her voice. "Where're we going? It's got to be past two."

"I'm making you a cup of tea. And"—he snagged her purse from where she'd dropped it onto the dining room table—"we'll need this."

"We'll need my *purse*?"

"We need what's *in* your purse."

"What's in my—?" Her eyes lit, watching him extract the thick packet. "Ohh. The letters." Ever since the fire, she'd been anxious to keep Sorrow Crabtree's letters safe and carried them with her, tied in a neat bundle that she kept wrapped in a Ziploc bag.

It wasn't just their historical value to her family and the town that had her so careful. As troubles around the lodge escalated, so did her feeling of connection with her great-great-great-grandmother. Her ancestor had faced struggles Sorrow couldn't begin to contemplate. So many of those pioneer women must have. And she figured, if her ancestor could weather the old days as a single mother, then *she* could buck up and deal with a little stress at the lodge.

"Don't think I haven't noticed how you read these every possible free moment." He helped her into the kitchen chair and gave her shoulders a squeeze. "Have you finished reading them yet?"

"No, I'm going slowly." She carefully pulled the collection from their layers of plastic and contemplated the paper, crisp and yellow with age. "Her story takes my mind off my troubles. I want to prolong it."

She wanted to savor every moment reading them, and the desire to understand what the older Sorrow endured had only intensified since Emerald's death. Why hadn't she ever asked Marlene's mother more questions? About how Sierra Falls used to be? About Marlene's childhood? So many simple things that'd never been asked and would never be answered now.

She half listened as Billy puttered around the kitchen, getting out tea bags and filling the kettle with water. He asked, "Would you read one to me?"

She popped her head up to make sure he was being serious. Her breath caught to look at him, scruffy in the dim light, wearing just his T-shirt and boxers. She couldn't believe this guy was hers. "Really?"

He stopped his bustling to pin her with his eyes. Standing still, he held the teakettle poised in midair over the stovetop. "I told you, I'm in this for keeps. What makes you happy makes me happy, too."

"Oh," she said simply. She darted her eyes back down, overcome with emotion. She couldn't remember the last time someone had expressed an interest in her happiness alone. "Okay."

"And hey, it's not exactly a stretch, either." Billy was still by the sink and hadn't caught her sudden shyness. "Those letters you found are amazing. To think Buck Larsen was prospecting for gold before he was elected as one of the first California representatives."

"I guess he must've bought his post with gold rush money." The man was infamous in California for having appeared out of the blue, replacing his political advisors with businessmen, then resigning midterm when elected life bored him. Rumors about bribes had followed him out the door. Larsen went on to build a railway empire, but not much was known about his life before he burst onto the scene.

"I guess all his money didn't come from bribes after all. Maybe some of it came from gold." The kettle whistled, and Billy poured their tea and joined her at the table. He gestured to the letters. "Where'd you leave off?"

She shuffled through. "Let's see . . . last thing I knew, Sorrow Crabtree had been bemoaning the town's judgmental biddies."

He gave a thoughtful shrug. "Can't have been easy, pregnant and alone. Life was hard and cheap back then—especially for women."

"Well, aren't you the strong, sensitive type?" She gave him a playful smile and squeezed his hand. He'd been right to bring out the letters—the more they chatted, the further away her troubles at the lodge seemed. "But you know, back then it wasn't just the men who made names for themselves. I read that some of those gold rush dancers made a fortune."

Billy leaned closer to scan the writing. "Maybe I've seen too many Westerns, but I bet there were other types of women than just dancers. You know, *those* kind of women."

She exclaimed, "A 'lady of the night'? She *couldn't* have been, could she?"

"Read it and see."

Sorrow traced her finger down the page to find her place. "Here's where I stopped. She wrote, *'Thank the Lord for Madame Lizzie. I know what you'd say, you'd be like to call her a harlot or worse. But, to me, she's my angel. She invited me to live with the Parlour Ladies, but she don't make me dance no more, nor worry about any of that other business on account of my swole belly. Swole with your child, Buck. Maybe I can see how you'd walk away from me, but I don't understand how you could walk away from your son.'"*

Amused, Billy raised a brow. "Doesn't make her do that *other business*?"

She put the letter down and met his eye. "Wow. She moved into a … ."

"A house of ill-repute?"

"Yeah, what you said." She put the page down to sip her tea thoughtfully. "It seems that the Madame was a *Madam* Madame."

Billy playfully guided her mug back down to the table and handed her the letter. "You can't stop reading now."

She gave him a broad smile and found her spot again. " *'Some folk carry a Bible in their hand and judgment in their eyes. But not the Madame. She has only kindness in her heart. Says we women need to stick together. I get the idea maybe she had a man who left her just like you did me. But I'm done being angry. It burned through me, and I've vowed to rid my heart of every last bit. Because each day goes by, and love fills my heart instead, feeling the strong kicks of my baby. My baby, Buck.'"*

She put the letter down. "Jeez, he sounds like such a jerk."

"I can't believe the infamous Buck Larsen knocked up a dance hall girl and left her alone and pregnant in a pioneer town. He's even more of a bastard than everyone thought."

"Pregnant, alone, and living in a *whorehouse*," she marveled. "At least it sounds like she didn't have to do the . . . extra duties."

"She must've done something to earn her keep."

Sorrow nodded and read on. "Wait, listen to this. *'Trouble came round this morning. I was in the parlour when some men came. They looked at me funny, all demanding like, wanting to buy my time. They said some nasty, un-Christian things, and I had to say a quiet prayer not to curse you, Buck. But then just when it seemed I was a goner, the Sheriff stepped in. I suppose Madame Lizzie done told him about my babe, and he sent those men packing.'"*

Billy grinned. "See, we sheriff types are good."

She beamed back at him. "Too bad Sorrow Crabtree ended up with the mailman instead of the sheriff. That would've been just too cool." She flipped through and saw they'd just about reached the end of that one. "Should I stop? It's getting late."

"No way. You can't stop now."

Sorrow felt her grin grow even wider. She loved these old letters, loved getting to know her ancestor this way, and she was positively tickled that Billy honestly seemed to enjoy them just as much. "Okay," she said, flipping to a new page full of cramped script. The beginning spoke about mundane things—the food, the coming weather—but then they finally reached a juicier bit. "You said she had do something to earn her keep; well here we go. *'Madame L says from now on I'm just to work at the cooking and laundry. It's hard work and my hands bleed from it, but it's better than lying under a man. Some of them come round with their suits and pocket watches, and they remind me of you. And I'd rather my hands bleed, Buck. How do you like that?'*

" *'One fellow came by yesterday, had with him a newspaper from Sacremennto. And whose name would you figure was on the front page? Mister Buck Larsen, all right. News is you were voted to Congress Man. My compliments. I guess the folk of California believed your promises just like I did. Fools, all of em.'*

" *'But I tell you, Buck, maybe it stung extra bad because today is an angry day. None of my dresses fit no more. I let them out all I could, and now I had to sew an extra panel just to cover my belly but all I had to use was an old bit of calico from my apron. And I tell you, Buck, that bit of calico makes me spitting mad. At you. Angry how you had your pretty words for me. You told me I was so lovely. Like a winter bloom on*

*the mountainside, you said. But you plucked that bloom and
left me, no good for no man now.'"*

She looked over the paper at Billy, making a funny face.
"Yikes. Pregnancy hormones, you think?"

Billy raised his hands in surrender. "I'm not touching *that*
comment with a ten-foot pole."

She laughed and read on. "'*I shoulda known watching you
glad-hand folk the way you did. You wanted me on your arm,
so pretty you said. Like a picture. You'da shown a picture more
care though. The moment the Rassmussens came to town, with
their fancy Foreignn money, you jumped fast enough for their
girl. 'Tis unkind of me to say, but I get comfort thinking of those
teeth of hers like a Truckee River Beaver, and trying to picture
you kissing on her. I swear, I hope you have a flock of beaver-
faced children. Not this babe in my belly though. Hes a fine
boy. I can feel it.'*

"'*And he's getting big too. I move slow now, but it don't
matter. Madame L lets me hide in the kitchen with my cooking,
and it's fine by me. I work and I think about the places I'll take
my boy some day.'*"

A sensation overwhelmed Sorrow, of a connection across
generations. "She liked to cook. It was an escape for her."

"Just like you," Billy said quietly.

She studied him. Stubble was faint along that strong jaw and
his hair went every which way. Being with Billy like this, in
the middle of the night serenity of the kitchen, she knew a fierce
stab of emotion. She felt loved and complete. "You get it, don't
you? Get me."

"Of course I do." He scooted his chair closer, and gently
swept the hair from her brow, tucking it behind her ear. "And
I'm the luckiest man alive that you've let me in to see."

Thirty-five

When Sully woke that morning, he knew at once—it was in the smell of the air, in the way he'd thrown the covers from the bed in the night. Spring had sprung, no doubt about it.

His bare feet hit the timber planks of his cabin's floor, and he drew up the shades. The snow had melted to a thin, crusty layer. Water dripped from the eaves, catching the dawn sunlight like crystal. The sky was clear, and the birds were chirping.

He'd been waiting for just such a day.

He made a quick call to Sorrow, and was surprised when she answered groggily. Usually she was the first up and at 'em. He smiled to himself—it was none of his business, but still, he hoped it was the sheriff who'd made her so sleepy that morning. The girl deserved to find happiness.

"No problem," she said, when he asked for a personal day. In fact, she sounded downright excited about it, and he'd suspected she would. Any excuse to get into that kitchen, cooking up an exotic breakfast confection sure to aggravate her father.

Anxious to surprise Marlene before she headed out for the day, he worked fast, making a picnic out of whatever basics he had on hand. Assembling a fruit salad, deviled eggs, bread, cheeses, juice, a thermos of coffee. Tossing it all in his pack.

On his way out the door, he cast a longing look at his Harley.

It might've been spring, but a woman like Marlene wasn't ready for the bike. *Yet.*

She answered the door, and it took his breath away. She was such an elegant lady, always pulled together, her clothes and hair just-so. But this morning, she wore jeans and a no-frills sweater, in a red that made her cheeks glow.

"Tom." She was shocked to see him. "What are you doing here? Is something the matter?"

"Yes, something's the matter." He knew what grief was like. Though Marlene still had her aunts, the routine she'd had with her mom would be hardwired into her. She'd be hopping up throughout the day, thinking it time to dress her mother, or feed her, or help with the bathroom, and maybe she'd make it all the way across the room before remembering that Emerald was no longer there to need her help. Marlene's days would feel long and empty for some time to come, and he'd help her avoid that emptiness if he could. He held out his hand. "You need to come with me."

She touched a hand to her cheek. "I need to finish putting on my face."

"Your face sure looks *on* to me. Prettier than this spring morning." He was certain he gaped at the sight—he couldn't peel his eyes from her, and if she didn't hear the truth in his words, then she was plum deaf. He repeated earnestly, "Come with me, Marlene."

"I'll get my coat." She nodded gravely, grabbing her jacket and purse from a rack by the door and joining him on the porch.

She'd jumped into action, and Tom forced himself to keep a straight face. She really was going with him.

Her hands fumbled with her keys, and he gently took them from her hands, locking the door for her. "Where are Ruby and Pearl?"

She widened her eyes, and it made her appear shell-shocked. "Shopping," she exclaimed. "They took the old pickup all the way to Silver City. There aren't even any sales right now."

"Good for them." He opened the car door for her.

"What's the emergency?" she asked once he'd gotten in. "It's not the lodge, is it?"

"Nope." He pulled out of her driveway, headed for Route 88.

"Where are you taking me?"

"The falls," he said.

"There's an emergency at the falls?"

"No, ma'am." He pulled his eyes from the road for long enough to savor her wide-eyed confusion. "There's a *picnic* at the falls."

"A picnic?"

"*Our* picnic." He gestured to the pack thrown onto the back-seat. "It's supposed to hit midfifties today. I thought we'd take a brisk walk out to the falls. We can sit on the rocks—they get nice and warm in the sun."

"We're hiking out to the falls?" She still sounded flummoxed, and it was endearing. "I don't have the right shoes for that."

"I've got snowshoes in the back," he said with a straight face, "but I don't think it'll come to that."

"Snowshoes?"

He laughed. "Marlene. I saw your shoes. They'll do just fine. I was out that way last week. The old fire road is clear, and the trail to the falls is pretty chewed up and dried out by now. Shouldn't give you any trouble. It's a short walk anyway."

The fire road was a longer walk—about two miles—but the day was glorious. Even though there hadn't been snow in days, thick blankets of it clung to the pine boughs, shrouding them in heavy silence. Once on the trail and in the trees, glimmering patches of ice and shards of sunlight made the land seem frozen in time.

They caught their first glimpse of the falls, and Marlene's breath caught. "It's magnificent."

She'd whispered, and the reverence and awe in her voice made his chest swell. *He'd* brought her here.

Her pace slowed as she took it all in. The water was flowing again after the long winter, but patches of ice still clung in shadows along the edges, an iridescent white blue. "It's like a fairy tale."

He took her hand. "Then come on, princess. Time for your feast."

The fresh air made their appetites boundless, and Marlene was devouring the countryside with her eyes as ravenously as she was eating her brunch. "I've never been here in the winter," she said finally.

He put down his fork, his interest only in her. The sunlight dappled through the trees onto her cheek, and her expression of awe made her seem twenty years younger. "It's my favorite time to come," he told her.

She took a bite of fruit salad and shook her head, staring at him as she chewed.

He raised a wary brow. "What is it?"

"Yet another surprise from you, Tom Sullivan."

"What do you mean?"

"You're not generally the biggest talker."

"I'm more a man of action," he said firmly.

She made a startled *oh* sound that gratified the man in him. He asked, "Is it the action part that surprises you?" He heard the huskiness in his voice and saw an answering flush on her cheeks. She seemed so uncertain, all he wanted was to wrap her in his arms and take care of things for a while.

"No," she said slowly. "It's that . . . just when I think I know you, you open your mouth and say the darndest thing."

"How's this, then?" He took her hand. "Marlene Kidd Jessup, once the weather warms up, I'm bringing you here on my bike."

She coughed as she swallowed. "Oh goodness. I could *never* ride a motorcycle."

"Why not?"

"Why not," she repeated, considering it. She opened her mouth, hesitated, then shut it again. "Well, I don't know why not, precisely."

"You can be your own woman, Marlene. Heed your own heart." He was thinking of her mother's last words, and he knew Marlene must've been thinking the same.

"I don't even know how I'd go about that," she said quietly.

"I could help you. We could figure it out together."

"Could we?" She sighed. "Sometimes I wonder if it's not over for me. I'm not sure how it happened or when, but I woke up one day and I was old. And now all I have in me is to mind my aunts, nag my grown children, and wait for the years to pass."

"Seems to me, your aunts do a damned fine job of minding themselves."

"Seems that way, doesn't it?" A grudging half smile spread across her face. "So there it is: my kids are done with me, my mother is gone, and not even my aunts need me, not really."

"Then you best get living for your own self." He wanted to touch her, to comfort her with his body. But there'd be time enough for that. He'd let her do some more grieving. Let her come to her own conclusions, get back on her own two feet. And then one day soon, he'd take Marlene, and they'd take off together.

"You're right." Her eyes brightened, clearer and more vivid than he'd ever seen them. "And you're on, Tom Sullivan. When the weather clears, we're getting on that bike of yours."

Thirty-six

"I am *so* sorry." Sorrow shepherded the couple out the door, doing her best to carry their suitcases with numbed fingers. Waking up to *screaming* tended to do that to a girl—dump adrenaline in her veins, leaving behind chilled and deadened limbs. "We'll refund your stay, of course."

"You bet you will," the woman said, looking as pinched as her buttoned-up collar.

Her husband angrily snatched back their roller bags, shoving them in the trunk of their car. "One doesn't expect to encounter *wildlife* on one's research trip."

Sorrow began to say, "We generally don't get bears" but the slamming car doors cut her off.

She stomped into the kitchen, muttering, "Newsflash, Professor. One *does* generally encounter *wildlife* in the damned *mountains*."

Her mom was standing at the sink where she'd been watching the proceedings from the window. "Good Lord in heaven, that woman has a scream to wake the dead."

Sorrow leaned against the counter and blew out a sigh. "I guess all their copious research didn't uncover how to handle a simple encounter with a black bear."

"Sit down, honey." Her mom led her to the table. "Your hands are shaking."

She shook them out. "I'm fine. I need to call Scott." Marlene's second oldest boy was their local park ranger. If there was a bear foraging through the trash cans of Sierra Falls, Scott Jessup needed to know about it.

She got up to pace, staring out the window as she called. She'd thought she'd fixed the stupid bear box, but it was swinging wide open again this morning, trash exploded everywhere—a veritable bear buffet. Someone must've tampered with it. There was no other explanation. Someone tampered with her bear box, knowing it'd summon every bear within sniffing radius. They were lucky there hadn't been a whole *gaggle* of them to surprise their lodgers.

"Scott's on his way," she told her mom as she put down the phone. "What do you call a group of bears? Like, there's a gaggle of geese, a murder of crows, and a *what* of bears?"

"Oh, honey. Relax." Her mom foisted a cup of tea on her. "Drink this."

Sorrow smelled it. Chamomile.

"*Drink it*, Sorrow."

"Dad's gonna flip out." As she took the mug, Sorrow cast another look out the window. "That couple couldn't get out of here fast enough. We could've used that money. And that mess . . ."

Her mom pointed to the table. "Sit yourself down for a second. The trash will wait. And your father will survive."

She thought about what Billy had said about Dad. Her father was from a very different generation, one that didn't have therapy or talk through their problems. No *Chicken Soup for the Soul* for men like Bear Bailey. There were a bunch of ways he could be more vital around the lodge—he just wasn't seeing them.

"You know," she said, sitting with her mom at the table, "Dad can't stand up for very long, but I bet if I dug out his old fishing stool and set him up with his tools, *he* could fix the bear box."

Her mom beamed. "That's a lovely idea. What a wonderful thing for you to think of."

Wow. Gauging from her mother's immediate and grateful reaction, Billy really had been on to something. "Yeah, no problem. I can think of other things, too." Her mind was already spinning with possibilities. "For sure."

"Sometimes," Mom began slowly, "I think your father has given up a little. Be patient with him. His bark is worse than his bite."

"I'll set him up just as soon as I clean up that mess. *Ugh*." She shuddered, just thinking about it. There were chicken carcasses, assorted bones, half-eaten bags of chips—it was a disaster. "Did you see it out there? Do we *really* have that many leftovers at the tavern? What a waste. I need to talk to Sully about that."

Mom stirred honey into her tea. "Where's your sister? Maybe she can help clean up."

"Laura? It's an *emergency*, Mom. Duh. For emergencies, Laura is nowhere in sight."

Mom reached across and put a gentle hand on hers. "Breathe, Sorrow. We're all in this together."

She blew on her tea, thinking how Billy had said some variation of the same thing. Maybe it *was* time for her to unclench, ask for help. "Okay, Mom. You're right again. I'll wait till Laura gets back to start the cleanup."

But a couple of hours passed, and when Sorrow felt like she could no longer wait, she called her sister's cell. "Where are you?"

"Running errands," Laura said, and then Sorrow heard her whisper "Thank you" to somebody.

"Where *are* you? I just needed you to pick up milk and some toilet paper. How long does that take?"

"I drove out to Silver City."

Sorrow froze in place. "For groceries? That's *my* car you took. If I'd known you were going to empty the tank I wouldn't have let you borrow it."

"My trunk's not big enough. I needed some other stuff, too."

"What other stuff?"

"Looks like I'm going to be staying in Sierra Falls for a while," Laura said, "but I totally don't have the clothes for it."

Sorrow thought her head might explode. "You went *clothes* shopping?"

"Yeah. Jeez, Sorrow. Chill out. You have things like hiking boots, why can't I?"

"Let me guess. You've decided to stay . . . because you saw an *opportunity to accessorize*?"

"What's that supposed to mean?" Laura's tone frosted over.

"It means you talk big about wanting to help around here, but I'll believe it when I see it."

"That is *so* unfair," Laura snapped. "I've come up with a million ideas, and you've shot down each one without even listening."

Sorrow didn't give her time to elaborate. She'd been harboring these feelings for years, and they burst to the surface, her voice coming louder, faster. "You took off for the city the moment you graduated, but it looks like you failed there, or at least I'm guessing you did because *you're* sure not talking, and by the way, saying you're taking a sabbatical, whatever the heck that is, tells me nothing, though apparently it involves you meandering home for a while where you can buy a new pair of hiking boots. You came home so that, *what*? So *we* can take care of you? You can't just drop in like nothing's happened, like it was no big deal that you disappeared for years. Like you're still the big sister in charge. It takes more than dressing like you live here to make you an active, contributing member of this household."

"I am totally an *active member*," Laura shouted, finally managing to cut in. "I'm practically pulling this festival together solo. But do I ever bug *you* about it? No. Did I have you help me do online publicity, or ask for money for the ads I placed in Bay Area newspapers? No. Did I—?"

Sorrow interrupted, her tone icy and measured, "I didn't ask you to do *any* of that stuff. All kinds of weird stuff is happening, the lodge is falling apart around us, and frankly, it shocks me that you haven't even noticed. So yeah, stupid *Buck Larsen* is the last thing on my mind at the moment."

"Ha!" Laura barked a sarcastic laugh. "Don't get all holier than thou on me. Our *lodge* is also the last thing on your mind."

"Meaning?" Sorrow grit her teeth, bracing for it.

"*Meaning*, you spend more time with that sheriff than you do in your own house."

Sorrow wanted to scream. "Are you so bored with your own life you came home to meddle in *mine*? Why are you even here?"

"To help the family."

"Oh, yeah, right." Sorrow rolled her eyes. "Because you're *sooo committed* to Mom and Dad. How do you expect me to believe you're here to stay when, way back, you fled town as fast as you could?"

"You want to be honest?" Laura asked in a flat voice.

Sorrow muttered, "This should be good."

"*I lost my job*, Sorrow. My *boyfriend* broke up with me. And I feel like a failure. I wake up every morning, and my life is empty. I've dated all the wrong guys, chased all the wrong things. I've got my stupid condo, and my stupid car, but there's nobody around who cares about me."

She had a moment of feeling stunned. But then she chalked it up to Laura just being dramatic. Again. Things were never that bad with her. *Boyfriend*—she'd probably only gone on two dates with the guy. Her sister was an expert with men, just like she was an expert with *everything*.

"Cry me a river, Laura. I am *so sorry* that driving your Beemer around San Francisco is giving you a crisis of the soul."

"I came home to get back to my roots, if you want to know. I need to figure my life out, and I need to be home to do it."

"I've heard your dramas before, Laura. But I've got my own dramas to worry about." She looked out the window and felt a pang of guilt. *Had* she been spending too much time with Billy? Was it so obvious she'd been paying less attention to business since he'd come into her life? "Look. I've got to go. Don't bring my car back with an empty tank." She hung up.

The new leaf Sorrow had meant to turn was turned back again. She angrily snapped on a pair of rubber gloves, grabbed a box of heavy-duty trash bags, and got to work.

Some time later, the door slammed, and Mom came out. "I thought you were waiting for Laura."

"Nope, dealing with it myself." Under her breath, she added, "Again."

Her mother wrapped her cardigan tight around her chest to ward off the cold. "Where is she?"

"I let her take my car to run a couple of errands." Sorrow used her forearm to wipe the hair from her brow. "But apparently she decided to disappear instead."

Would that *she* could disappear for a while. Would that *she* could go shopping—she'd get herself some sexy new lingerie. She'd shower off the stink of tavern scraps, put on bits of lacy silk under her jeans and sweater, and go to Billy's.

It had become her haven. *He* had become her haven.

She'd been going to his place a lot. She'd worried it was too much too soon, but he insisted he wanted her there as much as she wanted to be there. She worried they might get sick of each other, but instead of the magic wearing off, it intensified every time they were together. He came to the tavern almost every day for lunch, and every time she saw him, her heart skipped a beat. She was a goner . . . head over heels for the guy. And better yet, she had the impression he felt the same.

"Can Billy help?" her mom asked hopefully. Sorrow had been gazing into the distance, and the woman had clearly guessed what her daughter was thinking about.

She shook her head. "On duty."

"Can you call him?"

"Nah," she said, even though she knew she could. Billy would make time for her. But as much as she wanted to hear his voice, she made a point of not bugging him during his working hours.

They heard the phone ring, and her mom ran inside. A minute later, she was peeking out the door, her hand on the receiver. "It's Eddie Jessup," she said, sounding perplexed. "He says it's urgent."

"That's weird. Urgent?" Cold panic prickled up her arms— Eddie never called the house phone. Whenever she had construction issues, she contacted him or his brother Jack on her cell. She jogged inside, pulling off her gloves.

The call was quick. "Oh, God."

Her mother barely waited for her to hang up before she asked, "What is it?"

She met Mom's eyes. "There's been an accident."

Thirty-seven

Billy held Sorrow in the antiseptic waiting room. She leaned against his chest, and he willed strength into her. She'd need it.

"Thanks for coming to get me," she said.

He'd come over right away, speeding Sorrow to Silver City Memorial Hospital, with her parents following in Bear's truck.

He squeezed her closer. "What good is a police vehicle if I can't rush you to the hospital?" He kissed the top of her head. "We're lucky Eddie drove by when he did—he's got a work site near the Simmons place. He found Laura in the middle of nowhere, off Old Mine Road."

She nodded against his chest. "It's our shortcut. Old Mine hits a couple of back roads that eventually land you on 88 to Silver City."

"I know the route," he said. "It was a miracle Eddie saw the car. She'd rolled into a pretty deep ravine." The prospect chilled him. The road was thin and winding, shrouded by rock face on one side, sloping down to tall pines on the other. It was the foothills, and the drop off the eastern side got pretty steep in parts. "It's possible a few people drove by and didn't even see her."

Keri's accident flashed in his head. She'd been in Oakland, in the middle of the city. How many hundreds had driven by *her* accident site, rubbernecking for a glimpse?

He pulled Sorrow more tightly to him, holding on, thinking he might never let go. He knew firsthand just how lucky Laura had been. How lucky they all were that she'd survived.

The door to the waiting room swung open, and Sorrow looked expectantly at the nurse who'd appeared, but she was just calling in a patient. Her shoulders sagged. "I hate hospitals."

"Who doesn't?" He smoothed a hand over her hair. "Don't worry. You'll be able to see her the moment she's out of radiology."

"Do you think she broke her collarbone?" Sorrow asked, repeating the same question she'd asked not five minutes earlier. It was pure speculation, but he was happy to indulge in as much idle conjecture as she wanted, as long as it helped her pass the time.

And, for the moment, it was putting off the difficult news he needed to tell her.

"Whatever happens," he repeated for the umpteenth time, "she'll come through just fine. She'll be okay, and you two will be at each other's throats again before you know it."

At that, she burst into tears. Panic overwhelmed him, and he ran through his mind what he'd just told her, wondering what he'd said wrong. "What is it?"

"I said such horrible things to her the last time we talked. What if those had been the last things I ever said to her?" She scrubbed her face, and it was a relief to finally see her tears start to flow. The whole drive to Silver City, she'd been frozen, unable to cry, and he was beginning to fear it was shock.

"It's okay." He gently shushed her, rubbing her back and thumbing the tears from her cheeks. "I promise you, Laura will come through this just fine. She was lucky. It could've been a lot worse. I finally talked to the guys on the scene—your little GMC Jimmy is a pancake."

Dread and fear swept through him anew, a ball of ice in his belly. He'd lost one woman before; he'd not lose this one. He grabbed her chin, held her gaze, and told her in a grave voice, "I want you in a better truck. With air bags all over the place. And steel beams. One of those giant Ford Excursions. Or how about a tank? I need you safe, Sorrow."

She laughed, looking grateful for the flash of humor. A wave of emotion slammed into him, overtook him—this woman was so strong, so self-possessed. The words *I love you* burst into his heart, cut to the forefront of his mind. They were on his lips but still too frightening to say, so instead he hugged her more tightly, his voice cracking with intensity as he told her, "I feel so blessed it wasn't you behind the wheel." An accident had claimed his love once before, and he'd do everything in his power to prevent it from happening again.

Something shifted inside him, and the sheriff took over for the man. "We are lucky," he said vehemently, "and I intend on staying that way. There's something we need to talk about. Silver City PD told me some things you need to hear."

"What? Was it her fault?" She pulled away to look at him, looking afraid at what he was working up to. As well she should. "I still don't understand how the accident happened."

He took her hand, led her to a seat in the corner, away from the other people in the waiting area. He walked slowly, piecing together just the right words. "That's just it, Sorrow. It *wasn't* an accident. Your sister said a Hummer was on her tail. She slowed to let him pass, but as he was passing her, he slowed, too, and matched her pace."

"It sounds like something out of a movie," Sorrow said, looking confused. "You mean he was driving side by side with her?"

He nodded. "He, or she. Laura didn't get a look."

"So what'd the driver do?"

"A car approached from the other direction. When your sister saw it, she panicked. The Hummer managed to edge her over, off the road. That was how she lost control and flipped."

"Oh my God." She dropped her head into her hand. "Poor Laura. That should've been *me* doing errands."

"That's the point," he said, and the fierceness in his voice took them both aback. "Any other day it *would* have been you driving that car. Do you hear what I'm saying? Somebody did this on purpose. Somebody who thought *you* were driving."

Just the thought of it made him want to prowl the roads in his Sheriff's SUV until he found the son of a bitch.

Her eyes were wide, her skin blanched of its color. "This

has something to do with all the accidents at the lodge, doesn't it?"

In that moment, she looked so vulnerable, he wished he could scoop her up and hide her away, protecting her until this was all over.

He wrapped an arm around her shoulders, tugging her close and kissing her head. "I believe it absolutely does. Listen to me, Sorrow. As sheriff, this is my only priority right now." Technically, it was in Silver City's jurisdiction, but SCPD was being remarkably cooperative. And even if they weren't, nobody could stop him from investigating on his own.

She ran a finger under her eyes, drying the moisture and wiping away a smudge of makeup. She was visibly gathering herself, and it made him feel good to see it. She was a strong one, his Sorrow.

She inhaled and exhaled sharply. "Okay, tell me what I need to do."

"I need you to be strong. Lay low. Stay off the roads as much as you can. And, Sorrow . . ." He hesitated. She wasn't going to like what he had to say next. "I want you to stay away from Damien."

Her eyes popped wide. *"What?"*

Everyone loved Sorrow. Everyone wished her well. Everyone, with the possible exception of Damien.

"The accident happened near Simmons Timber land," he said, and let the statement hang for a moment. "Who might have a grudge against you?"

"Nobody! Especially not Damien or his family," she answered instantly. "They love me over there."

"Well, somebody doesn't. And they've upped the ante. First all those small incidents, then a fire, now a hit-and-run." He raised his brows. "Have you considered how you might've hurt your ex more than you realized?"

"Are you saying you think *Damien* tried to run me off the road?"

He gave her a noncommittal shrug. "Think about it."

"That's ridiculous," she said in a flat voice.

He wondered if her expression was confusion or anger. He'd

accept either. Sorrow could be mad at him all she wanted—he just wanted her safe. "It's fine for you to think that, but right now, for me, everyone is a suspect."

The intake nurse popped her head through the door. "Miss Bailey?"

Sorrow hopped to her feet. "Thank God."

"You're not mad at me?" he asked.

"Mad?" She looked down at him, her expression bewildered and rattled. "Of course I'm not mad. It doesn't mean I believe Damien had anything to do with this. But I trust you."

"I'll find out the truth."

"I know you will." She gave him a sad smile. She looked so tired, and it made his heart ache.

He stood up, cupped her cheek. "Don't think about this now. I'm on it. And I promise you, I *will* find out who did it. I won't stop until I see them behind bars."

She looked hesitant to leave him.

"You go to your sister," he told her.

"Do you want to come with me?" she asked in a small voice. "I could ask if it's allowed."

He kissed her forehead. "Family only." Though *he'd* be family soon, if he had anything to do with it.

For now, he had work to do. His mind was already two steps ahead, eager to track down the bastard who did this—and it all started at Simmons Timber.

But he wouldn't stress Sorrow by speculating about things she didn't need to hear, so he fudged the truth. "I need to get back anyway." He put his hands on her shoulders, fighting the urge to pull her in for another embrace. "Are you going to be okay here?"

She smiled weakly. "I'll get a ride with Mom and Dad."

He cupped her cheek. "I *hate* to leave you."

She inhaled deeply, and he read raw affection in her eyes. "You just go find the bad guy."

Thirty-eight

⁂

Sorrow stood in the doorway, watching her beautiful, vital, energetic, pain-in-the-ass sister, lying broken and sleeping on a hospital bed. The sight dredged powerful feelings to the surface.

Laura's left arm was in a sling, her shoulder was bound, and an IV tube was plugged into the other arm. Her face was bruised, and the sight of it shot a spear of anguish through Sorrow's heart. For all her bluster, Laura was so fragile. What if she hadn't survived? What if Sorrow had never gotten the opportunity to take back all those ugly things she'd said the last time they'd spoken?

Laura's eyes fluttered open, and the two sisters stared silently at each other.

"Hey, sleepy," Sorrow said finally.

"Sorry about your car." Laura's voice was small and cracking, and she coughed, clearing her dry throat.

Sorrow was beside her in an instant, easing onto the bed, pouring some water from a pitcher at her bedside. "Forget the car." She stroked the hair from her sister's head. "Hey, you did me a favor. It's a miracle the thing still ran."

"Remember when Dad got it?" Laura asked, and the girls laughed at the memory.

"Totally. He used to wax it every weekend, right before Sunday night football."

Laura rested her head back, a wistful smile on her face.

"There were times," Sorrow said, "when I wondered who he loved more, that car or us kids. I was shocked he handed it down to me. I thought for sure he was going to save it for BJ."

Laura's response was instant. "Nah. Of course it went to you." She looked away, her eyes suddenly glimmering. She gave a shuddering sigh, and Sorrow could tell her sister was trying to hold back the tears. "I always screw things up."

"Are you kidding?" Sorrow took her sister's good hand in hers and patted it. Laura was the favorite, the golden girl—the one who *never* screwed up. "That's just the painkillers talking. You know you're the family princess."

Laura pulled her hand away. "What are you talking about? You're Dad's favorite, you always have been."

Sorrow felt her jaw drop open, but darned if she could think of anything to say to *that*.

"Don't give me that look," Laura said. "Dad would never have let *me* take over the lodge."

Sorrow regained her voice. "As if you'd ever want to."

"Oh, please." Laura scooted herself up on the bed, looking ready to rant. "I'd have loved to work more around the place. But Dad *always* second-guesses me. Why do you think I took off? It's not easy being the oldest."

The room was silent but for the general muted buzz and whirr of the machines. Sorrow had spent years feeling abandoned by her sister. But what if Laura hadn't run from the family? What if she'd felt she had no choice but to leave, driven to prove herself?

"You really want to stay?" Sorrow asked finally. "Like, to *live* in Sierra Falls again?" She still didn't believe it.

"It's what I just said, isn't it?" Laura sighed.

"Seriously, Laura. *Permanently* permanently? As in, you're not going to get bored and take off again?"

"Permanently," Laura said. "I swear. I *pinky* swear it."

Sorrow saw her sister in a new light. "You're being serious." *Laura staying.* She sat with the notion a moment, remembering what Billy had told her. Why *not* let her sister help more? Sorrow had been too proud to see it, but finally the light clicked on.

Then Sorrow laughed outright, thinking of another side benefit. Sharing lodge duties also meant sharing the blame when things went wrong. "You know, actually, we *totally* need you. *Please* stay." She gripped Laura's hand. "You *must* stay. I don't know what my problem has been anyway. You'd be awesome—you have more business experience than the whole town put together."

Laura looked away, fiddling with her IV tubes. "Dad would never have it."

"Shut up!" She gave her sister a gentle nudge on her good arm. "Mom and Dad would be *thrilled* to have you around again."

"Okay," Laura admitted, laughing at Sorrow's vehemence. "You're right. I'm not being fair. But sometimes I think Dad respects me more in concept. Like, he can *think* about his eldest daughter out there, driving her fancy car, being Urban Business Barbie, but he doesn't need to be around to witness all the screwups." She blinked a few times, tears shimmering in her eyes. "And believe me, they are many."

"Well, forget that," Sorrow said. "You'll be the Sierra Falls *Rural* Business Barbie. And we'll screw up *together*." She beamed at her sister. "Oh my God, Laura. You don't understand. I'd give anything to spend less time with accounting ledgers, and plumbers, and snow shovels."

"I'd be happy to share it with you." Laura gave her a bland look. "I've been trying to tell you that since I got home."

"Girl, you want responsibilities, I've got them coming out of my ears."

Laura's answering laugh turned into a cough, and Sorrow was quick to bring the cup of water to her mouth.

"We just need to get you better." Sorrow watched her sister's trembling hand reach for the cup and the way her throat moved slowly and convulsively. "Thank God Eddie came along when he did. I'm going to give the guy a big kiss when I see him next."

Laura raised a brow. "Won't the sheriff be jealous?"

"Okay, *you* can give him a big kiss." Sorrow narrowed her

eyes on her sister. That she was staying made it a whole other ball game. "Maybe you should, Laura."

"Should what?"

"Go for Eddie. I've seen the looks between you two."

"Eddie?" Laura scowled, then grimaced from the pain of it. "If you saw me give Eddie Jessup any *look*, it was clearly either scorn or distaste."

"But he's so cute."

"I've learned my lesson—I'm staying away from pretty boys. If I date anybody, it'll be some nice businessman."

"What's that supposed to mean?" Sorrow tamped down a surge of anger. If Laura was going to be staying in Sierra Falls, she was going to need a massive attitude adjustment. "Not only have Eddie and his brother built a great business, but he's outside all day, working with his hands and body. I don't know, Laura, that sure seems pretty sexy to me."

"I'd never be interested in a man who uses tools."

Sorrow snorted with laughter. "You just lobbed me a softball."

Laura rolled her eyes. "Okay, Miss Dirty Mind, if we're being specific, I'd never be interested in a man who *works as a contractor*."

"So then why are you blushing?"

"I am *not* blushing," Laura snapped. "I haven't blushed since seventh grade."

"Maybe that's part of your problem." It came to Sorrow in a flash, exactly how best a girl's attitude got adjusted. "Maybe a good mountain man who makes you blush is just what you need. Give up on those city dorks in khakis whose idea of foreplay is talking about mutual funds."

Laura guffawed. "Who put a nickel in you? Jeez, the girl gets lucky with the town sheriff and all of a sudden she's Dr. Phil." Her sister's tone was joking, but Sorrow saw how she did consider it for a moment. But then Laura shuddered. "He drives a vehicle best suited for monster truck competitions. That giant red pickup. Can't go there."

"What's wrong with Eddie's pickup?"

"It's a kind of tacky, isn't it? Like he's overcompensating."

"You know what they say about the size of a man's truck," a deep voice said from the doorway.

Laura's cheeks flushed pink.

Sorrow grinned to see a couple of Jessup brothers. "Eddie, Mark, hi!" Under her breath, she sang, "Blushh-innng."

"We found the doctor," Eddie said, shoving his brother into the room. "But I don't know if you can trust him. I hear he sucks."

Mark shouldered him back, and the sight of a white-coated doctor roughhousing was comical. "You're just jealous I got all the brains."

Eddie flinched his shoulder away. "Whatever, dude. Mom likes me better." He got a wicked look in his eye and walked right up to Laura's bedside, putting a finger under her chin. "Plus I have the biggest truck. Isn't that right, sugar?" He winked.

Sorrow snickered to see the pink in Laura's cheeks flame positively crimson.

"Jessups," Laura said in a strangled voice. "They're all over the place."

"Can't get away from us." Eddie sat on the edge of her bed, and she inched away.

Mark snagged the chart that hung from the foot of her bed and flipped through. "Haven't seen you in a while, Laura."

"Not since you graduated high school," she said. "I was in eighth grade then. So, yeah. Long time."

"Wish the circumstances were better than a fractured clavicle."

Sorrow read over his shoulder. "You and me both, Dr. Mark."

"We need to figure out who did this," Eddie said in a steely voice, his shift in tone marked.

Sorrow nodded somberly. "Billy is investigating."

Mark raised a brow. "*Billy*, is it?"

It was Sorrow's turn to blush. "The sheriff and I have become friendly." She continued in her best business-as-usual voice, "He believes too much has happened around the lodge. And now, with the accident . . . it's just too suspicious."

Eddie pinned Laura with a look. "Good thing Miss

Fancy-pants here will be running off soon. Staying safe. Right on schedule."

Her sister resembled something like a deer in headlights, so Sorrow spoke for her. "Laura's sticking around this time."

"Oh, is she now?" Eddie's eyes glinted. "Sounds like something *I* need to investigate."

Thirty-nine

Billy needed to question Damien, and if he couldn't get the guy into an interrogation room, he'd do one better. A bar. The Thirsty Bear Tavern, to be exact. He'd considered meeting at a neutral spot like Chances across town, but when taking a man's measure, it was best to poke, prod, and provoke, targeting his most sensitive spots, getting under his skin. Which meant meeting at the tavern—ground zero for Damien's relationship with the Bailey family.

"Thanks for meeting me," he said when Damien came in. He forced an easy smile. The town of Sierra Falls seemed to love the guy, but from the start, he'd struck Billy as arrogant, slick, and too young to know better.

"Yeah. You bet." Damien pulled off his fleece jacket, his movements stiff. "Though why do I get the sense that this isn't a friendly visit?"

Because we're not friends? But instead of speaking his mind, Billy just laughed a carefree, rolling laugh. "Shall we get some drinks?"

Damien's posture loosened a bit, and with a nod, he headed toward an open stool at the bar.

But Billy headed him off, anxious for a little privacy. "How about a booth instead? That way we can kick back."

Damien's gaze skittered to the booth and back. "Whatever you say, Sheriff. How about I snag us a couple of beers first?" He laughed nervously. "I hope by drinks you didn't mean diet sodas."

The Simmons boy had always struck Billy as an entitled jackass, and nothing got a jackass's jaw flapping like a sit-down with his pal, Johnny Walker. He gave Damien a broad smile. "Why mess around? I'm off duty. How about a couple of shots with a beer back? My treat." He caught the bartender's eye. "My tab, Helen."

By the time Damien returned with the drinks, his features had hardened, his nerves under wraps. Apparently the guy knew the best defense was a good offense. He settled into the booth, leaning forward and sliding Billy's shot and beer across the table. "Cut the shit, Sheriff. Why am I here? Don't tell me it's because you need a new drinking buddy."

Billy raised his glass. "Points for the brass balls, Simmons." He tossed back his shot. "You're right. I'm not looking for a friend."

Damien's lip twitched, waiting for it.

He continued, "Just want to make sure it's all cool, this situation with me and Sorrow."

Damien's eyes narrowed to tiny slits. He threw back his own shot, then said, "Yeah, sure. It's cool."

"Good," he said, remaining as emotionless as possible. "Sorrow has enough on her mind without worrying about any bad blood. You'll have heard about the accident, I guess."

The guy's face was like stone. His head moved in the slightest of nods. "Tough break."

Simmons was going to be harder to crack than he'd anticipated. Time to bring out the big guns. "Hey, Helen," Billy called. "Why don't you just bring over the bottle?"

Damien raised his brows, like he was expecting a trick.

"Don't sweat it," Billy said easily. "My buddy Scott is coming by later. He'll drive us home."

"You're the sheriff," Damien said, his voice flat. He stared at his beer bottle, peeling and fraying the label. "So, she okay? Laura, I mean?"

Helen brought over the bottle of Scotch and her eyes lingered overlong on Damien. "I hear you're single now."

He didn't miss a beat before responding, "And I hear you're still married." As she walked away, Simmons pulled the bottle closer, tipping a solid slug into his shot glass. "Women," he grumbled.

Watching the amber liquid glug into the glass, Billy said, "That's the way," all the while thinking, *that's right, kid, time to get nice and loose.* He slid his own glass over for a pour. "I don't know how you and Sorrow left it," he said slowly. "She's no gossip, and what happened between you two is none of my business anyhow. But, as far as I can tell, there's no reason two men can't have a friendly drink."

Damien met his eyes and held them silently as he tipped the entire glass down his throat. "Or five."

Billy laughed. "Whoa, cowboy." Either the guy was more upset about the breakup than Sorrow knew, or he had something heavy on his mind. Guilt, maybe.

As sheriff, he knew that, if he wanted cred with the guy, he'd need to match him drink for drink, and so tipped his own shot back then slammed his glass down, exhaling hard. "Don't think you can drink an old man under the table."

Simmons actually cocked a half smile at that. *Progress.* "I bet I can, *old man.*" He stared in challenge. "Speaking of old, don't you think you're maybe a little *too* old for our Bailey?"

Billy barked out a laugh. "I'm not dead yet."

Damien was quick to wave the comment away with a brittle laugh. "Okay, you're right. Foul ball." He sighed, and the twenty-something guy suddenly sounded much older. "Hell, I don't know anymore." He poured himself another and raised it in a toast. "It pains me, Sheriff"—he clutched playfully at his heart, but there was truth in the jest—"*pains* me to say it." He grew oddly serious. "But I say this for *her* sake. I've known Bailey all my life. She's good people, and any friend of hers is a friend of mine."

That was unexpected. He ran it through his head, searching for some hidden edge or agenda, but it rang true. In his mind, he upgraded the kid from evil to just plain jerk. He clinked his glass with Damien's and tossed it back. They'd never be best buds, but Billy knew he had to keep his mind open to possibilities. Law enforcement's first lesson was that sometimes things weren't at all what they seemed.

Still, he reminded himself that it wouldn't do any good to

trust too easily. Which meant it was time to bring it back to the matter at hand. He was nonchalant, not even looking at Damien as he said, "So I hear the accident happened close to Simmons land. Hope that doesn't bring any bad publicity."

"Dad told me once, no publicity is bad publicity."

"Your father must know what he's talking about. He's successful enough."

"Truer words."

"You're lucky," Billy added, "having such an experienced man as a mentor."

"Who, Dad?"

"Do you work closely with him? I imagine he treats you like his protégé. You'll be the one to inherit Simmons Timber, after all."

Damien guzzled his beer, downing the second half of the bottle in one drink. "Sometimes I think Dad just wants me to be a suit."

Billy poured them each another, smaller drink, and then kept the bottle. The kid was pounding them too hard for his tastes. "A suit?" he repeated, encouraging Damien to say more.

"Yeah. A good old boy in a suit. He says it's the lynchpin of a business like ours. Hunting trips with the boys, that sort of thing. I have ideas, though." He snatched the bottle back, helping himself. "I try to be a good guy, a responsible guy."

"Responsible how?" *Like by running Laura Bailey off the road?*

Damien caught and held his gaze. "Newsflash, Sheriff: logging isn't exactly the most PC thing these days. I drive into the city and mention I'm in timber? Girls can't run away fast enough." He threw back his drink, and damn, the kid could hold his liquor—Billy would need to watch himself. But although the guy might not be slurring, the words *were* flowing more freely. He rambled on, "These days, all women wanna talk about is *composting*. Vegetarian food. Stuff like that. You'd think I was clubbing baby seals out there. Like cutting down trees is the devil's work."

Billy saw the kid in a new light. He was vulnerable, maybe even lonely. Sorrow probably *had* hurt him more than she'd realized. It was easy enough to imagine. If Sorrow were to leave *him*, he'd be shattered.

He'd need to tread carefully. "Seems to me, Damien, the ladies would love things like, well, let's be honest, like that car you drive."

"Yeah," Simmons said flatly. He caught Helen's eye and silently raised his empty bottle, requesting another beer. "Girls go for the money."

The kid sounded more jaded than the young, rich scion of a successful business should. He clearly didn't want the kind of girls who chased money. So then what *was* Damien's story? Seemed like there might be more to him than Billy had suspected. But why should that discovery surprise him? He had to give Sorrow a little credit—she wouldn't go out with a total numbskull.

When Billy spoke again, it was more as a fellow guy than as sheriff. "Have you tried to talk to your dad? I don't know much about running a big company, but it seems to me that change happens from within. Hell, I think sometimes environmental initiatives can be lucrative. Good press and all."

"I tried, man. I went to the Simmons board once, all I did was say the word *sustainability*, and they laughed me out of the boardroom. Like I was some kind of idiot. I know people need paper. Paper's not going anywhere . . . yet. I *know* that. I get it—I'm not stupid. But Dad, all he wants is to build, build, build." Damien laughed evilly, kicking back and peering out the window. "I think it drives him fucking *nuts* that Bear's sitting on so much prime land. I love it."

Billy froze. The Baileys were struggling—all this time, he'd just assumed that the only things they had were the tavern and the roof over their heads. "Are you saying that Bear owns land? And that it *borders* Simmons Timber?"

Damien laughed again, but this time he just sounded weary. "Yessir, Sheriff. Old Dabney Simmons calls it green gold."

Forty

❧

The lunch crowd was thinning, and Sorrow heard the tavern door whoosh open and shut as she stood at the bar, refilling the salt shakers. She glanced over her shoulder and held her breath. It was Damien, and he was making a beeline straight for her.

He came up beside her to lean against the bar. "I have a proposition for you."

"Hello to you, too." Her heart went to her throat. Billy and her ex had met for a couple of drinks the other night, and although Billy didn't come out of it as the biggest Damien fan, he no longer thought the guy capable of doing harm to her sister. According to his report, things were "all cool" among them. So then why this visit?

"Don't give me that look."

"I'm not doing a look," she said.

"Sure you are. You're doing your deer in the headlights thing." He laughed, surely seeing how flustered she was. "Relax, Bailey. I know you're off the market. I had a little pow-wow with your new boyfriend. Didn't he tell you?"

She nodded warily. "He told me."

"So then you know it's all good." He chucked her chin. "Your sheriff's not that bad even. For a relic." He gave her a pointed look that drew a smile from her. "Yeah, that's the Bailey I know. Here," he said, handing her a box. "I even brought you a peace offering."

She took it—it was one of those decorative tins—and she hefted it suspiciously in her hands. "What's in it?"

"Cookies. *Fancy* cookies. You should look for yourself. And before you thank me, don't. My parents got them for you."

She pried open the box. It was filled with chocolate-dipped madeleines.

He said, "Because of Laura's accident."

"Oh, wow . . ." She was speechless, touched by the gesture. To her it meant so much more than just them wishing her family well during this tough time. It meant that all was forgiven. She'd broken up with their only son, but they hadn't taken it personally themselves.

"I think they're from France," he said. "Your fancy-pants sister should like that."

She laughed. "They don't know Laura very well if they sent her cookies." But then she gave an automatic tug to the leg of her jeans—all the cooking she was doing for Billy was beginning to take its toll. "Or is it so obvious how much *I* like cookies?"

"No, goof. It's so obvious you deserve a treat." Seeing her suspiciously narrowed eyes, he quickly added, "I'm saying that as a *friend*. You're pretty as ever, but I told you, Billy and I had a meeting of the minds. We're all good."

"What's with you men? Everything is *'It's all good. It's cool.'*"

He gave her a broad smile. "That's because it is, Bailey."

She closed the tin. "So *this* is your peace offering? Some cookies that your mom picked out?"

"*No*," Damien said defensively. "Well, okay, partly. The cookies are gravy. I'm really here because I need to show you something."

"What?" she demanded, instantly on her guard.

"You have to come with me to see it."

She and Billy had agreed—Damien wasn't capable of such calculated evil as a hit-and-run designed to hurt her. But still, something niggled in the back of her mind. "Can't you just tell me? Why the mystery?"

Damien's eyes went cold. "Don't look at me like that, Sorrow. God, you make me feel like a criminal. I found something you'll think is cool. I wanted to surprise you with it. Sort of like one last hurrah for the two of us." At her skeptical glare, he added, "A *platonic* hurrah. Come on. Be a sport. I'll have you back in an hour."

Her misgivings transformed into pity. She felt ridiculous being suspicious of Damien—she'd known him all her life. But she did have an honest excuse. "I'm busy," she told him.

"C'mon, Bailey. The dinner crowd won't be here for hours. And Sully's back there, right? He can hold down the fort in the meantime."

She checked the clock on the wall—made from a slab of wood, it'd hung there for as long as she could remember. "I haven't even eaten lunch yet."

"Let's pack a couple of sandwiches." He grabbed the tin. "We can bring these, too. *Come on*," he pleaded again, making her smile. "I've got no meetings till three. Just sixty minutes, for an old friend. *Closure*, isn't that what you women are always clamoring on about?"

She barked out a laugh at that. It was the mischievous Damien she'd always known, and that was what decided it. It *would* be nice to have a little closure. She'd love to remain his friend, and an impromptu picnic seemed like just the right first step in that direction.

She whipped together a few sandwiches, grabbed a couple of apples, refilled her water bottle, and they were on their way. Some fresh air would do her good anyhow. She hadn't been out since Laura's accident, and spring was in full force, teasing her from outside the window. She was dying for a little blue sky. And, with him driving, she'd be safe. Whoever this mysterious bad guy was would assume she was at the lodge.

Her doubts burst back to the surface the farther they got from civilization. He was driving them down an old fire road, well off Irish Camp Road and deep into Simmons Timber land. "Where are you taking me?"

"I told you. I have something to show you."

She had to trust that Damien wouldn't hurt her. She *knew*

him. But still, she couldn't help but joke uneasily. "You're kind of freaking me out here."

He sighed heavily, pulling onto a dirt road, and stopped almost immediately, his sports car unable to go any farther. Hurt flickered in his eyes—he'd heard her unease. "You used to trust me, remember? What happened between us, Sorrow?"

She sat stiffly, not unbuckling. "Is that why you brought me here? To talk about our relationship? You need to bring me back home, right now."

He leaned back against the headrest, looking tired. "Give me just fifteen minutes. Then I'll take you back."

"First, you have to answer something for me." When Billy mentioned his initial reservations about Damien, she'd scoffed. But now, sitting in the middle of nowhere, everything Damien had ever said, every crisis at the lodge, every moment he'd happened to be right there to swoop in and save the day—it all came to her in a rush. There was just one too many coincidences. "Have you been sabotaging us?"

His face hardened into stunned disbelief. "What?"

She almost chickened out, but the words had been said. They were out there, hanging, with no going back now. She might as well let it all out.

"There have been so many freak accidents at the lodge," she said carefully. "And yet *you* always seem to be right there to help."

He stared in stunned silence. She'd expected the truth to flash in his eyes, but all she read was confusion, comprehension, and a surprising despair.

Finally, he spoke, his voice low and achingly heartfelt. "Jesus, Sorrow. I know I can be a jerk, but I would never sabotage you. *Never.*"

She watched him, plumbing those eyes for the truth. "How can I be sure?"

"How could you even think that? I've been trying to *help.* You've been so in over your head." He slammed his hands on the steering wheel. "Why would I *ever* hurt you? I care about you."

She racked her mind for possible reasons. "Maybe you're jealous."

"Of Billy? Yeah, sure, I admit, at first my gut twisted every time I saw his damned cruiser parked in your lot. I mean, what's the appeal? He's older, he doesn't try worth a damn—and yet every woman in town swoons for the guy."

"Seems to me, you're the one they're swooning for."

"I don't know. Maybe. It doesn't matter." He stared sightlessly out the front window, his voice gone soft. "You always talk about how you feel stuck, Sorrow. Abandoned in Sierra Falls by your siblings. But think how I feel." He met her eyes, and his were dark with anguish. "I'd give my left nut for a sibling. You think *you're* stuck, but I'm the one trapped with a golden boy rep and an empire whether I want it or not. What good am I, when my own girlfriend doesn't want me, and I'm the dude who supposedly has it all?"

Her eyes went wide. "Are you *kidding*? Damien, you're like . . . the *prince* of Sierra Falls. *You* were the star quarterback. *You're* the one who's going to inherit half the town."

"You still broke up with me."

"It wasn't because of you, though. You're amazing. It's just that I connected with Billy."

He gave a bitter laugh. "The old *'it's not you, it's me'* talk. But the thing is, Sorrow, it *was* me." He shook his head. "You don't get it. Billy Preston is the kind of man I could *never* be. Simple, loved."

"You're loved!"

"Sure thing, Sorrow." Damien's expression shuttered. "Forget all that. It's not what I came here for, whatever you might think. Look, I'm glad you found Billy. If *you* get off on the guy, I'm thrilled for you. If you're happy, I'm happy."

"Then what do you want?" she asked quietly.

"All I want, all I ever wanted, was to look out for you."

"Look out for me?" Ice rushed into her veins. "From what?" She looked out the window—they were surrounded by towering pines, and not another soul for miles. "You have me a little freaked out here."

He practically tore off his seat belt and pinned her with a look. "I keep being misunderstood, and I need to make it right."

Forty-one

≈

Damien got out and angrily flung open her door. He offered his hand, his arm extended rigidly. "Come with me. I swear I'll keep you safe." Something broke in his expression when she didn't take his hand right away. "I wanted this to be fun, and you're wigging out on me." His arm dropped, and he sighed, a tired, sad sound. "Hell, Sorrow, until that sheriff started showing his face around, I was the *only one* who gave a shit about whether or not you kept your head above water."

She stared up at him and saw emotions she'd never seen on Damien's face before—earnestness, anxiety, and even pain. It was in such contrast to the easy confidence she was used to. This was the Damien she'd suspected had been there all along.

She made her decision. Reaching up, Sorrow took his hand. "Fifteen minutes."

They hiked in silence. The trail was overgrown, and though they probably only went about a half mile, it was slow going.

She stopped to catch her breath. "So this is Simmons land?"

He leaned against a tree, pulling a water bottle from his pack, offering it to her first. "You don't know where we are, do you?"

She chugged, surprisingly thirsty, then looked around. Pine trees as far as the eye could see. "How could I?"

He pointed to the right. "See that over there?"

"See what?"

"That's *your* land."

"*My* land?"

"Bear's land, at least. There's a strip of it, extending south of the lodge. It's not enough to do much of anything with but sit on. Which is what the Baileys have been doing since, well, probably since the days of your Sorrow Crabtree." He took back his water and drank before returning it to his pack.

She laughed—there was no other response to such unexpected news. "Then why aren't we rich? Because it sure seems like a lot of land to me."

"You heard the phrase *land rich and cash poor*?" At her nod, he said, "Welcome to my world."

He walked on, and she followed. "What do you mean, *your* world?"

"Timber isn't exactly the thing to make your fortune in the twenty-first century. My family is *nothing* but land rich and cash poor."

He ducked through a thick patch of greenery, holding aside branches so she could follow. It looked like he was headed straight up.

She stared, aghast. "Are you sure this is safe?"

"I got you." He held a hand out. "I promise, you'll love it."

She practically had to crawl up, clutching his hand and clawing at roots to clamber up behind him. Finally, she made it to the top, and he held her shoulders to steady her.

"Careful." He led her along a narrow ledge. "I need you in one piece, so you can see"—he put his hands on her shoulders, angling her—"this."

She gasped. The path led to a black hole in the wall of the hill. Rotted timber posts at the entrance told her it was more than just a natural cave. "What's *that*?"

"An old gold mine," he said, sounding as giddy as a kid. "I'll show you."

She grabbed his shirt to stop him. "Is it safe?"

"Sure." He tugged her forward. "I've been here a bunch of times now."

As they got closer, she caught a glimpse inside, taking in

the deep hallway and timber scaffolding. "Wow, it really *is* a mine." The Sierra Nevada foothills were gold country—there must've been half a dozen gold rush tourist spots in El Dorado County alone—but she'd never been inside an actual mine. "Holy cow. And this is on *our* land?"

"Yup," he called from inside. "All yours. Too bad it's not worth a dime."

"I'll say." She followed him in, stopping to let her eyes adjust. It was dark, but not pitch-black. She sniffed, picking up a distant smell, pungent, like urine. "What is that? Is there, like, an army of homeless prospectors still down there?"

He laughed. "It's okay. Just bats. They won't hurt you."

She scowled, not buying it. "I guess."

He came back, guiding her shoulders. "I promise. It's totally safe. I've been hiking here since I found it."

Curiosity got the better of her, and she felt comfortable enough to look around. The place was in remarkably pristine condition, with regular wooden posts and tracks for a rail cart, just like in the movies. "How come not everyone knows about this?"

"I did some research down at Town Hall. The mine was a failure."

"*You* did research?"

"Yes, Bail. *I* did research." He walked in farther, leaning against a railing. "The Comstock Lode hit, and folks forgot about this place."

She went to stand next to him, then yelped and hopped back a step. He was standing at the edge of a narrow shaft. She registered the rusted pulley overhead, rotting ropes dangling from it like cobwebs. A ladder led one level down, dark enough that the floor below could easily have been just an illusion. "Creepy."

"I thought you'd like it." He picked up a rock and tossed it down. It landed on a platform just one story down, but the sound echoed and echoed.

"You're such a guy," she accused. "Don't do anything crazy, okay?"

"It's pretty safe, don't worry."

"*Pretty* safe?" She shivered, backing up another step. "I'll take your word for it. You're right, though. It is cool. How'd you even find it?"

"I didn't. Coop did."

"Your *dog* found it?"

"We were hunting. He scented a fox and wouldn't let it go. He followed her to a den just outside. There was a whole litter of kits—I swear there were a dozen of the things."

"Please tell me Cooper didn't eat them."

"Never fear. You know Coop wouldn't hurt a fly." Damien laughed. "It's why he's such a sucky hunting dog."

A quiet hissing sounded outside, and she went back to the entrance, glancing out to see a drizzle starting to fall. Nothing serious—just a gentle Sierra misting—but enough that she found herself a spot between rails and slid to the ground, leaning against the side of the tunnel.

He tossed down his backpack and joined her. "Hungry?"

"Starved." A light breeze billowed in, bringing the scent of damp pine needles. It was serene—and eerie, but in a pleasant way. She tucked into a turkey and Havarti sandwich and asked between bites, "So you really just wanted to show me this place?"

Damien gave his sandwich a critical once-over and opted for an apple instead. He took a huge bite, smiling as he chewed. "Maybe I wanted one more shot with you."

"Damien!" She nudged his foot.

He gave an exaggeratedly innocent shrug. "So. You sure it's over?"

"Yes, I'm sure." She narrowed her eyes at him "Hey, you said your intentions were innocent, bringing me here. You *lied*."

"I didn't lie," he said, smiling to match her glare. "I *didn't*."

She glared harder.

"Okay, okay," he admitted. "Maybe a little white lie. Can't blame a guy for trying."

She tried to be mad, but couldn't. It was just too classically Damien. Oddly, she felt a stab of affection for him because of it. Affection and, at the same time, total resolve. Damien was the same smooth-talking lady-killer he'd been in high school. But it wasn't high school anymore, and sitting there with him, she knew more than ever how she'd found her perfect man in

Billy. The revelation made her as comfortable with Damien as she'd ever been. "You just want to keep dating now that you know I'm a gold mine *heiress*," she said, ribbing him.

"Dream on," he said, ribbing right back. But then he grew thoughtful. "You really like that sheriff, huh?"

She finished the first half of her sandwich and dusted off her hands to reach for the second. "Yup. I really like that sheriff."

"He's a lucky man." He nibbled around the apple core, getting every last bit. The poor guy still looked famished.

The compliment made her feel shy, so she ignored it and focused on his choice of lunch instead. "I tell you, between you and my sister . . ." She nodded to his uneaten sandwich. "A carb and some mayo once in a while isn't going to kill you."

"A guy's gotta stay ripped." Damien smiled the confident old smile she knew. He cocked an eyebrow. "Especially now that I'm single."

"Hey, this was supposed to be a *hurrah*. I'd think, just this once, you could feed yourself something other than beef, berries, or protein shakes."

He laughed, pulling the cookie tin close. "Then screw the sandwich. If I'm eating processed, it's going to be sugar."

"Alert the media," she said gleefully, watching him shove an entire cookie into his mouth. "Damien Simmons, eating carbs. Eating *sugar*! Apocalypse really is nigh."

He laughed, too, and gobbled down a second cookie for good measure. "You should try one," he said, speaking over a mouthful.

"Very appetizing," she said sarcastically. "Don't worry, I will. If you can save me some."

Damien actually grabbed a third cookie, breaking off the chocolate end and popping it down. "That sheriff better take care of you. I worry about you in that lodge."

She stilled, her sandwich held in midair, studying him. "Why?"

"The place is a . . ."

"A *dump*? Is that what you were going to say?"

"No, of course not. It's halfway there, though. Why do you think I'm always coming by?"

The realization hit her with a sharp pang. She hadn't loved

Damien, but for a little while she'd enjoyed his company. Had felt wanted by him. "I'd hoped it was because you were my boyfriend."

"I *was*, Sorrow." He caught her gaze and held it, speaking earnestly. "I really do care about you. A lot. Say the word, and I'm back on board, baby. Your sheriff is lucky. Any man would be *thrilled* to call himself yours. But, no offense, where the lodge is concerned, you seem to be flying solo. You can't run the place alone. It's like a demolition zone. You need someone to look out for you."

The unexpected sentiment touched her, and for an instant, her eyes burned with unshed tears. Little did he know how much she needed *actual* protection. She was sure Billy would disagree, but she found herself confiding. "Billy thinks everything that's been happening . . . he doesn't think those are accidents."

He froze, his mouth gaping. "What do you mean, *not accidents*?"

"Think about it." She dropped her head in her hands, rattling it all off. "The tree branch, bear box, black ice . . . stuff like that can happen, sure. But a fire in the kitchen? That wasn't my fault. Sully and I keep a spotless oven, and you know it. And then there was Laura's hit-and-run. When she was driving *my* car." When she looked back up at him, he was wearing a peculiar expression. "What?"

"Just . . ." His brow was furrowed hard. "Who would want to hurt you?"

"I don't know." She stood abruptly and put a hand to her belly. It churned to think how someone was out there right now, waiting to do her harm.

"Are you sick?" he asked, sounding focused.

"No, I just . . ." She froze, watching his face. He had such a strange look on his face—at first, she'd thought it was just his shock, but saw now how he was breathing through his mouth. "Are *you* sick?"

"I feel kinda strange all of a sudden. I thought maybe you felt funny, too." He raked his hand through his hair, giving his head a shake. "What'd you put in that water bottle?" His laugh sounded only half joking. His skin was peaked, his face drawn.

It was unlike him—Damien was usually a powerhouse of fitness. "Oh shit." He lurched up and stumbled to the railing, leaning over the edge. "I think I'm gonna be sick."

She bolted over to him, rubbing his back. "Can you make it outside?" Trying for some comic relief, she added, "I don't know if the bats would like you puking in their territory."

He laughed weakly. "*Gross*, Bail. You know I can hold my water better than that." He tried to give her a smile, but his face grew slack. "I think I need some fresh air," he said, and the words came out sounding garbled.

When he tried to stand upright, he stumbled into her, and she leaned into the railing for support. He smelled like chocolate.

It set off an alarm in her mind. "Are you allergic to anything? Maybe there was a weird ingredient in the cookies." She grabbed his arms, trying to shuffle him away from the edge of the shaft. He needed to get fresh air, and she needed to call an ambulance.

"Sshhi—" He blinked his eyes open and shut, really slurring now.

"Can you breathe?" Her mind raced. Damien's cell would be in his pocket, but she couldn't grab it while he leaned on her like this. "Look, we need to call an ambulance."

He shook his head. "Ressep . . . resss . . ."

No cell reception. "Got it. Let's get you outside. Can you walk?"

He nodded, swallowing convulsively. She wondered if he might not get sick after all. The prospect spurred her to action.

"Ready? On three. One, two—" She pressed her back into the railing, trying to heave him off her chest so they might be able to shuffle out side by side.

Damien stumbled backward and fell on his bottom. There was a sharp crack, and Sorrow fell back, too. But all she met was open air.

Time suspended as she fell. But then she landed with a crash, and reality exploded to life. A horrific snap. Her arm. The sound was so hideous, she knew she'd never get it out of her head. She cradled it close, breathing through her teeth.

And then the strangest thing happened. Rather than panic,

the oddest, calmest clarity overtook her. She assessed her situation. Her whole body reverberated with pain, but nothing else seemed broken. It registered that Damien was shouting down to her.

"I'm okay," she shouted back. She looked around, praying she didn't see any of those bats he'd told her about. The floor was wider than she'd have guessed, with metal tracks leading away into the blackness. It was the eeriest thing she'd ever seen. She forced her voice to be steady. "I'm on some sort of a platform."

"Don't move," he said, and despite the slurring, she could hear how his voice had snapped taut with panic.

"The ladder." Using her good hand, she inched herself forward, reaching for it, but the wood crumbled in her fingers. Tears burned her eyes. "Rotted."

"Told you . . . don't move." He was speaking slowly, but she was grateful to hear his words were less slurred. "I'll . . . get help."

She yelled up at him, "No! You can't drive in your condition. I'll be okay." She heard him shuffling around up above, and shouted again, "Don't you dare leave, Damien Simmons!"

"It's . . . no good, Sorrow. I'm . . . been . . . coward . . . enough."

She heard his scuffling footsteps, and then nothing. Just the echo of her breath in a cavern twenty feet underground.

Forty-two

Billy stormed the tavern. He'd gotten a thirdhand message, delivered via police band. Dispatch calling with news from the EMT. An accident.

Just like Keri. All over again.

Not Keri, he assured himself. Sorrow hadn't been on the scene. But she was in danger all the same. And he had to find her.

The tavern door hit the wall, he'd opened it so hard. Everyone turned to stare.

Bear spun on his stool. "What the hell's gotten into you? Coming in here like a bat outta—"

He cut the man off. There was no time for bullshit grumbling. "There's been an accident. Damien, driving under the influence. He's injured and getting medevacked to Silver City, but he kept asking for me." Apparently through his slurring, all he did, over and over, was rant how they needed to contact the sheriff. Needed to find Sorrow. Needed to go to the mine. What the hell that all meant, he had no idea.

"All I know is, Sorrow had been with him, but now she's not. She's out there somewhere, and I think she's hurt. He said something about an Irish mine, and I need you to tell me what that means."

He cursed himself. Could he have done something to stop

it? For all he knew, she was lying broken at the bottom of a shaft somewhere.

Worse than Keri. Unthinkable.

He'd taken too long to put the pieces together. At first, he'd thought Damien was to blame for Sorrow's troubles. But then the kid had innocently spoken two words: *green gold.*

Then it hit him. Not Damien. *Dabney.* His father. If Dabney viewed Bear's property as valuable, for whatever reason, he'd swoop in to buy that land if anything happened to the owner.

Billy had the makings of a motive but he still didn't have proof, so he'd done some snooping. Damien had been down to the Town Hall, looking through old *mining* records. Later, thinking it Simmons Timber business, the clerk had innocently mentioned it to Dabney. Hearing there was an old gold mine on that land would've been as much of a shock to him as it'd been to Billy.

Mines meant gold. And yellow gold was a hell of a lot more valuable than the green kind. Valuable enough to kill for.

It was Dabney who'd been causing the trouble. Dabney behind the wheel of that Hummer.

The only missing piece had been *how.* Dabney didn't have the muscle to do it alone. That was when Billy checked with the El Dorado County parole officer. The fact that the Simmons family gardener had done time for breaking and entering was a big red flag. Surely Dabney did a background check on his employees, especially the household staff. Which meant Dabney knew he had a record—and now the guy had a new set of crimes to add to the list, and they were currently getting processed at the county lockup. The moment Billy tracked down Sorrow, he'd see that Dabney Simmons joined him there.

Edith was frantic. "What do you mean, Sorrow's hurt?"

"I don't know." His voice was hollow in his ears. Would it be just like with Keri? Not being there when she needed him? Losing yet another woman he loved? Because he loved Sorrow, more than he ever thought possible.

He'd come to Sierra Falls thinking to bide his years quietly. He hadn't expected to live any sort of a life at all. Instead, his feelings were deeper now than when he *was* married. He was older, his emotions more resonant, because he knew better than before, better than anyone, how it could all be taken in an instant. "I need to find her. Which means I need to find this mine."

These people could help. They knew Sierra Falls better than he did, and he was panicking them. His eyes swept the room, engaging every person in there. He took a deep breath and started again from the top. "The EMT said Damien was agitated, repeating Sorrow's name, and other things, too. He was fading in and out, so it was hard to follow, but he kept saying something about a mine. An Irish mine, maybe? Does that make sense to any of you? He must've meant Irish Camp Road, I can't think what else."

Everyone was quiet. Too quiet. He wanted to scream, to speed out of there without another word and drive till he found her. But instead, he forced his voice to be calm and slow—the most crucial thing right now was for him to play the role of *sheriff*, not frantic boyfriend. He pinned his eyes on Sorrow's father. "The mine, Bear. I need to find this mine."

The man nodded gravely. "I know the place."

"You do?" Edith asked, dumbfounded.

Helen piped up, "There's a mine in Sierra Falls?" By the looks on everyone's faces, she wasn't the only surprised one.

"If you follow Irish Camp out past 88, there's an old fire road. I played there when I was a kid. There was a lot of digging and panning back in the day. This particular mine closed back when *my* granddaddy was a kid."

Billy shoved his hat back on his head. "Then that's where I'm going. Edith, Bear, rally the troops. We'll need everyone's help tracking her down. Helen, call the hospital. No, call Dr. Mark. Maybe he can get some inside info, see if Damien's coherent yet. Hell, call everyone. And I mean *everyone*."

"Should we call 911?" someone asked.

"I *am* 911." He was getting aggravated now—hadn't he just said to call *everyone*? "But yeah, get the deputy on his cell, for sure. Scott can help, too. Maybe the Ranger Department knows the mine. Or at least they'll have some old survey maps lying around."

Edith hopped from her chair, following him to the door. She was visibly holding herself together, and barely. "Please bring my girl home."

He spared a moment for Sorrow's mom, giving her a meaningful look. "I'll find her."

Bear was right behind. "We'd be lost without her." Alarm gave an edge to his voice.

He contemplated the man with a hard look. Fear had stripped away Billy's filters, and he told him, "That's something you should try *showing* her once in a while."

Emotion wrenched Bear's features into those of an old, pained man. "Then bring me with you."

"You won't move fast enough for me."

Bear grabbed his coat from a hook by the door. "And you'll never find the mine without *me*."

"Then make tracks, old man." Billy stormed out the door with Bear on his heels, moving faster than he'd ever seen him.

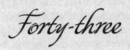

Forty-three

They sped to the trailhead, with Bear glowering in the seat beside him. "There's one thing I don't get," the old man said. "Damien drunk? This time of day? Doesn't sound like the kid I know."

Billy had to agree, but for different reasons. He'd bent his own elbow with the guy and knew from experience it'd take a hell of a lot to get Damien drunk.

"Let's just hope he had his wits enough to send us to the right place." The dirt road degraded until he could go no farther and his wheels spun and spat rocks against the vehicle's undercarriage. He slammed it into Park. "This is as far as she goes."

Bear peered out the window. "We're not close enough. You using your four-wheel drive?"

"I know how to drive in the mountains." There was no time for this. He unbuckled, jumped from the car, and leaning in, demanded, "Are you going to show me the mine, or do I need to find it myself?"

"Damned if I let you get all the glory." Bear hopped out, looking spry for a man half his age. Sure, he struggled with a limp, but he was keeping up remarkably well for someone who'd given up on good health.

The trail was slow-going, and Billy was going crazy with

frustration. But Bear had been right, the mine would've been impossible to find without help.

He stopped to let Sorrow's father catch up. The pace was maddening, his fear for Sorrow consuming, and he found himself speaking unchecked. "You want to know what I think?"

"Nope," Bear said between heavy breaths.

"I think that you're not as feeble as you worry you are."

The man didn't lift his eyes from the trail as he grunted, "I'm not feeble."

"I didn't say that. I said you *think* you're feeble. I think that stroke scared the hell out of you," Billy pressed. "I think you're afraid of testing your limits. But you were lucky. Many people don't survive it. You're lucky as hell you've got a kid like Sorrow who knew the signs and got you to the hospital early. You need to think on *that*, on how much you have, instead of focusing on what you've lost."

"Son, here's what I think: *I* think I'm done hearing your claptrap theories." The man looked like he'd swallowed a lemon, but his brow was furrowed in thought, and Billy had to hope his words had sunk in. Bear grumbled to himself, "I'm not afraid of you or anything, Sheriff."

A hill rose up beside them, and rather than continuing on the trail, Bear turned to face the steep incline, sighing heavily. "This is it."

Billy surveyed the rise, picking out a path of roots, rocks, and footholds in his mind's eye, "Up it is, then. I'll go first." What he didn't say was that he'd haul Bear up as he went.

Bear was trembling by the time he got to the top. "That way." He pointed along the ledge, trying to catch his breath. "You'll see it. On the right."

The man needed to gather his strength, but Billy couldn't wait. "You'll be fine here?"

"Right behind you," Bear said. "I told you. Not feeble."

If Billy hadn't been looking for the mine, he would've hiked right by it. Just a small black hole, etched into the rock face, it was no wonder folks had forgotten it through the years.

He shouted for her and strained his ears for a reply. Sorrow's answering yell came quickly, but her voice sounded strained and far away. Relief swamped him. She was alive. It was enough.

Billy burst into a run—it was a stupid, precarious thing to do, but he couldn't stop himself. He was desperate to get to her.

He burst into the mine, stopping short to let his eyes adjust. The air was close, cool pine breezes of the woods at his back mingled with the still scents of dirt and the abandoned nests of wild animals.

"Sorrow!" he shouted again, and bats exploded from inside the mine, a burst of shrieking and flapping.

Sorrow screamed.

He ran toward the sound, eyes scanning the ground. He'd been careless, but it'd be unforgivable if he fell to his death. "It's okay. Just bats. They won't hurt you."

"Easy for you to say." Her voice wavered, but her attempt at humor gave him hope.

He spotted the broken railing in the shadows, a timber skeleton holding vigil over a narrow black hole in the ground. He edged closer, not trusting the ground beneath him. It was a mineshaft, narrow as a well.

He dropped to his belly, scooting forward. "I'm here, babe." A ladder led up to the surface; she'd climbed halfway up, and he was startled to see her closer than he'd imagined.

"Help me," she said, and his relief turned to alarm.

He'd heard her pain and distress and assessed the situation, his eyes accustomed to the dark now. At least half the ladder rungs had crumbled to dust, and she held one arm tucked painfully at her side.

"*Stop*," he ordered. "Good God, Sorrow. What are you doing? You're going to kill yourself."

He eased over the ledge as far as he could go, stretching his arm out to her, but it was no good. She was just out of his reach.

He ran his hand down along the ladder rails. Between him and where Sorrow had managed to climb, there were only a couple of nubs where rungs should be. "Looks like you can't go any higher. Can you ease yourself back down?"

She gave a tight shake to her head. "A bunch of rungs snapped when I stepped on them."

And she was too high up to jump back down. Her arm was broken, and God knew what else. He couldn't risk further injury, which meant the only way for her to go was up.

He looked around frantically. The fragments of an old pulley system hung overhead, but the ropes had rotted decades ago. Why didn't he keep rope in the car? When they got out of there, he was going to do some serious reassessing of the safety gear he kept in the SUV.

Bear's scuffling footsteps announced his arrival. "You sure ran off half cocked," the old man said.

"Dad?" Sorrow's voice broke on the word.

"I'm here, girl. We're getting you out." Bear came and stood at the edge of the shaft, sucking on his teeth, deep in thought. "We'll need something for this."

"I could ease down the side maybe, if it weren't so tight." Billy considered the drop. He didn't care that he might break a leg—his concern was hitting her on the way down. He peered up at Bear. "Any ideas?"

"Be right back" was all the man said in reply.

Sorrow made a tiny whimpering sound, and as much as he wanted to soothe her, he knew the only way to handle it was to get her mind on other things. "Hold on," he said in a firm voice. "Talk to me, Sorrow."

She made a sound that was half laugh, half sniffle. "*Talk* to you?"

"Yeah, babe. You can start by telling me how you managed to get halfway up a mineshaft with a broken arm, using nothing but a decaying ladder."

She was silent for a moment, her breath echoing in the narrow passage. "A lot of shimmying," she said finally, her voice wavering with emotion.

She was trying, so he'd try, too. He kept his voice light as he said, "I'd like to see that sometime."

But rather than playing along, when she spoke again her voice was fragile, cracking as a child's might. "My dad really came?" But then she was quick to brush it off with a weak laugh. "I bet he's just worried I won't get the roast in the oven in time to feed the early birds."

Her doubt in her own lovability broke his heart. "Aw, hell, babe. Of course he came. He loves you. We all do."

The words had rolled off his tongue without thought, but he felt Sorrow hold her breath. She looked up at him, and her face glowed in the shadows, pale, beautiful, and dirt-smudged. "You do?"

"You know it," he said, his voice strong. "I do, Sorrow. I love you. And the moment we get you out of here, I'm going to show you just how much."

"Cool your jets," Bear grumbled from behind him. "Son of a gun, Sheriff, can't you control yourself for two minutes?"

Billy felt like slugging the guy. Until he turned and saw the giant branch Bear had dragged in behind him. His eyes goggled. "Where the hell'd you get that?"

"From a tree." Bear grumbled under his breath, "Fool city boys."

He rolled his eyes. "A *tree*, he says. I figured that, old man. But . . . how?"

"Just used my belt to pull it down." Bear tried to look nonchalant, but Billy read the pride in his eyes. "Back in my timber days, we called it tree fishing. Best way to clear the deadwood. We used rope, but a belt works just fine."

He gave the man an admiring look. "Apparently."

Bear went to the ledge and shouted down to his daughter, "Got to get you back for the early birds. They think you're making pot roast."

"Told you," Sorrow exclaimed, but Billy saw the humor in her eyes. It'd been just what she needed.

Billy lowered the tree limb down the hole—the thing must've been a good twenty feet long, and it scraped along the ceiling of the mine as he shoved it down. Dust and bits of rope showered onto Sorrow, and she looked away, shutting her eyes tight. Debris pelted his neck and back, but he didn't budge—he refused to take his eyes from her.

He worried the branch might snap, but it was dead not rotted, and thankfully still had enough resilience to bend. Unfortunately, that also meant it'd be too spindly at the top to support Sorrow's weight. But, leaned against one side of the ladder, it offered enough traction for her to shimmy up. He didn't need her to go far, just high enough for him to grab hold. She scrambled, and he held his breath. Finally she was within reach.

"Grab my hand, Sorrow. I got you."

"Reach, girl," her dad echoed. "You're there."

She hooked the elbow of her broken arm around the remains of one of the rungs, wincing with the effort. She strained her good hand up until her fingers brushed his arm. Billy grasped her forearm and scooted backward, hauling her up and over.

Still lying on the ground, he swept her into an embrace, careful of her broken wrist. He gazed at her, drinking in the sight of her, safe in his arms. Her face was filthy, there were cobwebs in her hair, and there was a goose egg on her head the size of a baseball. But Billy didn't see any of that—all he knew was that he was looking at his future bride. "You're one helluva woman, you know that, Sorrow Bailey?"

"I know it," she said, smiling broadly. "Oh, and Sheriff? I love you, too."

Bear turned to give them privacy. "If you kids are done, let's get the hell out of here. I've got a neck to wring. I plan on killing Damien Simmons with my bare hands."

"It wasn't Damien's fault," she said as Billy helped her stand. She swayed as she got her legs under her, and he held her close.

"Like hell it wasn't Damien," Bear snarled. "He brought you here, didn't he?"

"No, Dad. My falling was an accident." Sorrow clung to Billy for balance as they made their way from the mine, and he thought he might never let her go again. "I think he ate something that made him sick."

"Something from his parents, I'll bet."

"Wait"—she stopped—"What? Dabney and Phoebe sent us cookies. How'd you know?"

Billy pressed on, walking as he talked. "All the problems at the lodge, Laura's hit-and-run . . . it was Damien's *dad*. He's been sabotaging you all along." He felt her stagger, and hoisted her higher, taking more of her weight. "We need to get you to the hospital."

"You need to tell me what happened," she insisted. She was

striding along the path, looking nothing like a woman who'd spent the afternoon trapped in a mineshaft.

He shook his head—there was no stopping her. "Dabney wanted your land. At first he wanted the timber. But then he found out about the gold."

"But that mine isn't on our land," Bear said.

Sorrow added, "And Damien told me it was a failure anyway."

"It's true," Billy said. "The lode was played out, and that mine was a failure. Thing is, that wasn't the mother lode. The mother lode is on *Bailey* acreage."

"Holy cow," Sorrow exclaimed. "Are you saying there's gold on our land?"

"That's exactly what I'm saying."

"How do you know?"

"Once I learned that Dabney knew about the mine, from there, it was a no-brainer. There aren't many surveyors around. It took me fifteen minutes to track down the one he worked with, out of Sacramento. Modern technology makes things like prospecting a whole other ball game. They found gold—a high-grade vein."

"I still don't get how Dabney could've done all this," Sorrow said. "He was with us in the kitchen when the oven exploded. It was *his* car that got hit when Helen spun out on the black ice."

"Dabney didn't do it alone. He had help from his family gardener. The man has a record as long as your arm."

"Crazy," Sorrow exclaimed. "But you know what's crazier . . . we're *rich*."

"Easy," Bear said. "That ain't how it works. My granddad was panning for gold before Dabney Simmons was a light in his mama's eye. We're *all* sitting on gold out here. It's the mining of it that's hard. Dabney's too much the fool to know that." He turned to Billy, getting back on point. "So if it's my land, why pick on my daughter?"

Billy took a moment to help both of them navigate down the ravine. "It makes sense. Despite my doubts, it seems our Damien is a decent guy." He put his arm around Sorrow's waist, adjusting her arm to take most of her weight. "Every one of those accidents at the lodge drove the two of you closer. When you had trouble, Damien came to your rescue. The more accidents you had, the closer you got. If you'd eventually married the guy, the mine would've become just another part of the Simmons empire. Or at least your share of it would have."

"Well then why try to run me over? I can't marry Damien if I'm dead."

"The game became deadly when you had the great good sense to break up with Prince Charming. That meant it was time to sabotage the lodge and take it by force." He looked at Bear. "I imagine Dabney's long-term game was to drive your business into the ground and then make you an offer you couldn't refuse."

Sorrow staggered as they reached the bottom of the gully, and Billy simply swept her into his arms. "Put me down," she protested at once. "I'm too big to carry."

He gave her a little bounce, careful not to jostle her arm. She was soft and full and perfect in his hands. "You feel just right to me."

She wrapped her good arm around his neck, and the feel of her was like a missing puzzle piece clicking into place. She whispered in his ear, "Thanks for finding me."

Billy pointed his chin toward Bear. "Couldn't have done it without that man."

"Your mom and I would be lost without you, girl." Bear's lip twitched as he spoke, and Billy chuckled to himself, seeing how hard it was for the man to speak warmly. "Thought I'd have to come drag you out of that mine myself. Your sheriff was moving slower than molasses in January."

"Wow . . . rich or not, we're sitting on a gold mine," she repeated. "You know what that means? I'm definitely getting an assistant."

The men laughed and Sorrow did, too, and it was a wonderful sound. She tucked her head in his neck and he hugged her closer, managing to carry her effortlessly back to the car.

She'd been wrong—she was a feather in his arms. He could carry her forever if she let him. He hoped she would.

He'd never forget Keri—she'd been his first love, and there was no greater gift than that. But he'd aged a lifetime in a few short years, and his heart and soul had found peace there with Sorrow.

He let Bear walk ahead on the trail. Sorrow nestled close. "Thanks for carrying me."

"I was just thinking how there's nothing better than holding you." He hugged her even tighter, overwhelmed by the urge to have her, to make Sorrow his, wanting her with an intensity he'd never experienced before.

She nipped him on the ear, whispering, "I could think of maybe one thing that's better."

They went to Silver City Memorial, where she got bandaged up. Then Billy sped her back to his place, hoping to put that theory to the test.

"You sure you don't want to lie in bed?" Billy was torn. He wanted to be gentle with Sorrow. But he also wanted to take her, to have her and love her. To take care of her. To let her know he'd be there to do all of those things for the rest of her life if she'd let him.

Sorrow used her good hand to grab a pillow from his couch and toss it in front of the fireplace. "I'm sure I want to lie right here, with you, in front of the fire that you're about to make for me."

He added a couple of pillows to the mix, making a cozy nest for the two of them. "I'm about to make you a fire, am I?"

She nodded, settling under the afghan. "Mm-hm. A nice big hot one."

"I best get to it then." He squatted in front of the hearth, stacking kindling and logs. He glanced back at her as he twisted sheets of newspaper into rolls for tinder. The sight of her arm in a cast made him weak, but it could've been worse—she could've needed surgery. Or he might not have found her at all.

He forced such thoughts from his mind. He'd be there with her, enjoying the moment, looking with hope to the future while putting away regrets of the past.

"Hey, Sheriff." Sorrow had a saucy light in her eye, and it was one he'd already come to recognize. "You almost done over there?"

He chuckled. God, he loved this girl. "Oh, I'm done . . . with the fire, that is." He stood, wiping his hands on a rag. The kindling began to crackle and pop, warm at his back as he faced her. "I was thinking maybe you wanted me to do something else."

"How'd you know?" She pulled aside the afghan for him to join her. "You're going to join me."

"Join you?" He knelt beside her.

"Definitely. A girl gets cold on the floor. And lonely."

"Cold *and* lonely. We can't have that." He slid in next to her, and she turned to face him, wrapping her good arm around his neck. Their bodies fit like two puzzle pieces. "You okay?" he asked, helping her adjust her injured arm.

They settled her broken wrist on the floor over her head, nestled in pillows. "I'm good now," she said.

He sighed, a satisfied sound. "You *are*. You have no idea how good." He stroked his hand up her side. In the hospital, she'd been unable to pull her sweater back over her cast and had become chilled in just her tank top, and so he'd put her in his flannel shirt the moment they got back to his place. And, just as he'd imagined, she was sexy as hell in the oversized red and black plaid. "You warming up?"

Her hand found him beneath the blanket, and she caressed his leg. "It's getting downright hot in here."

"I'll say." He snuck his hand under the flannel, finding her breast and teasing her through the thin cotton of her tank.

She moaned, leaning close to nip at his jaw, then leaned in for a deep kiss. "Now I'm burning up," she whispered as she parted from him. Her eyes were glazed with desire.

He swept the hair from her face. "You're so beautiful." His eyes went to her mouth, so glistening and tempting. "I could kiss you forever."

Those lips curled into a sexy smile, "I was hoping you had other things in mind."

They kissed again, until they were both breathless. He tugged at her hem. "Maybe we should take this off."

"I think we should." She sat up a little, leaning on to his body for support, trying to wrestle off her top. But as he helped if off, the sleeve tugged on her cast, and she grunted.

He froze. "Wait, are you sure?" His body raged for her, aching for release after knowing such fear for her safety, but he didn't want to do anything she wasn't ready for. "I can wait."

"But I can't." She held his gaze, the firelight casting gold light along the side of her face. "Billy, I've never been more sure of anything in my life."

His heart was full as he smiled at her. "Then I know what we need to do." He rolled onto his back, and she gave a little surprised chirp as he swept her above him. "How about this?"

She gave him a naughty smile as she sat astride him, nestling him into just the right spot between her legs. "Mm. This." She leaned down to steal a kiss. "This is good," she whispered against his mouth. "There's just one problem."

"Is your arm hurting?" He gripped her hips, ready to swoop her back onto the floor.

"What arm?" She laughed, shaking her head. "Don't worry, I promise it's not the arm." She swayed her hips, grinding into him. "The problem is, too many pants."

He had to suck in a breath—he would *not* accidentally lose it in his uniform trousers like a teenager. "We'd best take care of this whole pants situation."

They made quick work of the rest of their clothes, and when he pulled her back atop him, he remained seated, keeping her straddled, facing him on his lap. The fire had warmed the room, and the afghan fell from her shoulders. He swept his fingers up her naked back, lacing them into her hair, luxuriating in the weight of it in his hands. "I need you closer."

"Mmm," she purred. "Closer is good."

He let those silky blond waves slide from his fingers and cradled her lovely face in his hands. "I'll keep you close forever, Sorrow. If you'll have me."

And she did.

Forty-four

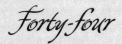

It was a gorgeous day for a festival, the sky a cloudless, robin's egg blue. Spring snowmelt had the falls rushing, visible in peekaboo glimpses from the picnic grounds.

Sorrow felt someone come and stand at her shoulder. She knew without looking that it was her sister. Tucking hands in pockets, she leaned back into her.

Despite all their sisterly bickering and rivalry, when the shift finally happened in their relationship, it'd been a quiet one. She saw clearly now how the lodge *was* Laura's place, and that it was *Sorrow's* turn to spread her wings.

It was a giddy day when she'd handed over her management duties. Her big sister's first order of business was putting Sorrow in charge of revamping the tavern menu. Dad had grumbled, but there was no arguing with a united front. As for Sully, he was as thrilled with the change as she was, claiming if he never baked another Prospector's Pie, it'd be too soon.

She and Laura had been a team ever since, and the festival was the latest thing to benefit. It was still early in the day yet, but the festivities were already an obvious, unabashed hit. For a few minutes, the two of them simply stood there, watching in contented silence. Between Laura's marketing savvy and Sorrow's talent with people and cooking, it was shaping up to be the most successful event the town had ever seen.

Laura wrapped an arm around her, giving her arm a squeeze. "You done good, baby sis."

"Me?" She edged away to catch Laura's eye. "You were the one doing all the work behind the scenes. This festival never would've happened without you." Sorrow raised a hand, silencing her sister's protests. "Seriously. This whole *town* wasn't the same without you. I was stupid not to see it sooner."

Their moment was broken by screams and laughter swelling in the distance. "That'd be the pie toss," Laura said, looking toward the games at the far edge of the field.

They caught sight of Ruby and Pearl Kidd headed their way, with Marlene and Sully walking several paces behind. The two were holding hands.

"How awesome is *that*?" Laura whispered.

"*Totally* awesome."

"Wonder what the old aunties think about it?"

Sorrow chuckled. "They probably think Marlene has become a fast woman."

"Well, good on her," Laura said. "We fast girls need to stick together."

As they watched Marlene's elderly entourage make their approach across the festival grounds, Sorrow whispered, "I'll regret to my dying day that I didn't get to see them the day I fell down that mine."

"You missed it all right," Laura said, stifling a giggle. "Those two ladies showed up like the SWAT team. They were quite a sight, speeding in, bouncing up and down on the bench of Marlene's old pickup, Ruby with a fistful of historical survey maps."

Sorrow had to dab tears of laughter from her eyes. "I think if Billy and Dad hadn't found me, Pearl and Ruby would've tracked down the mine and rescued me themselves."

"Don't you know it. You should've seen Mom's face. '*Good Lord, it's the Kidd ladies,*'" Laura mimicked, her voice a high-pitched exclamation that made Sorrow laugh even harder. "The way they peeled into the driveway, I thought for sure they were going to take out the porch."

"Shhh . . ." Sorrow said, trying to stop her convulsive laughter. They were headed their way. "They'll hear you."

"Congratulations to us!" Pearl exclaimed as they neared. "It's a smash!"

Ruby nodded enthusiastically—she and her sister were practically beaming. "There's record attendance, with both tourists and *historians*, too, from as far away as the Bay Area. I just wish Emerald were here to see it."

"Oh, Emmie." Pearl sighed. "She'd have thought this a hoot."

Marlene greeted the Bailey sisters with kisses on cheeks. "How right you are. Ma would've loved this."

Pearl interrupted with an impatient hand on Laura's arm. "Did you know, I heard a *reporter* from the *Sacramento Bee* is here."

"A reporter indeed," Marlene said. She faced Laura. "That has *you* written all over it."

"Could be." Laura shrugged, but couldn't conceal her smile. "I might've known someone who knew someone."

Sorrow chimed in, "The biggest news seems to be how our 'Buck Larsen Festival' turned into the first annual Sierra Falls Gold Rush Women's Festival instead."

Laura met her eye. "Can't hold a festival for someone who was a jerk."

Sorrow gave her a knowing smile. "Thanks for seeing the light. I like the new theme we came up with." At first, Laura had wanted to push the Buck Larsen affair, but in the end had trusted the youngest Bailey sister's opinion on the matter.

Laura nudged her shoulder. "What man in his right mind leaves a woman named Sorrow anyway?"

The comment made her feel a little shyly self-conscious, and not in a bad way. Only now was she realizing how loved she was in Sierra Falls, and it was Billy who'd opened her eyes to it. Seeing the community from an outsider's perspective, she recognized just how precious Sierra Falls was. And with its snow-capped peaks on the horizon, the lakes and the wildlife, the rush of the falls in spring, and those fragrant pines so thick all around, she saw with new eyes just how glorious her home was.

The mountains were in her blood. She wasn't trapped in the town, rather she carried the town inside her, in her heart. She felt connected to Sierra Falls, just as she felt connected to her thrice-great-grandmother. Sorrow Crabtree had been a woman, just like her, trying to find love and go her own way.

She held Laura's gaze a moment, before telling her, "It was a stroke of genius dedicating this to pioneer women."

"Except"—Sully spoke up, nodding toward one of the booths—"your father is over there complaining that you didn't bake enough for the cakewalk."

Everyone laughed, and Laura clapped her on the shoulder. "Dad's become her biggest fan."

She shrugged, no longer bothering to temper her smile. "Go figure."

"So Bear finally saw the light," Marlene said. "It's about time."

"And more power to her," Sully said. He looked at Sorrow with pride in his eyes. "The new head chef of the Thirsty Bear Tavern—it's about time, girl."

Their regular diners had all heard the news, too. It was hard to miss, seeing as Dad had taken to swaggering around the place, bragging about his youngest daughter's cooking and how folk better make a reservation now because they're booked solid through the month with her installed as their new head chef—and he always stressed the word *chef*, as though he were actually speaking French or something.

"Will you miss it?" Laura asked him.

"I'm all too happy to say good-bye to burgers for a while." Sully nestled Marlene closer. "The Harley is already in the shop getting tuned. Me and Marlene, we're going to take a tour come June. Maybe ride up to Oregon."

"We'll miss you," Sorrow said.

"You'll be too busy to miss us," Marlene said with a wink, implying more than just her kitchen duties.

Sorrow would never forget the day her parents announced their intentions to her. "You're going to cook," Dad had told her. "Every day of the week, if you want."

It was such an abrupt attitude shift, she didn't entirely believe it. "I thought you were upset, you know, thinking the oven got ruined on my watch."

"The oven? Aw hell, girl. Everyone knows the fire was that

damned Dabney's fault. Screw the oven." His gruff voice had turned ragged with emotion. "I could've lost *you* in that fire."

The sentiment had humbled her. And honestly, it'd shocked her, too. Something had happened that day at the mine. And part of the credit was owed to Billy, who'd had her father pegged all along.

"You're our baby," her mother had added.

Dad agreed—and it'd been tantamount to an emotional outburst. "We rely on you. We already have one kid so far away." His face had twisted up funny when he'd said that last bit. If it'd been any other man, the expression would've looked angry, but with her father, she knew, it was deep emotion he masked.

Even her mom was chiming in more than usual. She'd interrupted, saying, "What your father is trying to tell you is that we rely on you. How would we—how would *I*—have managed without you?" Mom gave Dad a chastising look. "I guess your father has held on to the past too tightly. Maybe he thought that a firm grip would keep you from running off like your siblings did."

"I'm not running anywhere. I just want to be given credit. Given responsibility."

Her father gave a gruff nod, visibly struggling with something. "It's been hard. The stroke."

"Oh, Daddy." She reached for him then, and he wrapped her in his arms. "It must be hard. Just because you're not out there chopping wood every morning doesn't mean you're not as strong, or as vital, or as important to us as before."

He'd given her a pat on the shoulder as they parted, looking uncomfortable at the sudden roiling emotions. "Fine then. You run a tight kitchen. Now get to it. Lunch crowd will be coming soon."

And that'd been that.

Sully's voice interrupted her thoughts. "Only makes good sense," he was saying. "Nobody packs the tavern with hungry diners like Sorrow here."

"And you taught her everything you know, didn't you?" Marlene took his arm. "Though it's a wonder Bear didn't see what was going on under his own nose. What a shock about Dabney."

"I guess Damien will get his shot at the helm of Simmons Timber sooner rather than later," Sorrow said. "His dad can't exactly run the company from prison, can he?"

"Prison," the Kidd sisters gasped, practically in unison.

"Just what we need," Laura said, not bothering to conceal her scowl. "Another Simmons male sitting on the throne."

Sorrow was quick to correct her. "Don't count Damien out yet. There's a good guy in there—he'll find his way out."

"Speaking of changes . . ." Marlene's gaze drifted across the grass to her grandson as he spread out a picnic blanket for him and his date. "Did you hear the news? Craig is headed to Chicago after graduation. Decided to go Navy. Said he was tired of being landlocked." She sighed.

"It's a good life." Sully tucked her arm more snugly in his, ignoring the scandalized glances Pearl and Ruby shot their way. "He's ready, Marlene. He's a man."

Marlene patted his hand, gratitude in her eyes. Those two made a great couple.

She glanced at her big sister to share a look, but when she saw those wickedly narrowed eyes, she braced herself.

Laura asked, "Where's *your* boyfriend?"

Boyfriend. Billy was so much more than just a boyfriend. He'd become her world. She'd have loved nothing more than to have him there for the entire day, but he was the sheriff, and his responsibilities never took a day off. And though they hadn't been together long, their bond was a powerful one. It was as though she felt him out there, their two hearts connected, no matter where they were.

But instead of saying all that, she just gave a casual shrug. "Once he saw the booths were all up and running, he said he had some quick department business to attend to."

It wasn't until later that afternoon that Sorrow got a taste of just what that pressing business was.

* * *

He hated leaving Sorrow's side on her big day. But it was just for a little while. And it was necessary.

Because Billy had a ring to pick up in Silver City.

He'd cut the timing close, but he wanted everything to be

perfect—perfect size, perfect fit—when he presented it to Sorrow. And man, that ring was just right.

He'd known the moment he saw it in the jewelry store window. It was an antique, a diamond surrounded by tiny sapphires in an engraved platinum setting. It was delicate and exquisite, but strong and solid, too. Not over the top. Nothing pretentious or splashy—a classic.

Just like Sorrow.

As Sorrow Crabtree's great-great-great-granddaughter and namesake, she'd been asked to join some of the other women in donning period dresses for the late afternoon supper show. A number of townsfolk had gotten into the spirit, dressing up like pioneers and prospectors from gold rush days. Everyone had migrated from the picnic grounds to the hall to enjoy the rousing music and saloon dance numbers just like the elder Sorrow might have performed.

Little did the audience know, they were about to get an even better show than they'd bargained for.

Unable to resist Sorrow and her enthusiasm in the days before the festival, he'd found an old-time sheriff's costume online. And, he had to admit, he felt like quite the badass clinking around the festival in his new spurs.

They'd talked around marriage, so he had an inkling he'd find a willing partner. Lately, though, he'd been avoiding the subject. Not because he was no longer interested, but because he'd wanted to keep his surprise.

His smile was wide, watching her laugh and fake her way through the old-time dance hall moves. For someone whose sense of responsibility and commitment to hard work and family was so hardwired, Sorrow sure did know how to experience joy. And the pleasure she took in her cooking was just the start of it. She embraced life with an easy, natural immediacy that'd paved the way for him to engage in his own life once more.

To engage his heart.

The number ended, and for a moment he lost sight of her amidst the milling, cheering crowd. He searched for her, and he knew a funny spurt of discontent until his eyes found her again, standing at the edge of the stage.

The buzzing of the audience came to him as though through

a tunnel. *She* was the reason he was there, happily wearing a silly getup with a diamond ring in his pocket.

He watched her, feeling calmed and contented by the very sight of her. Someone in the crowd had shouted something, and she was smiling down, one part of a three-way conversation that included June Harlan at the piano. Sorrow was open-hearted, generous, thoughtful, down-to-earth, and quick to smile . . . everyone in town loved her. How he got to be the lucky man who got to keep her was beyond him.

And she *was* the one. His heart was clear of all doubts on that score. He wondered if, in the deepest part of his soul, he hadn't known it all along. Sorrow had renewed that part of him he'd lost after Keri's death—that inner wellspring that he'd thought had died had simply been temporarily dried out, now replenished by her presence in his life.

She was the gift he thought he'd never receive—a chance at a second chapter. And this time, it was a love more profound than any he'd ever known, because he understood now just how precious, how valuable was such a treasure.

He couldn't stand it any longer. He went to her, parting the crowd as he made his way across the floor. The clink of his spurs amused him, widening the smile on his face.

He leapt up onto the stage and took her hand, distantly aware how the room had begun to hush.

She beamed. "Hey, stranger! There you are. I've been wondering—"

As he got down on one knee, the crowd gasped and the words froze on her lips.

An elderly voice exclaimed, "I knew it!" It'd been one of the Kidd sisters—Pearl maybe. Laughs followed. Other voices chimed in, cheering him on.

He didn't give any of them a second thought. His eyes were only for his Sorrow. The silence became complete.

He smiled up at her, so pretty and flushed from her dancing. Tendrils of curling blond hair had sprung free, framing her face. She was a vision.

She met his eyes, looking a combination of bewildered and thrilled. He could see from the tight bodice of her old-fashioned dress how her breath stuttered, caught.

He sighed as something unclenched in his own chest—she would say yes. She would be his, forever.

Calm and sure, he gave her hands a squeeze. He cleared his throat. "Sorrow Ann Bailey, would you do me the honor of becoming my bride?"

Whoops and whistles exploded through the hall. He heard Bear somewhere in the crowd boasting how he had a *lawman* in the family now.

She laughed and cried, nodding away, her eyes serious but her expression light. She was radiant—joyful and tearful and so perfectly herself. "Yes, yes," she repeated. *"Yes."*

That one word reverberated through his soul. He'd thought to be discreet—he was the town sheriff after all—but he couldn't help it. He stood and sealed it with a kiss.

The crowd erupted in cheers.

His next words were whispered for her ears alone. He knew how she longed to see the world, and he had to let her know she was free to do just that. He wanted nothing more than for Sorrow to follow her heart, and he'd happily follow *her* till the ends of the earth. All he needed was home, and that was right by her side. "We can go anywhere," he told her. "Live *any-where*. I'd even go back to the city, if that's what you wanted. You name it."

She cupped a hand on his cheek, and her touch was electric, crackling straight to the core of him. Those blue-green eyes connected with his, and the last ache in his heart melted away. "We'll travel," she said. "But I always want to come home with you. To Sierra Falls."

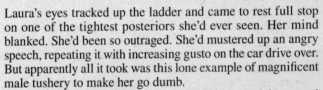

Laura's eyes tracked up the ladder and came to rest full stop on one of the tightest posteriors she'd ever seen. Her mind blanked. She'd been so outraged. She'd mustered up an angry speech, repeating it with increasing gusto on the car drive over. But apparently all it took was this lone example of magnificent male tushery to make her go dumb.

The ladder squeaked as the man shifted, looked down, and Laura caught sight of just whose ruggedly handsome face was attached to said magnificence.

She felt every muscle in her body stiffen. It was a Jessup. She was allergic to Jessups. To be precise, it was *Eddie* Jessup, the worst and most allergenic of them all.

He smiled broadly. "Can I help you?"

Her morning hadn't started this way. It'd started pretty great, actually, helping out with a bustling breakfast crowd. Her family's business was booming—visitors to the Big Bear Lodge were up, which meant diners aplenty at the tavern, and she was riding high as the new manager overseeing all of it.

Over the past several months, she'd thrown herself into her work. When her sister discovered a cache of letters dating from the gold rush era, Laura had used her expertise and Bay Area contacts to capitalize on the find. Now a film crew from the History Network was on their way, eager to shoot an in-depth piece. Which would mean even more visitors and more success for their family lodge.

But not if Eddie Jessup and his cursed Jessup Brothers Construction were actually doing what she'd heard they were doing.

It was a clear Indian summer day, and she shielded her eyes against the glare, watching as he climbed down the ladder. She was definitely *not* noticing the way his white T-shirt clung in places under the hot sun.

"You got something to say, or did you just come to ogle?"

That broke her silence. "I've got better things to do than ogle *you*, Eddie Jessup."

He laughed, and the easy confidence of it made her cheeks burn. Had he caught her staring? She shot her eyes down, making like she needed to check a text on her cell phone.

He jumped from the last few rungs, dusted off his hands, and faced her with a smile. "Well, darlin'? To what do I owe the honor?"

This particular Jessup had been getting under her skin since high school, but she was past that now. Back then, she'd looked only ahead, longing for the day she could hightail it out of Sierra Falls. Somehow Eddie had sensed it, and he'd upped his torment, always coaxing, teasing, and challenging her. It was a habit he'd never gotten over.

But *she* was over it. Big-time.

In fact, she liked to consider herself Jessup-proof. She was a college-educated, formerly incredibly successful Silicon Valley marketing professional who'd moved back home as a full-grown woman simply to get some perspective. She wanted only a change of scenery. No men—Jessup or otherwise.

She'd sworn off dating, just as she'd sworn off her old life in the city. She had an ex-fiancé she didn't miss and an old job she never thought about, and yet she'd once spent so much time chasing both of them. But why and for what?

She'd come home to figure out the answers. To determine what it was she wanted out of life, what made her happy. Because she'd learned the hard way that a man and a successful career didn't always go together in harmony.

She reminded herself that she was self-assured. Self-reliant.

Self-made. She put her hands on her hips. "I'm not your darlin'."

He gave her an assessing look. "More's the pity."

She resisted the urge to adjust her clothes under the intensity of that stare. "So don't call me that."

"Yes, ma'am." He'd said it with mock gravity, touching a finger to an imaginary hat. Before she could demand that he not *ma'am* her either, he continued, "So what would bring a fine, *not-your-darlin'* city girl like you to a construction site? Because I can see on that pretty face of yours—you've got something to say."

Fine . . . pretty. She refused to register the comments. Eddie probably spoke like that to every female within a ten-mile radius. And what *had* she come to say? It was in her brain somewhere.

She was confident. A pro with men. She refused to let the likes of Eddie trip her up. Every argument she'd rehearsed in the car shot to the forefront of her mind, and she demanded, "What are you doing here?"

He got an innocent look on his face. "I'm fixing a storm drain."

"I can see that. I mean, *what are you doing*?" She swept her arm, taking in the abandoned house and surrounding ranch property. "*Here.*"

"Ah." He met her eyes, and for once he looked serious. "You heard the news."

"Yeah, I heard about your Golden Slumbers Ranchlandia."

He laughed. "It's Sleepy Hills Resort and Spa."

"Whatever." She waved an impatient hand. "Sounds like a cemetery to me. Fitting, seeing as you're about to *bury* the Bailey family business."

"We have no intention of burying your business," he said in a kind voice. "It'll be good for the whole town. Fairview Properties contracted the Jessups. We bought our supplies from Tom's hardware store. Soon we'll hire extra workers. Workers who'll then go eat at *your* tavern. An influx of money all around."

She tapped a finger on her chin. "And hmm . . . let's see. Who do you think the big winners are in this whole thing?

Fairview, that's who. Because apparently they can just go wherever they want and install their giant resorts, meanwhile mowing down whatever stands in their way. What's next, a Hyatt?"

"Easy, Laura. I'm not the bad guy here."

His soothing tone had the opposite effect on her, and she stabbed her finger into his chest. "How about we kick the Kidd sisters out of their house and turn it into a Trump casino?"

"Nobody was kicked out. You know full well how Bob and Cathy abandoned this place for their swanky Sausalito condo years ago. It'll be good to fix it up." He took and held her finger, giving it a soft squeeze. "Look, Laura. I run a small business. We're working hard to get by, just like the rest of the town. We've got to take our jobs as we get them." Eddie's hand was calloused, and warm, and aggravatingly gentle.

She pulled her finger free. "How about *our* business? The lodge will never be able to compete with this." She glared at the traditional ranch house. It was a rambling one-story affair, in need of several coats of paint, probably entirely new electrical and plumbing systems, not to mention a whole lot of patching. "It's a dump, by the way."

"Nothing the Jessup boys can't fix."

"I hope you get overrun by raccoons."

"Don't get any ideas." He stood behind her, putting his hands on her shoulders, staring at the property with her. "Look, you see the size of the place. It's smaller than a regular hotel. The Fairview guys want it to be a boutique spa resort. High-end, marketed to people who like to think they hike, but wouldn't know a day pack from a day planner." He gave her shoulders a squeeze. "But you guys, your lodge is authentic. Tourists will always love it. You'll be fine."

She stiffened, stepping away before he had a chance to reach out and touch her again. The last time a man had told her *you'll be fine*, she'd ended up losing her job. "Eternal Slumbers here could put us out of business, and you know it."

Eddie's face fell, and she didn't trust it for an instant. "What do you want me to do?" he asked.

"I want you to get back into that ridiculous vehicle of yours, and call Fairview, and send them back to wherever it is they came from. Then they can go menace some other small town instead, and you can drive back to whatever rock you crawled out from under."

Instead of rising to the bait, he smiled an exasperating smile. "Not a fan of the pickup, are you?"

She only glared. "You're compensating."

His expression softened. "Look, Laura. I'm sorry. I really am. But if we hadn't been the ones hired for the job, it would've been someone else. Probably some out-of-town development company."

"At least *they* would've needed a place to stay." She stormed past him, back to her car.

Eddie followed her, and no matter how quickly she walked, his long strides kept up. "I really believe this'll be good for the town. More rooms can accommodate more visitors. More visitors means more diners—"

"Spare me." She hopped into a half jog, annoyed that he was following, and without so much as breaking a sweat. "I'm going to stop you."

He slowed, and if she didn't know his type better, she'd have thought she heard actual sympathy in his voice. "Come on, Laura. Let's discuss this."

She'd messed up a job before and she wouldn't fail again. She would show her family that she could be trusted with the business—better than that, she'd be more successful than they'd ever dreamed. Which meant she needed to stop Fairview Properties from building a competing hotel. And it all began with Eddie.

She flung open the door to her little BMW sedan. "Oh, I'll be back all right. I'm about to become your worst nightmare."